ONE MILLION A.D.

ONE MILLION A.D.

Edited by
Gardner Dozois

SCIENCE
FICTION

First Science Fiction Book Club printing December 2005

Published by Science Fiction Book Club, 401 Franklin Avenue, Garden City, New York 11530.

Visit the Science Fiction Book Club online at www.sfbc.com

Book design by Christos Peterson
ISBN: 0-7394-6273-3

Printed in the United States of America

For Tyler and Isabella, who *are* the future.

❖ Contents ❖

INTRODUCTION
Exploring the Far Future

The concept of the "far future" is a relatively new one. Before you can conceive of a time millions of years from now, you *first* have to have a sense of a past that stretches millions of years *behind* us, an intuition into what has been called "deep time," the kind of time, measured out in geological eras, in which mountains rise and fall, rock is laid down in patiently accumulating strata at the bottom of the sea before being thrust up into the air as naked new peaks, continents drift lazily around the globe, whole species of animals die, and new species evolve to replace them.

The idea of "deep time" didn't really become part of the intellectual armory of the human species until the late eighteenth and early nineteenth centuries, when thinkers such as Jean Louis Agassiz, James Hutton, Charles Lyell, and Charles Darwin began to challenge the church-sanctioned view that Creation had happened at 9:00 a.m. on October 26, 4004 B.C. (according to the calculations of Bishop Ussher in the seventeenth century), suggesting instead that the Earth was countless *millions* of years old, rather than a mere six thousand— a span of time so staggeringly huge, so dismayingly vast, that it is difficult for the human mind, used to measuring things on the Mayfly scale of our own eyeblink lives, to even grasp it.

Once you've had this vision of time stretching endlessly away behind us, it's perhaps inevitable that it will occur to somebody that this means that time will continue on *past* the current day and keep on go-

ing for millions of years to come . . . a concept which, through extrap-
olation, leads to the realization that changes as sweeping and dramatic
and vast as those that took place in remote geological ages past will
continue to happen in the *future*—that the Earth of the far future will
be as radically different from the Earth of today as today's Earth is
from the Earth of the Cretaceous or the Mesozoic.

And thus the concept of the "far future" was born.

Almost as soon as it was, science fiction writers were writing
about it, sailing into the far future on the wings of their imaginations
and exploring the strange and terrible wonders they found there. The
first such exploration may have taken place in the pages of H.G.
Wells's *The Time Machine* in 1895, written at a time when even the
concept that there *was* such a thing as the far future was radical, Cutting Edge stuff, and the concurrent idea that the Earth was millions of
years old rather than six thousand was still fiercely controversial,
hotly debated, and denied in both social and scientific circles. Wells
was soon joined in visits to the far future by visionaries such as
William Hope Hodgson (with his *The Night Land* and *The House on
the Borderland*), J.B.S. Haldane (with his "The Last Judgment"),
Olaf Stapledon (with his *Last and First Men*), and others—a tradition
that enters the hothouse of the genre SF market in the early '30s via
stories such as John W. Campbell's classic "Twilight" (written under
the pseudonym of Don A. Stuart) and the *Zothique* stories of Clark
Ashton Smith. By 1946, we come to the first great "modern" far-
future SF novel, Arthur C. Clarke's *Against the Fall of Night*, and visions of the far-future continue to appear throughout the twentieth
century in the work of writers such as Jack Vance, Brian W. Aldiss,
Cordwainer Smith, Gene Wolfe, Frederik Pohl, Michael Moorcock,
Poul Anderson, and others.

Here in the early days of the twenty-first century, I decided that it
was time to get a *twenty-first century* take on what the far future was
going to be like, and so I challenged a group of daring visionaries to
imagine life in One Million A.D.: a time so far ahead that the human
race and the Earth itself will have been altered almost out of recognition, and all our history and culture, everything we are, everything we
know and cherish, will have faded to dim and half-forgotten
mythology—if it's remembered at all.

Even within SF, where most stories are set at least some distance into the future, *far future* stories have always been relatively rare—few writers have ever had the imagination, poetic skills, and visionary scope required to write convincingly about what humanity might be like, what radical changes we might have undergone in nature and lifestyles, not just a few decades or even a hundred years from now, but a *million* years from now (always assuming, of course, that there *are* humans still surviving by then, or anything we'd recognize as human, anyway—but that's a different anthology!). To conjure up an evocative and poetically intense portrait of the far future calls for a degree—and a kind—of imagination rare even among science fiction writers.

I'm pleased to say that the writers gathered here, Robert Reed, Robert Silverberg, Nancy Kress, Alastair Reynolds, Charles Stross, and Greg Egan, have done a splendid job of meeting that challenge, providing along the way, not at all incidentally, some of the most vivid, evocative, entertaining, and mind-stretchingly imaginative science fiction you're ever likely to find. Enjoy!

—Gardner Dozois

ONE MILLION A.D.

GOOD MOUNTAIN

Robert Reed

Robert Reed sold his first story in 1986, and quickly established himself as a frequent contributor to The Magazine of Fantasy and Science Fiction *and* Asimov's Science Fiction, *as well as selling many stories to* Science Fiction Age, Universe, New Destinies, Tomorrow, Synergy, Starlight, *and elsewhere. Reed may be one of the most prolific of today's young writers, particularly at short-fiction lengths, seriously rivaled for that position only by authors such as Stephen Baxter and Brian Stableford. And—also like Baxter and Stableford—he manages to keep up a very high standard of quality* while *being prolific, something that is not at all easy to do. Reed stories such as "Sister Alice," "Brother Perfect," "Decency," "Savior," "The Remoras," "Chrysalis," "Whiptail," "The Utility Man," "Marrow," "Birth Day," "Blind," "The Toad of Heaven," "Stride," "The Shape of Everything," "Guest of Honor," "Waging Good," and "Killing the Morrow," among at least a half dozen others equally as strong, count as among some of the best short work produced by anyone in the '80s and '90s; many of his best stories were assembled in his first collection,* The Dragons of Springplace. *Nor is Reed non-prolific as a novelist, having turned out eight novels since the end of the '80s, including* The Lee Shore, The Hormone Jungle, Black Milk, The Remarkables, Down the Bright Way, Beyond the Veil of Stars, An Exaltation of Larks, Beneath the Gated Sky, Marrow, *and* Sister Alice. *His most recent book is a chapbook novella,* Mere.

Coming up is a new collection, The Cuckoo's Boys, *and a new novel,* The Well of Stars. *Reed lives with his family in Lincoln, Nebraska.*

Reed has visited the far future in his Sister Alice *stories and in stories such as "Whiptail" and "Marrow," but here he takes us deeper into the future than he ever has before, to a world whose origin is lost in the labyrinth of time, a world where, as a group of randomly thrown-together travelers is about to learn,* everything *is about to change—and not for the better.*

A DOT ON OLD PAPER

"World's Edge. Approaching now . . . World's Edge!"

The worm's caretaker was an elderly fellow named Brace. Standing in the middle of the long intestinal tract, he wore a dark gray uniform, patched but scrupulously clean, soft-soled boots and a breathing mask that rode on his hip. Strong hands held an angelwood bucket filled with a thick, sour-smelling white salve. His name was embossed above his shirt pocket, preceded by his rank, which was Master. Calling out with a deep voice, Master Brace explained to the several dozen passengers, "From this station, you may find your connecting trails to Hammer and Mister Low and Green Island. If World's Edge happens to be your destination, good luck to you, and please, collect your belongings before following the signs to the security checkpoints. And if you intend to stay with this splendid worm, that means Left-of-Left will be our next stop. And Port of Krauss will be our last."

The caretaker had a convincing smile and a calm, steady manner. In his presence, the innocent observer might believe that nothing was seriously wrong in the world.

"But if you do plan to stay with me," Brace continued, "you will still disembark at World's Edge, if only for the time being. My baby needs her rest and a good dinner, and she's got a few little sores that want cleaning." Then he winked at the passengers and began to walk again, totting his heavy bucket toward the stomach—up where the mockmen were quartered. "Or perhaps we'll linger here for two little

4

whiles," the old man joked. "But I don't expect significant delays, and you shouldn't let yourselves worry."

Jopale sighed and sat back against the warm pink wall. He wasn't worried. Not through any innate bravery, but because he had been scared for so long now, there was little room left for new concerns. Or so it seemed at that particular moment. Indeed, since his last long sleep, Jopale had enjoyed a renewed sense of confidence. A guarded optimism was taking root. Calculating how far he had come, he saw that most of the world lay behind him now, while it wasn't too much of a lie to tell himself that Port of Krauss was waiting just beyond the horizon.

Jopale even managed his own convincing smile, and watching his fellow passengers, he found one other face that appeared equally optimistic.

A young woman, built small and just a little short of pretty, was sitting directly across from him. She must have come onboard during his last sleep. Maybe at Which-Way, he reasoned. There was a fine university in that ancient city. Perhaps she was a student heading home, now that every school was officially closed. Her bags were few and small. A heavy book filled her tiny lap. Her breathing mask looked as if it had never been used, while a powerful torch rode on her other hip. Her clothes were comfortable if somewhat heavy—wool dyed green with thick leather pads on the knees and elbows. Bare black toes wiggled against a traveling blanket. Her leather boots had tough rubber soles, which was why she didn't wear them inside the worm. She looked ready for a long journey into cold darkness. But where could a young woman be going, and smiling about her prospects too?

There was one logical conclusion: Jopale caught the woman's gaze, nodded and offered a friendly wink. "Are you like me, miss?" he inquired. "Are you traveling to Port of Krauss?"

She hesitated, glancing at the other passengers. Then she shook her head. "I'm not, no," she told him.

Jopale thought he understood.

"But you're traveling through Krauss," he persisted. "On your way to some other destination, perhaps?"

He was thinking about the New Isles.

But she shook her head, a little embarrassed perhaps, but also taking some pleasure from his confusion.

No one else was speaking just then, and the intestine of a worm was a very quiet place. It was easy to eavesdrop and to be heard whenever you spoke. In quick succession, three young men offered possible destinations, picking little cities set on the auxiliary trails—each man plainly wishing that this woman's destination was his own.

"No," she told them. "No. And I'm sorry, but no."

Other passengers began to play the silly game, and to her credit, the woman remained cheerful and patient, responding immediately to each erroneous guess. Then the great worm began to shake around them, its muscular body twisting as it pulled off onto one of the side trails. Suddenly there was good reason to hurry the game along. The young men were leaving here; didn't they deserve a useful hint or two?

"All right," she said reasonably. "I'll remain on this trail until I'm done." Then she closed her book with a heavy thump, grinning as she imagined her final destination.

"Left-of-Left?" somebody shouted.

"We've already guessed that," another passenger complained.

"Where else is there?"

"Does anybody have a map?"

Jopale stood up. When their worm was young and quite small, holes had been cut through its fleshy sides, avoiding the major muscle groups. Each hole was fitted with progressively larger rubber plugs, and finally a small plastic window that looked as if it was carved from a cold fog. Through one of those windows, Jopale could see the tall buildings of the city and their long shadows, plus the high clear sky that was as close to night as anything he had ever known. What a journey this had been, and it wasn't even finished yet. Not for the first time, Jopale wished he had kept a journal. Then when there was time—once he was living on the New Isles, perhaps—he would write a thorough account of every awful thing that had happened, as well as his final triumphs.

A dozen travelers were now examining their maps, calling out the names of tiny places and abandoned cities. There was a time when people lived in the Tanglelands and points beyond, but that had been years ago. Only the oldest maps bothered to show those one-time destinations. A young man, very tall and shockingly thin, was standing close to the woman—too close, in Jopale's mind—and he carefully listed a string of places that existed nowhere but on a sheet of yellowed paper and faded ink that he held up to the window's light.

"Yes," said the woman, just once.

But the tall man didn't notice. He kept reading off names, pushing his finger along the black worm trail, and the woman was saying, "No, no, no," again, smiling pleasantly at his foolishness.

But Jopale had noticed.

"Go back," he said.

The tall man looked at him, bothered by the interruption.

Then a stocky old woman reached up high, hitting the fellow between the shoulder blades. "The girl said, 'Yes.' Didn't you hear?"

Another woman said, "Read backwards."

The tall man was too flustered to do anything now.

So Jopale took the map for himself, and in the dim light, he made his best guess. "What about Good Mountain?"

Once more, the girl said, "Yes."

"What kind of name is that?" the tall man asked, reclaiming his map, taking the trouble to fold it up neatly. "What does that word mean? 'Mountain'? I've never heard it before."

But the game was finished. Suddenly the old caretaker had returned, carrying an empty bucket with one bony hand. "This is the station at World's Edge," Master Brace called out.

The worm had come to a stop.

"My baby needs to breathe and to eat her fill," he reminded everyone. "So please, you must disembark. With your luggage, and with your tickets." Then a look of mischief came into the weathered face, and he added, "But if you will, please leave your hopes behind. I'd like to claim a few of them for myself."

A few passengers laughed at his bleak humor. But most just shook their heads and growled to themselves, or they quietly spat on the smooth pink floor.

The young woman was picking up her book and bags and her heavy boots, a joyous smile setting her apart from everyone else.

About her destination—the enigmatic Good Mountain—she said nothing at all.

A MOUTHFUL OF HISTORY

Every homeland was once new land, small and thin, pushed about by the willful winds. But the ground where Jopale grew up was still relatively young, and for much of its life, it had been a free-drifting body.

Jopale felt an easy pride toward his native wood—dense and fine—grained and very dark, almost black in its deep reaches, with a thick cuticle and the pleasant odor of sin-spice when sliced apart with steel saws. The wood's appearance and its telltale genetics made it the offspring of Graytell and Sweetsap lineages. According to the oldest nautical maps, an island matching that description first collided with the Continent near what was today Port of Krauss. But it didn't linger for long. In those ancient times, the Continent turned like a gigantic if extraordinarily slow wheel, deep-water roots helping to hold its green face under the eternal sunshine. This tiny unnamed body clung to the wheel's outer edge until it passed into the polar waters, and then it vanished from every record, probably drifting off into the cold gloom.

Unable to grow, the island shrank. Hungry, it drank dry its sap reservoirs. It could have brushed up against the Continent again, perhaps several more times, but some current or chance storm always pushed it away again. Then it wandered, lost on the dark face of the world. The evidence remained today inside its body. Its oldest wood was full of scars and purple-black knots—a catalog of relentless abuse brought on by miserly times. Not even a flicker of sunlight fell on its bleached surface. Starving, the island digested its deep-water roots and every vein of starch. Saprophytes thrived on its surface and giant worms gnawed their way through its depths. But each of those enemies was a blessing too. The tallest branches of the saprophytes caught the occasional breeze, helping the increasingly frail island drift across the quiet water. And the worms ate so much of the island that it floated easily, buoyed up by the air-filled caverns.

Finally the near-corpse was pushed into the storm belt, and the storms blew just so, carrying it out under the motionless sun. There the island turned a dark vibrant green again, dropping new roots that pulled minerals out of the nearly bottomless ocean—roots that flexed and rippled to help hold the island in the bright sunshine. And that's when new wood was built, and rivers of sugary sap, and a multitude of colonists began to find their way to its shores, including Jopale's distant ancestors.

Twelve hundred years ago, the island again collided with the Continent. But this time it struck the eastern shore, as far from Port of Krauss as possible. Its leeward edge pushed into the Plain of Perfect Deeds while another free-drifting island barged in behind, pinning it in place. Two more islands arrived over the next several years. Small bodies like those often splintered between shifting masses, or they were tilted up on end, shattering when their wood couldn't absorb the strain. Or sometimes they were shoved beneath the ancient Continent, rotting to form black muck and anaerobic gases. But Jopale's homeland proved both durable and extremely fortunate. Its wood was twisted into a series of fantastic ridges and deep valleys, but it outlasted each of the islands that came after it, its body finding a permanent nook where it could sit inside the world's Great Mother.

By the time Jopale was born, his land was far from open water. The sun wobbled in the sky but never climbed too high overhead or dropped near any horizon. By then, more islands and two lesser continents had coalesced with the Continent, and the once-elegant wheel had become an ungainly oval. Most of the world's dayside face was covered with a single unbroken lid too cumbersome to be turned. Competing wood had pushed the weakest lands deep beneath the Ocean, and like the keel of a great boat, those corpses held the Continent in one stubborn alignment, only the strongest currents and the most persistent winds able to force the oval toward the east or the west.

When Jopale was a young boy, disaster struck. The trade winds strengthened abruptly, and in a single year the Continent drifted west almost one thousand kilometers. Cities and entire homelands were plunged into darkness. Millions of free citizens saw their crops die and their homelands starve. The only rational response was to move away, living as immigrants on other lands, or as refugees, or in a few cases—like Port of Krauss—remaining where they were, in the darkness, making the very best of the tragedy.

To a young boy, the disaster seemed like enormous good fun. There was excitement in the air, a delicious sense of danger walking on the world. Strange new children arrived with their peculiar families, living in tiny homes given to them by charities and charitable guilds. Jopale got to know a few of those people, at least well enough to hear their stories about endless night and the flickering of nameless stars. But he still couldn't appreciate the fact that his own life was precarious now. Jopale was a bright child, but conventional. And he had a conventional family who promised him that the trade winds would soon weaken and the Continent would push its way back to its natural location. What was dead now would live again, those trusted voices argued. The dark lands would grow again. And because he was young and naturally optimistic, Jopale convinced himself that he would live to enjoy that glorious rebirth.

But the boy grew into a rather less optimistic young man, and the young man became a respectable and ordinary teacher of literature. During the average cycle, between one quiet sleep and the next, Jopale wouldn't once imagine that anything important about his world could ever change.

He was in his house, sleeping unaware, when a moderate quake split the land beneath him.

Early-warning sensors recorded the event, and Jopale happened to read about the quake in the morning newsbook. But no expert mentioned any special danger. The Continent was always shifting and cracking. Drowned islands would shatter, and bubbles of compressed gas were constantly pushing toward the surface. There was no compelling reason for worry, and so he ate his normal first-meal and rode his two-wheel over the ridge to work—a small landowners' school set on softer, paler ground just beyond his homeland—and there he taught the classics to his indifferent students, sat through a long department meeting, and then returned home again. Alone in his quiet house, he ate his last-meal and read until drowsy, and then he slipped his sleep-hood over his head and curled up in bed.

His house was small and relatively new, set in a corner of his parents' original farm. Jopale's property was part of a long prosperous valley. But since he was no farmer, he rented most of the ground to neighbors who raised crops and kept four-foots—milking varieties that were made into stew meat and bone meal once they grew old. The neighbors also kept scramblers for their sweet meat, and they used teams of mockmen to work the land and its animals, lending every waking moment a busy, industrious quality.

Jopale rose with the next cycle and went to work, as he did with the cycle after that, and the cycles that followed.

His homeland was blackish-green beneath its transparent cuticle of hard wax. The rough walls of the valley were covered with parasites and epiphytes that sprang from crevices and wormholes. There were even a few wild animals, though not as many as when he was a boy. With each passing year, people were more common, the forests more carefully tended, and like every inhabited part in the world, his home was becoming domesticated, efficient and ordinary.

For twenty cycles, Jopale went about his life without worry, unaware that the first quake was followed by a series of little events—rumbles and slow, undetectable shifts that let gas and black seawater intrude into the gap between his one-time island and the buried coastline. Nobody knew the danger; there was nobody to blame afterwards. Indeed, only a few dozen people were killed in the incident, which meant that it was barely noticed beyond Jopale's horizon.

He woke early that last morning and slipped quietly from his house. A neighbor woman was still sleeping in his bed. She had arrived at his doorstep at the end of the last cycle, a little drunk and in the mood for sex. Jopale enjoyed her companionship, on occasion, but he felt no obligation to be with her when she woke. That's why he dressed in a hurry and rode off to school. Nobody knew that the seawater and its poisons had traveled so close to the surface. But in the time it takes a lover's heart to beat twice, the pressurized water found itself inside a sap well, nothing above but an open shaft and the sky.

The resulting geyser was a spectacle; every survivor said so. Presumably the doomed were even more impressed, watching the tower of saltwater and foam soar high overhead, dislodged chunks of wood falling around them, and an endless thunder shaking the world as huge quantities of gas—methane laced with hydrogen sulfide—bubbled free.

Suffocation was the standard death, for people and everything else.

The entire valley was killed within minutes. But the high ridges trapped the poisons, keeping the carnage contained. Even before Jopale heard the news, the disaster was finished. By the time he rode home again, crews of mockmen dressed in diving suits had capped the geyser. Engineers were busy drawing up plans for permanent repairs. And it was safe enough that a grieving survivor could walk to the ridge above, holding a perfumed rag against his face as he stared down at the fate of the world.

Water covered the valley floor—a stagnant gray lake already growing warm in the brilliant sunlight. The forested slopes had either drowned or been bleached by the suffocating gases. From his vantage point, Jopale couldn't see his house. But the land beneath the sea was still alive—still a vibrant blackish-green. Pumps would have to be set up, and osmotic filters, and then everything else could be saved. But if the work happened too slowly, too much salt would seep through the cuticle, causing the land to sicken and die. Then the valley would become a single enormous sore, attacked by fungi and giant worms. If nature was allowed its freedom, this tiny portion of the Continent would rot through, and the sea would come up again, spreading along the ancient fault lines, untold volumes of gas bubbling up into the rapidly sickening air.

People had to save the valley.

Why shouldn't they? A rational part of Jopale knew what was at stake—what almost every long-term prediction said was inevitable. But he couldn't shake his selfish need to enjoy the next cycle and the rest of his life. This ground had always been a part of him. Why wouldn't he want it saved? Let other people lose their little places. Let the Continent die everywhere but here. That's what he told himself as he walked down the path, the perfumed rag pressed against his nose and mouth, a self-possessed optimism flourishing for those next few steps.

Where the gases hadn't reached, epiphytes still flourished. Each tree stood apart from its neighbors, like the hair on the head of an elderly mockman. That made for a tall open forest, which in turn allowed the land to receive its share of sunlight. A flock of day-yabbers watched him from the high branches, leathery wings folded close, bright blue eyes alarmed by nothing except his presence. Giant forest roaches danced from crevice to crevice. Wild scramblers hid in nests of hair and woven branches, calling out at him with soft mournful voices. Then the path bent and dropped, and everything changed.

More yabbers lay dead beneath their perches, and countless silverfish and juvenile worms had crawled up out of their holes before dying. A giant golden gyretree—one of Jopale's favorite specimens—was already turning black at its base. But the air was breathable again, the wind having blown away the highest poisons. Jopale wished he had his breathing mask, but had left it inside his house, floating in a cupboard somewhere close to his dead lover. That woman had always been good company. But in death, she had grown unreal, abstract and distant. Walking around a next turn in the trail, Jopale found himself imagining her funeral and what delicate role he might play. And that was when he saw the wild scramblers that had fled the rising gas, but not fast enough. They belonged to one of the ground-dwelling species; he wasn't sure which. They had short hairy bodies and long limbs and little hands that reached out for nothing. Crests of bright blue fur topped the otherwise naked faces. The gases had stolen away their oxygen, then their lives. Already they were beginning to swell and turn black, lending them a strange, unfamiliar appearance; and when Jopale looked into their miserable little faces, he felt a sharp, unbearable fear.

In death more than life, those scramblers resembled human beings.

Here was the moment when everything changed for this scholarly gentleman—this creature of tradition and habit, of optimism and indifference. Gazing into those smoky green eyes and the wide mouths choked by their fat purple tongues, he saw his own future. That he didn't love the dead woman was important: If they were married and had children, and if his family had died today, Jopale would have felt an unrelenting attachment to this tiny corner of the world. In their honor, he would have ignored the urge to run away, remaining even as the land splintered and bled poisons and turned to dust and dead water.

But escape was what he wanted. The urge was sudden and irresistible. And later, when he examined what was possible, Jopale discovered only one solution that gave him any confidence.

If he sold his parents' land to his surviving neighbors and relatives, and if he bled his savings blue . . . then he could abandon the only home he had ever known, and forsake the sun, as well as abandoning all of those foolish little scramblers who couldn't see past their next little while . . .

WORLD'S EDGE

The great worm had come to a stop, but its muscles continued to shiver, long ripples traveling the length of the body, its misery made all the more obvious by a deep low moan that Jopale didn't hear so much as he felt it in his bones.

World's Edge: In some past eon, the city stood on the Continent's shoreline, nothing beyond but darkening skies and bottomless water. For generations, this great port had served as a home for fishermen, and more importantly, for the brave souls who journeyed onto the trackless sea-hunting giant rust-fins and the copper eels and vicious many-mouths. Fortunes were made from every carcass brought home—great masses of inedible meat and iron-rich bone pushed into furnaces and burned away, leaving nothing behind but a few dozen kilos of precious metal. But new islands were always being born, oftentimes half a world away, and they grew as they wandered, eventually slamming into this coastline and sticking fast. Removed from its livelihood, the once great city fell into hard times. Most of the neighboring towns vanished completely. But World's Edge managed to survive, clinging to its outmoded name, and when times and the world's growing population demanded it, the city blossomed again, new industries and a relentless sense of commerce producing a metropolis where two million people could live out their busy, unexceptional lives.

Birth and growth, followed by death and rebirth—no story told by Man was as important as this.

Then the Continent suddenly drifted west, and again, World's Edge wore the perfect name.

Jopale considered the ironies as he carried his bags to the front of the intestine, then out through an artificial sphincter fitted into the worm's side. From there, it was a short climb to the station's high wooden platform. A bright sign flashed from the top of the greeting arch, displaying the present atmospheric readings, followed by the cheery promise, "No hazards, none foreseen." The sun hovered just above the eastern horizon, stratospheric clouds and low pollution obscuring only a portion of its fierce glare. Squinting, Jopale faced the sun. At least two large balloons were visible in the sky, suspended on long ropes, spotters busily watching the land for geysers or more subtle ruptures. Behind him, long shadows stretched toward lands rendered unfit for normal life. Not that nothing and no one could live out there . . . but still, Jopale felt as if he was standing on the brink of a profound desolation, and that image struck him in some innate, profoundly emotional fashion . . .

The caretakers walked on top of their friend and along the concave, heavily greased trail, examining the worm's gray skin and poking its long tired muscles, sometimes using electric wands but mostly employing nothing but their bare hands. The worm's reflexes were slow. The old caretaker said as much to the younger workers. "She's gone too far with too many in her empty bellies," Master Brace complained, gesturing at the milling passengers. "She needs half a cycle at least, and all she can eat."

Jopale realized their delay would be longer than he had anticipated. Pulling two tickets from his traveler's belt, he carefully read the deeply legal language. If he didn't reach Port of Krauss within another fifteen cycles, the worm's owners would refund half of the value of the first ticket. But that was an inconsequential gesture, all things considered. Because the second ticket promised him a small cabin onboard a methane-fueled ship that would leave for the New Isles two cycles later. Punctuality was his responsibility. If he was late, the ticket was worthless. And Jopale would be trapped in the Port with every other refugee, shepherding the last of his money while absorbing news from around the world, hoping that the coming nightmare would take its time and he could eventually purchase a new berth on some later, unpromised vessel.

What good would fear do him now? Or rage?

"No good at all," he said with a stiff voice, turning his back to the sun.

The station was a strangely quiet place. The only other worms were small or plainly ill, and even those specimens were pointed west, aimed at the darkness, as if waiting for the order to flee. Besides caretakers, the only human workers were soldiers. Older men, mostly. Disciplined and probably without families—exactly the sort of people to be trusted in the worst of times. Two soldiers stood farther up the worm, guarding the sphincter leading into the stomach. Mockmen waited in the darkness. Each creature had its owner's name tattooed on its forearms and back. Humans had to come forward to claim what was theirs, and even then, the soldiers questioned them with suspicious voices—as if somebody might try to steal one of these creatures now.

The mysterious young woman was standing with the other passengers, her book in one arm, eyes pointed in the general direction of the unloading.

"Which is yours?" Jopale asked.

She didn't seem to hear the question. Then he realized that her gaze reached past the mockmen, bright tan eyes staring at the night lands, her mind probably traveling on to her destination.

"Good Mountain, is it?" Jopale asked.

"I'm sorry, no." She was answering his first question, smiling in his general direction. "I don't own any of these creatures."

Jopale had brought a mockman from home, to help with his bags and his life, as well as giving him this ready excuse to stand where he was, chatting with this young woman.

With a quiet, gentlemanly voice, he offered his name.

She nodded and said, "Yes. Good Mountain."

They had found a pattern. He would ask some little question, and she would answer his former question.

"The word 'mountain,'" he said. "Do you know what it means?"

She smiled now, glancing at his face. "Do you?"

He allowed himself the pleasure of a wise nod. "It is an ancient word," he answered. "The oldest texts employ it. But even by then, the word had fallen into a rotten disuse."

"Really?"

"We have words for ridges and hills. With great clarity, we can describe the color and quality of any ground. But from what we can determine, using our oldest sources, 'mountain' implies a titanic uplifting of something much harder than any wood. Harder and more durable, and a true mountain rises high enough to puncture the sky. At least according to some expert interpretations."

She laughed, very softly. "I know."

"Do you?"

"That's why they picked the name," she explained.

Jopale didn't understand, and his expression must have said as much.

"Of course, there's no actual mountain there," she admitted. "It's just a flat plain shoved high by a set of faults and buoyant substrates. But there was a time, long ago, when the Continent pushed in from every side, and an entire island was buried. Buried and carried a long ways under the sea."

The woman liked to explain things. Was she a teacher?

"Interesting," Jopale offered, though he wasn't convinced that it was.

"That island is like a mountain in reverse, you see. It extends a long ways below the waterline. Like a fist sticking out from the bottom of the Continent, reaching deeper into our ocean than any other feature we know of."

"I see," he muttered.

But why she would call it, "Our ocean"? How many oceans were there?

"That's why the science station was built there," she explained. " 'A good mountain to do research.' That what my colleagues used to joke."

"What kind of research?" he asked.

"Land distortions and water cycles, mostly. And various experts who work with that submerged ground."

He said, "Really?" with a false enthusiasm.

The woman nodded, returning to her distant stare.

"Is that your specialty?" he asked, trying to read the binding of her book. "Prehistoric islands?"

"Oh, no." She passed the heavy book to her other arm.

"Then what do you do?"

It was an exceptionally reasonable question, but she was a peculiar creature. Smiling as if nothing had ever been funnier, she said, "Do-ane." She wasn't quite looking at his face, telling him, "That is my name."

He didn't have a ready response.

"You told me yours. I assumed you wanted to know mine."

"Thank you," Jopale muttered.

"I'm sorry, but I can't say anything else."

He nodded and shrugged. And then his mockman emerged from the stomach: A mature female with big blue eyes riding high on her broad stoic face. Jopale had recently purchased her from a cousin, replacing the mockmen he had lost when the valley flooded. For her species, she was smart and adaptable. By any standard, she was loyal, and in countless domestic tasks, she was helpful. And like every passenger from the worm's stomach, she smelled of acid and other unpleasant secretions. But at least this creature didn't want to play word games, or dance silly secrets before his eyes.

Jopale spoke to one of the soldiers, proving his ownership to everyone's satisfaction.

"My bags," he ordered.

The creature snatched each by its rope handle.

"This way," he said. Then with a minimal nod, he excused himself from Do-ane, pushing through the station, searching for some place where the noble refugee might eat a fit meal.

PARANOIA

Dining halls next to worm stations were rarely elegant. World's Edge was an exception: Using the local wood, artisans had carved long blocks into a series of omega-shaped beams, each a little different from the others, all linked like ribs to form a single long room. Woven gyre-tree branches created a porous roof. Heavy planks had been bleached white and laid out for a floor, each fastened to the foundation with solid pins made of dense black knot-wood. The tables and chairs were brightly colored, orange and gold predominating, everything made from slick new plastics—one of those expensive programs underwritten by some well-meaning government agency, public moneys helping lock away a few breaths of methane into this more permanent form. The usual indoor epiphytes clung to the overhead beams— vigorous plants with dark leaves that thrived in the artificial light, their finger-like roots drinking nothing but the travelers' nervous breathing. Jopale noticed a familiar figure planted at one end of a busy table, accompanied by two mockmen that sat backwards on turned-around chairs, eating their rations off their laps—a common custom in many places.

"May I join you?" asked Jopale.

"Please." The man was tall even when he was sitting, and unlike practically everyone else in the place, he wasn't eating. His old map was opened up before him, and with long fingers and sharpened nails, he measured and remeasured the distances between here and Port of Krauss.

Jopale set down his platter and handed his mockman two fresh rations of syrup-and-roach. The big female settled on the floor, legs crossed, hands and mind focused on the screw-style lids on both wooden jars.

Unsure what to say, Jopale said nothing. But silence proved uncomfortable, which was why he eventually picked the most obvious topic. "So why are you going to Port of Krauss?"

The thin man glanced up for a moment, apparently startled.

"You are going there, aren't you?"

"No."

"I'm sorry then," said Jopale. "I just assumed—"

"My trip doesn't end there," the thin man continued. "I have business, of a kind . . . business in another place . . ."

"The New Isles?"

Surprise turned to pleasure. "Are you going there too?"

Jopale nodded.

"Well, good. I knew there had to be others. Wonderful!"

Somehow that revelation didn't bring comfort. Jopale had the impression that his companion was difficult, and the idea of traveling with him across the rest of the Continent and then out over the Ocean felt daunting, if not out and out unpleasant.

"I need somebody to keep my confidence up," the tall man proclaimed.

What did confidence have to do with anything?

"My name is Rit."

"Jopale."

Rit didn't seem to hear him. Glancing over his shoulder, he observed, "There aren't any people working in the kitchen. Did you notice?"

Only mockmen were cooking and washing dishes. There wasn't even an overseer walking among them, keeping order.

"I don't know if I could make myself go to work," Jopale admitted. "All that's happening, even if it's far from here—"

"Not that far away," Rit interrupted.

"What? Has the news changed?"

"Aren't things awful enough as they are?" The tall man shuddered, then steered clear of that dangerous subject. He licked his lips and stared down at the big map, fingers stretched wide. Then with a tight voice, he asked the lines and tiny dots, "You do believe in the Isles, don't you?"

"Why wouldn't I?"

The narrow face twisted. "But have you ever seen the Isles? Or do you know anyone who's actually visited them?"

Jopale had never considered the possibility. "What do you mean? How could they not exist?" He immediately reached for the only book in his personal satchel—a leather-bound, professionally printed volume full of photographs and exhaustive explanations. With his voice rising, he said, "I haven't heard anything like that. Not even the rumor of a rumor."

Rit shook his head and began to fold up his map, saying to no one in particular, "I'm sorry. I have these panics. Always have."

The man was insane, or nearly so.

"It's just that in times like these . . ." Rit took a moment to compose himself. "When disaster reigns, deceitful souls prosper. Have you noticed? Criminals rise up like worms inside dead wood. They come from below to hurt good people, for profit and for fun."

There was an obvious, ominous counter to that logic. "We've never seen times as bad as these," Jopale said.

That observation earned a terrified but respectful look from his companion. "I suppose that's so."

"Why go to so much trouble to mislead us? With the worst happening, in far-off places now and maybe here soon . . . even a despicable thief knows he wouldn't have enough time to enjoy his money . . ."

"Unless he doesn't believe he will die." Rit leaned across the table, putting his bony face close to Jopale's face. "Most people still don't appreciate their mortality. They read about the deaths of

strangers. Places they don't know are poisoned or burning. But until
their lungs are sick and their skin is cooking, they think their chances
are exceptionally good."

There were stubborn souls in the world, yes. Jopale knew a history teacher—a brilliant man by any measure—who had openly
mocked him. "Nothing ever changes in the world," the colleague had
claimed. "The Continent will shatter here and there, and some old islands will be destroyed. But others islands will survive, along with the
people riding them. That is the irrefutable lesson of our past, Jopale.
Our world is tough, our species is lucky, and both will survive every
onslaught."

Jopale nodded for a moment, as if accepting that remembered lec-
ture. Then with an honest conviction, he reminded Rit, "There are easier and much cheaper ways to fool people. And steal a fortune in the
process, I might add."

His companion gave a grudging nod.

"I am like you," Jopale continued, knowing that he wasn't anything like this crazy fellow. "I've had some suspicions, yes. I wanted
to know: Were the New Isles really as strong and smartly designed as
their builders claim them to be? So I made inquiries before commit-
ting my money. And yes, the New Isles do exist. They were built at the
Port of Krauss, at the main shipyard. The last Isle was launched just a
year ago, and it's still being towed to its final destination. I even spoke
to workers at the Port, using a radiophone. And while they couldn't
promise that the Isles were located in safe places, or that I had an open
berth waiting for me and my mockman, they were definite about one
issue: They had done their best work, fabricating the largest, strongest
ships humans had ever known."

Jopale glanced at the cover of his book. From the bluffs overlook-
ing the unlit ocean, someone had taken a photograph showing a wide
vessel built from tough old wood. Some of the strongest, most enduring land in the world had been cut free of the Continent and floated
into position, then carved into a cumbersome but durable ensemble of
hulls and empty chambers. And to make the Isle even stronger, a fortune in refined metals had been fashioned into cables and struts and
long nails that were fixed throughout the Isle's body. Metal was what
Port of Krauss was famous for—the rare elements that could be fil-

tered from the cold dark seawater. With the best alloys in the world, insulated tanks were built, and they were filled with methane and dangled far beneath each Isle, using the sea's own pressure and cold to help keep the gas liquefied. That gas would eventually power lights and hydroponics, with enough energy in reserve to tear the seawater apart . . . to carve hydrogen from the precious oxygen, allowing everyone to breathe without any cumbersome masks.

With the surety of a good teacher, Jopale dismissed Rit's concerns. "These are genuine sanctuaries, and my new home is waiting for me. I just have to get there now. And I feel quite sure that I will."

Saying those words, he believed them.

Rit seemed to take it all to heart. He put away his map and found his own copy of the member's handbook, opening it to one of his favorite pages.

Finally, Jopale began to eat his meal. He had purchased two scrambler hands, fried but not too greasy, and a whitish lump of sweetcake and cultured algae in a salty soup, all washed down with a tall bottle of fermented sap imported from the Earlands. The drink was the most expensive item on the limited menu, and it was the most appreciated. The hard kick of the liquor was already working on his mood when his companion spoke again, using a sorry little voice to ask, "But what if?"

"What if what?" Jopale responded testily.

"What if these thieves and con artists did believe this world was coming to an end? And by promising berths to us and maybe a million others like us, they earned enough money to finance their own salvation."

Jopale grimaced, breathing through his teeth.

"What if a New Isle is waiting, but not for us?" Rit persisted.

Jopale felt a smile emerge on its own. Then with a bitter laugh, he told his traveling companion, "Well then. Then we aren't in any worse shape than the rest of the world. Now are we?"

ON AGAIN

Jopale had always excelled at school, including respectable grades earned in each of the three sciences. But he never achieved a profound understanding of genetics or selective forces. He learned what was absolutely necessary, relying on his clear memory when it came to the standard exams. Introductory classes demanded little else, while the high-level courses—those rarefied environments where professors wanted more than disgorged fact and holy equations—had never been in his future.

But one lesson Jopale took from science was this: Mockmen were wondrous creatures, pliable and creative by every genetic measure.

A glance around the station proved that truism. Most of the mockmen were big creatures, two or three times larger than a grown human. They had been bred for compliance and power when necessary and a minimal metabolism to help reduce the food bills. Yet some of these creatures were small and slender as a child. And a few of the kitchen workers were quicker than any human being—a blessing in this hurly-burly business. What's more, no two of them could be confused for each other, even though they might be siblings or a parent and grown child. All had an oval face and a protruding chin beneath a small, seemingly inadequate mouth. Yet each face was unique. Jopale's own girl had descended from giants that lived for generations on his family farm—a generalist by design and by training, her head topped with beastly red hair, a dramatic chin hanging from the parabolic jaw, and blue inhuman eyes gazing out at a world full of motion and incomprehensible purpose. If the creature had a voice, she would have commanded a vocabulary of several hundred easy words. But of course the larynx was pierced when she was a baby, leaving her able to communicate only with simple gestures and vaguely human expressions. A creature of habit and duty, his mockman was too simple to understand the dire state of the world—an ignorance that Jopale couldn't help but envy, at least now and again.

"Everything with a spine arose from a common ancestor," he had learned long ago. His biology professor—an ancient woman blessed with her own sturdy backbone—explained to the class, "A single creature must have been the originator of us all. On some ancient continent, long dead and rotted away, this precursor to humans ran about on two legs, climbing up into the saprophytes and epiphytes, grabbing what food it could with its primitive hands."

"Like a scrambler?" a student had asked.

Jopale didn't ask the question, thankfully. The professor reacted with a click of the tongue and a sorry shake of her head. "Hardly," she replied. "Scramblers are as far removed from our founding species as we are. As the mockmen are. Flying yabbers, copper eels, plus everything else you can name . . . all of these species would look at that vanished organism as being its very distant ancestor. That is, if simple beasts could ever think in such abstract terms."

"But where did the first vertebrates come from?" another student inquired. "From the sea? Or from some earlier continent?"

"Nobody knows," the professor replied. Then with the surety of age, she added, "And nobody will ever discover that unnecessary answer. Since there's no way to study the matter any further than it has been studied by now."

$$\bullet\bullet\bullet$$

Jopale had been sitting in the station for several hours, changing position as the plastic chair pushed against his rump. At that moment, he happened to be thinking about his biology teacher, long dead, and about the nature of surety. And to stave off boredom, he was studying the astonishing diversity of false humans who sat and walked among those who were real.

Suddenly a short, homely mockman entered the dining hall. It was female, dressed in the stiff uniform of a station worker. And like with a few of her species, some quirk of genetics had swollen her skull, giving her a genuine forehead under a cap of thick black hair. That forehead was remarkable enough. But then the newcomer opened her mouth, revealing a clear and exceptionally strong voice.

"The westbound worm is rested and ready," she sang out, the clarity of each word taking travelers by surprise. "Leave by way of the door behind me, sirs and madams. If you have a ticket. You must have a ticket. The westbound worm is fed and eager. She will be leaving shortly, my friends."

Most of the room stood up.

"That wasn't as long as I feared." An elderly woman wearing elegant clothes and amber gems was smiling at her good fortune. "I was ready to sit for quite a while longer," she admitted to her companion.

A handsome man, perhaps half her age, muttered, "I wonder why this is."

The rich woman had to laugh at him. "It's because we are special, darling. What more reason do you need?"

Jopale was among the last to reach the open doorway. Soldiers were waiting, carefully examining each ticket and every piece of identification. Meanwhile, the uniformed mockman stood beside the long line, smiling happily. Why did that creature make him feel so uneasy? Was it her face? Her voice? No, what bothered Jopale was the way she stared at the other faces, black eyes settling only on those who were human.

"Good journey," she said to Jopale.

Then to Rit, who was directly behind him, she said, "You are in trustworthy hands, sir. No need to worry."

She could read the man's fear.

A one-in-a-million creature, thought Jopale. Or there was another explanation, and far more sordid too. Glancing over his shoulder, he wondered if she could be a hybrid—a quirk of biology that wasn't destroyed at birth, but instead was fed and trained for this halfway demanding task. Nothing like her would ever happen in his homeland. It wasn't allowed. But World's Edge was a different part of the world, and Jopale's long journey had taught him many lessons, including that every place had its own culture, and cultures were defined by odd little customs understandable only to themselves.

"This way, this way!" the old caretaker cried out.

Jopale showed the soldiers what they wanted to see, his own mockman standing silently to his right.

Master Brace was at the end of the long platform, shouting for the passengers and waving both arms. Even at a distance, his face betrayed a look of genuine concern. Something bad must have happened. But their giant worm lay motionless on the greased trail, apparently sleeping. Its intestine was still jammed full of half-digested food. The worm's bloated shape said as much, and looking through the plastic windows, Jopale saw a rich dark mixture of masticated wood pulp and sweet knuckle-roots, happy muscles pressing the feast into new positions, the elastic walls working on the stubborn chunks and bubbles.

The passengers were being led up toward the stomach.

Jopale was disgusted, but compliant. The wealthy woman who talked about being special was now first to complain. Shaking an accusing finger at the caretaker, she said, "I did not pay for an acid-bath."

The caretaker had discarded his charm. He looked tired and perhaps a little scared, not to mention short of patience. "Her stomach isn't hungry anymore," he said with a loud, slow voice. "And it's thoroughly buffered, madam. You'll be comfortable enough inside there, I promise."

"But my mockmen—"

"Will ride above, in the open air." Brace gestured impatiently. The pilothouse was fixed on top of the long blind head, and behind it were ropes and straps and simple chairs. With a loud voice, Brace told every passenger, "If we waited for my baby to empty her bowels, we'd remain here until the next cycle. Which might be just as well. But word just came up from One-Time—"

An earlier stop, two cycles to the east.

"A new fissure has broken open there. The situation is dicey. And since there's room enough inside the stomach, I'm sure you can see . . . this is the best answer to our many problems . . . !"

The passengers turned together, gazing toward the east. While everyone was busily filling his own belly, the bright face of the sun had been covered over. Distant clouds seemed thicker than natural, and blacker, and the clouds were rising up like a great angry wall, towering over the green land that these people had only recently journeyed across.

A purposeful panic took hold of the crowd.

Jopale claimed his belongings from his mockman and ordered her to climb on top of the worm. Then he passed through the cramped sphincter and into the stomach, sniffing the air as an afterthought, pleased to find it fresh enough and even a little scented. The shaggy pink floor was a little damp but not truly wet. Worm stomachs were shorter than the duodenum, and most of the floor had been claimed. A simple latrine stood in back. Do-ane sat alone in the middle of the remaining space, hiking boots beside her. She showed Jopale a polite smile, nothing more. Where else could he go? Nowhere. Claiming the empty stomach to her right, he threw open his traveling blanket and inflated his pillow. Setting the pillow on the highest portion of his floor, he tried to ignore her. Then Rit knelt on the other side of the young woman, carefully laying out his blanket, preparing his fragile nerves for the next leg of this very long journey.

Jopale was terrified, genuinely terrified, right up until the moment when the alarms were sounded.

The sharp wailing of sirens began in the distance, diluted and distorted by the worm's body. Then the station's sirens joined in, and the floor rolled ominously. Was it a quake, or was the worm waking? Probably both reasons, he decided. Then the stomach sphincter closed, choking off the worst of the noise, and the giant creature gulped air into its long lungs and into its empty belly, needing little prompting to begin squirming against the trail's slick surface. Rolling muscle and the long powerful tail created a sound unlike any other in nature. Jopale was reminded of a thick fluid being forced down a very narrow drain. Slowly, slowly, the creature built its momentum, the trail's oils eliminating most of the friction, allowing its bulk to gradually become something swift and relentless.

Passengers held their air masks in their hands, waiting for instructions or the telltale stink of a gas cloud. Because there had to be gas somewhere close. A quake wasn't reason enough to sound the city's alarms. Yet curiously, in the midst of this obvious emergency, Jopale felt much calmer. He knew he had to remain vigilant and clearheaded. And gas was only an inconvenience to a man with the proper equipment. Standing beside one of the few stomach windows, he watched the station vanish behind them, replaced by broad government buildings and assorted shops, and then suddenly, by countless homes stacked three deep and set beside narrow, shade-drenched streets. A few mockmen were walking with purposeful shuffles; otherwise no one appeared in the open. Most of the homes were shuttered and sealed. If poisons were boiling up from below, private detectors would smell them; and people would huddle inside their little safe rooms, breathing filtered air or oxygen from bottles, or breathing nothing but the increasingly stale air. An awful experience, Jopale knew. There was no more helpless feeling in the world. Yet his overriding emotion now was a tremendous, almost giddy relief.

He had escaped again, just in time.

Do-ane joined him. The window was quite tiny, not designed for looking outside, but instead to let in sunlight and allow the caretakers to monitor the mockmen who normally rode here. Do-ane stood on her toes to look outside. She seemed prettier when she was nervous, and rather more appealing. In her hand was the most sophisticated gas-gauge that Jopale had ever seen. In a whisper, she said, "Hydrogen sulfide."

His own confidence fell to pieces. Methane was awful—suffocating and flammable—but the putrid hydrogen sulfide gas was far worse. There were places beneath the Continent where the dissolved oxygen had been exhausted. The living wood and dark currents couldn't freshen that water any more. And different types of rot took hold there, anaerobic bacteria creating a sour poison that could kill within minutes.

The city kept sliding past.

"Is that a body?" she asked suddenly.

What might be a mockman was lying on its side, tucked against the foundation of a long house. Or was it just trash dressed in a blanket? Jopale wasn't sure, and then they had passed both the body and the street. With his own quiet voice, he said, "It was nothing."

"It was human," Do-ane said.

"A sleeping mockman," he offered. "Or a dead one, maybe. But that means nothing. Disease or age, or boys out damaging property, maybe."

"Do you think so?" Do-ane asked hopefully.

"Oh, yes," he said. And because it felt good, he again said that word. "Yes." Then he added with his most reasonable tone, "If the gas was that terrible, the streets would be jammed with suffocating bodies."

She looked at him, desperate to believe those sordid words.

Suddenly Jopale couldn't remember why the young woman had bothered him. He smiled and she did the same, and with that, they leaned against the living wall, watching the city fall away and the countryside reemerge. Tall epiphytes spread their leaves to the waning light. Rain showers were soaking the land to the south. Maybe those clouds would drift north; that would lessen the chances of a fire, at least for a little while. Right? Meanwhile, Do-ane's sensor continued to record the fluctuating levels of sulfides, plus the usual methane and ethane that were pulled inside whenever the worm belched and swallowed more air. But none of the toxins reached a suffocating level, and except for a foul taste in the back of the mouth, they remained unnoticed by the other passengers.

Finally the sun merged with the horizon and the numbers began to fall again, working their way back toward levels that were normal enough, at least over the last few years.

Jopale sat on his blanket, enjoying his good fortune.

Then for no clear reason, he thought about the hybrid woman back at the station—the black-haired creature with the big lovely voice—and it occurred to him that unlike the human soldiers, she'd had no air mask riding upon her hip.

Had she survived?

And why, in the face of everything, did he seem to care?

PLANS OF ESCAPE

At the school where Jopale taught, the conclusion of each term meant a party thrown for the faculty and staff. Liquor was involved, and school politics, and during that final gathering, some extraordinarily raw emotions. Radiophone broadcasts had just reported a cluster of villages in the distant north destroyed by an eruption of poisons. Sober voices were repeating rumors—false rumors, as it happened—that the local engineers and mockmen crews couldn't stop the enormous jets of methane. The party soon divided itself into two camps: Some wanted to embrace their doom, while others clung to any excuse for hope. Jopale found himself on the fringes of the argument, unsure which stance to take. Then a colleague wandered past, his cup drained and his mind intoxicated. Listening to a few declarations of terror, the normally timid fellow found a buoyant courage. "The situation is not that dangerous," he declared. "Believe me, we can seal up holes ten times worse than what I've heard described in these stories!"

The optimists happily embraced those defiant words.

But the teacher shrugged off their praise. "You're as silly as the rest of them," he declared. "And at least as ignorant, too."

"What do you know?" someone asked.

"More than anybody else here, I can tell you that." Then the drunken man scanned the room. Searching for an escape route? No, he wanted the big bowl set on the central table—a leather bowl where sweet punch and fermented gig-berries created a small pond. "Look here," he called out. "I'll show you exactly what I mean."

His audience gathered at the table, maintaining a skeptical silence.

Using the thick decorative leaves of a hush-woad, the teacher began covering the pond's surface. And while he worked, he lectured about the wooden Continent and the bottomless Ocean and how things like rot and methane were the inevitable end products in a very ancient cycle.

Jopale understood it all, or he thought he did.

Then a third teacher—the most accomplished science instructor on their staff—cleared his throat before mentioning, "This isn't your professional area, you know."

"My area?" The lecturer with the leaves asked, "What is my area? Remind me now."

"Maps," the scientist said, that single word wrapped inside a smug and blatantly dismissive tone.

Anger showed on the colleague's face. But he didn't lose his temper. He just shook his head for a moment and set another layer of leaves on the pond. Then with a quiet, brittle voice, he said, "Jopale."

"Yes?"

"What do you know about the Man-and-Sky texts?"

Jopale had read excerpts in college. But even in these modest academic circles, it was best to appear well trained. "I studied them for a semester," he replied with a careful tone. "What about them?"

"How old are they?"

"No one knows."

"But judging by the different dead languages, we can assume they're probably several different ages . . . a mishmash of writings from a series of unnamed authors. Yes?"

Jopale offered a nod.

His colleague took a deep breath. "Scholars believe the Man-and-Sky offers at least three descriptions of the world, possibly four. Or five. Or even six. What's certain is that each description is not that much different from our world. There is a large continent and a motionless sun. Only the names of every location have been changed, and the peoples use different languages, and sometimes the animals and vegetation are not quite recognizable."

Like bored students, the teachers began to mutter among themselves.

The lecturer placed a hand upon the floating leaves. "My area . . . my intellectual passion . . . is too complicated for ordinary minds. I'll grant you that. Thousands upon thousands of islands coalesce into a single body, each island fighting with its stubborn neighbors to remain on the Ocean's surface, basking in the brightest possible sunshine. It makes for a grand, glorious puzzle that would baffle most of you . . ."

Feeling the insult, his audience fell silent.

"The Man-and-Sky texts give us the best maps of those earlier continents. And they offer some of the most compelling accounts of how the old continents fell to pieces." The geographer picked a pale yellow straw off the table, his mouth pressed into a wide, painful smile. "You probably don't know this. Those lost continents were barely half the size of ours. There is no evidence—none—that the islands in the past have ever managed to cover the entire day-face of our world. Which makes what is happening now into a singular event. An elaborate collision of random events, and perhaps selective forces too."

"What about selective forces?" the scientist grumbled.

"Which islands prosper?" their colleague asked. "The strong ones, of course. And those that remain on the surface for the longest time. Those that can resist the poisons in the bad times, and those that will endure the longest, darkest famines." Then he shrugged, adding, "In earlier cycles, the wood beneath us would have been dead long ago. The collapses would have come sooner; the tragedies would have been smaller. But this time—in our time—the islands have descended from a few durable lineages. And what's more, every other force at play in the world has pushed us to the worst stage imaginable."

Even in his blackest moods, Jopale didn't want to believe that.

"We don't know how much methane is under our toes," the lecturer admitted. "But even the median guesses are awful."

A small, sorry voice said, "The entire world could suffocate."

Jopale had offered those words.

"Oh, but it's far worse than that!" His colleague stuck the long straw into his mouth, then slipped the other end into a small wooden flask hidden in his coat pocket. He sucked up the liquid and covered the straw's upper end with his thumb, lifting the leaves until he could see the open punch, then he set the bottom of the straw against the sweet drink. "Of course I mean this as an illustration," he mentioned. Then he winked at the scientist, saying, "I know, I know. There's no genuine consensus among the experts. Or should I say specialists? Since there is, if you think about it, an important difference between those two words . . ."

"Don't," Jopale cautioned.

But the man struck a long match, making a yellow flame. Then winking at his audience, he said, "Of course, the Continent might collapse slowly, over many generations. A little gas here, a lot of gas there. People die, but not too many of us. And maybe we will marshal the necessary resources. Cut holes to the Ocean below and let out the bubbles in manageable little breaths. Or pump pure oxygen down under our feet, freshening the cold dead water." He waved the flame in front of his eyes. "Perhaps humans can do whatever it takes, and our atmosphere isn't destroyed when the hydrocarbons eat up our precious free oxygen."

"You're drunk," the scientist complained.

"Wonderfully drunk, yes." Then the teacher of city names and island positions laughed, and he lowered the flame.

Everyone stared at the leaf-covered punch.

Jopale assumed that the liquid from the vial was pure alcohol. But his colleague had decided to make a more effective demonstration of his argument, which was why he used a collection of long-chain hydrocarbons purchased from an industrial source—a highly flammable concoction that made a soft but impressive wooshing sound as it set the leaves on fire, and then the drunken man's hand, and a moment later, his astonished, pain-wracked face.

THE EVENING AIR

Left-of-Left was the next official stop—a safe station where the hard-pressed worm could catch its breath and empty its swollen bowels.

Most of the passengers had fallen asleep by then. The only light inside the crowded stomach came from a bioluminescent culture hung on an acid-etched brass hook. Do-ane hadn't bothered with a sleeping hood, curled up on her blanket, hands sweetly tucked between her pillow and face. Rit didn't seem able to relax, sitting up occasionally to adjust his hood or take another white melatonin pill. Only Jopale didn't feel tired—an illusion brought on by too much nervous energy—and that was why he stepped outdoors, using this brief pause to check on his mockman's health, breathe the open air, and absorb the depressing sights.

The station was empty and dark. Information displays had been turned off, while the offices and cafeteria had their doors locked. Master Brace was standing alone on the platform, watching his colleagues use electric wands to stimulate the worm's anus. Jopale approached, then hesitated. Was the old caretaker crying? But Brace sensed his audience. Suddenly wiping his eyes with a sleeve, he turned to the lone passenger, habit or perhaps some unflagging sense of duty helping him create a magnificent, heartening smile.

"A gloomy darkness, but a very pleasant climate," he remarked. "Don't you think so, sir?"

Jopale nodded.

"I've stood here at least a hundred times, sir."

"With our worm?"

"Oh, yes." Men like Brace often spent their professional lives caring for the same worm, learning its talents and peculiarities; and since worms were creatures of relentless habit, they were rarely asked to change routes or schedules.

"Pleasant," the old man said again.

Tall clouds stood on the eastern horizon, obscuring the last hints of sunlight. From a distance, the clouds resembled a thick purplish-red tower that was either extraordinarily lovely or extraordinarily terrible.

Jopale asked if the clouds were made from smoke or water.

Master Brace shrugged his shoulders. "We won't be staying long, sir," was all he said.

Left-of-Left was a small city, and judging by the spacious warehouses standing beside the various worm trails, it had been exceptionally prosperous. Great slabs of freshly cut wood waited beside the widest worm trails, mounted on sleds ready to be towed east by giant freight worms. But there was only one other worm in the station besides theirs, and it had dragged itself between two buildings and died, its pale carcass beginning to swell as it rotted from within.

"This wood—?" Jopale began.

"The finest in the world," the caretaker offered. "This ground is dense and durable—a sweet grain, and almost perfectly free of knots. It has been in demand, for centuries now. And when the Continent shifted east, the local miners adapted quickly." Brace gestured toward the south. "They poisoned the best of their wood with arsenic salts. Even if their land starved, they weren't going to allow any worm infestations. Beautiful planks were still coming out of this place . . . but you certainly don't want to breathe the sawdust, I can tell you."

Sprawling homes stood north of the station, yards sprinkled with tall poles. Gas-jet lights were strung high overhead—a cheat to bring light to a place without sunshine. But not one of the torches was burning now, and none of the windows on any house showed the barest hint of life.

Even the lowliest mockmen were missing.

"Because everybody left," the caretaker explained. "They went off . . . I don't quite know . . . maybe forty cycles ago? They were still here on my last trip through. Nobody warned me. But they were quiet while I was here, which was unusual for them. Very chatty folk, most of the time. Which makes me believe that they'd come to their decision already."

Their worm began to shake now. Intestines contracted and the long body grew longer, the creature beginning to clear its bowels. The stink of the process was horrific, yet it bothered no one but the lone passenger.

Jopale turned his face away. "What decision was that?" he asked, one hand thrown across his mouth and nose.

"These people had their escape prepared," the caretaker replied. "Probably years ago. A lot of these little communities . . . out here in the dark . . . they have schemes. Sanctuaries, special ground."

"Is that so?"

"Oh, yes," Brace replied, as if this was common knowledge. "People living in the night know what disaster means. They have experience and common sense. Like Left-of-Left here. One lady told me, with a confidential voice, that her family had built themselves a fireproof shelter and surrounded it with a deep moat. When the air soured, they would breathe bottled oxygen. And if the fires came, they'd flood the moat with water and spray it over their heads."

Jopale almost responded.

But the caretaker saw doubt in his face. "Oh, I know, sir. I realize. That doesn't sound workable. This would be no ordinary fire, and this dense ground is sure to burn hot and long. If that miserable time should come." He laughed amiably for a moment, then added, "She was definitely lying to me. I know that now, and maybe I knew it then. You see . . . I would normally remain here for a cycle or two. We like to give this worm a long sleep and a chance to fatten up, and that local woman would let me share her bed. A wonderful lady, and a good friend, and she wanted me to know that she had arrangements made. But she didn't tell me enough so that I could find her. Which is reasonable, and I shouldn't be hurt. Wherever these people have gone, they don't have extra room for their occasional lovers."

Jopale didn't know what to say, so he remained silent.

Then the caretaker turned back to his colleagues, and with a sharp, accusing tone, he called out, "Leave those turds on the trail. You hear me?"

A young woman was standing in the worm-greased trail. Spiked boots kept her from falling, and she held a special stick used to shove the foul wastes to the side. "But the regulations—" she began.

"Regulations?" the old man interrupted. Forgetting about Jopale, he stepped to the edge of the platform, throwing out a few curses before reminding his crew, "Our first concern is our own worm. Our second concern is our passengers. And we are not wasting any time rolling crap out of the way of worms and people who are not going to be coming.

"Do you hear what I'm saying to you?"

A LAST MOMENT PLEA

Friends and colleagues were remarkably supportive of Jopale's decision to leave home. Most offered polite words, while a few posed the most obvious questions. "Where did you learn about the New Isles?" they asked. He had come across an article in a small journal that catered to the wealthy. For a fee, he was able to purchase an introductory book filled with photographs and useful descriptions. "And they had space available?" people wondered. "At this late date?" But a New Isle was being built every few years—the process guaranteed to continue until the disaster came or the danger passed. So yes, there was space enough for him. "But how does a teacher afford it?" they pressed. "How could you afford it?" Jopale offered a shrug and shy smile, mentioning his substantial inheritance. He always made that confession warily, expecting others to be openly jealous or envious or even noticeably bitter. But people absorbed the news with surprise and resignation. Which was a little disappointing, curiously enough. It would have made Jopale feel more secure about his solution—more optimistic by a long measure—if what he was doing caused pointed hatred in the people that he was prepared to leave behind.

Acquaintances and fellow teachers always seemed to have their own escape routes planned—hopeful schemes wrapped around the local civil protection service or private bunkers. And there was some good reason for hope: Throughout the district, old worm holes were being sealed and stocked with provisions. If the fires came, locals would hunker in the dark, sipping bottled air, while the ground above was saturated with pure water and complex foams guaranteed to shoulder all but the most catastrophic heat.

The problem was that if the fires came, the heat would turn catastrophic. The worst fires to date were in the south, not far from the polar zone. Epiphyte forests were being consumed in an instant. The normally inflammable cuticle boiled away soon after that. Then the deep living wood caught fire and burned off, allowing drowned, half-rotted islands free to spring to the surface, bringing up fresh methane that only caused the fires to grow larger. After that, the soggiest, most rotten wood was soon baked to a crisp and set on fire, and despite an army of mockmen and brave firefighters, that circular zone of total destruction was spreading outwards, eating a kilometer with every cycle, engulfing abandoned villages and useless farms in a roaring, irresistible maelstrom.

Yet Jopale's friends put on hopeful, brave faces. "We'll get the upper hand soon," they claimed, sounding as if they were fighting on the front lines. "And we'll beat the next twenty blazes too. You just wait and see."

But nothing happened quickly in the world. Cycle after cycle, the southern fire continued to spread, and new ones exploded to life in other distant places. The steady, irresistible disaster gave everyone time enough to doubt his most cherished beliefs. That's when people found themselves admitting to their very lousy prospects, particularly in conversation with their oldest friends.

"I keep telling people that I'm staying," announced one of Jopale's neighbors. A bachelor like Jopale, bright and well-read, he admitted, "I'm always saying that the fires will be put out, or they'll miss us. But when it comes down to it, do you know what I'll do? Run. Run east to the Ocean, just like you're running west. If I can slip past the provincial guards and disappear into the chaos . . ."

"Maybe," Jopale replied, unsure what that would accomplish.

But the fellow had written himself into an interesting story. "All those last islands that merged with the Continent? Well, I've heard their citizens are burying explosives inside the old fault lines. And when the time comes, they'll set off the biggest blasts in history."

Again, Jopale said, "Maybe."

He didn't want to attack the man's dream. But doubt must have crept into his face, because his friend bristled, asking, "What's wrong?"

Jopale was no expert. But in every account he had read, those giant fires were accompanied by fabulously strong winds. The winds blew toward the flames, feeding them the oxygen critical to their survival. You could shatter the old fractures from end to end, chiseling the islands free of the doomed Continent; but those enormous masses of wood and scared humanity would still have to move into the open water, pressing against that roaring gale.

"Well then," the friend responded. "They'll think of that. Probably they'll blow their way free long before the fire comes."

And release any methane trapped under their feet, starting their own deadly blaze. But this time, Jopale found the tact to say, "That's reasonable, sure." Then he added, "I don't know much about technical matters."

"Keep that in mind, Jopale." Shaking a finger, the old friend said, "You don't know much about anything."

True enough.

Jopale's relatives surprised him with their calm, stubborn dismissal of his New Isles plan. Uncles and older cousins thought he was a fool for surrendering to popular despair. Poisons and fires would kill distant strangers and burn up portions of the world. But not their good ground, no. They couldn't imagine their lucky island being changed in any lasting fashion. At the very worst, forests and farms would burn up, which would bring a famine that would quickly silence the extra mouths in the world. But that would be a blessing and a grand opportunity, they maintained. To his considerable astonishment, Jopale learned that his family had been preparing for years: Secret lockers were stuffed full of dried scramblers and wooden tubs jammed with pickled fruit, plus enough roach cakes and syrup to keep the most useful mockmen alive. There would be a few hard years, they agreed. Only the prepared would survive to the end. But that's what they intended to do. Survive at all costs. Then life would settle back into its comfortable, profitable, and entirely natural routine.

"Stay with us," they pleaded, but not too hard. Perhaps they'd decided that Jopale was one of those extra mouths.

One old aunt assured him, "You will go insane in the darkness. Starlight has that effect on people, you know."

That wasn't true. Humans were adaptable, and besides, the New Isles were lit up with blue-white lights very much like sunshine. Yet his response was deflected with a cold pleasure. "You *will* go insane," his aunt repeated. "Don't for two moments think otherwise, my boy."

Then a pair of young cousins—a twin brother and sister—explained what was plainly obvious to them. "When the time comes," they said, "the Spirit of Man will rise from the Ocean's center to save all of the good people."

It was an old faith, half-remembered and twisted to fit the times.

"Only true believers will be spared," they promised. "How about you, Jopale? Will you join us with the reborn?"

"Never," he responded, amazed by his sudden anger. His cousins were probably no more mistaken about the future than those with well-stocked bunkers. But he found himself panting, telling them, "That's a stupid creed, and you can't make me buy into it."

"Then you will die horribly," they told him, speaking with one voice. "And that's precisely what you deserve, Jopale."

But people rarely got what they deserved; wasn't that the central lesson of the modern world?

With his critical possessions packed and his precious tickets and papers in easy reach, Jopale walked to the nearest worm station, accompanied by his only remaining mockman. No well-wishers were waiting to send him off. Thank goodness. He and a few other travelers stood on the open platform, looking off to the east. The huge gray worm appeared on schedule, sliding in on the side trail and stopping before them, deep wet breaths making the entire station shake. Travelers formed a line, ready to prove themselves to the waiting soldiers. Then a single voice called out, "Jopale." It was a woman's voice, vaguely familiar. Jopale looked over his shoulder. He had grown up with this woman—a natural beauty who hadn't spoken ten words to him in the last ten years—but there she stood, dressed to travel and smiling only at him.

Jopale assumed she was heading west, perhaps even to the New Isles.

But no, she explained that she didn't have any ticket. She'd heard about his plans and simply come here to speak with him now.

"Please," she implored, touching her wide mouth, then running a hand across her long, elegant scalp.

He stepped out of line.

"This is difficult," she admitted. Then with a deep, soul-wrenching sigh, she added, "I wish I'd done what you've done."

But she hadn't, of course.

"If I stay here, I'll die here," she told him and every other person in earshot. "But I'll ask you, Jopale: Is there any way I could travel with you?"

There wasn't. No. "All the berths on the New Isles are taken by now. I'm quite sure. And I'm bringing only what I'm allowed to bring. Even with these little bags here, I'm pressing against my limits."

The woman wrapped her arms around her perfect chest, shivering as if chilled. Then quietly, through a clenched mouth, she said, "But there is a way."

"What?"

Standing beside Jopale was his red-haired mockman. The beautiful woman glanced up at the gigantic creature. Then with a stiff, somewhat angry voice, she said, "Leave it behind. Take me instead."

Did Jopale hear that correctly?

"I'll ride inside the worm's stomach with the mockmen," she promised. "And I'll carry your luggage for you too."

"No," he said.

"I'll even eat mockman rations—"

"No."

The woman began to cry, tears rolling down her lovely, pain-wracked face. "I'll do whatever you wish, Jopale. I'll even relinquish my legal rights, and you can beat me if I'm slow—"

"Stop it," he cried out.

"Please, Jopale! Please?"

Then a soldier stepped up, asking to see their papers. What could Jopale do? He was startled, off-balance. This unexpected idea hadn't had time enough to take root in his head. The woman could never survive the life she was begging for. Besides, he had never lived without a mockman on his right side. And if he ever needed new money, this was a valuable creature on any market.

Jopale's only rational choice was to turn away from the woman, saying nothing else. He silently handed his identification to the armed man and then his precious ticket to an elderly fellow wearing the gray uniform of a worm caretaker.

"Master Brace" was written over the chest pocket.

"All the way to the Port of Krauss, sir?" asked the old fellow.

"Yes, I am."

Offering a wink and jolly laugh, Brace said, "Well, sir. You and I should get to know each other by the end of the line, sir. I should think."

"IT IS COMING"

The sky was cloudless and absolutely dark, save for a single point of soft yellow light—one of the Four Sisters slowly dancing about the hidden sun. The distant stars were too faint to be seen through the thick window—a few hundred specks that only scientists had bothered to name and map. Stars meant very little to Jopale. What captured his mind was soft country beneath: The Tanglelands. Relentless pressures had crumbled this wood, exposing every old seam and any line of weakness. Long ridges and single hills had been erected through a series of unending quakes. As a result, the trail was far from a straight line, and the climb as well as fatigue kept slowing the worm's progress. But there were no fresh breaks or blockages on the trail, at least so far. The waking passengers seemed thrilled to be alive, or at least they pretended to share a renewed confidence. And of course everyone wanted at least a glimpse of the tall saprophytes that grew beside the trail, watching the exotic forest passing by for a moment or two, then returning to their blankets and more familiar distractions.

Jopale had never seen country like this, save in picture books.

He mentioned his interest to Do-ane, and she responded as he hoped. "I've seen the Tanglelands," she admitted. "Several times now. But I still think they're lovely. Just wonderful."

The girl had a buoyant, joyful attitude when she wanted to.

Jopale stood beside her, watching the pale, many-hued light pouring out of the dense foliage. Sometimes he asked about a particularly bright or massive tree. Do-ane would warn that she didn't know her fungi as well as she would like. But every time, she named the species. Then when the rest of the passengers had settled on the stomach's floor, leaving them alone, she quietly asked her new student, "Do you know why this country is so rich?"

"The old islands are broken into hundreds of pieces," he offered. "Plenty of fresh surfaces ready to rot away."

"That's part of it," she allowed. "But as much as anything, it's because of the moisture. Three large islands were compressed and splintered to make the Tanglelands, and each one had tremendous reserves of fresh water underground. Which the saprophytes need as much as they need food, of course."

He nodded amiably.

"And besides, rain likes hilly country," she continued. "Given its choice, a storm will drop its wealth on broken ground."

"How about your Good Mountain? Is it very wet . . . ?"

She shook her head. "Not particularly. That country is very flat and very boring. And beneath the surface, the wood is exceptionally dry."

"Why?"

"Because the island on the surface can't reach the Ocean any more." Do-ane put one tiny hand beneath the other, as an illustration. "I think I mentioned: There's a second island resting under it, thick and solid, blocking almost every root."

"That's your Mountain? The underneath island?"

She hesitated, making some kind of delicate calculation. Then she looked out the window again, saying, "No," in the tone people use when they want to say a good deal more.

Jopale waited. Then he said, "Tell me more."

She squinted, saying nothing.

"About your undersea mountain," he coaxed. "What do you do down there?"

"Research," she allowed.

"In biology?" he asked. And when she didn't responded, he offered a mild lie. "I was once an avid biology student. Some years ago now."

Do-ane glanced at the passengers. Rit was sleeping. None of the others were paying attention to the two of them. Yet the young woman whispered so softly that Jopale could barely hear her words. "No," she said. "It's not really biology that I'm studying, no."

"Not really?" he pushed.

She wasn't supposed to speak, but she also wanted to explain herself. With a slender smile, she said, "I can't."

"I don't mean to interrogate," he lied.

The young woman's life was wrapped around her work. It showed in her face, her manners. In her anxious, joyful silence.

"Forget it," he muttered. An enormous fungus stood beside the trail—a pillar topped with fruiting bodies that bled a bright purple light. It was a common species whose name he had already forgotten. Staring at that apparition of rot and death, Jopale remarked with the coldest possible voice, "It's not as if the world is going to end soon."

"But it won't end," Do-ane said.

He gave a little sniff, and that's when he discovered that he was crying. It was the sort of manipulative gesture Jopale might have attempted and would have failed at. But his tears were as honest as anything he had ever done, a fabulous pain hiding inside him, any excuse good enough to make it surge into public view.

"This disaster has happened before," the young woman promised.

"So I've heard."

"But it's true. A new continent always grows on the sunlit face of the world. The water below is always choked of its free oxygen. Old wood compresses and shatters, and the methane rises up through the fissures and holes."

"What about wildfires?" he asked.

"There have been big fires before." She smiled to herself, betraying a deep fascination, as if describing an enjoyable novel full of fictional tragedies. Then she added, "These world-consuming fires have come seventeen other times."

Not sixteen times, or fifty thousand.

Jopale invested several long minutes contemplating her precision. Then he asked, "How do you know that? An exact number?"

"I can't," she said.

"You can't tell me?"

"No."

He stared at her face, letting his own anger bubble up. "This place where you're going," he started to ask. "This peculiar mountain . . . ?"

"Yes?"

"Your colleagues, those scientists who discovered the feature . . . I don't think they used the old word 'mountain' because it reaches in any particular direction. Toward the sky or toward the world's core, either."

Do-ane avoided his weepy eyes.

"My guess? The object was named for its composition. That's another quality inherent in the word. The mythical mountain is supposed to be harder and far more enduring than any wood. Am I right?"

The young woman was standing on her stocking feet, staring through the window again. The Tanglelands were beginning to thin out and turn flat, stretches of empty dead ground between the occasional giant fungi. Now the brightest stars were visible through the window, twinkling and jumping as the worm slid along. Do-ane was standing close enough to Jopale to touch him, and she was taking quick shallow breaths, her face growing brighter even as the empty land around them turned blacker.

Jopale held his breath.

Then very quietly, his companion said, "The great fire," and touched the plastic of the window with the tips of two fingers.

Do-ane announced, "It is coming . . . !"

THE HEART OF THINGS

When a worm like theirs was a baby, it was abused in the most awful ways—or so it might seem to somebody who didn't concern himself with the rough necessities of the world. Stolen from its mother, the newborn creature was cut through in several places and the wounds were kept open until they became permanent holes, ready for the first in a series of increasingly large sphincters. Then its diet was strictly controlled while professional handlers assessed its tendencies and potential uses. Intelligent and mild-tempered worms were given over to passenger duties. Many of the candidates didn't survive the conditioning of their digestive tracts or the additional surgeries. Among the alterations, inflatable bladders were inserted into the region directly behind the head, producing a series of permanent cavities where individual caretakers could live, each fitting with a rubber doorway leading into a narrow, astonishingly dry esophagus.

Jopale stood beneath a glow-light, shouting Brace's name. A voice called back to him. A few moments later, the old caretaker stepped from inside one of the little rooms, wiping his sleepy face while asking what was wrong.

With words and manic gestures, Jopale explained the situation.

For an instant, the caretaker didn't believe him. The weathered face looked doubtful, and the pursed lips seemed ready to downplay what he was being told. But then one of the worm's drivers ran down the narrow esophagus, shouting the same essential news.

"Where are we now?" the caretaker asked her.

The woman offered a number and letter designation that might as well have been in another language.

But the old man instantly absorbed the knowledge. "We'll stop at Kings Crossing," he ordered. "The station's gone, but the ground is up on the last ridge. We'll be able to see how bad things are. And any good news too."

Jopale couldn't imagine anything good.

Then the caretaker turned to him, saying, "Sir," with a firm tone. "I need to know. Have the other passengers noticed?"

"Just one. The girl—"

The caretaker hesitated for a moment. Then he said, "Say nothing. I'll see if I can raise some voices on the radiophone, get the latest news . . . and then I'll walk through the belly and offer a few words . . ."

Brace's voice fell away. What kind of encouragement could he offer anyone now?

There was tense silence, then a deep slow rumbling. The sound that came and then came again, making the great throat shiver.

"What is that?" Jopale had to ask.

"That would be the worm's heart," the caretaker offered. He tilted his head and held his breath, listening carefully. "And you can hear her lungs working too. Which is why we live up here, sir. So we can keep tabs on our baby."

Jopale nodded.

Then the caretaker touched the rough pink wall, and the driver did the same, both using that pause to fight back their own tears.

●●●

Do-ane had abandoned the window, sitting alone on her blanket, using her electric torch to read her book. Everyone else was sitting too, including Rit. The old map was unfolded before him. Glancing up, he said nothing to Jopale. Then he looked down again, asking the map, "What's wrong?"

"Nothing," Jopale lied, as a reflex.

The tall man glanced at Do-ane, and with the heightened senses of a paranoid, he announced, "Something is wrong."

She started to look at the window, then stopped herself.

But Rit noticed. He decided to take his own look, pulling his long legs under his body, taking a deep breath, and another. But there wasn't enough courage inside him to stand. His legs stretched out again, and a long hand wiped his mouth dry, and then he carefully fixed his eyes on the old map, nourishing his own faltering sense of ignorance.

"Did you tell?" Do-ane whispered, closing the book on her thumb.

Jopale nodded.

She stared at his face, his eyes. Something about her expression was new—a hard stare meant to reach down to his soul, seemingly. Then she made her decision, whatever that might be. Opening the book again, she flipped through pages until she found what she wanted. Placing her back to Rit, she pushed the book toward Jopale and handed him her torch, giving his face one last study, just to convince herself that her feelings were right.

The page was blank.

No, it unfolded. Jopale found a corner bent up by use, and he lifted the slick paper and gave the book a quarter turn, an elaborate drawing showing what looked to be the configuration for some type of worm.

"Is it—?" he began.

"The mountain," she interrupted, fingers held to her mouth.

Rit seemed to notice nothing. No one was paying attention to the two of them. The wealthy old woman who had complained at World's End was making her male companion look out the window. But she only wanted to know what was approaching, and he only looked ahead, reporting with a matter-of-fact voice, "There's some long slope. And that's all I can tell."

Was the mountain a worm? Jopale wondered.

He returned to the diagram, finding a scale that gave him a sense of size. But surely there was a mistake here. Even if the scale were wrong by a factor of ten, this worm would be larger than a dozen rust-fins set in a row. And if the scale were right, then the mountain would dwarf a hundred and twenty full-grown rust-fins . . . making it larger than most cities, wouldn't it . . . ?

He looked up. "Is it alive?" he whispered.

Do-ane had no simple answer for that. She shrugged and said, "It isn't now," in a soft voice. And then even softer, she said, "Look again."

He was no expert about worms. But he knew enough to tell that the mountain shared little with the creatures he had grown up with. Its mouth was enormous but without true jaws, forming a perfect circle from which every tooth had been removed. The throat was straight and wide, and then like a funnel, it collapsed on itself, becoming too tiny to show on this diagram. The anus was equally tiny, opening at the very tip of the tail. And between mouth and anus was a digestive tract that filled only a portion of the worm's enormous body.

"What are these?" he asked.

She touched the lines and the spaces within them, saying, "Chambers. Cavities. Rooms, of a kind."

He didn't understand. "How could a creature survive this much surgery?" he asked. And when she didn't answer, he looked up, realizing, "But this isn't any species of worm, is it?"

She mouthed the word, "No."

"It is a machine," he muttered.

She tilted her head, as if to say, "Maybe."

"Or is it alive?"

"Not now, no. Not anymore. We think."

The worm carrying them was attacking the last long slope, slowing as it crawled higher. Another person stood to look outside. But he was on the north side of the worm, and from that angle, nothing was visible behind them.

"The tail and some of the midsection cavities are flooded," Do-ane told him.

Those were drawn with blue ink.

He asked, "Is the tail the deepest part?"

She nodded.

"And the mouth?"

"Buried inside a fossil island," she reported.

"Choked while eating its lunch?" He meant it as a joke, forcing himself to laugh.

But Do-ane just shook her head. "We don't know what it ate in life," she reported. "But this organism, this machine . . . whatever it was . . . it probably required more energy than you could ever pull out of wood pulp and stolen sap."

Jopale closed the book and turned it in his hands, examining the binding. But there was nothing to read except a cryptic "Notes" followed by a date from several years earlier.

"What I am," Do-ane began.

He reopened the book and unfolded the diagram again. "What are you?"

"In the sciences, I have no specialty." She smiled, proud to say it. "I belong to a special project. A confidential research project, you see. My colleagues and I are trained in every discipline. The hope is . . . was . . . that we could piece together what this thing might be . . ."

"It's metal," Jopale guessed.

"Within its body," she said, "we have found more iron and copper and zinc than all of the peoples of the world have gathered. Plus there's gold and silver, and elements too unusual to have common names."

Jopale wanted to turn through the pages, but he still couldn't make sense of this one.

"Yet the body is composed mostly other substances," she continued. "Plastics and compounds that look plastic. Ceramic materials. And lining the mouth and what seems to be the power plant . . . well, there are things too strong to cut samples from, which means we can't even test them in any useful fashion . . ."

"And what are you?" he asked again.

"One member of a large, secret team trying to make sense of this." She showed him a grim smile, adding, "I'm just a novice still. Some of us have worked forty years on this project."

"And have you learned anything?"

A hopeful expression passed across her face. But again, they had reached a juncture where Do-ane didn't want to say anything more. Jopale sensed that she'd already told him too much. That they were pushing into codes and laws that had to be obeyed, even when Catastrophe walked across their world.

Again, their worm was slowing.

Passengers noticed, and in a moment, they grew uneasy.

"Where?" Jopale asked.

Do-ane ran a finger over the giant mouth. "What are you asking?"

"Its origin," he said. "Do you know that much?"

"Guess," she whispered.

He could see only two possibilities. "It comes from the world's center," he offered. "There are metals down there. I remember that much from school. Deep inside the world, the temperatures and chemistries are too strange for us to even imagine."

"What's the second possibility?"

He remembered what she had said earlier. "Our Ocean," she mentioned, as if there could be more than one. Then he pointed at the sky.

"In my little profession," she sighed, "those are the two islands of opinion. I'm one of the other-world people, and I believe that this object is a kind of ship meant to cross from star to star."

Jopale closed the book and pushed it back to her.

By then, their worm had pulled to a stop, and the passengers were looking at each other, plainly wondering what was happening. But Master Brace was absent, probably still listening to the radiophone. Which was why Jopale took it upon himself to stand and say to the others, "This is Kings Crossing."

Rit pulled the map to his face, asking, "Why here?"

Like any good caretaker, Jopale managed to smile. But he couldn't maintain the lie past that point. Shaking his head and looking at the warm damp floor, he reminded everyone, "We're alive still." And then he started marching toward the still-closed sphincter.

FIRE

The night air was cool and dry, and it blew softly toward the east—a breeze at this moment, but gaining strength and urgency with the passage of time. Years ago, a tidy little city had grown up on this ridge, but then the sun vanished, and the city had died. Homes and shops quickly became piles of anonymous rubble. But the worm station must have survived for more years. The facility was only recently stripped of its metal, but otherwise it had been left intact. Only a few saprophytic weeds were rooted in the softest planks, while the damp faces of the main building were painted with a rough fungus. Regardless of color, every surface glowed with a steady red light. Jopale read "Kings Crossing" on the greeting arch, painted in a flowing script that was popular back when he was a child. Behind him, the other passengers were slowly stepping onto the platform, talking in breathless whispers. He didn't hear their words so much as he listened to the terror in their voices, and Jopale did nothing for the moment but stare at the planks beneath his feet and at his own trembling hands. Then when he felt ready—when no other choice seemed left for him—he forced himself to breathe and turn around, staring wide-eyed at the burning world.

Jopale once toured a factory where precious iron was melted inside furnaces built from equally precious ceramic bricks. He remembered watching the red-hot liquid being poured into thin syrupy ribbons that were quickly attacked by the artisans in charge. He decided that this wildfire possessed the same fierce, unworldly glow. It was crimson and brilliant enough to make eyes tear up, and it seemed as if some wickedly powerful artist, inspired by his malevolent urges, must have pulled molten metal across the entire eastern horizon.

Every passenger had left the confines of the worm. Most of the caretakers were busy breaking into a nearby warehouse, presumably under orders to claim any useful supplies. "How far away is that?" a young fellow asked. Jopale couldn't gauge distances, but others gladly threw out numbers. Optimists claimed the fire was just a few kilometers behind them, and it was really quite small. While Rit admitted that the flames were enormous, but trying to be positive, he thought they might be as far away as World's Edge.

"Oh, it's closer than that," the old caretaker called out. "As we stand here, Left-of-Left is being incinerated."

With a haughty tone, Rit asked, "And you know that how?"

Swollen eyes studied the horizon. Master Brace had been crying again. But he had dried his face before joining the others, and he managed to keep his voice steady and clear. "I was listening to broadcasts, where I could find them. From spotters near the fire lines, mostly."

Every face was sorry and scared.

"That quake we felt? As we were crawling out of World's Edge?" Brace shook his head, telling them, "That was an old seam south and east of the city. It split wide, along a hundred kilometer line. I didn't know this till now . . . but so much gas came from that rupture, emergency crews didn't have time to dress. They were killed, mostly. And the methane kept bubbling out. For a full cycle, it was mixing with the air. Then something . . . a person, or maybe lightning from a thunder-storm . . . made the spark that set the whole damn mess on fire."

"What happened to the city?" Jopale asked.

Brace glanced at him for a moment, then stared at the planks. "I talked to a spotter. She's riding her balloon east of World's Edge. The city's gone now, she says. Including the ground it was sitting on. From where she is, she sees open water where millions of people should be . . ."

"Open water?" Rit asked. "Does that mean the fire is going out?"

Brace hesitated.

Do-ane said, "No." The woman looked tiny and exceptionally young, her boots back on her feet but still needing to be buttoned. Clearing her throat, she explained, "If too much methane saturates the atmosphere, and the local oxygen is exhausted or pushed aside . . . there can't be any fire . . ."

Jopale closed his eyes, seeing the beautiful station and the black-haired woman with that lovely, lost voice.

Brace nodded, saying, "There's two fire lines now. One's racing east, the other west. In the middle, the water's bubbling up so hard, huge chunks of rotten wood are being flung up in the air. So the methane . . . it's still coming, yes sir. And the spotter told me that our fire . . . the one that's chasing us . . . it just now reached to the fringes of the Tanglelands . . . and then I lost her signal . . ."

Some people wept; others appeared too numb or tired to react at all.

Two drivers were standing near the worm's head. One of them suddenly called out a few words, her voice barely legible.

The other caretakers had vanished inside an unlit warehouse.

Master Brace turned to the drivers. "The full dose, yes," he shouted. "Under the vestigial arm."

"But the flames don't look that tall," said the wealthy woman. She shook her head, refusing to accept their awful prospects. To her com-panion, she said, "Perhaps the fire's just burning off the forests."

Her young man muttered a few agreeable words.

But Do-ane said, "No, you're confused. It's the smoke that fools you."

"Pardon me, miss?"

"That land is definitely burning," she said. "Huge volumes of green wood are being turned to smoke and ash, which help hide the tops of the flames. And of course that scorching heat will lift everything." She pointed at the sky, asking, "Can you see what I see?"

Jopale hadn't noticed. But the eastern half of the sky had no stars, a dense black lid set over the dying world. Flood this landscape with daylight, and half of the heavens would be choked beneath a foul mass of boiling, poisonous clouds.

"Are you certain?" the old woman asked doubtfully. "What do you know about any of this?"

Do-ane hesitated.

"The girl's a scientist," Rit interjected. "She understands everything that's happening to us."

"Is that so, miss?"

Do-ane glanced at Jopale, eyes narrowed, as if blaming him for making public what she had told him in the strictest confidence.

But he hadn't said one word.

"She and her friend here thought that I was napping," Rit confessed. "But I wasn't. I heard every word they said."

Do-ane looked embarrassed, shrinking a little bit, and her tiny hands nervously wrestled with one another.

Jopale tried to find a reply—gentle words to help deflate the palpable tension. But then a hard prolonged shock came through the ground, everybody's legs bending, and the land beneath them fell several meters in one steady, terrifying moment.

When the falling sensation ended, the old woman asked Do-ane, "Would you explain that, dear? What just happened?"

"This ridge," Do-ane began, opening her hands again. "We're standing on the last slab of the Tanglelands. It's the largest slab, and it reaches back to the east, deep underwater, ending up under Left-of-Left." Like a teacher, she used hands to help explain. "As the ground above is burned away, and as methane rushes to the open surface, this land's foundation is being torn loose."

As if to prove her words, the ridge shook again.

Jopale looked over his shoulder, but Master Brace had slipped away. He was standing beside the worm, he and the two drivers busily manipulating a leather sack filled with some kind of dense liquid. The sack was connected to a hose, and the hose fitted into a needle large enough to push through two grown men. The trio was having trouble with the work, and noticing Jopale, the caretaker cried out, "Sir, would you help us? Just for a moment. She knows we're up to something, and she isn't cooperating."

The others glanced at Jopale, surprised he would be called, and perhaps a little impressed.

The worm had stopped against the trail's closer edge. But there were still a few steps of greased ground to cross. Generations of worms had laid down this thick impermeable oil—the same white gunk that its wild counterparts used to lubricate their enormous tunnels. On soft-soled shoes, Jopale let himself slide down to the creature. He hadn't touched a worm since he was a boy, and he didn't relish touching one now. He could smell oil and worm sweat—a rich mingling of distinct odors—and he looked up at the vestigial limb, crooked and thin and held flat against the huge gray body.

"Take this extra wand, sir," said Brace. "Like I'm doing. Just stroke her belly, if you will."

The rubber wand ended with a metal electrode, batteries strapped to a spicewood handle. The drivers had set a tall ladder beside the worm, spikes driven through the oil and into the ground. The woman driver climbed quickly and her colleague followed—a boyish fellow carrying the enormous needle as if it was a spear. The ladder was topped by a narrow platform. The woman grabbed the limb and pulled hard, and Brace ran his wand back and forth against the worm's slick belly, small blue flashes producing what must be a pleasurable tingle.

The woman forced the limb to extend.

"Why there?" Jopale asked, mimicking the old man's motions.

"It's a good blood-rich site," he said quickly, as if speaking one long word. "And besides, there's no time to open the usual veins."

The other passengers had come to watch and listen. Except for Do-ane, who drifted to the far end of the platform, studying her magnificent fire.

"Is this a drug?" Jopale wanted to know.

"I like the word 'medicine,'" the caretaker admitted. Patting the sack, he said, "We keep this stuff for drivers more than for the worm. Of course, there's enough in this sack to kill a thousand people. But what it is—"

Somebody cursed, and a second voice shouted, "Watch out!"

The long needle fell between Jopale and Brace, landing flat on the oil.

"It's a stimulant, sir." The caretaker picked up the needle, and with a quick voice explained, "It will make our girl faster, and she won't need sleep, and it may well kill her. But of course, we don't have any choice now."

"I suppose—"

"Two more favors, sir. Please?"

"Yes."

"Take the needle up. All right?" Then he asked for a second favor, promising, "It should help quite a lot."

Jopale had never enjoyed heights, but he didn't hesitate. There were twenty rungs to manage, and the breeze seemed to grow stronger as he climbed higher. Over his shoulder, he saw the rest of the crew returning from the warehouse, nothing worth stealing in their hands. Then Jopale was standing on the narrow platform, and the driver had the vestigial limb extended as far as she could, and her assistant took the needle with both hands, starting to jab its tip into the exposed flesh while shouting, "Now!"

A tiny pump began to sing.

"The hand, sir," Brace called out. "Please, sir."

The worm's arm was tiny compared to its enormous body, but it was far longer than any human limb. Perched on the end of it were three fingers fused into a knobby extrusion and a stiff little finger beside it. And there was a thumb too. Not every worm possessed thumbs; Jopale had read that odd fact once or twice. And more unusual, this particular thumb could move, at least well enough to curl around his hands as he clasped hold of the worm. Then he squeezed its hand as tight as he could, trying to make certain that his grip was noticed, letting the great beast feel a little more ease, at least until the medicine found its home.

WORMS

Then they were moving again. The pace felt swift, but the worm was sliding down a considerable slope. Without landmarks, the casual eye had trouble discerning their true speed. But later, when they were crossing a flat empty plain, Jopale was sure they were making swift progress. Wandering up into the throat again, he listened to the hard swift beating of the heart, and he was sure that, whatever else, the creature's body was expending a fabulous amount of energy.

Returning to the stomach, he found every passenger gathered around Do-ane. "Show us that book of yours," Rit was saying. "Show us your machine."

"We're very interested," said the rich woman's companion. Then with a wink, he asked, "What harm would it do?"

People were scared and miserable and desperate for any distraction. Jopale sat next to Do-ane.

She seemed to consider the possibilities. Then she said, "Here," and opened the book to a fresh page—a page showing photographs of giant chambers and smooth-walled tunnels. Holding her torch above, she explained what she had already told Jopale, and a little more. "We think these were living quarters. It's hard to realize how big everything . . . but this is a colleague of mine, here, standing in the background . . ."

The scientist was little more than a dot on the grayish landscape.

"If this machine was a ship that traveled between the stars, as some believe . . . as I believe . . . then its engines would have produced an acceleration, and this would have been the floor." She pulled a fond finger over the image. "This was taken ten years ago. Do you see the dirt in the corner?"

Some people nodded, but those in the back could see nothing.

Do-ane turned the page. The next image was a large black-and-white photograph showing a skull and ribs and a very long backbone that had curled up in death. The earlier colleague was present again, standing on the giant skull. And again, he was still little more than a dot on this bizarre landscape.

"That's a dead worm," Jopale whispered.

Do-ane glanced at him, then at the others.

"This machine came from another star," Rit said, repeating her verdict.

"Yes," she said.

"A spaceship, you're saying?"

"It seems obvious—"

"And that's where our worms came from too?" The tall man was kneeling on the other side of her, his expression doubtful but focused. "They came from this spaceship of yours?"

Do-ane said, "Yes."

Then she said, "No."

"Which is it?" Rit demanded.

The young woman sighed. And then a second time, she sighed. Finally she looked up, telling everyone, "Suppose that we built a starship, and we went out hunting for a new home. Even a machine as powerful as this needs a great deal of time to cross from one sun to the next. And if that new sun didn't happen to have an inviting world, we'd have to travel farther. And if that next sun didn't offer a home, then we would have to travel farther still. And if we could never find a planet like our old home, at some point, wouldn't we have to make due with the best world that was in reach?"

Jopale tried to study the worm's skeleton.

"I don't know any of this as fact," she said. "But we've learned this much. This starship's crew was nothing like us. Not like people, or anything simply organic." She ran a finger along the edge of the fossil skull. "What looks like bone is not. It's ceramic and very tough, ancient beyond anything we can measure. And what organs we find aren't livers or hearts or lungs. They're machines, and we can't even begin to decipher how they might have functioned when they were slipped inside a living body."

Rit started to make a comment, then thought better of it.

"These creatures were built from metals and ceramics, plus rare earth elements that exist to us only in the tiniest amounts. Scarce beyond measure. But if you look deeper into the galaxy, into the spiral arms, you see suns with more metals than our sun has. And presumably, the worlds circling them are built from similar bones."

She breathed, breathed again.

"Our sun, you see . . . it is very large and bright, and it is metal-poor and rather young. By many measures, it won't live long at all. Less than a billion years, which is a short time in the universe." She lifted her torch higher, allowing more people to see the bizarre skeleton. "I don't know any of this for sure. I'm telling you a story, and maybe it's all wrong. But what I think happened . . . what many of my colleagues, the true geniuses in this endeavor, feel is self-evident . . . is that this starship journeyed all the way to our world and could go no farther. It landed on the Ocean and tasted the water, tasted the air, and its crew took what they had in reach. Metals were scarce, as were silicon and all the other heavy elements. But at least they could borrow the oldest genetics inside their own bodies. To build a full functioning ecosystem, they wove a thousand new species. Humans. Mockmen. Copper-eels and many-mouths. Plus all the little scramblers. And they used the other species that were brought with them. We've found spores and dead seeds on the ship, so we're sure that our ancestors brought plants with them. They devised giant plants that could thrive on the Ocean's surface, roots reaching deep to bring up the scarce minerals. And think of our forest roaches, too. We have found little versions of them dead in the ship's darkest corners, hiding in the cracks. Incredible as it sounds, perhaps they rode here as pests."

"But where are the human bones?" Jopale asked.

She looked at him, her face sad for a brief moment, but then drifting into a cautious amusement.

"I mean the crew that piloted this starship," Jopale continued. "What finally happened to them?"

Judging by the murmurs, others had made the same obvious assumption.

Do-ane shook her head. Then she said, "No," with a grim finality. "Think if you can in these terms: You fly from star to star. Your body is as much a machine as it is flesh. And everything you need comes to you with the help of your loyal machinery. With that kind of freedom, you can acquire any shape that you wish. Which is why you might allow your limbs to grow smaller with the eons, and why you perhaps would decide, finally, to let yourself become a worm.

"Assuming that we began as human beings, of course. Or something that resembles humans, back on that other world of ours.

"This lost, unnamable home."

GOOD MOUNTAIN

Caretakers began to hurry through the stomach, in twos and threes, carrying buckets of salve and sacks of buffering agents back into the now-empty intestines. Jopale guessed what this meant, and he felt sure when another pair of caretakers arrived, hurriedly dismantling the latrine and its privacy curtain. But where would the worm's next meal come from, and how much time would they spend waiting for her to eat her fill?

Capping the nearly filled latrine, the caretakers began wrestling it towards the esophagus. That was when Jopale decided to confront them, and that was when Master Brace finally reappeared.

The old caretaker wore a grimacing smile. He tried to wink at Jopale, and then he noticed Do-ane sitting among the passengers, flipping from page to page in her enormous book.

"Are we stopping now?" Jopale asked.

Brace nodded. With a distracted voice, he said, "There's an emergency locker up ahead. Always stocked with knuckle-roots and barrels of sap. Or at least it's supposed to be stocked."

His voice fell away.

"How long will this take?" Jopale wanted to know.

Brace heard something in his tone. Speaking with absolute surety, he admitted, "My girl needs food. Badly. If we don't give her sugar, we won't make it off this wasteland. Fire or not."

Jopale nodded. "All right. I see."

"Good Mountain," said the caretaker. "That's where we're stopping."

A dozen faces looked up.

Realizing that he had been noticed, Brace straightened his back and took a deep breath. Then without hesitation, he said, "Everyone will disembark. The feeding will be done as fast as possible. And from this point, everyone rides on top of the worm. Up where the mockmen are sitting now."

The old woman bristled. "But where will my mockmen ride?"

"They will not, madam." With squared shoulders, the caretaker faced the spoiled creature, explaining to her and to everyone, "This is an emergency situation, if ever there was. And I'm using the powers of my office, madam. Do not try to stop me."

The woman shrank a little bit.

But her companion, smelling his duty, climbed to his feet. "We can't just leave these creatures behind," he argued.

Brace smiled. Then he laughed, quietly and with considerable relish. And he opened his arms while gesturing at the surrounding stomach, admitting, "Oh, I don't intend to leave them. Not at all."

◉◉◉

There was no station at Good Mountain, abandoned or otherwise. There wasn't even an auxiliary trail for a worm to pull to one side. But the foundations for homes were visible, plus markings lain out to define a network of streets. The only signs of recent habitation were the promised locker—an underground facility little bigger than a worm's stomach—and standing to the north, a beacon tower built of wood and capped with an enormous bone-lined bowl. A reservoir of fats and cured sap was burning slowly, yellow flames swirling with the wind. In other times, this would have been the brightest light for a hundred kilometers—a navigation point to help any lost souls. But the firestorm to the east made the fire seem quite weak. Against that rushing, sizzling wall of scorching fire and vaporized wood, everything about the world seemed small and feeble.

The wind was blowing harder now, and with it came a chill from the west, causing Jopale to shiver.

Caretakers worked frantically, breaking open the locker, rolling barrel after barrel onto the trail directly in front of the worm. And other caretakers ordered the mockmen off the worm's back, gathering them together on the dusty, dry ground, loud voices warning them not to take another step.

Jopale thought he could hear the firestorm, even though it was still ten or twenty kilometers behind them.

It sounded like water, oddly enough. Like a strong current flowing over a brink, then falling fast.

Do-ane appeared suddenly, almost close enough to touch him. Her boots were buttoned. Her book was cradled under one arm. She studied his face for a moment. Then she regarded the firestorm with the same speculative intensity. And finally, she said to Jopale, "Come with me."

He wasn't surprised. For a long while now, he had imagined this invitation and his response. But what startled him was his own reaction, feeling decidedly unsure about what to do.

"My colleagues are there now," she continued, pointing at the still-distant tower. "Behind the beacon is a little hut, and there's a shaft and elevator that will drop us all the way to the starship—"

"What about me?" Rit interrupted.

Do-ane gave him a moment's glance. She seemed unprepared for his entirely natural question.

"Your starship is huge," Rit reminded her. "Huge and empty. Don't you think your friends would welcome me, too?"

She tried to speak.

Then the old wealthy woman stepped forward. "There isn't much time, miss. Where's this sanctuary of yours—?"

"Beyond that tower," Rit offered.

"Thank you." Then to her companion, she said, "Help me, will you dear? I'm not sure I can manage such a long walk."

Her young man was holding their essential bags, a faint smile showing as he stared off to the north. With an agreeable tone, he said, "I'm sure you'll do fine." Then he winked, adding, "Start right away. As fast as you can." And with the strength of youth, he ran off into the ruddy gloom, dropping his bags and hers in his wake.

Other passengers began to follow him.

"Well," the old woman muttered. Then with a shuffling gait, she tried to keep up.

Rit glared at Do-ane. Appalled by the circumstances, he asked, "So just how big is this elevator? And how fast? And will it take all of us at once?"

She tried to answer, but her voice kept failing her.

Rit looked back at the worm, then focused on the tower.

"Where are you going?" Master Brace hollered. He was still up near the worm's mouth, but moving toward them as fast as he could manage. "What are you people doing? What in the hell are you thinking?"

Do-ane saw him coming. Then she threw down everything but her precious book, and glancing at Jopale one last time, she turned and sprinted across the empty plain.

Rit considered Jopale, plainly doubting his good sense and sanity. Then he was gone too, his long stride letting him catch up to Do-ane, then the old woman, leaving both of them behind.

"Sir," said Brace, staggering up next to Jopale.

He would say his good-byes; then he would run too. Jopale had made up his mind, or so he believed.

"Don't," was the caretaker's advice.

"Don't what?" Jopale asked.

Brace took him by the shoulder. Panting from his run, he said, "I like you, sir. And I honestly meant to warn you before now."

"Warn me?"

"And then . . . then I saw the girl talking to everybody, and I didn't think . . . I couldn't imagine . . . that all of you would actually believe her—"

"What is this?" Jopale cried out.

"She's ridden my worm in the past, sir." Brace looked across the plain. The fire to the east was tall enough and bright enough to illuminate each of the fleeing passengers. Tiny now. Frantic little shapes soon to be lost against that great expanse of dead dry wood.

"I know she's ridden this way," Jopale said. "Of course she has. She comes here to study the secret mountain."

Brace shook his head.

"No, sir," he said.

Then he looked Jopale in the eye, saying, "She does this. She has that book of hers, and she befriends a man . . . usually an older man . . . convincing him that everything she says is real. Then she steps off at this place and invites him to join her adventure, and of course any man would happily walk off with a pretty young thing like that.

"But she is insane, sir. I am sure.

"On my worm, she has ridden west at least five times now. And

61

three times, she has set off a flare to make us stop here and pick her up on our eastbound leg." He gulped the cool air. "That's what people do in this country when there is no station, sir." Offering a grim smile, he added, "But sometimes we haven't brought her, and it's her men who set off the flares. We've rescued several gentlemen of your age and bearing, and they're always angry. 'She showed me this big book,' they'll say. They'll say, 'I was going to explore an ancient starship and look at the bones of gods.' "

Jopale wrapped his arms around his chest, moaning softly.

"That girl is quite crazy, sir. And that's all she is." Brace placed a comforting hand upon Jopale's shoulder. "She takes her men walking in the darkness. She keeps telling them that their destination is just a little farther now. But there's nothing to find out there. Even the most foolish man figures that out. And do you know what she does? At some point, she'll turn and tell him, 'You are the problem. You don't believe, so of course we can't find it.'

"Then those fellows return here and continue their journey west. And she wanders for a little while, then comes and waits here for the next eastbound worm. Somehow she always has money. Her life is spent riding worms and reading her book, and when she forgets that nothing on those pages is real, she comes back this way again. And that's all that she does in her life, from what I can tell."

Jopale was confused, and he had never been so angry. But somehow none of this was a perfect surprise.

"I should have said something," Brace admitted. "In my baby's stomach, when I saw her talking to everybody . . ."

"Should we chase after them?" Jopale asked.

But the caretaker could only shake his head, telling him, "There isn't time, sir. And honestly, I don't think we could make those people listen to reason now. They're chasing the only hope they've got left."

"But we should try to do what's right," Jopale maintained. "Perhaps we can convince one or two of them to turn back—"

"Sir," Brace interrupted.

Then the old fellow laughed at him.

"I don't know if you've noticed this, sir. But there is an exceptionally good chance that we ourselves won't be alive for much longer."

Again, Jopale heard the soft watery rumbling of the fire.

"Yes. Of course . . ."

TOWARD PORT OF KRAUSS

Brace began walking toward the worm's head.

The worm was slowly crawling forward, gulping down the big sweet barrels as she moved. Farther ahead, several dozen mockmen were being coaxed down onto the trail. At a distance, they looked entirely human. They seemed small and plainly scared, clinging to one another while their bare feet slipped on the white grease.

Jopale caught Brace, and before he lost his own scarce courage, he made an enormous request.

"I know it's asking a lot," he admitted.

"That won't make much difference," the old man said, offering a dark little laugh. Then he paused and cupped his hands around his mouth, shouting new orders into the wind.

The red-haired female was separated from the other mockmen.

Jopale rejoined his companion, and the two of them grabbed his bags and then a rope ladder, climbing onto the worm's wide back.

Without prompting, the mockman claimed one of the low chairs, facing forward, her long legs stretched out before her. If the creature was grateful, it didn't show on her stoic face. Either she was too stupid to understand what he had done, or she was perceptive enough to despise him for saving only her, leaving her friends to their gruesome fate.

The worm's bare flesh was warm to the touch. Jopale sat directly behind his mockman, letting her bulk block the wind. He could feel the great spine shifting beneath his rump. Facing backwards, he didn't watch the rest of the feeding, and save for a few muddled screams, he heard nothing. Then the worm began to accelerate, drugs and this one meal lending her phenomenal energy. And after a little while, when they were racing across the empty landscape, Master Brace came and sat beside him.

"But the book," Jopale began.

"It certainly looks real enough," the old man replied, guessing his mind. "And maybe it is genuine. Maybe she stole it from a true scientist who actually knows where the starship is buried. Or maybe it's an ancient manuscript, and there was once a starship . . . but the ship sank to the core ages ago, and some curious fluke has placed it in her strange hands."

"Or she invented everything," Jopale allowed.

"Perhaps." Watching the firestorm, Brace nodded. "Perhaps the girl heard a story about space flight and lost worlds, and she has a talent that lets her draw elaborate diagrams and play games with cameras. And these times are what made her insane. The terrors and wild hopes tell her that everything she can dream up is real. Perhaps."

Or she was perfectly rational, Jopale thought, and the starship really *was* waiting out there. Somewhere. While Brace was the creature whose sanity had been discarded along the way, his mind lying to both of them, forcing them to stay onboard his treasured worm.

"But the name," Jopale muttered.

"Sir?"

" 'Good Mountain.' She told me why the scientists used that old word. And honestly, I can't think of another reason for placing that noble name on this ridiculous place?"

"First of all, sir—"

"Call me Jopale, please."

"Jopale. Yes." Brace held both of his hands against the worm's skin, listening to the great body. "First of all, I know this country well. If there were a project here, a research station of any size, it would not be a secret from me. And I can tell you frankly, Jopale . . . except for that one strange girl and her misguided men, nobody comes to this wasted space . . ."

A small quake rolled beneath them.

When it passed, Brace suggested, "We might be in luck here, sir. Do-ane may have told you: There's a dead island under this ground. There's a lot of wood sitting between us and the methane. So when the fire gets off the Tanglelands, it should slow down. At least for a little while. This wood's going to burn, sure, but not as fast as that damned gas does."

Jopale tried to feel encouraged. Then he repeated the words, " 'First of all.' "

"Sir?"

"You said, 'First of all.' What's second of all?"

Master Brace nodded in a thoughtful fashion, then said, "You know, my mother was a caretaker on a worm exactly like this one. And her father was a driver on a freighter worm that crawled along this same trail, bringing the new iron back from Port of Krauss. It was that grandfather who told me that even when there was sunlight here, this was an awful place to live. Flat like this. Sapless. Hard to farm, and hard on the soul. But some greedy fellow bought this land for nothing, then sold pieces of it to people in more crowded parts of the world. He named his ground 'Good Mountain' because he thought the old word sounded strong and lasting. But of course, all he wanted was to lure fools into his trap . . ."

Jopale reached back over his head, burying one of his hands into the mockman's thick hair. Then he pushed with his legs, feeling a consuming need to be closer to her, grinding his spine hard up against her spine.

"It's just one old word," Brace was saying. With his face lit up by the endless fire, he said, "And I don't know if you've noticed this, sir. But words . . . what they are . . . they're just sounds and scribbles. It's *people* who give them meaning. Without us, the poor things wouldn't have any life at all."

And they pressed on, rushing toward the promised Ocean, with the End of the World following close behind.

A PIECE OF THE
GREAT WORLD

Robert Silverberg

*Robert Silverberg is one of the most famous SF writers of
modern times, with dozens of novels, anthologies, and collections to his credit. As both writer and editor (he was editor of
the original anthology series* New Dimensions, *perhaps the
most acclaimed anthology series of its era), Silverberg was one
of the most influential figures of the Post New Wave era of the
'70s, and continues to be at the forefront of the field to this
very day, having won a total of five Nebula Awards and four
Hugo Awards, plus SFWA's prestigious Grandmaster Award.*

His novels include the acclaimed Dying Inside, Lord
Valentine's Castle, The Book of Skulls, Downward to the
Earth, Tower of Glass, Son of Man, Nightwings, The World
Inside, Born with the Dead, Shadrack in the Furnace, Thorns,
Up the Line, The Man in the Maze, Tom O'Bedlam, Star of
Gypsies, At Winter's End, The Face of the Waters, Kingdoms
of the Wall, Hot Sky at Morning, The Alien Years, Lord Pres-
timion, Mountains of Majipoor, *and two novel-length expan-
sions of famous Isaac Asimov stories,* Nightfall *and* The Ugly
Little Boy. *His collections include* Unfamiliar Territory,
Capricorn Games, Majipoor Chronicles, The Best of Robert
Silverberg, At the Conglomeroid Cocktail Party, Beyond the
Safe Zone, *and a massive retrospective collection* The Col-
lected Stories of Robert Silverberg, Volume One: Secret Shar-

ers. *His reprint anthologies are far too numerous to list here, but include* The Science Fiction Hall of Fame, Volume One *and the distinguished* Alpha *series, among dozens of others. His most recent books are the novel* The Long Way Home, *the mosaic novel* Roma Eterna, *and a massive new retrospective collection,* Phases of the Moon: Stories from Six Decades. *Coming up is a new collection,* In the Beginning. *He lives with his wife, writer Karen Haber, in Oakland, California.*

As an author, Robert Silverberg has always seemed fascinated with the far future, and he has returned to far-future milieus again and again throughout his career in stories such as the Hugo-winning "Nightwings" (which was later melded with two other far-future novellas into the novel Nightwings), *"At Winter's End," "A Long Night's Vigil at the Temple," "Homecoming," "Dancers in the Time-Flux," "This Is the Road," "Red Blaze in the Morning," the Nebula Award-winning "Sailing to Byzantium," and many others, as well as in novels such as* Son of Man *and the stories and novels of the* Majipoor *sequence.*

All of which made him one of the very first authors I thought of when assembling this anthology. A confidence he amply justifies with the fascinating and exotic story that follows, in which we visit a future Earth just awakening again after sleeping through a million-year winter, and where we soon discover that even in a fresh new springtime world, there may be some cold pieces of winter left behind . . .

The expedition to the ancestral cocoon would be setting out very soon now. Nortekku was still deep in the task of preparing for it, studying up on the accounts of the events of two centuries before. For weeks he had been poring over the accounts of the emergence of the People from the cocoons when the Long Winter had finally ended—out into that strange, empty world, where the debris flung up by the death-stars still hovered in the upper levels of the atmosphere and a rippling mesh of color streamed in the sky, rainbow nets of amethyst, copper, topaz, crimson, radiant green. He had read too of the famous trek across the continent to the ruins of ancient Vengiboneeza, and of the founding of the first cities of the New Springtime. By then he had become so caught up in the story that he kept pushing his research backward and ever backward across the ages, digging hungrily, compulsively.

There was so much to absorb. He wondered if he would ever master it all. The years fluttered before him, going in reverse. He moved step by step from the tale of the Time of Going Forth back to the era of the cocoons itself, the 700,000 years of life underground during the Long Winter that had preceded the Going Forth, and from there to the dire onslaught of the death-stars that had brought on the deep snows and black winds of the Long Winter. Then he went farther back yet, to the glorious civilization known as the Great World that the winter of the death-stars had destroyed, when all was in motion and great caravels circled the globe laden with merchandise of fabulous richness and splendor, and onward even into what little was known of that shadowy era, millions of years before the Great World had existed, when the vanished human race had dominated the world.

Nortekku had never cared much about all that before—he was an architect by profession, looking toward the future, not the past. But Thalarne, who was an archaeologist, did, and he cared very much about Thalarne, with whom he was about to go off on an expedition of the highest archaeological significance. So for her sake he went tunneling deep into these historical matters that he had not thought about since his schoolboy days.

He studied the way of life of the cocoon era until he began to feel like a cocoon-dweller himself. Those snug cozy burrows, insulated chambers deep in the ground, self-sufficient, sealed away from the cold, carved out by the patient labor of generations—what marvels of architecture they must have been! A maze of passageways twisting and forking like serpents, a network of intricate ventilation shafts providing fresh air, clusters of luminescent glowberries for lighting, water pumped up from streams far underground, special chambers for raising crops and livestock—

Soon he and Thalarne would be venturing into the holiest cocoon of all, the one from which Hresh and Koshmar and the rest of the great city-builders had come. When all of the planning was complete, a week or ten days from now, they would set out from Yissou in a cavalcade of motor vehicles on a journey that would take them halfway across the continent in search of the supposed site of the ancestral co-coon. Together they would uncover its buried secrets. Thalarne would be at his side, a woman like no woman he had ever known, beautiful slender Thalarne of the emerald eyes and the dark sleek fur, Thalarne of the quick, questing mind and the elegant vibrant body—Thalarne—oh, how he loved her!

But then everything fell apart.

First, practically on the eve of departure, they quarreled. It was over a trifle, an absurd trifle. And then, just as Nortekku was beginning to believe that everything had been patched up, Thalarne's mate Hamiruld came to him unexpectedly with news that the expedition was cancelled.

"Cancelled?" Nortekku said, amazed. "But I'm almost finished with all the arrangements! How—why—?"

Hamiruld shrugged. He appeared scarcely to care. Hamiruld was marvelously indifferent to almost everything, up to and including Nortekku's months-long romance with his mate. "She asked me to tell you that something else has come up, something more important. That's all I know."

"All because of that stupid argument we had?"

Another shrug. Hamiruld's bland reddish-gray eyes seemed to be gazing into some other dimension. Idly he patted down a tangle in his fur. "I wouldn't know about that. Something more important, she said."

Nortekku felt as though he had been punched. Cancelled? *Cancelled?* Just like that?

"If that's so," he said to Hamiruld, "I've got to talk to her right now. Where is she? At home, or at the Institute?"

"Neither one," Hamiruld said.

"Neither?"

"I'm afraid she's gone," said Hamiruld mildly.

"Gone? Where?" This was bewildering. Nortekku wanted to shake him.

"I don't actually know," said Hamiruld, giving Nortekku a quick, pallid little smile. "She left very quickly, last night, without telling me where she was going. I didn't see her. All there was was this message, asking me to let you know that the expedition was off." There seemed to be a glint of malice behind the smile. Perhaps Hamiruld isn't quite as indifferent to things as he leads one to believe, Nortekku thought.

Cancelled. Something more important has come up.

What do I do now, he wondered?

●●●

It was his engagement to the Princess Silina of Dawinno—or, rather, an indirect consequence of his impulsive breaking off of that engagement—that had brought Nortekku into contact with Thalarne in the first place. Giving him not the slightest hint of his intentions, Nortekku's father had arranged a marriage for his only child with the vapid but highborn Silina, whose ancestral line went back to some helmet-wearing chieftain of the Beng tribe that had played such a key part in the early days of the city-founding era.

The elder Nortekku was one of the wealthiest and most successful members of the merchant class that was coming to wield the real economic and political power in Dawinno. For him the mating would provide his family with the touch of aristocracy that was the only asset it lacked. To his son, though, it felt like an intolerable intrusion on his freedom of choice. He had never been involved with any one woman for very long, had never even considered taking any of them as his mate, had not even been thinking about such things. And he had seen enough of silly Silina over the years, in the course of the regular social round of the Dawinnan upper classes, to know that she was close to the last woman he would want as his mate, assuming he wanted one at all.

He tried to keep those feelings hidden. He did try. But then, with plans for the nuptials already far along, it all suddenly overflowed in him. Angrily Nortekku told his father that he rejected the entire arrangement and was indignant that it had been set up without consulting him. He would never marry, he said, never, never, never—not the Princess Silina, not anyone. All of which was met, just as heatedly, with a blazing glare, a snarl of fury, and a quick, explicit threat of disinheritance.

"As you wish," Nortekku replied, without a moment's hesitation. He had never had any interest in his father's wealth or in the dreary commercial pursuits that had created it. He had taken up architecture as his profession instead of going into the family firm because he wanted to accomplish something in his own right, not simply become the passive beneficiary of the older man's boundless riches. Yearning to penetrate deep secrets, he had aspired originally to be an astronomer; but although there was poetry in him there was not quite enough mathematics, and so the choice had fallen upon architecture instead. "Keep your money, father. Give it to the poor. I'm not for sale."

"So you'll go to her family, then, and tell them to their faces that you're breaking off the betrothal? Just like that, sorry, it was all a mistake, goodbye, *poof!* What do you think Prince Vuldimin will say?"

That was a difficult one. Prince Vuldimin, the shrewd and powerful cousin of King Falid of Yissou, was Nortekku's most important client at the moment, and Nortekku's whole professional relationship with him was an outgrowth of the marital negotiations. Vuldimin had come to Dawinno earlier in the year in search of an architect to design a new palace for him in the countryside outside Yissou, a palace that would favor the bright, airy, swooping look of modern Dawinnan architecture rather than the crabbed and somber style typical of Yissou.

That project fell to Nortekku because Vuldimin was distantly related to Silina's father, who was, for all his lofty ancestry, an impoverished aristocrat eager to see Silina married off to a man of wealth and importance. He saw the job of designing Vuldimin's palace as a useful step in the building of his future son-in-law's career, and arranged a meeting between Nortekku and the prince. It went very well: Vuldimin spelled out his ideas for the new palace, Nortekku dared to make some suggestions for bettering them, and Vuldimin showed what appeared to be unfeigned enthusiasm. And so two contracts were drawn up, one pledging the troth of Silina and Nortekku, the other engaging Nortekku as the architect of Vuldimin's palace. The voiding of one contract now might well cause the other to be broken as well, with disastrous results for Nortekku's career.

Well, there was no helping any of it. If his father refused to name him as his heir, if Vuldimin withdrew the commission for designing the palace, so be it. Nortekku wasn't going to spend the rest of his life listening to the Princess Silina's whinnying laughter and mindless girlish chatter.

The day he went to pay the ceremonial call on Silina's family to explain his reluctance to undertake the mating, it happened, just to make everything worse, that Prince Vuldimin was there. But there was no turning back. Silina's parents and brothers and cousins and uncles, perhaps anticipating what he was about to say, stood arrayed before him like a court of inquisition, every one of them glaring at him with those eerie crimson Beng eyes of theirs, while he lamely told them that he had looked into the depths of his soul in the past few weeks and seen how hastily, carried away by his infatuation with Silina's great beauty and fascinating personality, he had allowed himself to plunge into the marriage contract.

He understood now how rash that decision had been, he said.

He did not see how the marriage could be a success.

He told them that he felt unready for mating, that he was too callow and flighty to be able to offer a splendid woman like Silina the sort of life she deserved, that he felt covered with shame and chagrin but saw no alternative but to withdraw from the contract. It was his hope, he said, that the Princess Silina would before long find a mate more worthy of her than he could possibly be.

This produced an immediate uproar, loud and intense. Nortekku considered the possibility that there might even be violence. Silina, sobbing, rushed from the room. Her parents puffed up in rage like infuriated adders. The brothers and cousins and uncles shook fists and shouted. Threats of legal action were uttered.

There was something almost comic about it, Nortekku thought, although he knew that the developments following upon his repudiation of Silina were not likely to be in any way amusing. He stood stock-still in the midst of the clamor, pondering how he was going to manage to make his escape.

In the end it was Prince Vuldimin, who had witnessed the whole scene from the side, who rescued him. The prince, a short, stocky older man of almost regal presence and authority, cut through the hubbub with a few quick pacifying words, delivered in a tone that could not fail to gain attention, and in the moment of shocked calm that ensued took Nortekku by the elbow and led him swiftly from the room.

When they were outside, Nortekku saw that the prince was smiling, even choking back a giggle. A great flood of relief washed over him.

I have an ally here, he realized.

The prince, who must understand his kinsmen here as well as anyone, had plainly sized up the situation in a moment and his sympathies
were all with Nortekku. Thanks be to all the gods for that, Nortekku
told himself.

"What a pack of buffoons," Vuldimin murmured. "How did you
ever get entangled with them, anyway? Were you really so very infat-
uated with the princess?"

"Not for a second," Nortekku said. "It was all my father's doing.
He arranged it and told me about it afterward. —But I'm in trouble
now, aren't I? What do you think will happen next?"

"Nothing that you're going to like. If they're wise, they'll hush the
whole thing up and try to find another husband for their girl before she
gets branded as unmarriageable. But, as you see, they aren't wise. So
there'll probably be a noisy lawsuit, breach of contract, defamation of
character, the gods only know what else. They'll want to portray you
as a worthless adventurer, an evil seducer, a shameless social
climber—"

"I seduced no one here. And if I'm such a shameless social
climber, why would I back out of a mating with a Beng princess, however much of a ninny she may be? There's no sense to any of that."

"Maybe so. But there'd be plenty of sense to suing you if the real
goal is to squeeze a couple of million units out of your father to settle
the suit."

Nortekku gasped. "He's already threatened to disinherit me if I
don't go through with the wedding. He's certainly not going to pay my
legal bills. And I don't have a unit of my own to my name."

Vuldimin seemed to know that already. There was an almost fa-
therly warmth in his golden eyes as he looked up toward the much
taller Nortekku and said, "Then the best thing for you is to get out of
town for a while. Come up to Yissou; stay at my estate for a month or
two. We'll say that you need to begin surveying the site of the country
palace. There's truth in that, after all. And process-servers from Dawinno have no jurisdiction up there, so the lawsuit will be stalled for
however much time you're out of town, and perhaps in your absence I
can talk my kinsmen here into forgetting about the whole unfortunate
event without making it even worse by suing. Once they realize that

your father isn't going to underwrite any settlement they may be willing to be rational about things. But in the meanwhile, get yourself to
my place in Yissou and wait it out. What do you say?"

"I couldn't be more grateful, your grace," said Nortekku, and
thought for one wild moment that he was about to burst into tears.

●●●

That night he left for Yissou, not aboard the regular evening train
but—at Vuldimin's suggestion—as a passenger on a freight caravan,
where no Dawinno bailiff would be likely to look for him. In Yissou
he was given lavish quarters at Vuldimin's sprawling dark-walled
palace just off an enormous square known as the Plaza of the Sun, and
during the succeeding weeks was treated by the prince's huge staff of
servants as though he were a visiting member of some royal house.
Vuldimin himself returned from Dawinno shortly, assured Nortekko
that his problems with Silina's family would in one way or another be
overcome, and made it clear that his breaking of the marriage contract
would in no way affect the commission to build the new palace.

Nortekku had never cared much for Yissou, which was far to the
north of Dawinno and had a much colder climate, especially now, in
winter. One's first view of the city was utterly off-putting. Its entire
core was surrounded by a colossal, brooding wall of black stone, a
wall of enormous height and breadth that had been constructed nearly
two centuries before by one of the earliest kings of the city, who
feared all manner of enemies both real and unreal and had devoted a
reign of many decades to raising that wall ever higher and higher, until its implacable shadow came to dominate almost the whole of the
city within.

Once you were inside the wall things were no prettier. Nortekku's
architect's eye was offended by the cramped and twisting alleyways
that passed for streets and the squat, ungraceful, ponderous stone
buildings that filled them, each jammed up against the next, low thick-
walled ground-hugging boxes with the narrowest of slits to serve as
windows. Marketplaces had been situated with seeming randomness
throughout the city, so you were assailed everywhere by the smell of
produce that was no longer fresh and seafood that had spent too many
days away from the sea. And one whole quarter of the city was popu-

lated by Hjjks, those giant yellow-and-black insect-creatures that were the only one of the Six Peoples of the Great World that had survived the cataclysm of the death-stars. Nortekku had no great fondness for Hjjks, even though the ancient threat of warfare between the hive-dwellers and the People had subsided more than a century ago. He was displeased by the look of them, their dry, harsh, chittering voices, their icy alien reserve. But there were very few of them in Dawinno, far to the south, and he rarely encountered one there. Here in Yissou, much closer to the bleak Hjjk homeland that spanned the northern half of the continent, one saw them everywhere, tall menacing-looking six-legged creatures with formidable claws and beaks. He greatly disliked rubbing shoulders with them in the streets.

Still, life in Yissou had its compensations. Vuldimin's palace was handsome and comfortable, and so long as Nortekku stayed indoors the ugliness and dank coldness of the city were no problem for him. Vuldimin himself was warm and friendly in a quasi-paternal way, and clearly had taken a liking to him. Nortekku, who had never known much in the way of affection from his own blustering, churlish father, found that very welcome. And it was the prince, rather than Yissou's monarch, his gloomy cousin Falid, who was at the center of Yissou's social and political life. Vuldimin was a man of great cultivation and progressive ideas, unarguably superior in intellect and vision and charisma to the cautious, reactionary king, and it was to him that Yissou's brightest and most interesting people flocked. Thus it came to pass that Nortekku, at one of the regular assemblages of industrialists and scientists and artists one evening at Prince Vuldimin's palace, found himself face to face with the brilliant young archaeologist Thalarne and had his life turned upside down between one moment and the next.

He had noticed her from the far side of the room, engaged in an animated conversation with six or seven persons who, Nortekku observed, all happened to be men. She was an instantaneously compelling sight: tall, nearly as tall as Nortekku himself, with a fine figure and a thick, gleaming pelt of dark fur spotted here and there by oval splotches of dazzling white.

Every aspect of her commanded attention. Her eyes were of a rich emerald color, glistening with an inner light; her features were delicately and beautifully formed, her expression a searching, mobile one; her stance was alert and dynamic. She wore the vivid yellow sash that Nortekku knew indicated membership in Yissou's Institute of Scientific Study, the counterpart of his own city's great research center, the House of Knowledge. Several of the men surrounding her wore the yellow sash also.

Nortekku drifted closer.

She was speaking of the tendency of sophisticated people in Yissou nowadays to regard the stories of the People's past as just that stories, mere myth. Indeed Nortekku had encountered the same phenomenon among his friends in Dawinno, who brushed the popular historical tales aside as the stuff of legend. Had there ever really been a Long Winter? Did the People actually live once upon a time in underground cocoons? Had the Great World truly been as magnificent as the legends would have it?

"We have the evidence of the Chronicles, of course," one of the men said.

"So we do," said another, "but how do we know that they represent actual history? They may be no more reliable than the history plays we see in the theater."

"Yes. *Torlyri and Trei Husathirn,*" said a third man. "*The Boyhood of Hresh. Hresh at the Nest of Nests.*"

"And there's that play about Nialli Apuilana and her captivity among the Hjjks, and how she faced down the Hjjk Queen and defeated Her," said another.

"You speak of them as though they're just fiction," the first man said. "These people actually existed. They really did the things that they're credited with doing. Otherwise, how did we get here? Who led us from the cocoon, if not Koshmar and Torlyri? Who founded the cities, if not Hresh and Harruel and Salaman? Who drove back the Hjjks when they wanted to take over all our land? Why, Thalarne here is a direct descendant herself of Taniane, Hresh, Thu-Kimnibol—"

"They were real, yes," said the second man. "But can we be sure that any of their great deeds actually took place? What if it's all just a bunch of children's fables?"

It was at that point, by which time Nortekku had brought himself to the very edge of the circle around Thalarne and was standing directly opposite her, that she said, in a deep, throaty voice that made him tingle with delight, "Which is exactly why all the evidence of the Chronicles needs to be challenged, reviewed, subjected to modern scientific examination. And the first step in that, I think, is to retrace the great trek, eastward all the way to the Hallimalla, and find the original Koshmar cocoon. Which is what I intend to do."

"How soon will you be leaving?" one of the other sash-wearers asked.

"Two months, maybe three," she said. "However long it takes to get the funding together and acquire the equipment."

"Excuse me," Nortekku said then. "I couldn't help overhearing your discussion. I'm Nortekku of Dawinno, an architect, here to design a palace outside the wall for Prince Vuldimin." He was addressing himself directly to her, as though the others weren't there at all.

"Thalarne Koshmar," she said.

His name, his link to his father's vast wealth, didn't seem to mean anything to her. But she was looking straight back at him, very intently indeed. He knew what an intense stare like that usually meant. He knew, also, that he was probably staring at her the same way.

"And did I hear correctly that you're planning an expedition to the original cocoon?"

"Yes," she said. "Yes, I most certainly am."

"Well, then," said Nortekku at once. "I wonder if there might be room in your group for someone who isn't himself an archaeologist, but who—"

●●●

The words were out of his mouth before he had given the thing half a thought. He had no idea what use an architect would be to a bunch of archaeologists, but that hardly mattered. Four or five weeks, even a couple of months, perhaps, out there in the back woods with this wondrous Thalarne—why would he hesitate for so much as a moment?

"Are you serious?" she asked, with a little flurrying show of surprise.

"Positively! To be part of a project like that—why, it's the most fascinating idea I've heard in years, Thalarne!" Shamelessly he said,

78

almost believing it for the moment, "History has always been one of my great interests, as a matter of fact."

"Ah, has it? Why, that's wonderful!" she said, as though she might not be entirely sure of his sincerity, but wanted to be.

"And to be on hand when scientists enter the original Koshmar cocoon—to help recover whatever artifacts our forefathers might have left behind at the Time of Going Forth—to gain new knowledge of the early days of the People—!"

His mind went racing ahead, looking for reasons that might make his presence on the expedition plausible. As an architect, he would be well equipped to map and sketch the intricate layout of the underground chambers that had been inhabited so long. They surely went great distances into the earth. He might even be able to provide technical aid with the excavations. And he could offer financial support too, if that was needed—by way of his father's many business enterprises he was well connected among the princes and great merchants of Dawinno, many of whom claimed to have a profound interest in matters of antiquity.

But it was unnecessary to muster any of those arguments. He could see right away, from the sudden brightness in Thalarne's eyes and the sudden quivering of her sensing-organ and the unmistakable rising of her lustrous black fur, that Thalarne wanted him on the expedition as much as he wanted to be on it, and for the same reasons, which had very little, actually, to do with archaeology.

Over the weeks that followed his mind dwelled on the adventure to come to the exclusion of almost everything else. Enamored of her and newly enraptured by the science to which she had devoted her life, he flung himself into his belated study of antiquity, the better to understand her.

She loaned him books. Worlds were revealed to him: worlds piled on worlds, worlds without end—the world of the humans, of which not the slightest speck remained, and the Great World, whose merest outlines alone survived, and the hidden world of the now abandoned cocoons in which the People, created out of simple apelike animals by the humans to be the successors to the Great World, had waited out the Long Winter. And now, rising atop those strata of antiquity, the brave new world that the People had created for themselves since the Time of Going Forth. Was that, too, destined to thrive awhile and decay and vanish, and be replaced by another, Nortekku wondered? Probably. The earth changes, he thought. Mountains rise, are ground to dust, give way to plains and valleys. Shorelines are drowned; new islands are thrust upward out of the sea. Civilizations are born, die, are forgotten. The planet alone abides, and all that dwells upon it is transient.

Contemplating these things, he felt much the richer for all his freshly acquired knowledge. He felt that for the first time he comprehended, at least in some small way, the great chain of existence, stretching across time from misty past to unborn future. And in the months ahead, he told himself, that comprehension would only grow and deepen as Thalarne and he made their way, side by side, into the ancestral cocoon.

These months in Yissou were the happiest of his life. He and Thalarne had become lovers almost immediately, and soon after that became twining-partners also, even before he discovered that she already had a mate, a certain Hamiruld, who was yet another kinsman of the king of Yissou and of Prince Vuldimin. The fact that Thalarne was married did not appear to be a serious obstacle. Nortekku quickly came to see Hamiruld as a sly and effete man, who appeared to have no particular interest in Thalarne and displayed no overt signs of love for her. Why he had married her, the gods alone knew, but he seemed not to be in any way possessive. Indeed, he seemed to go beyond complaisance into indifference. Quite likely he would step aside if asked; for Nortekku, for the first time ever, had mating on his mind. Thalarne's stunning beauty, her soaring spirit, her keen intelligence—

But that was for later. Finishing the plans for the expedition was the central thing now. Nortekku busied himself putting together the financial backing and purchasing the necessary equipment—Prince Til-Menimat, the famous collector of antiquities, provided most of the money—while Thalarne assembled her team of fellow archaeologists and worked out the details of the route to the ancestral cocoon.

Her ancestral cocoon, anyway, for Thalarne was highborn, not just a member of the aristocratic Koshmar line but of the House of Hresh that was the leading family of that line. Therefore she could trace a direct line of descent from several of the leaders of the little band of

People that had come forth at the end of the Long Winter to found both Yissou and Dawinno. Nortekku himself had no clear idea of his own ancestry. All that his father had ever been able to discover was that they had sprung from one of the minor People groups—he wasn't sure which one, maybe the Stadrains, maybe the Mortirils—that had been eking out a scruffy existence in the hinterlands at the time when Hresh and Koshmar and Harruel and the rest of those heroes of long ago, semi-mythical by now, had made their epic trek westward to found the two great city-states of the coastal strip.

They were ten days or so away from the departure date. And then came the quarrel.

It was a preposterous thing: a new opera was having its premiere, *Salaman*, about the tempestuous life of the second king of Yissou, he who had built the great wall. Tickets were scarce—it would be the social event of the winter season—but Prince Vuldimin was able to obtain a dozen of them and gave a pair to Nortekku, who offered one to Thalarne. He thought she would be pleased. She had already spoken of the new opera in some excitement, and Hamiruld, who notoriously had branded opera as a decadent amusement on several recent occasions, was unlikely to want to attend. Nortekku was excited too: it would be their first public outing as a couple.

"But surely you realize that I'll be going to the opera with Hamiruld!" Thalarne said.

Nortekku was taken aback by that, and let it show.

She gave him a puzzled look. "Why do you seem so surprised, Nortekku?"

"That you should be going with Hamiruld? He doesn't have any more interest in opera than that chair over there!"

"But we have tickets. He feels that he ought to go. It's an important evening. He's a direct descendant of King Salaman, you know."

"So is half the nobility of the city. What does that have to do with it?—He's deliberately doing this because he doesn't want us to be seen here in public together, isn't he?"

Her expression darkened into annoyance. "That's ridiculous, Nortekku. Has he ever shown any sort of jealousy? But he's my mate, don't forget. If he wants to go to the opera with me, why shouldn't he? And why should you read all sorts of dark motives into it? He sees it as a social obligation. And if he does, it's simply a matter of good form that I be seen attending the opera with my husband instead of with my—my—"

"Your lover," he supplied, as she faltered into silence.

"My lover, yes," she said, and Nortekku could not mistake the frosty edge that she had put on the word.

He suspected that he was getting ever deeper into trouble, but he drove recklessly onward, unable to hold himself back. "The whole city knows about us already. Everybody is aware that you and I are about to set out on a trip lasting many months and that Hamiruld doesn't care in the slightest. So what difference can it make if you happen to be sitting next to me in the opera house one night next week?"

"What I might be doing next month along the banks of the Halli-malla, far from this city and all its busybodies, is very different from what I choose to do next week in the opera house of Yissou."

"Nevertheless—"

"No. Listen to me, Nortekku."

"You listen to me."

"Please, Nortekku—"

"You know he hates opera." He waved the tickets about. "I insist—"

"You *insist*?"

It got worse from there. Very quickly they were shouting at each other; then they grew more calm, but it was the calmness of cold fury, and then she turned and walked out. Nortekku realized instantly how stupid he had been. Hamiruld and Thalarne were husband and wife; this was their native city, where they were people of some importance; he was an interloper in their marriage and so long as they were still living together he had no claim on her. And what did next week's opera matter, anyway? She herself had reminded him that soon enough he and Thalarne would be far from Yissou and Hamiruld, with time aplenty for making love. To be raising such a fuss over a purely symbolic thing like a night at the opera together now was completely idiotic.

He sent her a letter of apology, and a gift. When no reply came, he sent a second letter, not quite so abject as the first but definitely conciliatory. She agreed to meet with him and gave convincing signs of having accepted his expressions of contrition. Even then there was still some distance between them, which at the moment he made no attempt to bridge, but it seemed to him that the damage was well on the way toward being repaired.

He had to spend the next two days doing the final surveying work out at the site of Vuldimin's new palace in the country. When he came back, Hamiruld was waiting for him with the news that the expedition was off and Thalarne had left the city for points unknown, and the realization that he had no choice but to take himself back to Dawinno and face whatever it was that Silina's people, or his father, or both, had in store for him.

He was still pondering his dilemma that evening when a burly, deep-chested man of middle years, with coarse thick fur and a fierce, glowering visage, hailed him by name in the street. Only after he had actually walked a few steps past him did the preoccupied Nortekku recognize him as Khardakhor, one of his father's great commercial rivals, a dealer in metals and precious stones.

Once, many years back, Khardakhor and Nortekku's father had been partners. Something had gone wrong between them, though. There had been a bitter and vindictive dispute and a court battle of some sort, and the name of Khardakhor was no longer mentioned in Nortekku's house. But Nortekku had never known or cared very much about any of that and he saw no reason to snub Khardakhor now, this far from home. He halted and acknowledged the other man.

Khardakhor seemed amiable enough. He proved to be not nearly so fierce as he looked, greeting Nortekku like a long-lost nephew rather than as the son of an enemy. Evidently he had come north on business, and evidently, too, he had spent some time recently with Prince Vuldimin, because he knew about Nortekku's having been hired to design a palace for the prince, and—wink, nudge, hearty grin—he knew about Nortekku's affair with the beautiful Thalarne as well. "Quite a choice piece, that one is," he said. "Saw her at Vuldimin's a year or two ago, one of those dinner parties of his. If I were a little younger I'd have gone for her myself. I understand you and she have been cutting quite a swathe lately. —But why haven't you gone off to Bornigrayal with her?"

"Bornigrayal?" Nortekku said blankly. What did Bornigrayal have to do with anything? He wondered whether he had heard correctly. Bornigrayal was a city on the other coast. He knew practically nothing about it, only its name and that it was one of the Five Cities back there. Everyone knew their names—Cignoi, Gharb, Gajnsiuelem, Thisthissima, Bornigrayal—but rarely did anyone from the two western city-states have any reason to visit one. Unknown tribes, emerging from unknown cocoons on the far side of the Hallimalla, had founded them after the Long Winter. For citizens of Dawinno or Yissou, they were all so distant that they might just as well have been on some other planet. "I don't follow you. We didn't have any plans for going to Bornigrayal. What we were about to do was to set out for the Hallimalla, to hunt for the old Koshmar-tribe cocoon."

"Yes, of course. I heard about that project from Til-Menimat back in Dawinno. He expects you to find all sorts of marvels for his collection, I understand. But that's been called off, hasn't it? I ran into Thalarne's husband Hamiruld yesterday"—wink, nudge, grin—"and he told me that he had put Thalarne aboard an airwagon bound for Bornigrayal, a few days back. There's been some kind of discovery out that way that completely puts the cocoon thing in the shade."

Nortekku shook his head. He felt as though a thick mist had wrapped itself about him. It seemed to him that he was moving from bafflement to bafflement these past few days, hardly having a chance to absorb one confusing thing before two or three more presented themselves.

"Well, maybe so. But Hamiruld didn't say anything to *me* about her going to Bornigrayal," Nortekku muttered, after a moment. He had difficulty articulating the words, like someone who was just coming up from sleep. "He told me she was gone, but he didn't know *where* she had gone. Didn't have any idea, is what he said."

"Which is what he told *you*, anyway," said Khardakhor, grinning broadly. "To me, he said something different. I can't see where he'd have had any reason to lie to me. Maybe he just didn't want you going off to Bornigrayal after her." The fierce eyes narrowed a bit. "Well, you didn't hear it from me, did you? But the girl's in Bornigrayal. I have it on the best authority."

This was incomprehensible. Nortekku felt a heavy pounding in his chest. Carefully he said, "And what could be in Bornigrayal that might interest her, do you think?"

"How would I know? Never been there, never thought much about the place. I don't do any business there." Khardakhor was studying him very closely. In the narrow glinting eyes Nortekku saw amusement, pity, even, perhaps, just a little envy. "Odd that she didn't say anything to you, if you and she were really as thick with each other as all the rumors around town had it. But if that was how you and she really were, shouldn't you be heading off to Bornigrayal to look for her?"

"Bornigrayal," Nortekku said, hopelessly befuddled. The other end of the continent. It was frightening to think that she was that far from him, and frightening also to contemplate the notion of going there after her. It was an unimaginable distance. He had never traveled anywhere except up and down the Western Coast between Dawinno and Yissou. The journey to the banks of the Hallimalla would have been the grandest peregrination of his life. Why Bornigrayal? What could have possibly taken her there, on the spur of the moment, giving him no warning? To get away from him and all the complexities he had introduced into her marriage? It would hardly have been necessary to go to the ends of the Earth for that. Simply telling him it was over would have sufficed.

Bornigrayal, he thought, in wonder. Why? Why?

"I should go, yes," he said. "Find her. Talk to her. Get all of this straightened out."

Khardakhor was beaming now. "Absolutely, boy. Absolutely! Go to Bornigrayal. Do you know our ambassador there, Samnibolon? He'll help you. He's a very good man, is Samnibolon. You tell him you're a friend of mine, that you're looking for your girlfriend, that I told you she's in Bornigrayal. Go, boy. Waste no time. Bornigrayal may be only the first stop for her. She may be planning to go even farther than that."

●●●

It was all becoming something very dreamlike. He felt himself being drawn onward and onward, surrendering all volition. If this man Khardakhor thought he should go to Bornigrayal after Thalarne, who was he to say no? *Go, boy. Waste no time.*

Prince Vuldimin appeared to feel the same way. The prince knew nothing about Thalarne's hasty departure and had no idea whatever of what could have drawn her to Bornigrayal, though he too seemed to know that that was where she had gone. Unhesitatingly he provided Nortekku with money for the trip. He provided a coachman, too, the following morning, who took Nortekku out to Yissou Sky Harbor, an enormous barren expanse of land far beyond the city walls, with two great concrete runways down its center and a huge gray airwagon sitting at the end of one of them. And within an hour Nortekku, who had never flown anywhere, who had never so much as thought of undertaking a journey by air, found himself aboard that great vessel as it made ready for takeoff.

The airwagon was a very large elongated metal box with wings, a thing of gigantic size. There must have been two or three dozen other passengers on board, perhaps even more. Nortekku was unable to understand how anything this massive could ever be capable of rising into the air. It was only about thirty years since the first experimental flying wagons had made the first tiny uncertain hops between one village and another, and already they were able to traverse the entire continent, which was impressive progress indeed; but for Nortekku transcontinental travel by air was simply something that one might read about, one more of the many technological miracles of modern times, not anything that had any real relevance to one's own life.

Would he survive the voyage, he asked himself? Did it matter?

He had no assurance that he would be able find Thalarne at all when he got there, or if he did, that she would welcome his having pursued her across all this great distance. It might well be that this whole enterprise would prove destructive to the very thing he hoped to accomplish. Maybe, he thought, she had gone off like this to sort out her feelings about him, and his going after her would serve only to convince her that he was still an adolescent in some ways, an interesting choice for a brief fling but too troublesome to remain involved with for very long.

From beneath him rose a terrifying rumble. From each side of the airwagon came a low throbbing sound that rapidly expanded into a deafening roar.

Without even pausing to consider the incongruity of what he was doing Nortekku, who had never had a moment of religious feeling in his life, murmured a quick spontaneous prayer to all the ancient tribal gods. He called upon Yissou the Protector to look after him, and then asked Mueri the Comforter to ease his journey, and then, for good measure, begged the surveillance of Friit the Healer and Emakkis the Provider as well, and even Dawinno himself, the deity of destruction and transformation.

The airwagon began to move forward. And suddenly, astonishingly, unbelievably, it was aloft.

Nortekku had no clear sense of the point at which the wagon made the transition from ground to sky. But there could be no doubt that it *had* made the transition, for he was looking down at treetops and the metal-roofed sheds of Yissou Sky Harbor, and then, as the wagon banked and wheeled eastward, he saw Yissou City far below, a clenched fist of a place, an ugly huddled maze of tangled streets held in a constricting grasp by the formidable medieval wall that encircled them, with a chaotic sprawl of latter-day suburbs spreading outward from it. From this height it was possible clearly to make out the perfectly circular outline of the city: the first settlers had built the place inside the rim of one of the giant craters that had been formed when the death-stars struck the Earth.

Yissou diminished quickly and was lost to sight somewhere behind them.

In its jarring, lurching way the airwagon sped on through the sky. Red sparks streamed by the windows like frantic scarlet insects. The steady metallic screaming of the engines, disconcerting at first, came to seem familiar and almost welcome. Below, all was a green wilderness, with great blankets of snow on the highest elevations. From time to time Nortekku saw a great circular scar, a brown-walled cicatrice in the midst of the greenness: one of the innumerable pockmarks left on the face of the Earth by the falling death-stars.

As he looked down he was struck by an inrushing awareness of the vastness of the world, and of its antiquity, and of the succession of races that had come and gone upon this planet. Down below there was nothing at all, now, but trees and stones. But once all that wilderness had been inhabited, he knew, by the myriad denizens of the long-lost Great World civilization, the unthinkably rich and glorious era of the

Six Peoples whom he had studied in school long ago and then again lately in the first flush of his affair with Thalarne: the Hjjks, the Sea-Lords, the Vegetals, the reptilian race known as the Sapphire-Eyes people, the Mechanicals, and the most enigmatic ones of all, the Dream-Dreamers, who might perhaps have been the last vestiges of the humans who once had ruled this world in a previous epoch.

For some unknowable length of time—half a million years, a million?—the huge cities of the Great World, full of quivering vitality, astounding in their opulence and size, their myriad windows sparkling in the sun, had covered the landscape below. They had come, they had flourished, they had disappeared, he thought. And it will be the same with us, as it was for others who had lived before them. More strongly than ever before he understood that we are all just visitors here. Though our time of stay may last for millions of years, we are merely temporary residents all the same.

As Nortekku passed high above that landscape he sought with second sight to pry open the eons and thrust his mind into that ancient world, and the worlds that had lived before it, but without success. Nothing remained of it now except some vague traceries of foundation-lines and a few ruined structures. Now and again he thought he could make out the spidery outlines of one of those lost ancient cities below, but perhaps that was only an illusion. Those cities were long gone, right down to their roots. The death-stars had come, dropping in swarms from the sky to stir up dark clouds of debris that blotted out the sun and brought on a winter seven hundred thousand years long, and all the Great World peoples had perished, all but the Hjjks, who manifestly could survive anything, even the end of the world.

There were half a dozen Hjjks aboard this very wagon. Nortekku saw their bristling antennae rising from seats not very far in front of his. He wondered what they were thinking and feeling as they looked down toward the uninhabited plains where their ancestors had dwelled in the Great World's time of majesty. Nostalgia for that vanished epoch? Pride at its accomplishments? Grief over its destruction? Nothing at all, perhaps. Who could say what sort of emotions a Hjjk might have? They kept their feelings to themselves, if they had any.

But his own feelings were in turmoil again. Contemplating the antiquity of the world had stirred fresh yearnings for Thalarne in him. He wanted to sweep into his arms all those millions of lost years whose faint traces he imagined he could see down there, all that richness of a vanished world, as though to embrace the whole of Earth's past, because by embracing that incomprehensible past he was embracing Thalarne, whose goal it was to comprehend it. And for him Thalarne was the future.

Bornigrayal would tell the tale.

He was surprised at how swiftly the day grew darker as they continued eastward. It was winter, of course, and days were short; but the airwagon had taken off in the morning, and already the sky had the dull cast of afternoon, though they had been aloft only a couple of hours. Such a foreshortening of the day perplexed him for a time. But then Nortekku realized that the sun, rising out of the east, was in motion just as they were, already past him and rushing off beyond the cities of the west into the Western Ocean even as they went roaring on in the opposite direction toward the gathering night. The hour must be later the farther east one went; in some places out there, night had already fallen. In Bornigrayal, Thalarne might even now be sitting down to her evening meal, while for him it was not much past midday. Strange, he thought, that it should be early afternoon here, and night already there. He had never considered such matters before.

A meal was served; and then the wagon began to descend. Landing at Bornigrayal so soon? Fine. He had already had more than enough of this trip. But no, no, not Bornigrayal: it was a place called Kundalimon, they told him, a town he had never heard of, somewhere in the middle of nowhere. Three passengers disembarked; seven new passengers came on board, five People and two Hjjks. The airwagon, he realized, must not have the capacity to fly all the way across the continent in a single burst, and, in any case, the inhabitants of places like Kundalimon must sometimes need to travel also. Within fifteen minutes the wagon was aloft again.

The hours went past. The sky became ashen with dusk and then grew entirely dark. Sometimes isolated villages came into view below, little sprinklings of lights, thin white rivulets of smoke curling upward. Otherwise he could no longer see anything down there. For all he knew they had already by this time passed above the Hallimalla, the great southward-flowing river that cut the continent in half. They might have gone right over the ancestral cocoon, even. But all was blackness below. Nortekku fell into a doze, and dreamed that he was wandering through a fabulous city, a place of gigantic shining towers and gleaming bridges that looped through the air without apparent means of support. In his dream he understood it to be Vengiboneeza, the one city of the Great World that had survived the Long Winter almost intact, and in which the Koshmar tribe of People, Thalarne's ancestors, had dwelled for a few years after the Time of Going Forth. Dreaming about Vengiboneeza was nothing new for Nortekku; every architect speculated about Vengiboneeza, trying to reconstruct in his imagination how it must have looked. The descriptions left of it by those who had seen it while it still existed led one to think that its buildings were unparalleled for beauty and brilliance of design, crystalline cloud-piercing towers, arrayed on grand boulevards. But nothing remained of the place now. The Hjjks had occupied it after the People had moved on south to found Yissou and Dawinno, two centuries back, and in the war that soon followed between the Hjjks and the People the great Koshmar warrior Thu-Kimnibol had pounded those priceless ruins into oblivion, using potent Great World weapons that his brother, the famed wise man Hresh, had obtained for him by excavating ancient sites. Those two, Thu-Kimnibol and Hresh, were directly ancestral to Thalarne, Nortekku knew. He wondered whether her passion for archaeology was in some way a means of atoning for the destruction of great Vengiboneeza that her famous ancestors had brought about.

The airwagon made another stop, and another. Another meal was served. Nortekku slept again, and when he awakened the morning sunlight was in the sky and the wagon was landing once more.

Another brief stop, he thought. We will go on and on, for days, for weeks, for months, until this machine finally brings us to Bornigrayal. If ever it does.

But no: this place was Bornigrayal, even now, here, actually, truly, journey's end. Rumpled and blinking, he joined the line of passengers leaving the wagon, descended the staircase that took him to the runway, shaded his eyes against the sudden flinty brightness of the day. This was the northernmost of the Five Cities of the Eastern Coast, and it was cold here, very cold, colder even than in Yissou. The Borni-grayal sky-harbor was situated practically at the shore of what must surely be the Eastern Ocean. A ferocious brutal wind, knife-sharp, came roaring in off the dull gray surface of that immeasurable body of water. The chill was like a bit of the Long Winter, long after its time, obstinately lingering here in these high latitudes. That wind cut right through Nortekku's dense covering of fur and struck at the skin beneath, so that he began to shiver. None of the other debarking passengers seemed to be affected by the cold, not just the Hjjks, who were impervious to cold, but the various People too. Yissouans, naturally, were accustomed to hard winters, and so also must be the passengers who had boarded in mid-flight. But Nortekku had grown up in golden Dawinno of the balmy breezes, where true winter never came, where the only distinction between one season and another was that during the winter months the days were shorter and there was occasionally a little rain. For love of Thalarne he had subjected himself to a winter in Yissou, and now, it seemed, still for love of Thalarne, he was going to have to endure even worse weather than that.

Carriages were waiting to take the arriving passengers to the Borni-grayal proper, which could be seen against the western horizon as a distant row of white flat-topped towers glinting in the hard morning light. On the eve of his departure Nortekku had mentioned to Prince Vuldimin that the merchant Khardakhor had advised him to seek out the Dawinnan ambassador, Samnibolon, upon his arrival, and Vuldimin had at once given him a letter of introduction. The ambassador was, he said, an old friend of his. It was amazing how everybody of any importance in the two city-states of the Western Coast turned out to be an old friend of Vuldimin's, if not an actual kinsman. But it should hardly be surprising that close ties of kinship would unite most of the highborn of both cities, since their ancestors had all come out of just two cocoons, the Koshmar one and the Beng, and Koshmars and Bengs had intermarried steadily since the union of the two tribes in the early days of the Going Forth.

"I should warn you," Prince Vuldimin had said, "in case you're not already aware of it, that Prince Samnibolon is connected by marriage to the family of the Princess Silina. Quite probably he doesn't know a thing about your unfortunate little interaction with them. But I wouldn't go out of my way to mention it, if I were you."

"I wouldn't think of it," said Nortekku. "Not to him, not to anyone, not ever."

Prince Samnibolon was a small-framed man, gray-furred, whose office in the embassy quarter of the city was as elegantly appointed as any prince's chamber should be, with painted scrolls on the wall and glass cases that contained the sort of small Great World artifacts that so many highborns were fond of collecting. The ambassador sat at a circular desk fashioned of strips of rare woods, raised on a gleaming bronze dais. Nortekku knew him to be a member of the House of Hresh, Dawinno's dominant family, who held most of the highest posts in Dawinno's government. He was reputed to be a suave and subtle man, a diplomat of diplomats. Through the Hresh connection he was related in some way to Thalarne.

The ambassador skimmed quickly through Nortekku's letter of introduction and said, "Building a new palace for Vuldimin, are you? He does have a taste for comfort and luxury, that man!" Then, with a knowing smile: "But if I had to live in a ghastly place like Yissou, I suppose that I would too. —You've been up north for quite some time, then?"

"Most of this past year. I bring you greetings from your friend the merchant Khardakhor, who is currently in Yissou. It was at his suggestion that I came to you."

Samnibolon delicately raised one eyebrow in a brief show of surprise. He would know, certainly, about the bitter commercial rivalry between Khardakhor and the elder Nortekku. But he said nothing of that now, merely murmuring a word or two about hearty old rough-hewn Khardakhor and moving smoothly on to ask what it was that had brought Nortekku to Bornigrayal. To which Nortekku responded that he had come to have a small role in an archaeological project under the direction of Thalarne Koshmar of Yissou's Institute of Scientific Study. She was currently here in Bornigrayal on a matter of family business, he said; and, since certain unexpected problems now had arisen regarding their project, he needed to locate her and apprise her of the new developments. It was a story that he had carefully rehearsed all morning and he delivered it unfalteringly.

"Ah, Thalarne!" the ambassador said. "One of the great ornaments of the Yissouan branch of my family, so everyone says."

"You know her, do you?"

"Alas, no. I haven't had the pleasure. But I've heard many good things of her: said to be a most attractive woman—most! And brilliant and learned as well. As no doubt I hardly need to tell you." Samnibolon pointed out that as a citizen of Yissou she was outside his official sphere of responsibility, and therefore she would not have had any reason to contact him since her arrival. So he could not confirm that she was actually in Bornigrayal at this very time, but if Nortekku wished him to make inquiries about her at the Yissouan Embassy, he definitely would. Nortekku did so wish. He gave the ambassador the address of the hostelry where he had found lodgings, and, after a few pleasant minutes of exchanging gossip about certain high figures of Dawinno who were known to them both—Nortekku noticed that throughout the interview Samnibolon had made no mention of Nortekku the elder; he must be aware of their estrangement—he took his leave.

●●●

Late the next day a courier from the Embassy came to him bearing the address of the place where Thalarne was living.

It was, Nortekku learned, halfway across the city from his own place. Which meant a considerable distance, for Bornigrayal had turned out to be a diffuse, far-flung city, endlessly proliferating itself over a succession of islands linked by bridges as it sloped down toward the ocean. Because of the cold, he had not cared to explore the city at all thus far—indeed he failed to understand why anyone had been mad enough to found a city in such a chilly site—but he saw now, as a hired carriage took him on what proved to be an hour-long journey to Thalarne's lodgings, that considerable ingenuity and skill had been expended on the layout and construction of this place, and in fact it was a city of some grandeur, in every way the equal of grand Dawinno itself. One might regard all those tall flat-topped white buildings as stark and monotonous; but, just as readily, one might find great power in them, much rugged strength.

According to the message from Samnibolon, Thalarne had found rooms for herself in the faculty lodge of Bornigrayal University. Nortekku, apprehensive over the meeting, had not sent word ahead to

Thalarne that he was coming to see her. He realized that he half hoped she would be somewhere else when he arrived.

The University was dramatically situated on a high craggy out-cropping rising above the city's central island. His driver dropped him off in the wrong place, and Nortekku needed to do much dreary trudg-ing about from building to building before he located the right one.

That same apprehension, that same uneasiness about coming face to face with her, still gripped him as he knocked at her door. How would she react to his showing up like this on her doorstep? With amazement, no doubt, that he had followed her all the way across the continent. But then what? Displeasure, resentment, irritation, anger?

He heard footsteps. The door opened. For a moment, standing there facing her, Nortekku had to fight back the temptation to turn and flee. But then he saw that she was smiling. Her eyes were warm and bright with surprise and pleasure.

"So you got here at last!" she cried. "Oh, Nortekku, what could have taken you so long?"

And drew him quickly across the threshold, and enfolded him in her arms, and touched her sensing-organ to his in a greeting of un-qualified delight.

He was too befuddled to be able to speak at all. Fearing the worst, he had never dared to expect anything like this. For a long while they embraced in silence; then, as she released him, he stepped back and looked at her in wonder, and said, finally, "What—took—me—so—long? Thalarne, what can you possibly mean? I had to find out where you had gone, first. And then make arrangements to get here. And then—you know how long the trip takes—then I had to track you down. —You aren't upset that I came, then?"

"Upset?" She sounded mystified. "I've been waiting for you all week. If you hadn't turned up in another couple of days, I would have had to continue on without you. The ship is due to sail at the end of the week, and—"

"The ship?" he said. "What ship?" There was a lot to sort out here. "Wait a minute, Thalarne. This isn't making sense. Can we back things up a little? Hamiruld came to me and told me that you had left town without saying a word to him about where you were going, and that he was instructed to simply inform me that our expedition was off."

"No. That isn't true, Nortekku."

"What isn't true? That he told me—"

"No. That I left any such message for you." Something close to panic flared in her eyes. "Oh, Nortekku, Nortekku, this is all so badly garbled! What I asked him to let you know was that there's been a new discovery, something that has a much higher priority than anything you and I could have done at the cocoon site, and that I was leaving straight-away for Bornigrayal. You were supposed to take the next flight out."

He felt numb. "He said nothing whatever like that. Only that you had gone off somewhere, and the expedition was cancelled. And I thought—that perhaps, because of that imbecilic quarrel I had with you—"

"The quarrel was over and done with."

"I thought so too."

"Hamiruld lied to you," Thalarne said. She seemed to be trembling. "Deliberately and cold-bloodedly lied to you. I can hardly believe it."

By second sight Nortekku felt waves of sincerity radiating from her. To use second sight on another person without permission was im-proper in Dawinno, always had been, but the Yissouans had no such prohibition, and he and Thalarne had allowed themselves that commun-ion almost from the beginning. He felt it now. There could be no doubt.

He said, "I thought he had no feelings of jealousy about us. But that isn't so, is it? I wanted to think so, but obviously that isn't true. He deliberately withheld the key part of your message and distorted the rest of it, hoping to cause trouble between us. I see now that I've never really understood your relationship with Hamiruld."

She was silent a moment, frowning a little, as though debating how much she wanted to tell him. Then she said, "Hamiruld has no physical interest in women, Nortekku. He never has. I don't know why: that's just how he is. But he claims to love me, and I think he does. I'm a kind of trophy for him, perhaps: something to be proud of, a woman whom every man in Yissou seems to desire for one reason or another, most, I guess, for my looks, maybe some for my mind. Or both. And so he's been willing to countenance my—affairs, provided I'll go on living with him."

My affairs. Well, he thought, of course he hadn't been the first. Of course not.

"And you?" he said. "You're perfectly willing to have that kind of marriage? Do you love him, Thalarne?"

Something close to evasiveness crossed her features. "Love? How can I say? It was never an issue, before you came along. We were, well, happy. We got on well together. We enjoyed each other's company. We went to the year's social events as a couple. To the parties at court. To the opera—you saw what a problem it created when you wanted to take me. He didn't get in the way of my research. If I felt like amusing myself with another man, he didn't interfere."

"Up to a point, it would seem."

"Up to a point, yes. But clearly he was unhappy about the proposed cocoon expedition, or at least with your being a part of it, and even unhappier when I announced I was going to come out here. And so he suppressed my message to you, which I find tremendously distressing. He's never done anything like that before. It's a complete violation of the rules of our marriage."

Nortekku glanced away from her. All of this, this series of unwanted glimpses into the intimacies of their life together, was beginning to make him exceedingly uncomfortable.

The less he knew of the rules of their marriage, the less he knew about their marriage at all, the better, he thought. He had taken care never to question her about any aspect of it. It had seemed unlikely to him that they coupled—indeed Hamiruld didn't appear to be the sort of man who cared much about bodily passion—but Nortekku had not presumed to pry. Did they twine? He certainly had not wanted to know that. And now—having heard everything that had just poured out of her—

We got on well together. We enjoyed each other's company.

Hoarsely he said, "We've taken ourselves completely off the track with this discussion of how Hamiruld handled that message of yours. The important thing is that I still don't know why it is that you went to Bornigrayal, or wanted me to come here. A new discovery, you said—a higher priority than excavating the cocoon site—"

"Yes." She looked relieved to be changing the subject also. "Do you know where the Inland Sea is, Nortekku?"

"Approximately, yes."

From the uncertainty of his tone she must have realized how approximate that knowledge was. Nortekku knew that there were other continents in the world, of course, somewhere on the far side of the Eastern Ocean, and that two of them were separated by a great land-rimmed sea that was almost a third ocean in itself. But that was all. One never thought much about the other side of the world. The Five Cities of this coast were remote enough; the continents of the other hemisphere were beyond consideration.

She sketched a quick map for him. "Our continent, here. Yissou, Dawinno." A line down the middle for the Hallimalla River. Five dots along the eastern seaboard for the Five Cities. Then emptiness—the Eastern Ocean—and then, far off at the left end of the sheet, two amorphous land-masses, one above the other, with another emptiness, this one long and oval, between them. "The Inland Sea," Thalarne said, tapping the sheet. "And here, on its southern coast, where the weather is very warm, a little colony of Sea-Lords has been living ever since the Long Winter began."

She said it quite calmly, as though telling him that she had learned of some interesting new inscription that had been discovered there, or some unusual Great World artifact. But for him it was like an earthquake. Sea-Lords? Still living somewhere, a little colony of them on the far side of the Eastern Ocean? There were no Sea-Lords anywhere, he thought. The Sea-Lords were gone, every last one of them, like all the rest of the Great World except the Hjjks.

Nortekku's recent historical studies had told him very little about the Sea-Lords. One of the Six Peoples of the Great World, yes, a race of intelligent amphibious mammals, sea-going merchant princes who had held sway over the extensive maritime commerce that had flourished in Great World times. That was all he knew of them, other than that they were all supposed to have perished when the darkness and cold of the Long Winter fell upon the Earth. The books that Hresh and other historians had written about that era had dealt mainly with the reptilian Sapphire-Eyes, the dominant race of their time, and provided some knowledge of their servants the Mechanicals, and of the floral Vegetals, and, in abundance, of the Hjjks, whose subterranean hives had sheltered them without difficulty throughout the interminable icy years. But of the Sea-Lords virtually nothing was known. They were the most mysterious of the Great World races, other than the totally baffling Dream-Dreamers.

"You mean to say they're still there? Living as they always did?"

"Still there, yes. Living as they always did, no. From what I've been told, I suspect that they're pitiful impaired creatures, decadent, degenerate, whatever word you want to use—half crazy, most of them. Bestial. Sad. They've retrogressed, gone some distance backward toward the animals they once were."

That saddened him. Attuned to ancient history as he had lately become, he had often longed for some miracle that would restore at least a part of the Great World to life, in all its wonder, for him to see and experience. Still, the fact that they had survived at all—

"They're definitely Sea-Lords, though? Not just some contemporary species of marine mammal?"

"Oh, yes. Definitely Sea-Lords. They speak what is thought to be a Great World language, or at least a debased version of it. The Hjjks who were in the discovery party claim to be able to communicate with them. Legends of the Great World have survived among them. They know what they once were, it seems."

"This stands everything that we know about the end of the Great World on its head, doesn't it?" Nortekku said.

"Much of it, anyway. We thought that the oceans everywhere had grown so cold that it became impossible for the Sea-Lords to survive. Apparently not so. And if there's a band of them still alive on the coast of that southern continent, who can say what still survives farther south? A bunch of Sapphire-Eyes, maybe? Vegetals? It's only two hundred years since we came out of the cocoons, Nortekku. We think we've achieved a lot, with our cities and our universities and our air-wagons and all of that. But the truth is we've only just begun, really, to explore the world around us. Off in Dawinno and Yissou, it seems to us that cities of the Eastern Coast like Bornigrayal and Thisthissima are worlds unto themselves, far off beyond our ken. Actually we should look upon them as being next door to us, though. There's a whole huge continent south of us that we know just about nothing about—"

"South?"

"South, yes. Going on and on, right on down to the Pole, maybe.

There have been some voyages to it from Cignoi, but the Cignese haven't been saying anything about whatever they may have found there. And in the east, across this ocean here, there are two continents far larger than this one, with cities of the People on them—we know the names of two or three—with which Bornigrayal has regular commerce, though they haven't been talking much about that either. Beyond those two—"

"Even more continents?" Nortekku said. This was dizzying.

"Who knows? Nobody's ever been there. But it's a round planet, Nortekku. You keep going east, sooner or later you reach the Western Ocean's far side, and if we could sail across it we'd be back at our own coast again. I find it hard to believe that there's nothing but empty ocean west of us."

"The Sea-Lords," he said. "Come back to the Sea-Lords. You told me, when I first came in, that there's a ship due to sail from here at the end of the week, and you're planning to be on it. To go and look for that colony of Sea-Lords, is that it? And you want me to accompany you?"

"Of course," Thalarne said.

◆◆◆

It was too much, flooding in all in a single moment like this. His head was swimming. One day he had simply been trying to repair a spat with his lover, and the next, practically, he found himself aboard an airwagon heading for the other side of the continent, and then—new continents—living Sea-Lords—a voyage to the eastern hemisphere, to the shores of the Inland Sea—

She sat him down and poured wine for him, and she told him a little about the arrangements she had made for the new expedition and her hopes of what they would find out there across the ocean, and her fears, too, and of a good deal else, while he listened spellbound, though only partly convinced that any of this was really happening. Perhaps, Nortekku thought, he was still back in Yissou, lost in some fever-dream. Perhaps he had never even left Dawinno.

But the whiplash sound of an icy wind against the window reminded him that he really was in wintry Bornigrayal, and that the dark, emerald-eyed woman beside him actually was Thalarne, whom

he had not lost after all, and that he and she were talking quite seriously about taking passage aboard some ocean-going vessel and
crossing the sea in quest of survivors of a race that had thought to be
extinct for seven hundred thousand years. He moved closer to her. By
imperceptible stages they found themselves embracing, and then, after only a moment of shared uncertainty—shall we couple first? Or
twine?—they made their choice and slid to the floor and were hard at
it, coupling for the first time in—what, two weeks? Three? She arched
her back against his chest, pressing herself close, and awaited him.
How good it was to reunite with her now! First the coupling, the simpler communion, the basic one, the old primitive thing that all creatures enjoyed. And then later, he hoped, they would twine. But for now
he lost himself in her rich scent, in the warmth of her. He clasped her
tight, and cupped her breasts in his hands, and from her came a gasp
of joy as he thrust himself into her.

And afterward, when they had coupled, and rested, perhaps even
dozed a little while, their sensing-organs came into contact, idly,
nudging playfully, at first, and then touching in what was not a playful
way at all, and they entered twining mode, made ready for the true
union of souls, the joining that only the People could do, the linking
of their perceptors in the deepest, most intense, most intimate contact
that was possible between one person and another. The essence that
was Thalarne came flooding into him, and all that was Nortekku into
her. He felt her love—no question of it—and her excitement at everything that was opening before them now, the new quest and their own
companionship in the weeks to come.

They slept, then. They rose and put together a sort of a meal. They
coupled a second time. No twining, this time—one did not twine often; it was too intense—and then they slept again, and when Nortekku
woke just after dawn there was a light carpeting of shining snow over
the grounds outside the building. Nortekku had never seen snow at
such close range before. Snow was wholly unknown in and around
Dawinno, certainly, where it was summer all year round, and even up
by chillier Yissou it was a once-in-a-decade event, so they said. Since
the end of the Long Winter the world had grown warmer year by year,
and, having spent his whole life in the benign climate of the Western
Coast, Nortekku had come to assume that all the world now enjoyed

similar temperate weather. Not true, it seemed. Here on the other side of the continent things were different. They were not as distant yet in Bornigrayal from the days of the Long Winter as were those who lived on the other coast.

Since Thalarne was still asleep, he went downstairs and walked in the snow for a time. Scooped some up in his hand: it burned like flame against his bare skin. He shivered and wrapped his arms about himself. This must have been what the Long Winter was like, he thought, something like this snowy morning, though on a much greater scale. Snowdrifts many times higher than a man's head; vast expanses of blinding whiteness, stretching off as far as anyone could see; black icy winds, relentless, remorseless, raking the land like scythes. No leaf in sight, no blade of grass. How awful!

He cast his mind back across the ages, tried once again, as he had so many times before, to imagine the Long Winter's onset: the death-stars plummeting from the sky—the legend had it that they came every twenty-six million years, clusters of jagged stones falling out of the heavens, crashing down to engender such clouds of dust and smoke that the sky turned black and there was darkness on the face of the Earth and its inhabitants were cut off from the warmth of the sun for century after century. Whole races had died out in that terrible winter and those that survived did so by creeping off into safe hiding-places until the agony of the planet was over. And when it was over the Great World was gone and the inheritors of the planet were the simpler folk who called themselves the People.

The Great World peoples could have saved themselves, so said the Book of Hresh that that great wise man had set down toward the end of his life, in the first generation after the Time of Going Forth. Their wisdom would have been equal to that task. But they had calmly chosen to die instead, all but the Hjjks, who, like insects of every sort, seemed to intend to endure until the end of time. According to Hresh, though, the others had convinced themselves that it was the great design of divine Dawinno to replace old races by new ones from time to time in the course of the world's history: the ancient humans had given way to the peoples of the Great World, and now it was the turn of the Great World peoples to vanish in favor of the furry folk of the cocoons, whose turn it would be, so Hresh supposed, to yield the stage eventually themselves some day. Dawinno was the deity of transformations, was he not? He destroyed and then he created, all in the service of eternal change and renewal.

So the Sapphire-Eyes and the Vegetals, who were not in any way fitted to withstand cold, had done nothing to protect themselves against it, and the Mechanicals, those intelligent machines, saw that they would have no purpose once the others had died, and let themselves be overtaken by the snowfall in open country, where their rusted remains could still be found all these many years later, and the Dream-Dreamer race disappeared somewhere also, except for those few who settled among the People in the cocoons, and those did not outlast the Long Winter. And, though scientists knew that the oceans themselves had not completely frozen over during the Long Winter, it was believed that the Sea-Lords, too, had found the new climate too much for them.

Evidently not, if Thalarne's tale of that degenerate band on the southern shore of the Inland Sea had any substance to it. To some small extent they had defied Dawinno's great plan of extinction, just as the Hjjks had done. What, Nortekku wondered, would old Hresh have made of that?

❧

He had had enough of walking through the snow. He went back inside and found that Thalarne had awakened.

"Did you enjoy it, the snow?" she asked.

He rubbed his tingling hands together. "An interesting experience, I suppose. But a little of it goes a long way."

"You'll find it much warmer where we're going. More like your own city."

"Good," he said. "Excellent."

While they breakfasted she told him more of the details of the venture on which they were about to embark.

The sea voyage would take two weeks, possibly three. That was staggering in itself: cooped up for such a long time in what he envisioned as some sort of wooden container, tossing on the turbulent breast of an ocean so great in size that his imagination was unable to encompass it. He was restless by nature. It would be difficult, he knew, to get through the days and nights of such a long voyage without growing a little fretful, maybe more than a little. But he did not share his anxiety about that with her.

And he would have to prepare himself, Thalarne said, for a certain amount of discomfort. Did he know what seasickness was? The winter seas in these latitudes were not easy. Nortekku brushed that part of it aside also, making a fine show of not thoroughly heartfelt bravado. They would be together: what could a few bothersome storms matter? Their initial destination, she said, was Sempinore, a port city on the southern coast of the northern continent. There they would spend a week or so replenishing their supplies, and then they would set out southward across the Inland Sea, a journey of only a few days, to the secret location of the Sea-Lord colony on the northern shore of the other continent.

It was all going to take much longer than he had expected, he saw. Nortekku fidgeted a bit, thinking about the expenses. After a time he said, "I hate to bring this up, but I'm not sure how I'm going to deal with the cost of this much traveling. You ought to know, Thalarne, that I'm not a rich man. My father is, yes, but he and I—"

"There won't be any expense," she said crisply. "The entire expedition is being underwritten by a syndicate of wealthy and prominent Western Coast individuals, both from Dawinno and Yissou, which is how I happened to learn about the project at all. Our friend Prince Til-Menimat, for one."

"So he's behind this one, too? How did *he* get to be part of it?"

"He's currently financing the excavations in Thisthissima, right down the coast from Bornigrayal. The Bornigrayan archaeologists who made the Sea-Lord discovery are connected with that work too. Thisthissima, you know, is built right on top of a major Great World city, and some very fruitful digging has been going on the past couple of years. So the Bornigrayal people came to Til-Menimat and said, 'Listen, your grace, we're on to something very big over across the Eastern Ocean, but we need serious funding in order to go ahead with it, and therefore—' "

Nortekku began to feel just a little dazed. He understood the hunger to unearth the buried remnants of the world's forgotten epochs, here in these constantly burgeoning years of the New Springtime. But only since becoming involved with Thalarne had he come to understand how fierce that hunger was. There was something ugly about it. Highborns from every city seemed to be competing frenziedly with one another in the race to uncover the secrets of all those lost yesterdays. Til-Menimat was a charming, cultured man, but in his lust to own pieces of the Great World he seemed to have greedy tentacles outstretched everywhere.

He walked to the window. The morning sun was high, now, painting a fiery orange track across the snowy fields below.

"So this is just an artifact-hunting operation, then?" he asked.

"Not *just* an artifact-hunting operation. That part of it won't be any concern of yours or mine. But we'll be there to do scientific work. Studying the Sea-Lords."

"While these other archaeologists do the treasure-hunting. These Bornigrayal people."

"Yes," she said. "A man and a woman, Kanibond Graysz and his mate Siglondan. I've had a little correspondence with them, and I met them for the first time the other day, but I don't really know much about them. It seems that they were in Sempinore consulting the archives there when some local Hjjks came to them and said that they had made a very interesting discovery over on the other side of the Inland Sea. So Kanibond Graysz and Siglondan went over with them to have a look, and there were the Sea-Lords. They hurried back to Bornigrayal, and then down to Thisthissima when they heard that Prince Til-Menimat happened to be back east touring the Thisthissima excavations just then. And that was when they told him about the discovery and got him to put up the money for this new expedition."

Nortekku nodded distantly. One aspect of the story had begun to bother him as this part of her story unfolded. "But you were right on the verge of setting out on our cocoon expedition, which Til-Menimat was also underwriting. Why would he have wanted to pull you off that and send you flying out to Bornigrayal?"

"He didn't," Thalarne said. All resonance had suddenly fled from her tone, and her voice sounded hollow and dead. "It was Hamiruld who got me mixed up in this."

"Hamiruld?" he said, in a voice as suddenly leaden as hers.

So he was in this too. The revelation came with the force of a blow. Every one of these highborns seemed linked to each of the rest in their worldwide dealings. They were all over the place. You came upon one where you didn't expect him and then you saw that there was another of his kind standing right next to him. For all he knew, Prince Samnibolon was part of the group too. And had been quietly smiling within while Nortekku went on and on, the other day at the Embassy, about Thalarne's having come to Bornigrayal on "family business."

Speaking a little too quickly, Thalarne said, "Prince Til-Menimat invited him into the syndicate, you see. They've gone into a lot of these things together. But Hamiruld pointed out that an out-and-out artifact-collecting expedition would raise some ethical problems, considering that what was involved was a bunch of actual living Sea-Lords. I mean, it's one thing to dig up artifacts on an uninhabited site a million years old, and another thing entirely to take them from living people. Some archaeologist whose interests were purely scientific ought to go along also, Hamiruld said, for the sake of keeping an eye on the two Bornigrayans and make sure that everything was carried out in an appropriate way."

"Someone like you," Nortekku said.

"Someone like me, yes."

"Even though the artifacts are going to get taken anyway, whether you're keeping an eye on things or not?"

She gave him a pained look. "Don't press me too hard on this, Nortekku. If I want to be part of the expedition at all, I can't make myself too much of an obstacle. I know there are problems here. I'll do whatever I can."

Everything was falling into place now for him. Hamiruld not only had known all along about her running off that way to Bornigrayal, he had engineered her leaving town himself. Unwilling, despite his pretense of indifference, to have Thalarne and Nortekku spend cozy weeks or even months digging things up together out by the Hallimalla, Hamiruld had maneuvered her into a place on this Sea-Lord expedition. Til-Menimat would surely have seen the importance of the discovery, and it might not have been hard to convince him that the cocoon venture could always wait for some other time, that the Sea-Lord journey must come first, and that Thalarne's presence on it was necessary to provide scientific cover for the real purposes of the project. And then, after having shipped Thalarne safely off to the other side of the world, presumably far beyond Nortekku's reach, Hamiruld would prevent Nortekku from finding out where she was by coolly pretending to him that he had no information whatever about where she had gone.

Nortekku could understand all that easily enough. Hamiruld must have been more annoyed by Thalarne's affair with him than he wanted to admit. Any man, even one who had countenanced the sort of things in his marriage that Hamiruld evidently had, might be expected to react in that way to an affair that gave the appearance of going well beyond the previously defined bounds of their arrangement.

Well, he had thwarted Hamiruld's scheme—but only because Hamiruld had been careless enough to tell Khardakhor that Thalarne had gone to Bordigrayal, never dreaming that Khardakhor would share the news with the son of his worst enemy. What still disturbed him, though, was the agitation Thalarne had displayed when she discovered that Hamiruld had blatantly altered the message she had given him about going to Bornigrayal, and the hesitation she had shown in revealing to him that Hamiruld was actually a key player in this Sea-Lord enterprise.

In his quiet way Hamiruld held plenty of power over her, he saw. On some level she must still be uneasy about his presence as a third partner in her marriage—that the marriage itself still had more of a hold on her than she would like him to think, that she seemed eager to gloss swiftly over anything that might demonstrate to him that Hamiruld still played a significant role in her life. It was clear now that Hamiruld intended to fight to keep his marriage intact; what was not so clear, Nortekku thought, was what Thalarne's own position on the future of that marriage might be.

"You're very quiet," Thalarne said, in something more like her normal tone of voice.

"You've given me a lot to think about."

"The risks of the trip? The part about collecting artifacts? The fact that Hamiruld is involved?"

"All of it."

"Oh, Nortekku—"

They stood facing each other across the room for a moment. He had no idea what to say. Neither, it seemed, did she.

But only for a moment. The same bright glow came into her eyes that he had seen at their first meeting, back in Yissou, what felt like eons ago. She stretched her arms toward him.

"Come here," she said.

⬤⬤⬤

The ship was much smaller than Nortekku had expected—a tubby, wide-bodied vessel, oddly square-looking, fashioned from thick planks of some kind of blackish wood, that sat low in the water along a weatherbeaten pier at the harbor of Bornigrayal. It was hard to believe that a clumsy little craft like that, which seemed scarcely big enough to pass as a riverboat, would be able to carry them all the way across the immensities of the Eastern Ocean in anything less than a lifetime and a half.

Once he was aboard, though, he saw that he had greatly underestimated the vessel's size. There was much more of it below the water line than was visible from dockside. Two parallel corridors ran its length, with a host of small low-ceilinged cabins branching off from them, and a series of spacious cargo holds at front and back. Nortekku and Thalarne were going to share a cabin near the ship's bow. "This will be a little complicated," she told him. "Kanibond Graysz knows that I'm the wife of one of the backers of the expedition. I've booked only one cabin, and they've let me know that they can't or won't make another one available. But I don't dare try to pass you off as Hamiruld."

"Shall we just say we're very good friends?" Nortekku asked.

"Don't joke. I've let it be known that we're brother and sister. When we're in public, make sure you behave that way."

"I hate telling lies, Thalarne. You know that."

"Tell this one. For me."

"Can we at least be a particularly friendly brother and sister, then?"

"Please, Nortekku."

"What if anyone passing our cabin at night happens to hear

sounds coming out of it that might not be considered appropriate for a brother and sister to be making?"

"*Please*," Thalarne said, as irritated as he had ever heard her sound. "You know how badly I wanted you to accompany me on this expedition. But stirring up a scandal won't achieve anything for anybody. I don't think anybody's going to care, but we need to observe the forms, anyway. Is that clear, brother?"

He forced a grin. "Completely, sister."

Their cabin was ridiculously tiny. The two narrow bunks, one above the other, took up more than half of it. They had one small cabinet for their possessions, and a washbasin. There was scarcely room to turn around in the middle of the floor. The atmosphere in the room was pervaded by the thick, piercing odor of some caulking compound, close to nauseating at first, though Nortekku found himself rapidly getting used to it. A single slitlike opening, not even a hand's-breadth wide, was their window to the outside world. When he pushed the shutter aside a harsh stream of cold air, salty and acrid and unpleasant, drifted in through it, filling the room with a rank, heavy smell that cut through the other one. The smell of the sea, he thought. Of multitudes of fishes, of seaweed, of scuttling sea-creatures moving about just beyond the hull. He had never smelled anything like it before, insistent, commanding, hostile.

The Bornigrayans, Kanibond Graysz and Siglondan, had the cabin just across the corridor. They would have made a far more plausible brother-sister pair than Nortekku and Thalarne: indeed they might almost have been twins. They both were small and fine-boned, both were white-furred, though not from age, both had small alert close-set eyes, his a sharp yellow, hers blue-green. Their faces were cold and pinched, and when they looked at you out of those small bright eyes it was in what struck Nortekku as a shifty, calculating way, as though they were measuring you for some kind of swindle. He found himself taking an instant irrational dislike to them.

But they were affable enough. They greeted Thalarne warmly and showed no sign of surprise that she had suddenly produced a brother as a traveling companion. Wisely, she introduced him as the architect that he was, rather than as any sort of archaeologist, but explained that he had a deep and abiding interest in Great World history—a hobby of his since childhood, she said and had begged her to be taken along. If they had any misgivings about that, they said nothing about them. They talked mostly about the excitement of what lay ahead, the great discoveries that were certain to be made. Not that Nortekku had an easy time understanding them: the language spoken in Bornigrayal was essentially no more than a dialect of that of the West Coast, but the pronunciation and placing of accents differed in a number of significant ways, words were often slurred, other words were entirely unfamiliar, and at all times the two Bornigrayans spoke so quickly that Nortekku found himself lagging a sentence or two behind. Still, they produced a flask of superb Bornigrayan brandy, of a truly extraordinary smooth ness and tang, and the four of them solemnly raised a toast to each other and to the success of the expedition. No one who would share brandy of that quality with people they barely knew could be altogether bad, Nortekku decided.

As the Bornigrayans poured a second round there came the shattering sound of the ship's horn, three mighty blasts. Then the whole vessel began to quiver and from somewhere far below came the drumbeat pounding of the engines. The journey was beginning.

Within moments Nortekku heard a frightful creaking sound that he realized must be the first movements of the ship's two great paddlewheels. They went up on deck to watch as the ship pulled out. There was room for perhaps eight people up there, along with a couple of lifeboats, a sputtering oil lamp, a bell hanging in the bow. The planks were stained and unevenly laid. A flimsy-looking rail was all that guarded the deck's margin.

The day was cold, the sky bleak, a few wisps of snow swirling about. Ominous green lightning was crackling far out at sea. Quickly, but with a troublesome sidewise swaying motion, not quite sickening but distinctly unsettling, the ship moved away from Bornigrayal and on into the gray, unwelcoming ocean. This close to land the water was fairly calm, but dismaying-looking waves were curling along the surface out by the horizon. There would surely be worse to come. The sea is very wide, Nortekku thought, and our ship is so small.

"You look unhappy," Thalarne murmured at his side.

"I think this is scarier than flying, and flying is scary enough. But if your airwagon falls out of the sky you die right away. I suspect that drowning is slow and hideous."

"No doubt it is. So let's try not to drown, all right?"

Gloomily he said, "Wouldn't one good wave be sufficient to turn this ship upside down?"

She looked entirely unperturbed about that: amused, even, by his fears. By way of dismissing them she invented even worse ones for him, slimy sea-monsters rising from the depths and swarming across the deck, or gigantic ocean-going birds swooping down from on high to carry off unsuspecting passengers, or a sudden whirlpool in the sea that would suck the ship down like a ravening monster. He admired her casual attitude—outwardly casual, at least—toward the perils of the sea, and felt abashed for his own faintheartedness. But he went on feeling miserable all the same, and before long returned to their cabin, pleading chill.

At twilight the eastern sky dimmed swiftly, deep blue streaked with red, then a brooding grayish purple, then black. All sight of land had disappeared. They were alone in a seemingly endless expanse of water.

But as one day slid into the next no sea-monsters turned up, nor whirlpools or other menaces, and though a storm swept over them on the fourth or fifth day out, lifting awesome waves that went crashing across the ship's bow, the crewmen behaved as though they were unconcerned and nothing untoward occurred. Nortekku felt himself sliding into the rhythm of the voyage. His fears subsided. Despite all the constraints that their brother-sister masquerade entailed, it was delightful to have Thalarne close beside him all the time, delightful to know that night after night he could climb down from his upper berth and find her welcoming arms outstretched to him.

He was discovering, though, that that closeness was not without its drawbacks. In the cramped cabin they got on each other's nerves all too easily. She had brought a little collection of books, as much as she could gather on short notice about the Great World and Sea-Lords in particular the day she had left for Bornigrayal. During the long hours of the day Nortekku studied them avidly, for what little good that did: they all had the same information, most of it sketchy and speculative. Often, though, Thalarne wanted to consult them too. Somehow whichever book he happened to be reading was the one she needed to look at, right now—or the other way around. Often that led to sharpness between them.

They would heal these little conflicts, frequently, with bouts of coupling. But even that was hampered by the need not to be vocal in their taking of pleasure with each other lest they reveal to the Bornigrayans across the hall, or to some passing member of the crew, that their relationship was somewhat more intimate than that of brother and sister ordinarily should be.

Not that it was at all certain that they had anyone fooled. On a morning when the sea was especially rough Nortekku was passing the time in the ship's little lounge, and Thalarne had gone above—they tried now to give each other as much space as they could—when a couple of crewmen came down the stairs and one said to him, in that thick-tongued Bornigrayan dialect that Nortekku still had so much difficulty understanding, "You ought to go up. Your woman is sick on deck, pretty bad."

There was nothing unusual about that. The weather had mostly been stormy, eternally gray and windy, with much rain and sometimes sleet, and one or another of them had had a bout of seasickness practically every day. But Nortekku took exception to the phrasing.

"My *sister*, you mean."

"Your sister, yes." There was mockery in the man's unfriendly blue eyes. "Up there, sick, your sister, on deck." He winked suggestively. The other began to laugh.

Well, let them laugh, Nortekku thought. Having to pass himself off as Thalarne's brother hadn't been *his* idea.

He went up on deck. She was finished being sick, by then, but she looked dreadful. Nortekku laid his hand on her wrist and lightly rubbed the thick fur up and down by way of comfort, and she managed a faint, unconvincing smile.

"Bad?" he asked.

"Worse than seeing five sea-monsters crawling up on deck. But it's over now."

Just then the sea bucked beneath them, though, and the ship seemed to skip and hop above it, and from Thalarne came a dry ratcheting sound, followed almost at once by a little moan. She turned away from him, huddling miserably into herself. He held her, gently stroking her shoulders, and the spasm passed without further incident. With a game little grin she said, "I wonder how much longer this voyage is supposed to last."

"Only another four years or so," he told her. "Maybe three, if we remember to say our prayers every night."

Seasickness did not seem to afflict him. But as the days went by the restlessness that had plagued him since boyhood grew to a level that was barely tolerable. He prowled constantly from deck to deck, up, down, up, down, standing a long while in the sleety air abovedecks, and then, half frozen, descending to their cabin, where Thalarne sat poring over some map of Great World sites and looked anything but pleased to see him, and then up again, down again to the tiny lounge in the stern, up, down.

The time did pass, somehow. And it became evident, not many days later, that the worst of the voyage was behind them. Each day winter yielded a little more to spring, and the path of the ship had been trending all the while toward the southeast, so that now the skies were a clear blue the whole day long, no more rain fell, and the air was taking on some warmth. Birds were common sights overhead. Siglondan, who appeared to know something about natural history, said that they were shore-birds, coming out from the eastern continent just ahead of them.

She and Kanibond Graysz, with whom Thalarne and Nortekku took their meals every day, were speaking more openly now about the approaching fulfillment of the goals of the expedition. They seemed more slippery than ever, still cagy about what was actually supposed to be achieved. But what was becoming clear was that they had been bought, that their chief interest lay not in what could be learned about this handful of Sea-Lords that had so surprisingly endured beyond their supposed time of extinction, but in how much profit they could turn by prying loose rare artifacts for which the sponsors of the venture would pay extremely well. From something careless that Kanibond Graysz had let slip, Nortekku concluded that whatever collectible objects they brought back with them would be distributed among Til-Menimat and Hamiruld and the other backers according to some prearranged system, and the two Bornigrayan archaeologists would be given bonuses according to the quantity and quality of what they brought back for them.

A grimy business, Nortekku thought. And he knew what Thalarne thought of it as well. But she seemed able to balance her qualms against the advantage of being able to gain access to these improbable survivors from antiquity. He only hoped that she would emerge from the project with her own scientific reputation still untarnished.

The ship moved on, into warmer and warmer weather. Then there was a darkness on the horizon, which rapidly resolved itself into the skyline of a city.

"That's Sempinore there," Siglondan said. They had completed their crossing of the ocean; they were staring out at another continent, at a totally new world.

●●●

The city of Sempinore occupied a long looping crescent around a curving bay of sparkling blue water under a warm, inviting sun. He was unable to see either its beginning or its end. Its population, he thought, must be enormous. He felt awed and overwhelmed.

A grand boulevard ran along the shore parallel to the wharves, with swarms of wheeled vehicles moving swiftly up and down it, and porters guiding patient-looking red-furred beasts of burden that moved heedlessly among them. The air was sweet and fragrant, laden with the aroma of strange spices. There was noise everywhere, the shouts of the porters, the rhythmic chants of peddlers pushing heavily laden carts, the dissonant clash of unfamiliar music. Nortekku counted six wide, straight avenues radiating from the shoreline boulevard into different parts of the city: the main arteries, it would seem.

It was good to eat fresh tender meat that night, to drink sweet young wine again, and cool water from a nearby mountain spring, to fill one's mouth with the flavors of fruits and vegetables that hadn't spent weeks stored in casks. Good, also, to be at rest in a place solidly rooted in the ground, that didn't sway or pitch or heave on the bosom of the sea. At the hotel Nortekku and Thalarne were given separate rooms, as befitted brother and sister; but he came to her after dinner and they slept that night side by side, in an actual bed, in one another's arms. He left before dawn and returned to his own room, taking care not to be seen, though he doubted that any of their fellow travelers believed any longer that their relationship was what they had claimed it to be.

During the idle week they spent in Sempinore Nortekku devoted much time to a study of the city's architecture. The place had a profoundly alien look, and though he knew he should have expected that, it was a source of constant amazement for him.

Its buildings—whitewashed clusters of high domes, spidery aerial bridges high above the ground linking spiky-tipped towers, massive dark octagonal stone structures surrounded by the delicate traceries of pink fretwork walls—had a kind of consistency of style from one block to the next, but it was an alien consistency, a style that reminded him curiously of the imaginary Vengiboneeza that he had seen once in his dreams. They had been designed and built by people whose experiences had been nothing like those of his own people, whose history was in every way different, other than that they too had waited out the Long Winter in cocoons.

Those who dwelled here were folk who knew not Hresh, nor Koshmar nor Torlyri nor Thu-Kimnibol, nor any of the great Bengs, and they spoke a different language, a sibilant, whispering thing of which Nortekku couldn't comprehend a single word, and when they had reached the city-building stage of civilization they had built a city that reflected all those differences. There are only certain ways one can handle the enclosing of space, Nortekku knew—that was what architecture was primarily about, he believed, the enclosing of space. And there are only certain things one can do with light, with form, with proportion. And yet, given all that, many sorts of variants were possible within those basics: variant materials, variant strategies of structural support, and variant kinds of ornament, of cornices, windows, facades, pediments, colonnades. Wherever he looked here, he saw variants from what he considered the norm. Everything, *everything*, was different here. Yissou was different from Dawinno, yes, and Bornigrayal different from both of those in other ways, but this place was—does the phrase make sense, he wondered?—more different still. He felt a kind of vertigo of the soul, walking among its infinity of strange buildings. This too was like a dream, the oddest kind of dream, in which one could not only see but also touch, and feel.

Thalarne sometimes accompanied him on these walks, sometimes not. When she was with him he tried to make clear the impact that this place was having on him. Sempinore had produced an odd reversal in their relationship: when the center of their discourse had been the world's ancient past, she was the teacher, he the novice, but now he was leading the way, endlessly analyzing and explaining the unfamiliar and sometimes almost unbelievable structural assumptions by which the buildings of Sempinore had been put together, and she followed his discourses as well as she could.

At last the reprovisioning job was complete and the time had come for the next stage of their journey.

Two Hjjks had come on board now. Nortekku glumly watched them arrive: like all their kind they were towering figures, taller than any man, with long gleaming bodies marked horizontally with bands of yellow and black, fearsome-looking beaks, narrow tapering heads topped by great feathery antennae, glittering blue-black eyes, deep constrictions marking the boundaries between head and thorax, thorax and abdomen. They were, he supposed, their guides, the two who had discovered the Sea-Lord colony across the Inland Sea. Apparently they were going to sleep on the main deck. They laid out a little Hjjk domain for themselves there, nailing talismans of plaited grass to the planks, setting up small wooden shrines that contained some smooth egg-shaped white stones, installing a cupboard that held a stock of the dried fruit and sun-parched meat that was their food.

He knew he would never understand Hjjks, nor come to have any liking for them. It was, he supposed, some kind of inherent racial animosity, something that had run through him from birth, inbred in blood and bone. To him they were unsightly, ominous things, dry and cold of soul, alien, remote, dangerous. Some of that feeling was a legacy of the things he had been taught in school about the early wars between People and Hjjks for territory in the first years of the New Springtime, but that was just history now. The Hjjks posed no sort of menace at all. The old system of dominance by a central Queen operating out of a central Nest had been shattered by a civil war; the Queen of Queens had been put to death by her own military caste, in a punitive action typical of the icy Hjjk mentality, after a rebellion by the lesser Queens.

Now, Nortekku knew, each Nest was independent and the People's old sense of the Hjjks as an implacable monolithic entity had been replaced by an awareness that, divided as they were, they could no longer be any sort of threat. The two species lived together, not exactly in friendship—never that—but with a sort of cool mutual toleration. There was commerce now, not warfare, between the two species. Hjjks moved freely through the cities of the People and had taken up residence in certain sectors of them. It was too warm and humid for them in Dawinno, but you saw them wherever you went in Yissou, and there had been many of them in Bornigrayal, too. Even so, Nortekku still felt a reflexive stiffening of his spine whenever he was near one; and now there would be two of them as his companions for the rest of the voyage.

Kanibond Graysz and Siglondan could be seen up on deck with them most of the day, huddling in close conversations conducted in low, conspiratorial tones, the two Bornigrayans muttering in their rapid-fire Bornigrayan way and the Hjjks answering in their own harsh, chittering manner. Nortekku saw much sketching of diagrams, and handing of them back and forth, and a good deal of gesturing and pointing. There was something oddly secretive, almost unsavory, about these discussions that Nortekku found very puzzling. They made no attempt to draw their fellow archaeologist Thalarne into them, let alone Nortekku. He never even learned the names of the two Hjjks, if indeed—he had never been sure on that point—Hjjks had individual names. Well, he thought, whatever the Hjjks and the Bornigrayans had to say to each other was no concern of his. He was here to see the Sea-Lords; that, and to be with Thalarne.

❧❧❧

The second voyage was wholly different from the first one. The Inland Sea was the most placid body of water imaginable, waveless, tideless, a shimmering blue pathway offering no challenges of any sort. The whole day long the sun filled the sky like a beacon, bright, huge, astonishingly warm, drawing them on to the south.

From the side of the deck Nortekku could see the creatures of the depths in all their abundance, great schools of silvery fish swarming almost at the surface, occasional solitary giants hanging motionless nearby like underwater balloons and feeding, it seemed, on the great wads of seaweed that lay in clumps all about, and swift predators with the fins along their backs raised up into view like swords cutting the air. Once a mountainous turtle paddled close beside the ship, extended its long neck to stare at him in a glassy, unintelligent way, and slowly closed one eye in a grotesque parody of a wink. Such a profusion of maritime life, Nortekku realized, could not have developed just in the relatively few years since the thawing of the world. Whatever havoc the Long Winter had worked among the citizens of the Great World, it must not have brought complete devastation to these denizens of this warm sea.

In just a few days the shore came into view ahead of them, a long low line of sand and trees. The air was warm and soft. It was easy to believe that in this blessed place the Long Winter had never come, or, if it had, that it had brushed the land with only the gentlest of touches. They coasted westward past white beaches lined with trees of a kind Nortekku had never seen before, thick stubby brown trunks jutting upward from the sand to culminate in a single amazing explosion of long, jagged green leaves at the summit, like a crown of feathers. Farther back he saw wild tangles of vines all snarled together, blooming so profusely that they formed great blurts of color, a solid mass of magenta here, a burst of brilliant orange there, a huge spread of scarlet just beyond.

Late that afternoon they pulled into a protected cove where steamy mist was hovering above the water. Bubbles were visible along the western curve of the little bay, suggesting that a stream of heated water must be rising here from some volcanic furnace below the sea.

Large brown animals, perhaps as many as ten of them, were splashing about in the surf, diving, surfacing, beating the water with their flipperlike limbs, uttering loud trumpeting snorts. Nortekku assumed at first, carelessly, unthinkingly, that they were nothing more than seagoing mammals—akin, perhaps, to the good-natured barking bewhiskered beasts that often could be seen frolicking off the coast near Dawinno. But then, as the ship's dinghy carried him closer to the shore, he saw the luminous glow of what had to be intelligence in their sea-green eyes, and realized with a quick hard jolt of understanding and something not far from terror what these beings actually were.

It was as if a doorway in time had rolled suddenly open and a segment of the ancient world had come jutting through.

Of course the two Hjjks who stood distressingly close by him in the dinghy were survivors of the Great World themselves, but one took the survival of the Hjjks for granted: they had never gone away, they had been part of the landscape from the first moment when the People began coming forth from their cocoons. Sea-Lords, though, were a dead race, extinct, the next thing to legendary. Yet here they were, seven, eight, ten of them close at hand in the steamy pinkish water of this cove, and more appearing now on shore, emerging from the trees that lined the beach and clumsily moving down toward the edge of the water on their flipperlike hind legs.

They displayed no sign of fear. The ones that had been in the water ceased to splash and snort, and now had gathered in a silent group to watch the dinghy's approach, but they seemed quite calm. So too did the ones on shore, collecting now in five or six groups just at the fringe of the sea. They were handsome animals, Nortekku thought, telling himself instantly that he must not call them animals, must never think of them that way. Their kind had been among the rulers of the world when his own ancestors had been apes chattering in the trees.

There might have been sixty of them all told, though others, possibly, might be lingering on the far side of the line of shallow dunes that rose just behind the trees, or out of sight at sea. They were gracefully tapering creatures, sturdily built, bigger and obviously stronger than men, with powerful, robust bodies that had a dense layer of sleek brown fur plastered close to their skin. Both their upper and lower sets of limbs were flipperlike, though Nortekku saw that their hands had capable-looking fingers with opposable thumbs. Their heads too were tapered, long and narrow, but with high-domed foreheads that indicated the force and capacity of the minds housed within.

"Such sadness," Thalarne said softly. "Do you see it, Nortekku? That look in their eyes—that misery, that pain—"

Yes. It was impossible not to perceive it, even from a distance: a look of the deepest sorrow, almost of grief. Those big glossy eyes, so close in color to her own, seemed without exception disconsolate, desolate, shrouded in lamentation. There was a touch of anger in those eyes, too, he thought, a hot blast of fury plainly visible behind that sadness. He asked himself whether he had any right to project emotion of any sort on these beings of another species, whose true feelings probably could not be read with any accuracy. And then he looked again, and it was the same as before: sorrow, grief, heartbreak, rage. They were strong, agile, handsome, graceful beings: they should have been happy creatures on this happiest of coasts. But that did not appear to be the case.

The dinghy came to rest in the shallows. "Is there a village here?" Thalarne asked Sjglondan, as they scrambled ashore.

"We didn't find one last time, if by a village you mean permanent structures. They live mostly in the water, though they come up on shore for some part of every day and settle down for naps under the trees."

"Then they have no tools, either? Nothing that we'd call a culture?"

"Not any more. But they have language. They have a knowledge of their own race's history. We think that they may keep some shrines containing objects of Great World provenance somewhere not very far inland. They've pretty much reverted to a natural existence, but there's no doubt that they're genuine Sea-Lords." Pretentiously Siglondan added, "It's almost impossible for one to comprehend the full awesomeness of the discovery."

"Awesome, yes," Thalarne said. "And sad. So very sad. These pitiful creatures."

The Bornigrayan woman gave her an odd look. "Pitiful, did you say?" But Thalarne had already begun to wander off. Nortekku moved along after her. He glanced down toward the group of Sea-Lords by the shore; then, hastily, he glanced away. The thought of transgressing on the privacy of these beings whom he had come such a great distance to behold made him ill at ease. That expression of deep-seated melancholy mingled with rage that he imagined he saw in those huge glossy green eyes, whether it was really there or not, was something that suddenly he could not bear to see.

He considered what small stock of information he had about the Sea-Lord civilization of the Great World days. About all there was was the account in the book that Hresh had written, he who so many years ago had penetrated the ruined cities of the ancients and looked with his own eyes on their way of life by means of machines of theirs, no longer functional now, that had given him glimpses of their actual time.

The Sea-Lords, Hresh said, had been created by the humans out of some species of intelligent sea-going mammal, just as they had created the People out of apes. Like all mammals they breathed air, not water, but they were much more at home in the sea than on land, where they moved about with some degree of difficulty. When they were on land they traveled in cunningly made chariots that moved on silver treads, controlling them with manipulations of their flip per-fingers. Mainly, though, they lived at sea, guiding the vessels that carried all manner of costly merchandise from one part of the Great World to another. The other Great World races depended heavily on them. When they were in port, Hresh said, in the taverns and shops and waterfront restaurants that they frequented, they behaved like the bold, swaggering princes of the sea that they were.

And now—to have retrogressed to the simple life of watergoing beasts—

The crewmen were putting up tents under the trees. Nortekku watched them for a while. Not that the sight of tents being raised was so fascinating, but just now he wanted to avoid coming close to the Sea-Lords, or even to look in their direction.

Siglondan and Kanibond Graysz didn't appear to feel any such inhibition. They and their two Hjjk confederates went quickly down to the nearest Sea-Lord group and involved themselves in what looked very much like a conversation with them. Nortekku could hear the clicking, buzzing sound of Hjjk-speak, then the quick chatter of the Bornigrayans, and then the Hjjks again, speaking in brief outbursts with long spans of silence between them. From time to time the Sea-Lords seemed to reply, with a sort of clipped grunting that had the cadence and phrasing of language. After each burst of it the Hjjks spoke again to the two Bornigrayans, as if interpreting what had just been said.

But how had the Hjkks learned the Sea-Lord language? By second sight, perhaps. Hjjks, Nortekku knew, had a kind of second sight that was much more powerful than that of the People. They were able to speak directly to minds with it: that was how they had first communicated with the newly emerged People in the early days of the Going

Forth. Perhaps they had used it to develop some understanding of Sea-Lord speech, too.

Thalarne now had joined the group and was listening attentively. Curiosity overcame Nortekku's uneasiness: it felt foolish to hang back like this. He took himself down the sloping strand to the place close by the water where the others were gathered but the gathering broke up just as he arrived. The Sea-Lords headed into the water and the two Bornigrayans, with the pair of Hjjks, went off up the beach. Thalarne alone remained.

She gave him a stricken look as he approached.

"What was all that about?" Nortekku asked.

She seemed to be struggling to shape an answer. Then she said, "There's something very bad going on here, but I'm not altogether sure what it is. All I can tell you is that we aren't just imagining what we think we see in their eyes. One good look will tell you that. It's very clear that these people are aware of their own tragedy. They know what they once were; they know what they are now. You just have to look into those eyes and you know that they're the eyes of people who can't understand why they're still alive, and don't want to be any more. People who wish they were dead, Nortekku."

◆◆◆

Who wish they were dead? For a moment Nortekku made no reply. He had never seen her look so deeply unnerved. It was easy enough to believe that there was something tragic about the expression in these creatures' eyes: he had seen it himself, from far away. But how could she be certain of this startling interpretation of it? The grunting speech of the Sea-Lords and the mind-speech of the Hjjks were closed books to her, Nortekku knew.

"You heard the Hjjks tell this to Kanibond Graysz and Siglondan?"

She shook her head. "I got there too late to hear anything important. It was all winding down by then. I'm speaking purely intuitively."

"Ah. I see. And you trust that intuition, Thalarne?"

"Yes. I do." She was steadier now. "I looked into those eyes, Nortekku. And what they were saying was, *We want to die. Show us how to do it. You are great ones who can cross the mighty sea; surely you can give this little thing to us. Surely. Surely. Surely.*

That was going much too far, Nortekku told himself. This was hardly the method of science, as he understood that concept. The look in their eyes: was something like that a sufficient basis for so fantastic a theory? But Thalarne seemed wholly carried away by it. He had to be careful here. Cautiously he said, "You may be right. But I just can't help but think that you're making an awfully big intuitive leap."

"Of course I am. And I've already told you I'm not fully sure of it myself. Just go and stand close to them, though, and you can see for yourself. Those eyes are sending a message without any ambiguity at all. They're pleading for it, Nortekku. They're crying out for it."

"For death."

"For death, yes. For the extinction that somehow was denied them when the rest of the Great World was destroyed. They want to die, Nortekku, but they don't know how to manage it. It's almost as if they're saying they want us to kill them. To put them out of their misery."

"But that's insane!" Nortekku said, brushing at the air as though to push the concept away.

"Well, then, so they're insane. Or half insane, anyway. Or perhaps they're so terribly sane that to us they seem crazy."

"Asking to be killed—asking to be made extinct—"

Perhaps there was something to it. He had seen those eyes himself. She was simply guessing, but the guess had a cold plausibility about it. But was Thalarne hinting, then, that she felt that their wish ought to be granted?

Surely not.

The idea was repellent, unthinkable, horrifying. It was a violation of all she believed, and he as well. She was a scientist, not an executioner. She had come here to investigate this surprising remnant of the Great World, to learn all that could be learned about it, not to extirpate it. And for him the survival of these Sea-Lords was a marvelous boon, a miraculous restoration of a small piece of a vanished world.

With short, quick, troubled steps he began to pace back and forth, ankle-deep, at the margin of the gentle surf. Thalarne, moving along beside him, said, "Their whole context is gone. They're all alone in a world they are no longer part of, one that they don't like or understand. They have the intelligence their race had in the old days, or nearly so, but there's nothing to apply it to, no framework to fit into, no world to belong to. So they swim and copulate and catch fish all day. Does that sound good to you? Then try it. Try it for ten, twenty, fifty years. Watch your parents growing old in such a life. Watch your children entering into it. They live a long time, Nortekku. They try not to bring new generations into being, but it happens. They think their gods have forgotten them. Their life is meaningless, and it goes on and on and on. It's driven them halfway to madness. And so they want to die. If only they knew how."

"Well, maybe so. We can't really know. But of course, even if that's what they want, we couldn't possibly—"

"No. Of course not," she said quickly. "How could we even consider it?"

That much was a relief, he thought.

"But that's why this situation, if I'm right about it, is so tragic," she went on. "And that's why we need to find out much more about them."

"Yes," Nortekku said. "Yes, definitely." He would have said anything, just then. He wanted to get away from this whole subject as fast as he could.

"Come with me," Thalarne said abruptly. "Up there, behind those dunes, where Siglondan thinks there may be shrines. Places where artifacts are kept."

That made him uneasy too. "Should we go there, do you think? Wouldn't it be sacrilege?"

"Just to look. Siglondan and Kanibond Graysz surely will, before very long."

Getting over the dunes was no trivial task. Very little vegetation of any kind grew on them, and the loose sand slipped and slid beneath their feet. Thalarne pointed out places where the Sea-Lords themselves had worn deep tracks, compacting the dunes with their flippers, and they followed those. On the far side the air was still and very warm, heavy with the stifling interior heat of this continent: nowhere could they feel the sea breeze that made the strip by the shore so pleasant. Strange spiky plants were growing here, tall, stiff-armed, leafless, bristling with spines. These stood everywhere about, like guardians in the sandy wasteland. It was hard to follow the track here, but after a little searching Nortekku found something that had the look of a path, and they took it.

By trial and error they made their way to a place where, no question about it, many flippered feet had passed. The sand was packed down hard. There was a second row of dunes here, much more stable ones, tightly bound by low sprawling shrubs interwoven with gray clumps of tough, sharp-edged grass.

"Look here," Thalarne said.

Three bare metal frameworks sat in a row at the foot of the dunes: mere shapes, the fragile outlines of things rather than the things themselves. But from those shapes it seemed clear that these were the remnants of three of the vehicles—"chariots," Hresh had called them—by which the ancient Sea-Lords had traveled when ashore. The ghostly hints of levers, of wheels, of seats, all gave credence to that idea.

There was a sign, also, of a passageway into the dune, a tunnel roofed over by wooden arches. Nortekku and Thalarne exchanged glances. He saw her eagerness.

"No," he said. "We mustn't. Not without their permission."

"Even though Kanibond Graysz and Siglondan will—"

"Let them. We can't. This has to be a sacred place."

He knew that Thalarne conceded the strength of that argument. But in any case the decision was taken from their hands, for a Sea-Lord had appeared from somewhere, an elderly one, it seemed, a male, stooped and bowed, with silvered fur and veiled, blinking eyes, who came shuffling up to them and took up a stance between them and the three chariots. The custodian of this place, perhaps—a priest, maybe. He had the sadness in his eyes too, and possibly also the anger that Nortekku believed lay behind it, but mainly they were tired eyes, very old, very weary. The Sea-Lord said something in a barely audible tone, low and husky, and, after a brief silence, said it again.

"He wants us to leave, I think," Nortekku said. But of course the old Sea-Lord could have been saying almost anything else.

Thalarne agreed, all too readily. "Yes. Yes, that has to be it."

She smiled at the Sea-Lord and turned her hands outward, apologetically, and the two of them moved away, back toward the encampment by the water. The Sea-Lord remained where he was, watching them go.

"Will you tell the Bornigrayans about this?" Nortekku asked.

"I have to," said Thalarne. "We're not here as competitors. They've shared a lot of things with me. They'll find it by themselves before long, anyway. You know that."

"Yes," he said. "I imagine they will."

The eyes of that old Sea-Lord haunted him as they picked their way back over the outer dune. Thinking of him, Nortekku felt again a sense of the great age of the world into which his own people had erupted so recently. *His* world was new and young, only two centuries old, bursting with the vigor that came with having been let free of the cocoons after seven hundred thousand years in hiding. But now he saw more clearly than ever that the world of the New Springtime was but a thin overlay masking the dead, used-up world that had preceded it— masking a whole succession of dead, used-up worlds, going back to who knew what pre-human mysteries.

So you are back to that, he thought. The transience of everything, the eternal cycle of decay and extinction. That is a grim and cheerless way of looking at things, he told himself. It is a vision devoid of all hope.

But in that same bleak moment came once again the opposite thought, the compensating and comforting one, the thought that the world is a place of constant renewal through billions of years, and that that renewal was a never-ending process that held out the promise of eternal life. World after world, world without end.

I will cling to that idea, Nortekku told himself. I must. I must.

◉◉◉

The next morning Thalarne led the two Bornigrayan archaeologists to the site on the far side of the dunes. Nortekku was still displeased about that, but grudgingly he accepted her argument that it would be unethical for one member of the expedition to conceal an important find from the others. He had to bear in mind, she reminded him, that she was here—and he as well—only because they had invited her along.

There was something wrong with that line of reasoning, but Nortekku did not feel like taking the matter up with her. She was here, in fact, because her husband had wanted to send her somewhere far

away, someplace where her lover wouldn't be able to find her: it was
for that reason, and no other, that Hamiruld had arranged to have her
included in what was fundamentally an expedition designed to produce new plunder for those wealthy highborn collectors of antiquities
who were paying the venture's expenses. Whatever scientific information might be gathered was strictly incidental. And so, even though it
struck Nortekku as folly to be worrying about ethical issues when
dealing with such people as Siglondan and Kanibond Graysz, he
wasn't in a good position to be urging her to conceal finds from them.
The truth of the situation was, he conceded, that he and Thalarne were
fundamentally helpless here.

Helplessly, therefore, they accompanied the Bornigrayans to the
place of the chariots. The old Sea-Lord custodian was nowhere in
sight. That was a blessing, Nortekku thought. Helplessly they looked
on as Kanibond Graysz, using a power torch, went slithering into the
tunnel that entered the dune. Helplessly they watched him emerge
with objects: a rusted helmet that had an air of immense age about it,
a knobby-tipped rod of scabby yellow metal that might have been a
scepter, a battered bronze box inscribed with curvilinear writing of a
Great World sort.

"Nothing else in there," Kanibond Graysz reported. "Just these
three things, scattered about at random. But it's a start. We'll need to
excavate to see if other things are buried beneath the floor. Tomorrow,
perhaps."

Little was said by anybody as they returned to camp. But once
Nortekku and Thalarne were back in the tent that they shared—the
pretense that they were brother and sister had long since been
abandoned—he found, to his horror, that he could not keep himself
from raising the issue that he knew he must not raise with her.

"That made me sick, what happened today. It's theft, Thalarne.
You said yourself, back in Bornigrayal, that it's one thing to collect
objects from a site that's abandoned for a million years, and
something very different to steal them from living people."

"Yes. That's true."

"And yet you just stood there while he went in and took those
things. Even leaving the ethical issues out of the question, I ask you,
Thalarne: is that good archaeological technique, just to walk in and

pick up objects, without recording stratification or anything else?—
But then there are the ethical issues too."

She made no attempt to hide her anguish. "Let me be, Nortekku. I
don't have any answers for you."

He pressed onward anyway. "Is it your position that since these
people don't care a hoot whether they live or die, it doesn't matter
what we do with the things that belong to them? We aren't sure that
that's how they feel, you know. It's just a speculation."

"A very likely one, though."

"Well, then—granting that you're right—can we really feel free to
help ourselves to their possessions while they're still alive?"

"Let me be, Nortekku," Thalarne said again, tonelessly. "Can't
you see that I'm caught between all sorts of conflicting forces, and
there's nothing I can do? *Nothing*."

He saw that it was dangerous to push her any further. There was
nothing she could do, nor he, for that matter. Nor would she allow any
further debate about this. It was as though she had pulled an impene-
trable curtain down around herself.

The days went by. Nortekku stayed away, most of the time, when
the Bornigrayans went over the dunes to poke in the caches of hidden
artifacts back there. Usually Thalarne went with them, sometimes not,
but when she did go she had little to report to Nortekku about anything
they might have found there. It couldn't have been much, he knew:
Kanibond Graysz said something about that, one night at dinner, re-
marking on how scrappy and insignificant most of their finds had
been. The sponsors of the expedition were going to be disappointed.
Too bad, Nortekku thought, but he kept his opinions to himself.

He still could not bring himself to go near the Sea-Lords. They
spent much of their time in the water, often far out from shore where
it would not have been possible to go, but when they returned to the
beach he kept his distance from them. The unhappiness that they em-
anated was too contagious: being near them plunged him into gloom.
Now and then he would see one of them looking toward him with that
poignant, yearning stare of theirs. He would always look away.

His estrangement from Thalarne saddened him as much as what
the archaeologists were doing in the dunes. They still shared a tent,
they still would couple from time to time, but there was no lifting of

the invisible barrier that had fallen between them. Since he was unable to discuss anything with her involving the Sea-Lords, about all that was left to talk about was the weather, and the weather was unchanging, warm and sunny and calm day after day.

It surprised him not at all when the two Bornigrayans returned from a trip to the inner dune one morning, accompanied by their two Hjkks, who were carrying one of the Great World Sea-Lord chariots on an improvised litter of planks that had been brought from the ship. Of course they would take one of the chariots: of course. There had been so little else of any note to bring back. The chariot was a major prize, worthy of the finest collection.

The Sea-Lords who were nearby didn't seem to be in any way upset as the chariot was stowed aboard the dinghy and transported to the ship. Shouldn't they be protesting this flagrant theft of one of their most sacred objects? Apparently they didn't care. They looked on in the same uninvolved, passive way they had greeted everything else since the landing of the expedition on their shore. Either the chariot wasn't really sacred to them, or, as Thalarne believed, they had so thoroughly divested themselves of all will to live that its removal couldn't possibly make any difference to them. If so, then he had been wrong to berate Thalarne after the Bornigrayans' initial intrusion into the artifact cache, and he needed to tell her that. Even if the Sea-Lords didn't care, though, he did, and it saddened him greatly to watch what was happening.

Siglondan herself admitted to some vestigial guilt over the removal of the chariot. In a rare moment of openness she said to Nortekku, as they stood together by the shore watching the dinghy return, "I can't help feeling that this is hurting them. That chariot is practically all that they have left to remember their ancestors by. We haven't ever excavated a site that still has living descendants of the ancients on it before. But Kanibond Graysz thinks it's such an important object that we simply have to take it. It's not as though it's their only one."

It was the first sign Nortekku had seen of any compassion for the Sea-Lords in her, or of the slightest disagreement on a policy issue between Siglondan and her mate. Kanibond Graysz seemed all greed, all ice. Siglondan, at least, had revealed some flickerings of conscience just now.

He said, feeling some elusive need to reassure her, "Well, if they just don't care about anything, if they even regret that they're alive at all—"

It was the wrong thing to say. The Bornigrayan woman shot him a peculiar look. "That wild fantasy of Thalarne's, eh? That they want to die? That they're a bitter people who think their gods have forgotten them? That they're looking for a way to get us to put them out of their misery? You believe it too, do you?"

"I don't know what I believe. I have no evidence to work with."

"Neither does she."

"So you think she's wrong?"

"Of course I do. Kanibond Graysz and I have had conversations with them, you know."

"But everything gets filtered through the Hjjks, and who knows what distortions the things that they're saying pick up along the way?"

She shrugged. "This isn't a matter of translation. This is a matter of understanding the realities that are right here around us. The notion Thalarne is trying to put forth is crazy, Nortekku, completely crazy. The Sea-Lords have given us no indication whatever of a death-wish. If she tries to propose such an idea publicly, we'll oppose her at every step." He could feel Siglondan drawing back, closing down. The openness of a few moments before was gone now. Her voice had taken on a cold, formal intonation. She was angry and defensive. "Has your— sister—told you that she not only believes they want to die, she's willing to help them achieve it?"

"She told me that we mustn't even consider it."

"Well, she *is* considering it, regardless of anything she might have told you. I know that she is. But even if her theory about them is right, and there's no reason to think that it is, we couldn't possibly allow any such thing to happen. You understand that, I hope. These beings are infinitely precious. They're the last few of their kind, so far as we know, the only survivors of a great ancient culture. We have to protect their lives at all cost. We're preservers of the past, Nortekku, not destroyers." And with a barren little smile she moved on toward her tent.

He stood looking after her, bewildered. He had no idea where he stood in any of this. After hearing Siglondan's scornful dismissal, Thalarne's theory did indeed seem wild, fantastic, almost frightening in its arbitrary assumptions. And yet, when you studied a Sea-Lord's eyes, when you saw that terrible look that could only be an expression of intolerable grief and rage and longing and despair, it didn't seem all that arbitrary. But as for enabling the Sea-Lords to die, as an act of compassion, if that was what Thalarne was advocating—and she had denied that, had she not?—the concept was too absurd even to consider. To kill the very creatures they had come here to find—no—no—

As he struggled with these matters Nortekku became aware of figures moving up the beach toward him—a couple of Sea-Lords, females, by the size of them, and one of the Hjjks trailing along a few paces behind. Automatically he turned to go. Even less than ever, now, did he want to be in any sort of proximity to a Sea-Lord.

But before he could take more than a few steps the bigger of the two Sea-Lords, moving with surprising swiftness, closed the distance between them in a few long sliding strides. One of its flippers shot out and grabbed his arm. The webbed fingers tightened around his wrist. Grunting, barking, it pulled him roughly toward it, swinging him around so that they stood face to face.

He was too amazed even to feel afraid. For a moment he was conscious only of the fishy reek of the creature, and of the great shining bristles that jutted from its muzzle, and—yes—of its huge glistening eyes, close to his own, staring at him with a frightful intensity. There was no way he could break its grip. The Sea-Lord was as big as he was, and much stronger. He leaned away as far as he could, holding himself rigid, averting his head. A further series of low barking grunts came from it.

"Tell it to let go of me," Nortekku said to the Hjjk, who was standing by in utter unconcern.

"It will release you when it is ready to release you," said the Hjjk in that dispassionate Hjjk way of theirs. "First it will finish what it is saying."

Saying? Yes. Nortekku observed now that those grunts had a structured rhythm to them, the balance and even the audible punctuation of what must surely be a language. It was indeed trying to say something to him. But what?

"I can't understand you," Nortekku told the Sea-Lord futilely. "Let me go! Let go!" And, to the Hjjk: "What's it saying, then?"

The Hjjk replied, evasively, in the clickings and chitterings of its own tongue, which Nortekku had never mastered.

He glared at the insect-man's great-beaked face. "No," he said. "Tell it so I can understand."

"What it is is the usual thing," said the Hjjk, after a moment. "It is asking for your help."

"My—help?" Nortekku said, and a monstrous realization began to dawn in him. "What kind of help?"

The Sea-Lord was finished with its oration, now. It loosed its hold on Nortekku's wrist and stepped back, watching him expectantly. Nortekku turned once more to the Hjjk.

"What kind of help?" he demanded again.

Once again the Hjjk answered him, maddeningly, in Hjjk.

Nortekku snatched up a driftwood log that was lying near his right foot and brandished it under the Hjjk's jutting beak. "Tell it the right way, or by all the gods, I'll pull you apart and feed your fragments to the fishes!"

The Hjjk showed no sign of alarm. Crossing its uppermost arms across its thorax in what might have been a gesture of self-protection, but which had more of an aura of unconcern, it said blandly, "It would like to end its life. It wishes that you would teach it how to die. This is the thing that they always are saying, you know."

Yes. Yes, of course. *Teach it how to die.* Precisely what he had not wanted to hear, precisely what he would prefer not to face. Precisely what Thalarne had already guessed. *It is the thing that they are always saying.*

◆◆◆

Thalarne did not seem surprised at all, when he told her of his encounter with the Sea-Lord. It was as if she had been expecting vindication of this kind to come at any moment.

"It *had* to be, Nortekku. I felt it from my first glimpse of them." Wonderingly she said, "It wants us to teach it how to die! Which means they can't achieve it on their own—they probably don't even have the *concept* of suicide. So they've been asking and asking, ever since we got here. And of course those two have been suppressing it. The Sea-Lords are their big asset, their key to fame and fortune and scientific glory. They'd never permit anything to happen to them."

"And you would?"

"No. You know I wouldn't. Couldn't. It isn't possible to take a responsibility like that into one's own hands."

He nodded. He wished he could hear more conviction in her voice.

She went on, "What I would do, what I *will* do—is file a report with the Institute about all this when I get back. And with the government of Yissou, and I suppose with the Presidium of Dawinno also. And let *them* decide what to do about the Sea-Lords."

"You know that Kanibon Graysz and Siglondan will file a dissenting report."

"Let them. The powers that be can hire their own Hjjk interpreters and send their own expedition out here and find out themselves what the Sea-Lords do or don't want. The decision's not up to us. But how good it is, Nortekku, that you discovered what you did. I was sure of it, but I had no proof. And now—"

"Proof? All you have, Thalarne, is the word of a Hjjk that that's what the Sea-Lord was saying."

"It's a step toward understanding what's happening here," she said. "A very important one. And why would a Hjjk invent anything so fantastic? The Hjjks aren't famous for their great imaginations. I don't think they tell a lot of lies, either. Neither one of them would have volunteered a word about this on its own, but when you asked for a translation—"

"It gave me one. Yes. And an accurate one, I suppose. They're too indifferent to want to tell lies, aren't they?"

It wishes that you would teach it how to die.

No. No. No. No.

❥❥❥

He and Thalarne agreed to say nothing more about any of this, neither to each other nor, certainly, to the Bornigrayans, until they had returned to their home continent. Siglondan had made it quite clear where she and her mate stood on the subject of Thalarne's Sea-Lord theory. There was nothing to gain but trouble by debating it with them now.

Later in the week, as it became clear that the visit was winding down, Nortekku heard the sound of hammering coming from the ship as it sat at anchor off shore. The ship's carpenters must be doing some remodeling on board. Then came Kanibond Graysz's announcement that the ship would leave the next morning: the only thing that remained, he said, was to round up the Sea-Lord specimens that they were taking back, and put them on board the—

"*What* did you say?" Thalarne asked incredulously.

"To round up the Sea-Lord specimens," the Bornigrayan said again. And then, in a droning, official tone: "Our charter empowers us to bring up to four Sea-Lords back with us to Bornigrayal, where they will be placed in a congenial environmental situation so that they can undergo careful study in the most sympathetic surroundings possible."

"I don't believe this," Thalarne said. Her whole body had gone taut. "You're going to take *prisoners*? Intelligent autonomous beings are going to be collected by you and brought home and turned into zoological exhibits?"

"That is in our charter. It was the understanding from the beginning. I can show you the authorization we have—the signatures of such important figures as Prince Samnibolon of Dawinno, and Prince Til-Menimat—"

"No," Thalarne said. "This can't be."

"And of your own husband, lady, Prince Hamiruld of Yissou—"

"Hamiruld doesn't have the rank of prince," said Thalarne, absurdly, in the faintest of voices. She looked stunned. Turning from the Bornigrayan as if he had uttered some vile obscenity, she hurried off up the beach toward the tents. Nortekku went running after her. He caught up with her just outside the tent.

"Thalarne—"

Panting, wild-eyed, she whirled to face him. "Did you hear that? This is outrageous! We can't let them do it, Nortekku!"

"We can't?"

"We could make a case out for *killing* the Sea-Lords, if that's what they genuinely want. But to put them on display in a zoo? Coddled, peered at, *imprisoned*? Their lives will be even more nightmarish than they already are."

"I agree. This is very ugly."

"Worse than ugly: criminal. We won't allow it."

"And just how will we stop it, then?"

"Why—why—" She paused only briefly. "We'll explain to the captain and his men that what these two want to do is illegal, that he and his whole crew will be making themselves accessories to a crime—"

"They'll laugh in our faces, Thalarne. Their pay comes from Kanibond Graysz, not from us. The captain takes his orders from Kanibond Graysz."

"Then we'll prevent the ship from setting out if it has any Sea-Lords aboard."

"How?" Nortekku asked again.

"We'll figure something out. Damage the engine, or something. We *can't* let this happen. We *can't*."

"If we make any sort of trouble," Nortekku said quietly, "they'll simply throw us overboard. Or at best put us in irons and keep us chained up until the ship has docked at Bornigrayal. Believe me, Thalarne: there's isn't any way we can stop this. None. None. None."

He made her see it, finally, though it took some time. He got her to see, also, that he was as horrified by Kanibond Graysz' scheme as she was, that he was in no way condoning it when he said they must simply abide by what was going to occur. There were just the two of them against a whole crew of burly Bornigrayan sailors who weren't going to collect their pay until they had fulfilled their obligations under their contract with their employers. And it struck him as far from implausible that he and Thalarne would be dumped into the middle of the ocean if they made themselves sufficiently obstreperous. Kanibond Graysz could tell any sort of story he pleased. *The woman fell overboard during rough weather*, he could say, *and the man jumped in to rescue her, and then—they were surrounded by flesh-eating fish—there was nothing we could do to save them—nothing—*

It was a shameful affair, hideous, morally repugnant. But it couldn't be halted. He and Thalarne would have to stand by and watch it happen, which in effect turned them into accomplices. He had never felt so powerless in his life.

This is Hamiruld's revenge, he thought.

◦◦◦

Helpless once more, he watched stonily as Kanibond Graysz pointed out four of the Sea-Lords on the beach, two males, two females, to the crewmen of the ship. Eight or ten of the crewmen, wielding electric prods, surrounded one of the female Sea-Lords and hustled her into the water and aboard the dinghy. Nortekku expected her to resist, to fling the crewmen away from her as though they were discarded dolls—even the females, smaller than the males, were powerfully muscular creatures—but, no, the prods never were needed, there was no resistance at all, not even when the Bornigrayans produced a thick rope and swiftly wrapped it about her upper flippers to prevent her from escaping. She remained quiescent as they heaved her into the dinghy, as they rowed back to the ship, as they pulled her up on deck. It went the same way with the other three. Neither the other female nor the two males, huge and brawny though they were, gave any indication of being aware of what was taking place.

It is true, then, about their wanting to die, Nortekku realized. Life is already over for them; nothing remains but the actual moment of termination. What happens to them between now and then is of no concern to them whatever.

Still, it had been sickening to watch the capture. The Sea-Lords might not care, but *he* did, and, of course, Thalarne, who was so strongly affected by it that it was several days before she came up far enough from her depression even to feel like speaking.

By then they were well out to sea. The continental coast behind them dwindled to the most imperceptible line and then vanished altogether. The course was a straight westerly one: they would not be going back to Sempinore, either to reprovision or to drop off the two Hjjk guides, but would, rather, leave the Inland Sea as soon as possible and head right across the Eastern Ocean to Bornigrayal with their booty.

Nortekku knew now what the hammering aboard the ship had been. They had converted the two storage holds at the ship's stern into one large tank for the Sea-Lords. Some kind of siphon arrangement brought fresh ocean water up into the tank each day. Thus the four captives would have access to the environment in which they preferred to spend most of their time. At mid-morning each day they were brought out for exercise on the desk—a solemn ritual in which they flapped up and back for half an hour or so—and then they lay basking until it was time for them to return to their cabins. The ropes with which they had been pinioned had been removed. It would have been simple enough for them to leap over the rail and make their way back to their home at the edge of the southern continent; but either they believed that they were already too far from home to be able to accomplish the journey, or, what was more probable, their being prisoners here aboard the ship was of no consequence to them. All four seemed to be living in some private world. They paid no attention to their captors. Mostly they were silent; occasionally they spoke with one another in their language of grunts and barks, but once, when Thalarne asked one of the Hjjks for a translation, the Hjjk merely stared at her as though her own language were unintelligible to it.

The westward crossing was far easier than the eastward voyage had been. Spring had come to the ocean, now, and the air was nearly as warm as it was when they were in the region of the Inland Sea. There were no storms, only occasional gentle showers. An easy wind came from behind them, helping them along.

Nortekku and Thalarne were standing on the deck as the ship docked at Bornigrayal Harbor. Suddenly she caught her breath as though in shock, and grasped his wrist tightly with both her hands. He turned to her, amazed.

"Look! Look! Down there, Nortekku!"

He glanced down, toward the quay, where the deckhands were tying up the ship.

Hamiruld was standing there.

Thalarne could barely speak. Only choked monosyllables came from her. "How—why—"

"Easy, Thalarne. Easy."

Struggling to regain her self-control, she said, "But what's he *doing* here? What does he want? He should be back in Yissou. He's got no business being here!"

Nortekku, feeling shaken also by the presence of Thalarne's mate here, so far from their home, stared toward the slight, wiry figure of Hamiruld and was appalled to see him cheerily smiling and waving at them. The loving husband showing up at the pier to welcome his wife and a friend of hers as they returned from a little trip, yes. How sweet of him.

This is very bad, Nortekku thought.

As calmly as he could he said, "He's come to claim you back, I suppose. Someone must have told him I flew out to Bornigrayal after you. Khardakhor, perhaps. Or even Prince Vuldimin." Could that be, he wondered? Would he have cared that much? A more reasonable possibility presented itself. —"Or perhaps he's just here to represent the syndicate. I suspect they'd want to check up on our two Borni-grayan friends, and make sure that when the ship is unloaded they don't go walking off with any Sea-Lord finds that don't belong to them."

Either way, it was the worst finish to the voyage he could imagine, except, possibly, if the ship had gone down at sea with the loss of all aboard. First to discover the dolorous state of the little Sea-Lord colony, then to have to participate, however involuntarily, in the capture of the four who had come back with them, and now to be confronted in the moment of their arrival by Thalarne's mean-souled, spiteful little husband—

Hamiruld was courtesy itself, though, as they landed. He came sprinting up on deck as soon as the boarding ramp had been laid down, saluted the captain, warmly embraced Thalarne—she held herself stiffly away from him as he hugged her—and even clapped Nortekku exuberantly on the shoulder. He proffered no explanation for being here on this side of the continent. He let them know that had already heard reports of the great success of the expedition and that he wanted to hear all the details, that night, at the hotel in town where they would all be staying. He had rented the finest rooms; there would be a grand celebratory feast.

"I will be spending the night aboard the ship, I think," said Nortekku coolly. He assumed that Hamiruld would sweep Thalarne up into his own luxurious suite at the hotel, and the last thing he wanted was to be under the same roof. "There are a few details I have to finish up—I need to organize my notes, to do some final packing—"

Hamiruld looked a little surprised at that, but not greatly troubled. All his attention was focused on Thalarne.

She, though, said just as coolly, "I will be staying aboard the ship tonight also, Hamiruld."

At that a flash of quick fury came up into his eyes, like a goblin-face appearing at a window. Then, just as quickly, he grew calm again. "You will? And why is that, Thalarne?"

"I'd rather speak with you privately about that," she said. — "Nortekku? Would you excuse us for a moment?"

She was in full command, now. Obediently Hamiruld allowed her to march him off toward the ship's bow, and just as obediently Nortekku swung around and walked to the other side of the ship, where he could look outward into the harbor instead of having to observe their conversation from a distance.

It went on a very long while. It was one of the longest moments of his life. Then she returned, grim-faced, her jaw tightly set. Glancing across, Nortekku saw that Hamiruld was gone from the deck, that he had descended once again to the pier.

"Well?" Nortekku asked.

"I told him that we had brought four living Sea-Lords back with us, and that I wanted him to have them released. I told him that I would leave him, if he didn't."

The conditional nature of that threat left Nortekku feeling chilled. But all he said, when she did not continue, was: "And then?"

"And then he shrugged. He said, 'You're going to leave me anyway, aren't you? So why should I let them go?' And that was all. He's going back to the hotel now. I'll stay with you aboard the ship."

◦◦◦

In the night Thalarne awakened him and said, "Do you hear noises, Nortekku?"

"Noises?" He had been in the deepest of sleeps.

"Thumps. Shouts. A scream, maybe."

Nortekku pushed himself upward through the fog that shrouded his mind. Yes, there *were* noises. Muffled thumpings. A panicky outcry. Another. Then deep-voiced grunting sounds that could only be the bellowings of Sea-Lords.

"Someone's in there with them in the tank," she said. "Listen—that sound's coming from a Sea-Lord. But that one isn't."

"Hamiruld?" Nortekku suggested, pulling the idea out of the blue. "Could it be that he's come on board, and—"

But she was already up and on her way out of the cabin. Nortekku ran madly after her, down the corridor, up the little flight of well-worn stairs, and down the upper corridor that led toward the stern of the ship and the tank of the captive Sea-Lords. The door of their hold was open. The light was on inside.

Hamiruld, yes.

What was he doing on board? Who knew? Here to gloat over his invaluable prisoners, maybe? Or simply making sure that Thalarne and Nortekku weren't going to release them in the night?

But he seemed to be under attack. He was at the back of the hold, up on the narrow boardwalk that ran along three sides of the room around the edges of the tank, and the four Sea-Lords stood crowding around him, jostling him roughly. They were clustered close, pushing fiercely at him with their shoulders, buffeting him from one to another, and Hamiruld, crying out in terror and pain, was trying to get out from among them. The two big males seemed to be letting the females do most of the shoving, but even they were bigger than Hamiruld, and when they thrust themselves against him he went ricocheting back like a flimsy toy.

"They'll kill him!" Thalarne cried.

Nortekku nodded. It was hard to believe, these gentle, passive creatures wanting to kill, but surely the rough sport they were having with Hamiruld was doing great injury. And very likely they would kill anyone who tried to intervene, too. He hesitated, uncertain of what to do, looking around for something he could use to push the Sea-Lords back from him.

Then came footsteps in the corridor. Crewmen appearing, five or six of them, the night watch belatedly putting in its appearance.

Nortekku pointed. "Don't you see what's happening?"

They could see it, yes, and, seizing electric prods from a case mounted just inside the door, they ran into the room and headed down the boardwalk.

At the sight of them, the Sea-Lords closed in even more tightly.

Hamiruld was completely hidden by them now. Out of the center of the group came a single horrible shriek, high-pitched, cracking at the end. Then the crewmen were in the midst of the melee themselves, jabbing at the Sea-Lords with the prods, trying to push them back into the water of the tank. One of the males swung a broad flipper at the nearest crewman and knocked him on a high curving arc into the tank. The other men danced backward, then approached with their prods again. There came the hissing sound of electrical discharges—the bright flash of light at the tips of the prods—

"No!" Thalarne called. "Not maximum! Don't use maximum!"

Everything dissolved into confusion, then—Sea-Lords and crewmen lurching back and forth on the narrow platform, prods hissing, lights flashing, Hamiruld nowhere to be seen—and then, abruptly, it was over.

Two of the crewmen were in the tank. The rest stood gasping against the wall. All four of the Sea-Lords lay sprawling on the boardwalk, motionless. The crumpled figure of Hamiruld, broken and bent, was face-down at the edge of the tank, motionless also.

Nortekku and Thalarne, who had remained in the doorway throughout the struggle, moved out along the boardwalk now. Thalarne knelt beside Hamiruld. She touched his shoulder with the tip of a finger, very gently. Then she looked up.

"Dead, I think."

"I imagine he is," said Nortekku. He had reached one of the Sea-Lord females. "This one is, too. And this. They all are, all four. These idiots did have their prods turned to maximum!"

"Dangerous animals," one of the crewmen mumbled. "Gone berserk. Anything could have happened. Look, they killed that man who came from the city—"

"Yes. So they did. And they're dead too."

So four of them, at least, had had their wish. The Sea-Lords at rest were awesome, mysterious, calm. There was a rightness, he thought, about their death. They were creatures out of place in time, who should have died when the Great World ended. They had carried on their backs the whole burden of the world's past ages, and now they had relinquished it at last.

Nortekku looked toward Thalarne. "That was what they wanted

most, wasn't it? To die? It's why they attacked him. They did it deliberately, to set things in motion. So that someone would come rushing
in to defend him, someone who would kill them for the sake of pro-
tecting Hamiruld. Don't you think so?"

"I think you're right," Thalarne said, her voice hardly more than a
whisper. She was still kneeling by Hamiruld, holding his limp arm at
the wrist. Letting go of it, she rose and looked about, surveying the
carnage. "What a ghastly scene, though. Dead, all of them. And
Hamiruld too."

"He shouldn't have been in here," said Nortekku. "He had no right
to be aboard." But that only made it all the worse, blaming Hamiruld
for his own death.

Some ungovernable impulse made him ask her, as he had asked
her once before, "Did you love him, Thalarne?"

"I suppose I must have, once. In some way, yes, I did. After a
fashion. But what difference does that make? I told him this afternoon
I could never forgive him. For lying to you, for sponsoring this expedition, for agreeing to the capture of the Sea-Lords. I told him I
wanted nothing more to do with him. Maybe that was why he came
here tonight."

"We'll never know what really went on in this room, will we?"

"No," she said. "We'll never know."

"Come. Let's get out of here."

He led her up on deck. The night air was warm, the moon was
high and nearly full. The ship rocked gently against the pier. Out here
it was as though none of the horror below had really happened.

He felt very strange. He had never been in the presence of violent
death before. And yet, shocked and dazed as he was, he felt that what
had happened had not entirely been a thing of horror, that some necessary act of liberation had taken place this night. Those four Sea-
Lords would not now go onward to a humiliating life as exhibits in a
zoo; and whatever forces had driven the tormented Hamiruld were at
rest now also. Perhaps all of them, Hamiruld and the Sea-Lords both,
had found in that terrible melee in the tank room that which they had
been seeking most.

And for him everything that he thought he believed had been
transformed in one moment of violence.

What now? Now, Nortekku thought, it is up to us to finish the job.

Thalarne moved close up beside him. He slipped one arm around her and they stood that way in silence.

"You said you'd file a report with the governments of Yissou and Dawinno, and let them decide what to do with the Sea-Lords," he said, after a long time had passed. "But you know who has the last word in what those governments decide: Prince Til-Menimat, and Prince Sam-nibolon, and maybe Prince Vuldimin, and Prince This-and-That, all the rest of them who paid for this expedition so they could add Sea-Lord artifacts to their collections. Do you know what they'll do, when they find out that the first try at bringing some live Sea-Lords back has failed? They'll organize another expedition right away."

"Yes. That's exactly what they'll do."

"We have to get there first, don't we?" He looked at her. "Tomorrow morning," he said, "we'll speak to the captain, and ask him if his ship is available for making a voyage right back to where we just came from."

She nodded. She understood. "Yes. We should go back there."

"And we will," he said. "We have to. Because now we have to show the rest of those Sea-Lords how to die."

MIRROR IMAGE

Nancy Kress

Nancy Kress began selling her elegant and incisive stories in the mid-'70s and has since become a frequent contributor to Asimov's Science Fiction, The Magazine of Fantasy and Science Fiction, Omni, *and elsewhere. Her books include the novels* The Prince of Morning Bells, The Golden Grove, The White Pipes, An Alien Light, Brain Rose, Oaths and Miracles, Stinger, Maximum Light, *the novel version of her Hugo and Nebula-winning story,* Beggars in Spain, *a sequel,* Beggars and Choosers, *and a popular recent sequence of novels,* Probability Moon, Probability Sun, *and* Probability Space. *Her short work has been collected in* Trinity and Other Stories, The Aliens of Earth, *and* Beaker's Dozen. *Her most recent books are two new novels,* Crossfire *and* Nothing Human. *Upcoming is a new novel,* Crucible. *She has also won Nebula Awards for her stories "Out of All Them Bright Stars" and "The Flowers of Aulit Prison."*

Many far-future stories show the inhabitants of the future continuing to live much the same sort of day-to-day life, on a basic human level, that we do now, in spite of all the hundreds of thousands of years that supposedly have gone by—-some far-future stories even have a retro *tinge, so that people are shown as getting around on horseback, drinking in torch-lit taverns, staying on straw mats in half-timbered roadside inns, cooking their meals over open campfires, and so forth, much as they might have in the Middle Ages of our own society's past.*

*Nancy Kress is too smart for this, though, and the intricate
pavane of identity and loss that follows clearly demonstrates
that the people of the far future will lead lives that are nothing
whatsoever like our own—except, perhaps, for a few simple
things such as betrayal, conspiracy, redemption, and love.*

When the message from Seliku reached me, I was dreaming in
QUENTIAM. No, not dreaming, that can't be right—the upload state
doesn't permit dreaming. For that you need a biological, soft tissue of
one sort or another, and I had no biology until my next body was done.
I had qubits moving at c, combining and recombining with themselves
and, to the extent It will permit, with QUENTIAM. I should not have
been dreaming.

Still, the subprogram felt like a biological dream. Something
menacing and ill-defined chased me through a shifting landscape,
something unknowably vast, coming closer and closer, its terrifying
breath on my back, its—

Message from Seliku, magnitude one, QUENTIAM "said" to
me and the dream vanished. The non-dream.

From Seliku? Now?

Yes.

It's not time for Seliku. And certainly not at a magnitude one.

QUENTIAM didn't answer. It gave me an image of Seliku gazing
at an image of me from out of a mirror, a piece of rococo drollery I
was all at once too apprehensive to appreciate. It was nowhere near
time for me to hear from Seliku, or from any of my sister-selves.

"Akilo," she said in agitation. Her image had the faint halo of
real-time transmission. Seliku wore the body we all used for our
bond-times, a female all-human with pale brown skin, head hair in a
dark green crest, black eyes. Four coiled superflexible tentacles were
each a meter long, the digits slim and graceful. It was the body of the
woman we would have become had our creation occurred on a quiet
planet—not that we could have been created on a quiet planet. We
called the body "human standard," to QUENTIAM's great amusement. We didn't understand that amusement, and It had declined to
explain.

For my image, QUENTIAM had used my last body, grown for my fish work on ^563, just before this upload. Four arms, tail, gills. I'd never liked the body and now I tweaked its image to a duplicate of Seliku's. We gazed at each other within my usual upload sim, a forested bedroom copied from ^894, where I'd once adjusted a particularly appealing species of seedings. It had been some of my best work. I'd been happy there.

Seliku said, "Akilo, you must come to Calyx. Now. Immediately."

"What has happened?" She was scaring me.

"I don't know what happened. I mean yes, I do, we do, it's Haradil—you must come!"

I recognized fear in her jerky, elliptical blurtings—we all spoke that way when genuinely terrified. "Bej—"

"Bej and Camy are here."

"Where is Haradil? Seliku, *tell* me!"

"I . . . sorry, I'm sorry, I thought I . . . Haradil is at the Mori Core. Or she *was* there. They arrested and tried her already—"

"*Tried* her? For what?"

"The Mori First One called me. The First One himself. He said that Haradil destroyed a star system."

Stunned, I tried to assimilate this. *A star system*—an entire star system. How? Why?

"*Why?*"

Seliku was more coherent now, calmed a bit by sharing the disaster. That, too, I recognized. She said, "The First One wouldn't tell me except in person. You know how they are. Akilo, the star system was inhabited. There was life there."

"Sentient?"

"Yes, although primitive. And Haradil . . . they've exiled her to a quiet planet for life."

For life. For taking life. "I—"

"Come *now*, Akilo. We're waiting for you. Please come now."

"I'm in upload, my new body isn't done—"

"I know you're in upload! Come when the body's done!" Anger, our habitual response to helplessness. Seliku's image vanished without waiting for agreement; she knew that of course I would come.

I turned my share of our anger on QUENTIAM. *Why didn't you tell me about Haradil when it happened?*

You didn't ask.

We have a group flag on anything significant involving any of us!

Haradil overrode it half a year ago, QUENTIAM said.

Overrode it. Haradil hadn't wanted her sister-selves to know what she'd been doing.

What *had* she been doing? Who were the sentients that Haradil had given over to death? How had she, who was genetically I, done such a thing? *Destroyed a star system . . . exiled for life . . . a quiet planet*. Where now Haradil, too, would die.

As children we had played at "death." One of us would lie absolutely still while the others whispered above her, kicked her softly, pretended to walk away and leave her alone forever. The game had left us breathless and thrilled, like playing "nova" or "magic." Children enjoy the impossible, the unthinkable.

I said to QUENTIAM, *When will my next body be done?*

At the same moment I named when you last asked me that.

Can it be sooner?

I cannot hurry bio-nanos. I am a membrane, Akilo, not a magician.

How had she, who was I, done such a thing?

❦

I stood before a full-length mirror in the vat room of the station, flexing my new tentacles with distaste. This body had been designed for my next assignment, on ^1864. After Seliku's message arrived, QUENTIAM had directed the nanos to make some alterations, but I'd been unwilling to take the time to start from scratch. On ^1864 the gravity was 1.6 standard and the seedings I'd been going to adjust were non-sentient, semi-aquatic plants. This body had large webbed feet, heavy muscles in the squat lower body, and relatively short tentacles ending in too many digits of enormous flexibility. Most of QUENTIAM's last-minute alterations had occurred in the face, which was more or less the one Seliku had worn in her transmission, although 1.6 gravity dictated that the neck was practically nonexistent.

"I hate it," I said.

"It's very practical," QUENTIAM said. Now that I had down-loaded, his voice came from the walls of the small room, furnished only with the mirror and the vat from which my body had come. "Or it would have been practical if you were still going to ^1864."

"Are you sending someone else?"

"Of course. It's been nearly a thousand years since their last ad-justment."

No one knows what QUENTIAM calls a "year." It doesn't seem to correspond to any planetary revolution stored in Its deebees, which suggests that the measure is very old indeed, carried over from the previous versions of QUENTIAM. Some of the knowledge in those earlier versions appears to have been lost. I can't imagine any of the versions; QUENTIAM has been what It is in the memory of everyone I've ever met, no matter how many states they've inhabited. It's just QUENTIAM, the membrane of spacetime into which everything else is woven.

QUENTIAM Itself says Its name is archaic, once standing for "Quantum-Entangled Networked Transportation and Information Artificial-Intelligence Membrane." I'm not sure, beyond the basics, what that encompasses. Seliku is the sister-self who chose to follow our childhood interest in cosmology, just as Camy and Bej chose art and I chose the sciences of living things.

And Haradil . . .

A clone-set, like any living thing, is a chaotic system. Initial small differences, small choices, can lead to major divergences lifetimes later. That is why all clone-sets from my part of the galaxy meet every two "years." The meeting is inviolable. One can't be expected to keep track of lovers or friends; there are too many choices to pull them away, too many states to inhabit, too much provided by nano, over too long a time. There is always QUENTIAM, of course, but the only hu-man continuity, the only hope of genuine human bonding, comes from sister- or brother-selves, who share at least the same DNA. All the other so-called "family structures" that people periodically try have been failures.

Well, not all. Apparently the Mori have, in the last thousand years, worked out some sort of expanding kinship structure to match their expanding empire. But it seems to be maintained partly through force, which is repugnant to most people. Anyway, a thousand years—QUENTIAM's mysterious "years"—isn't long enough to prove the viability of anything. I'm half that old myself.

Of course, the Great Mission also considers itself a "kinship structure." But they're not only repugnant but also deluded.

QUENTIAM said, "Your shuttle has docked."

"How many others are going on it?"

"Five. Three more new downloads and two transients."

"Transients? What are transients doing on this station?" It was small and dull, existing solely as a convenient node for up/downloading near the t-hole.

"They're missionaries, Seliku. I'll keep them away from you as long as I can."

"Yes. Do," I said acidly, even as I wondered what QUENTIAM was saying at that same moment to the missionaries. *"Seliku isn't going to be easy for you to talk to, but your best chance is to approach her through her work"*?

Probably. QUENTIAM, of course, gives all people the information they want to hear. But It would do as It said and keep the missionaries away from me. I was not in the mood for proselytizing.

The wall opened and nano-machinery spat out my traveling bag onto the floor. I opened it and checked that everything was there, even though no other possibility existed. S-suit, food synthesizer, my favorite cosmetics, a blanket—sometimes other people had strange notions of comfortable temperature—music cube . . . I strapped the bag around my very thick waist, stepped toward the door, and hit my head on the ceiling. "Ooohhhhh!"

"Are you injured?" QUENTIAM asked.

"Only my dignity."

"Your body is designed for 1.6 standard gravities," It intoned, "whereas your previous assignment featured a planet with only—"

"O, burn it, QUENTIAM." I rubbed my head, which this time around appeared to have a thick skull case. "What is a 'standard gravity,' anyway?"

"I don't know. Possibly that information has been lost."

"I don't really care." Carefully I reached the door, which slid open, leading directly to the shuttle bay.

The other five passengers waited beside the shuttle. Two of the three recent downloads, easy to pick out, echoed my own awkwardness with their new bodies. We stepped gingerly, took a second too long to focus vision, gave off that air of concentration on motions that should be automatic.

The person in the four-legged body of a celwi was, incongruously, the most graceful. He must have used that configuration before. Celwi bodies are popular for their speed; it's a lovely sensation to gallop full-tilt across a grassy plain. The two-legged woman wore a clear helmet in preparation for some alien atmospheric mixture. She and I exchanged rueful glances and tried not to bump into each other.

The third download moved easily in a genderless machine body equipped with very impressive cutting tools and, I suspected, a full range of imaging equipment. It had my admiration; I had only inhabited a machine once and had found the state subtly unpleasant. But some people like it.

That left the two missionaries, both close to what my sister-selves called "human standard," but much smaller. Each stood no higher than a meter. So they were going Out, as far beyond a t-hole as a real ship could get them, to carry out the Great Mission. Mass mattered on such trips. I didn't make eye contact.

"Please board now for the t-hole," the shuttle said pleasantly. It was, of course, one of QUENTIAM's many voices, this one light and musical. The machine body raised its head quickly as if it had received more information than the rest of us, which it probably had.

The shuttle seats were arranged in four rows of two, so everybody got a window view. I hung back, trying to get a seat beside the woman in the helmet or, failing that, alone, but I hung back too long. When I climbed in, last, the four-legged celwi had taken up two seats and the machine body's cutting tools were extended across one whole seat in an unfriendly manner: *I don't want company.* The missionaries had split up, the better to bother other passengers. I settled in beside one of them, felt the seat configure around me, and closed my eyes.

That didn't stop her. "All the good of Arlbeni save you, sister."

"Hhhmmmfff," I said. I was not her sister. I kept my eyes closed.

"I'm Flotyllinip cagrut Pinlinindhar 16," she said cordially, and I groaned inwardly. I had been on Flotyll. No place in the galaxy had so embraced the Great Mission.

Not to answer her would have been the grossest discourtesy. I said shortly, "Akilo Sister-Self 7664-3," omitting my home planet, Jiu. None of us had remained on Jiu past childhood; it wasn't really home. We've never understood people who form an attachment to their birth planet, but the Flotylli are famous for it. It's a pretty planet, yes, but the galaxy is full of pretty planets. Home is one's sister-selves.

Haradil . . .

I transmitted to QUENTIAM through my implant: *I thought you were going to keep the missionaries away from me.*

You sat next to her.

"We're going to seed another world, my friend and I," Pinhead 16 said. "Praise Arlbeni and the emptiness of the universe."

"Mmmhhhfffff," I mumbled. But no mumbling stops missionaries.

"Before I joined the Great Mission, I was nothing. We all were. Are you a student of history, sister?"

"No."

A mistake. Her face lit up. I could feel it even with my eyes closed, a stretching of the air that probably registered on the machine body's sensors as elevations in everything from thermals to gamma rays. But if I'd said yes, I was indeed a student of history, she probably would have replied *"Then perhaps you are aware . . . "*

She said, "Then perhaps you aren't aware just how Disciple Arlbeni saved us all, thousands of years ago but still fresh as ever. We had everything due to nano and QUENTIAM, and to have everything is to have nothing. From evolution to sentience, from sentience to nano, from nano to the decay of sentience due to boredom and purposeless. Humanity was destroying itself! And then Arlbeni had his Vision: Against all physical laws, the universe was empty of any life but human life, and so to fill it must be our purpose. The universe was Divinely left empty because—"

I had to cut this off. I opened my eyes and looked directly at her. "Maybe not as empty as Arlbeni thought."

I watched her expression freeze, then constrict.

"There have been reports," I went on, apparently artlessly, "of newly discovered planets that bear life which we didn't put there. Non-DNA-based life. Not our seedings. Native life of some sort, maybe blown in from space, seeded by panspermia on worlds far from the t-holes."

"Lies," she said. Her eyes had narrowed to two cold slits.

"Have you checked personally?"

"I don't need to."

"I see," I said, with import, and looked away.

But she was more tenacious than she looked. "Have *you* checked personally on such reports?"

"No," I said. "But, then, I don't care if the galaxy holds other life besides our seedings."

"And *your* life—what gives it purpose?"

"Observing and caring for the life that's here, no matter how it got here. I'm an adjustment biologist."

"And that's enough? Just life, with no plan behind it, no Divine purpose, no—"

"It's more than enough," I said and turned away from her with such discourtesy that even she, the Arlbeni-blinded, left me alone.

I did recognize that my disproportionate fury was not solely due to the stupidity of faith that refused facts. *More than enough*, I'd said of my life . . . but was it? I made adjustments to life planted millennia ago by Arlbenists. I added genes to improve species, altered ecosystems for better balance, nudged along developing sentients. Then I left, usually to never see the results of my tinkering. Was my work actually helping anything at all?

The doubt was an old ache. I turned to the new one.

QUENTIAM, the life on the planet that Haradil destroyed—what was its seeding number?

QUENTIAM, of course, answers everything instantly. But it seemed to me that a long moment went by before he answered. In that moment all the rumors I'd ever heard blasted into my mind, like lethal radiation. Life that humanity had not seeded, life borne in on the winds of space from who-knew-where, life hated or denied by the followers of Arlbeni and the Great Mission . . . But, no, Haradil couldn't have committed genocide for that reason. Even if she'd become an Arlbenist, she couldn't have eliminated a star system just to destroy evidence of panspermia . . .

Life on the planet destroyed by Haradil was Seeding ^5387 of the Great Mission.

I breathed again.

But I was still left with the great Why, as empty of answers as the galaxy that Arlbeni had thought he had all figured out.

●●●

"Five minivals until t-hole passage," the shuttle said in its pleasant voice. I looked out my window, but of course there was nothing to see except the cold steady stars. The station was still only a few hundred meters away, but it was on the other side of the shuttle and I would not turn my head toward the missionary beside me.

"You are the least flexible of all of us," Bej had teased at our last bond-time, and she was probably right. Seliku's cosmology, Bej and Camy's art, seemed too soft to me, too formless, without rigorous standards. Artists could create without limits. QUENTIAM could fold the fabric of spacetime to create t-holes and information transfer; It could control endless nanomachinery operating at countless locations throughout the galaxy; It could be directed to manipulate matter and energy right up to the physical constants of the universe. Biology was not so flexible. Life needed what it needed: the nutrients and atmosphere and protection of its current form, and if it did not get those things, it died. Not even QUENTIAM could change death, once it had happened. Life/death was a binary state.

Yet there had been a time, when my sister-selves and I had been young, when I had played at art and studied Arlbeni and considered cosmological history. The seeds for all these pursuits had been in me. I had chosen another path, for good or not, but it was precisely because I knew myself capable of religious thought that the missionaries angered me so much now. I had looked past that easy meaning to something more uncompromising—why couldn't they?

"One minival to t-hole passage . . . t-hole passage completed."

No sensation, no elapsed time. But the stars now had different configurations, and a planet turned below our orbit. Blue and white, it was a lovely thing, as was the yellow star that nourished it. The single continent in all that ocean of blue drifted into view, still lit with the densely clustered lights of the night city. QUENTIAM, of course, is everywhere, and so humanity has no real center. But Calyx, by sheer numbers of inhabitants, comes closest. Slowly it had accreted people who wanted to be with other people already there, each new addition changing the shape of the city, like the lovely shell reefs I had seen on in my fish work on ^563.

The other missionary, the one not sitting beside me, screamed.

I whipped my head around. The machine body had fallen across the missionary, nearly crushing him. His head protruded from under the heavy metal body, the face distorted by pain, and one arm flailed wildly. The machine body lay completely inert, stiff as a dead biological.

"QUENTIAM! What's happening!" I hadn't realized I'd spoken aloud until my yell mingled with the rest in the small cabin.

"I don't know!" QUENTIAM said, and silence descended abruptly as a knife.

I don't know.

I don't know.

I don't know.

There are many things QUENTIAM does not know—It is not a magician, as It enjoys telling me—but the status of a machine body is not one of them. The machine state—I have inhabited it myself, for environments where no biological will suit—is the next closest thing to an upload. A person in machine state was connected to QUENTIAM not by a single soft-brain implant but by shared flows of energy and information. Everything the machine sensors picked up, at all wave lengths, was processed through QUENTIAM and back to the machine body's computer brain. It wasn't possible for QUENTIAM to not know what had just happened.

The machine body moved and sat up. "What . . ."

No one but me said anything. "You fainted," I said, the word so absurd in this context that I felt blood warm my face. Then came a sudden rush of sound and activity. The fallen-upon missionary was examined for damage, found to be bruised but not hurt, his nanomeds already active. The shuttle docked at the orbital which, apparently, was the destination of both missionaries and of the machine body, and they all disembarked. A few minivals later the four-legged body and the woman in the helmet left after the shuttle had taken us through a second t-hole to a second orbital. Only I was left aboard.

QUENTIAM—what happened to the machine body?

I don't know.

The shuttle descended to Calyx.

The city had changed completely in the half-year since our last bond-time. It was no less lovely, just different. Then the entire continent had soared with high, curving shapes, undulating buildings connected with sinuous bridges, the whole a city in the clouds done entirely in subtle shades of white. Shortly after that Bej and Camy, working together for the first time, had gotten the art contract. Apparently it was decided by some sort of vote, although I didn't know of whom.

My sister-selves had made Calyx the opposite of what I'd seen. The nanos had been reprogrammed to replace shimmer and purity with a riot of living foliage, so that it was difficult to see the buildings under the flora. Maybe the buildings *were* flora. Low flowering plants overgrew everything, even the moving walks. The dominant colors were dark, the purple of the photosynthetic bacteria plus dark reds and blues, but the effect was not somber. It was sexual. I stepped from the shuttle into a tumult of inflamed pollination.

Camy and Bej stood waiting amid the flowers. We hugged and I said, "So you're in love."

Bej laughed unhappily. "I told you she'd know immediately," she said to Camy, who neither laughed nor answered. The horror of Haradil's act lay in her eyes, plus perhaps something else.

I said, "It's beautiful, sisters."

"Thank you."

"Have you heard any more about . . ."

"A little. Come with us."

They led me to a moving walk, which took us a short distance to the beach and a low structure covered with long, sinuous vines wild with magenta flowers. The city represented the intemperance we were all capable of, all my sister-selves. We did nothing by halves. Of course Camy and Bej, if they were in love, would create this sort of unrestrained living art. Just as I, working on a seeding on some planet long unvisited by the Great Mission, would stubbornly work for uninterrupted days and nights and days again on some adjustment to a species. Seliku had showed the same extravagance in cerebral form. Her theory of the origin of the universe was once so far beyond the usual thinking that all five of us had been ridiculed for at least two centuries. Now the Seliku Cosmology was widely accepted. And Haradil—

"Have some tea, Akilo," Bej said. We sat on cushions that looked like giant blossoms, or were giant blossoms, and sipped a thin, musky drink that also tasted flowery. I set my cup down when Seliku walked in through a tangle of vines.

"Akilo! How are you?"

Camy said bitterly, "How are any of us?" as I hugged Seliku. O, the comfort of physical contact with one's sister-selves! It doesn't matter how long or how far we've been apart, we are still an indivisible whole. That which we are individually grows greater as time goes on, but it can never be greater than what we are together. What one does, all do, and I have always had difficulty understanding the essential loneliness of those singletons for whom this isn't true. What anchors them? How do they survive with only QUENTIAM, who is not human? How do they bear the isolation?

Seliku let me go and accepted a cup of tea from Bej, asking gently, "He's gone?"

It was Camy who answered. "Of course he's gone! Would *you* stay with us now?"

Seliku didn't have to answer. So Bej and Camy's lover—they always chose together, and always insisted the person adopt a male body if not already wearing one—had fled. Well, I couldn't blame him. A city created in celebration of sex could not compensate for a sister-self who'd destroyed a whole worldful of people. Not to an ethical person. Both Bej and Camy were taking their lover's desertion hard. They have always stayed together, and so few differences distinguish one from the other. Still, I sensed that Camy was more bitter than Bej.

Seliku sat on a flower-cushion and said, "I don't know much more than I did before. QUENTIAM still blocks all Haradil's former interactions with It, of course, and the information It would give me from the Morit records is sparse. You know how the Mori are. Their little corner of the galaxy is considered *theirs*, and they limit contact even with QUENTIAM to the absolute necessities. In fact, implants are now forbidden at the Mori Core."

"Forbidden!" I said.

"For the last century," Seliku said. *Century*—another of QUENTIAM's inexplicable, archaic terms. But I knew what time span it denoted: 60.8 years on my natal Jiu. I tried, and failed, to picture life unconnected to QUENTIAM, or connected only through external devices.

"I finally got another Mori to speak to me," Seliku continued, and her cup trembled slightly in her hand. "It wasn't easy."

Bej said, "How did you . . . o, your reputation, of course," and smiled apologetically. Bej and Camy were good local artists, but they were known in no more than a handful of star systems, and I was an unknown laborer among the seedings. But Seliku is famous.

She said, "The Mori I just talked to repeated what the First One told me: Haradil blew up the system by destroying the star, a G3 on the very edge of the Morit territory. In fact, to say it was Morit is debatable, but QUENTIAM awarded it to them. The Great Mission apparently seeded the planet so long ago that not even QUENTIAM had a record of the seeding, which is the only reason that the Mori could claim it at all."

I said, startled, "QUENTIAM didn't have a record?"

"It was either one of the very first seedings, when QUENTIAM was just establishing sensors everywhere, or . . . I don't know. It seemed strange to me, too, but that's what It said. Anyway, the inhabited planet was a cold, small, iron-core world with an atmosphere and lakes heavy on methane. The seedings were adapted anaerobes with a nervous system highly enough evolved to swim in communities. The Mori report indicated the evolution of language, including some imaginative communication that they decided was poetry."

My sister-selves looked at me. I said, "It was probably a combination of sound and motion to convey nonliteral ideas." I'd seen that among many seedings. My throat constricted. Sentients with poetry.

"After that last report," Seliku continued, "the Mori closed the system, like all the rest of their empire. They don't know, or won't say, how Haradil got interested in it. But she built a missile out of an asteroid, aimed it at the star, and ducked back through a t-hole before it hit. The missile badly . . . badly warped spacetime around the star just before it—the missile, I mean—burned up. I saw the Morit data on the explosion. The warping somehow blew up the star."

" 'Somehow'?" Camy cried. "What do you mean 'somehow'? How did Haradil know how to make such a thing?"

"I don't know," Seliku said. Her hand now trembled so much she set her cup on the spongy floor. Moments before, I had had to do the same.

Bej said, "Seliku, could *you* have made such a thing? With all your knowledge of quantum blending?"

Seliku said carefully, "It's been theoretically possible for a while. But QUENTIAM doesn't know how to translate that into nano programming. And It wouldn't have done such a thing, anyway. Not blown up an inhabited system."

There was a long moment of silence while each of us did the same thing: *QUENTIAM, do you know how to create a working missile that can warp spacetime around or inside a star so as to make it explode?*

No.

Seliku waited without rancor. She herself would have checked on the statement, had she not already known the answer. That was us.

Camy said, "Do you think the Mori know how she did it?"

Bej burst out, "Or *why*?"

Seliku said, "They don't know either answer. But immediately after the explosion, QUENTIAM of course identified Haradil as the cause and delivered her to the Mori. They ran whatever their equivalent of a judgment process is, decided she was guilty, and put her down on a quiet planet. They wouldn't tell me where it is, but I combed all the data QUENTIAM has on recent t-hole use and I think she's on ^17843."

"Where's that?" Bej asked.

"On the outer galactic rim, on the Jujaju Arm. It's a new discovery, and one clearly attributable to the Mori, so they've claimed it even though it's nowhere near their territory. QUENTIAM has accepted its designation as a quiet planet."

"So—" I said, and stopped.

"So that's that," Seliku said, and we all shifted on our cushions and said nothing. QUENTIAM does not overhear our thoughts unless we direct them to him via implant. Only in the upload state, and one other, is mental privacy lost. But my sister-selves and I didn't need to overhear each other's thoughts; we shared them.

We were going to break the prohibition on that quiet planet. We were going to go get the only person who could tell us what had actually happened in that star system explosion: Haradil herself.

●●●

There are many reasons why people grow bodies without implants. Most people try it, at least briefly, in their youth, just to define the boundary between themselves and QUENTIAM: What is It and what is me? We five had done that for a few years, a long time ago. Others do it for religious/philosophical reasons, as apparently the Mori had decided. Still others with adventurous genes like to amuse themselves with the challenge of survival without QUENTIAM. Not all of these survive their adventure. There are artists (although not Bej and Camy) who dislike the bond with QUENTIAM, feeling it less a connection than a tether. Finally, there are assorted crazies who just don't like being a part of anything else, not even the membrane woven through all of spacetime.

I stood on the beach, Camy and Bej's lovely flower-strewn beach, and watched the warm small waves roll between softly planted islands.

QUENTIAM, I want the basic data-set on ^17843.

Seliku believes that is the place where Haradil was sent.

Yes. Give me an external durable.

If QUENTIAM was surprised by my request for a durable, I would never know it. It directed me to the nearest slot for the nanomachinery buried below Calyx, which produced a thin, flexible, practically indestructible sheet of carbon tubules covered with writing.

I can read. It had been a few of QUENTIAM's "centuries" since I had done so, of course, but we had all learned. I assumed that the intriguing, archaic skill was still with me. I was wrong.

The sheet in my hands was dense with symbols and numbers, and only a few looked familiar. I felt my new face grow warm.

Give me the basic set directly.

* ^17843 is a transformed and seeded satellite orbiting a class 6 gas giant, which in turn orbits a type 34 star at an average distance of 2.3 PU. The moon is called by the inhabitants "Paletej," which means roughly "unwanted" in Mori. It has .6 gravity, class 9 illumination, a diameter of 36 filliub, type 18 planetary composition, pressure of gk8, axial inclination of two degrees. There are two small equatorial continents and an even smaller polar one, with temperature range of 400-560.*

I translated all this into human terms. Haradil's prison would be seasonless, warm, adequately lit. No moons, since ^17843 was itself a moon, but the gas giant would loom huge in the sky.

QUENTIAM continued. *Paletej is served by one t-hole, in close orbit with the Mori station. The Mori seeded the moon liberally with Level 3 plant life, which have completely covered one continent and have begun to spread to a second through wind and water. There is no animal life above Level 4.*

Level 3 plant life was pre-flowering. Flowers begat fruit, which is much more concentrated nutrition than greens. With no animal protein available above the level of worms, the prisoners would have to spend nearly all their time in food-gathering and eating, unless their bodies had been adapted otherwise. I doubt that they had.

My tentacle closed tight on the durable, which crumpled but did not crease.

QUENTIAM was not finished. *Paletej has also been densely seeded with nanospores that consume all atoms with a Konig designation higher than 45. A hundred meters below the surface, counter-nanos stop atom consumption, to prevent danger to planetary composition.*

No metals. No way to make any tools more primitive than wood, stone, maybe basic ceramics. And, of course, no nanomachinery.

I stared blindly at the soft sea. *What . . . what sort of bodies were made for the prisoners?*

That information is not accessible to you.

Burn you, QUENTIAM! Do the bodies at least have nanomeds? Tell me!

That information is not accessible to you.

But I already knew the answer. Quiet planets had no nanomeds for anyone but transients, had no nanomachinery of any kind, had no implants to connect to QUENTIAM. That's what made them quiet. That's what made them death.

I stumbled along the beach, barely able to see from rage. *Grow four bodies for me and my sister-selves. Conform each to the best possible fit to basic data set of ^17843.* I would not call the cursed place "Paletej." Haradil was not "unwanted." *Grow the four bodies with full nanomeds but *without* implants.*

Akilo, you and your sister-selves cannot get down to Paletej. The atmosphere, too, is densely seeded with the engineered spores.

How do the prisoners get down? Any shuttle would be consumed and crash.

That information is not available to you.

There must be a t-hole on the surface, one restricted to the Mori alone. QUENTIAM's parameters permitted that, part of its delicate balancing of group possession with preservation as the greatest good of the universe. But what Haradil was enduring was not preservation, was not life, was not endurable.

Who had programmed the moral parameters of QUENTIAM's remote ancestor, all those hundreds of millennia ago? My own barely human ancestors, of course. And the basic principles had been carried forward as QUENTIAM constantly recreated itself, extended its' penetration of spacetime, became intertwined with human consciousness itself. How had justice, in that evolutionary progression, become corrupted? No beings should "own" a t-hole. Down that gravity well lay blind possessiveness, so that you ended up with the Arlbeni disciples, who had perverted a sense of purpose into believing that they alone owned morality. To disagree with Arlbeni was to be unethical, evil. No matter what the evidence said about Arlbeni himself being wrong about the emptiness of the universe.

What I was really afraid of was that QUENTIAM was wrong. That, unknown to It, Haradil had somehow discovered on the planet she'd destroyed some evidence of non-DNA-based life, existing right alongside the seeded anaerobes. I was afraid that she had blown up the place for precisely that reason. That she had become an Arlbenist, melded to the Great Mission, and lost to us.

If there had been panspermic, non-seeded life there, QUENTIAM should have known about it. QUENTIAM had had enough sensors in that star system to transmit detailed explosion data, including what Seliku had called "warping." We had all asked QUENTIAM, Seliku and Bej and Camy and I and probably also the Mori, if the planet had held non-DNA-based life. It had said no. QUENTIAM could withhold information, but It could not lie.

Of course, if the panspermic life was very new, and in an isolated corner of the planet, it's possible that QUENTIAM might not have known about it and Haradil had.

Grow the bodies I specified, QUENTIAM.

I have already begun. But, I repeat, you cannot get down to Paletej in them.

We can get as far as the t-hole above it.

Yes. It is a universal t-hole.

As they all should be.

It didn't answer. Uncrumpling the durable in my hand, the sheet of symbols I could not understand, I realized that probably Seliku could read them. She was a cosmologist. I went to look for my sisters, my other selves, my solace in this suddenly icy city by the soft sea.

●●●

By the time our bodies were ready, so was our shuttle. Nano-built on one of Calyx's many orbitals, it was a sprawling thing, fragile as a flower except for the tough nano-maintained force shield that surrounded it. The shield was protection against stray meteors and other cosmic junk. The shuttle, which didn't need to survive an atmospheric entry, didn't need to be durable.

Our bodies did. They turned out to be pretty much as I'd envisioned, and not too different from the one I was wearing now except for being much lighter and less muscular. Short, two legs, four tentacles ending in superflexible digits. My current webbed feet had been replaced with tough feet with prehensile toes, complementing the prehensile tail, in case ^17843 had plants large enough to climb. We weren't sure what specific flora to expect there, and the Mori weren't sharing information.

The new body's ears could detect the widest possible range of sound waves; electromagnetic sensing was as good as feasible in a biological; smell was stronger than even in celwyns. A double layer of fine, shit-brown fur made us as weatherproof as we'd need to be for the temperature range, although at the upper end, we might be a bit uncomfortable.

"Not very pretty, are they," Camy said, gazing at the full-grown bodies in their clear vats. "The faces are so flat."

"You could have ordered modifications earlier," I pointed out, "but you said you didn't care."

"I don't care."

Seliku said, "QUENTIAM, are you ready to begin uploads?"

"Yes." Its deepest, most authoritative tone; It was offended.

"We're ready, too." But the co-vats had begun to assemble even before she finished speaking. I climbed into mine, lay down, and was instantly asleep.

When I woke, an unknowable time later, the download was complete. I climbed out of my vat simultaneously with my sisters. It was a hard climb; we were now engineered for a gravity one-third less than Calyx's. But that wasn't the reason that we gazed at each other in dismay.

"Are . . . are you all right?"

"Yes," Seliku said. "Are you?"

"Yes, but . . ."

But I'd had to *ask*. Looking at Seliku, Camy, Bej as we stood in our new dull fur, our new flat faces, I hadn't automatically known that, yes, they were all right because otherwise QUENTIAM would have told me. I'd had to look, to question. Camy put her hand to her head and I knew what she was thinking: QUENTIAM was gone. We were without implants. We were on our own, not even able to image each other in real-time if one of us stepped into the next room.

"It feels very strange," Bej said softly. "How will we . . ."

"We will," Seliku said. "Because we must."

I felt myself nodding. We would, because we must.

162

QUENTIAM said, "The shuttle can take you up to the orbital now, and your t-hole shuttle is ready there."

"Not yet," I said, not without pleasure. It's hard to surprise QUENTIAM, but I guessed that we were doing it now. "There's more things I want to prepare."

"More things?" Definitely offended. I saw Bej grin slightly at Camy.

"Yes," I said, savoring the moment. "We'll be ready to go soon."

The four of us waddled laboriously—curse this gravity—to my lab. I had set it up days ago in a room grown near the vat room. Ostensibly the lab's purpose was to study the microbiology of the flowers Bej and Camy had designed and QUENTIAM had created for Calyx, just as if they were biologicals or cyborgs that had naturally evolved from seedings. And I had done some of that work, storing the data in QUENTIAM, carefully packing and storing both specimens and experimental materials in opaque canisters for any future biologists who might want them. But that was not all I had done.

QUENTIAM, give me—

Give me nothing. It couldn't hear me. I had no implant.

The eeriest sensation came over me then: *I am dead.* It was a thousand-fold-stronger version of what I had felt moments before, in the vat room. I was detached, unconnected, alone, in the supreme isolation of death.

But of course I was not. My sister-selves were there, and I clutched Bej's hand. She seemed to understand. We were not alone, not cut off, not dead. We had each other.

This must be what Haradil felt. And she did not have the rest of us.

For a brief moment I hated QUENTIAM. It had done this, It and Its parameters for permissible human behavior. QUENTIAM had gone along with this brutal Morit "justice," and now Haradil . . .

Camy said quietly, "It must be even worse for her. Because . . . you know."

We all knew.

There are five possible states for a human being. Without implants, as we were now. Implanted, which is the normal state. A machine body, which is really just a much heightened version of implants plus a virtually indestructible body. Upload, which is bodiless but still a separate subprogram within QUENTIAM, with its own boundaries. And merged, in which individual identity is temporarily lost in the larger membrane-self of QUENTIAM. Few humans merge, and most never return. Those that do are never really the same.

Haradil, three bond-times ago, had merged with QUENTIAM.

It had been after a bad love affair. We all took those hard; I thought of Camy and Bej's ravaged looks when I'd landed on Ca-lyx. We were all intemperate, single-minded in romance as in all else. But Haradil, who had never really chosen a field of work, had been the one who tried to handle the emotional pain by merging with QUENTIAM. And she had come back calmer but almost to-tally silent, unwilling to tell us what it had been like. "Not unwill-ing," she'd finally said. "Unable. It's an experience you can't put into words." It had been the longest speech she'd made since re-turning.

I'd been afraid for her then. We'd all been afraid. But she had con-tinued calm, silent, remote during the next two bond-times. With us and not with us. Neither happy nor unhappy, but somehow beyond both.

"Not human," Bej had finally said, and we'd turned on her in anger, because we'd all thought it ourselves.

But not destructive, either. In fact, the opposite. Gradually we'd come to sense optimism of some kind under Haradil's silence, and our anxiety had been at least partially allayed, and then Haradil had blown up a star system containing sentient life.

Now Seliku said, "Let's get to work."

We had the nanomachinery create a cart. The cart loaded onto it-self the canisters I indicated. Seliku, Bej, and Camy hadn't been able to make their lesser preparations until after they were without implants, and there were things I wanted to add to the cart as well, so we dragged around in the monstrous gravity for another day. QUENTIAM ob-served everything, of course, but It had no reason to stop us. And it asked no questions about anything we had the nanos manufacture.

There were many moments when I started to ask It something: *QUENTIAM, is the—* and then I remembered. But there were no more moments like the terrible, deathlike one in the lab. All day my sister-selves and I worked beside each other, tentacles reaching out to touch and pat, and at night we slept in a heap, tails and legs tangled together in the too-warm, fragrant air of Calyx.

"I hope I never see another flower again," Seliku said when we were finally aboard QUENTIAM's shuttle on our way upstairs. And then, "O, sorry, Bej and Camy, I didn't mean—"

"I don't want to see flowers, either," they said in unison, and then laughed unhappily. Below us the planet dwindled to a soft blue-and-white bauble.

We would see no flowers on ^17843.

The gravity on our orbital-grown shuttle was a relief; it matched ^17843's. "QUENTIAM," Seliku said, "take us through the t-hole to ^17843."

I thought It might speak to us for the first time since we'd left the vat room, but It didn't. The shuttle moved away from the orbital toward nothing, apparently went through nothing, and emerged into a different sky.

A huge gas giant, ringless and hazy, filled half the sky. Ugly—the pale planet looked as ugly as the fuzzy tumors of a seeding biology gone very wrong. As I watched, a large moon emerged from behind the planet. Clouds, oceans, but none of the beauty of Calyx. To my present state of mind, those feature, too, looked like primitive biological deformities, the clouds crawling like parasites across a landscape diseased with what did not belong there.

The shuttle was equipped with full orbital sensors. I imaged the continent with flora as it turned repeatedly below us. Large animal activity showed up on half a dozen different readings. And there was only one large animal on ^17843. I gave Seliku the right coordinates.

Seliku said calmly, "QUENTIAM, take this shuttle as low as is safe."

"This is as low as is safe. You are within the upper atmosphere."

"All right. Sister-selves?"

"Yes," Camy said, speaking for all of us.

And so it began.

We unpacked the canisters we'd brought with us. Each of us tied on cloth belts containing nonmetallic tools, blankets, rope, concentrated food pellets, collapsible ceramic cups, the rest of our prepared items. Then we pushed the remaining four opaque canisters toward the airlock.

"What are you doing?" QUENTIAM said. "It is not permitted to descend to Paletej."

Seliku said, "It is not permitted for you to take us through a t-hole to the surface. It is permitted for us to leave the shuttle to go into space."

"You will die," QUENTIAM said. Did I hear regret in Its voice, or anger?

Seliku merely repeated, "It is permitted for us to leave the shuttle. We have nothing that can be destroyed by the metal-eating spores in the atmosphere. And we have nothing with us that connects us to you, QUENTIAM, or anything else forbidden on the surface of a quiet planet."

"Your bodies contain nanomeds."

"They are not forbidden to visitors to quiet planets."

"This quiet planet never has visitors."

"Until now."

"You will die outside the shuttle. We are well within the gravity well. You will fall to your deaths."

Seliku opened her canister, laid the lid on the floor, and stepped inside. "You will open the shuttle door over these coordinates, as soon as feasible after seventy-five millivals."

"But—"

"You will open the door."

"Yes," QUENTIAM said. It had no real choice. A human being may destroy herself, although not others, if she so chooses.

Bej, Camy, and I opened our canisters, laid the lids on the floor, and stepped inside. Our gazes all met. "I love you," Camy said, for all of us, as the membranes in the canister began to grow around us.

Biological membranes, not the spacetime that is QUENTIAM.

I had found them on ^22763, a planet seeded back in the very beginnings of the Great Mission, when humans had been willing to subject living things to a far greater range of environments than they did later on. So many of those hapless seedings died, and so many suffered. ^22763 had been lucky, winning the blind lottery of evolutionary mutation. They were light, air-filled creatures, non-sentient, floating through a world with no sustenance except sunlight, in temperatures just high enough to keep their atmosphere from freezing. All my data on them had of course been stored in QUENTIAM, but I had memorized it, too, because it had been so interesting.

On Calyx, with the help of programmable nanos, I had recreated the floaters and stored them as spores in opaque canisters. The mature floaters, biologicals, were not forbidden on ^17843, although they would die there. But first, unless I had misremembered data, they would get us down to the surface. If I had misremembered, we would die along with the creatures.

The membrane sealed around me just before the shuttle door opened.

When did QUENTIAM realize what we were doing? It's possible It knew from the very beginning. It may have had no choice but to permit this because of its "parameters," or because preservation is the first law, or even because of "love." Who can understand the mind of QUENTIAM? It moves in mysterious ways.

As the air left the shuttle, the four floaters were blown into space. The shuttle orbited as low as possible without encountering the metal-consuming nanos. The floaters, which had fed voraciously on the light inside the shuttle, now fed on the abundant reflected light from the gas giant. They swelled with the breathable gases that were its carefully re-engineered waste products. I had held my breath for too long; now I breathed.

In the clear living bubbles, which were already dying, my sister-selves and I began the long float down to the surface of the transformed moon.

◦◦◦

Pain. Fear. A rushing in my head like rapids, water that would sweep me away, kill me . . .

The rushing receded, although the pain did not. There was no water. I hung at a steep incline, head lower than my legs, in the fronds of a giant, prickly fern. The rushing became the voices of Bej and Camy somewhere below me in the eddies of green.

"Akilo! Akilo, answer us!"

"I'm . . . here. I'm all right," I said, although clearly I was not. As sensation clarified, the pain localized to my head and one leg.

"You're only three or four meters above the ground," Bej called. "Drop and we'll catch you."

I did, they did, and the world blackened for a moment, then returned. I lay on a forest floor, a bed of thick, damp, pulpy plants as unpleasant to lie on as a dung heap. Not that any of my sister-selves had ever seen a dung heap. I was the biologist, and a fine job I'd done of adapting the floaters that had died and disintegrated before we'd actually reached ground.

"I'm sorry," I croaked up at Bej and Camy. "Seliku?"

"I'm here," she said, striding into my circle of sight. "You're the only one hurt, Akilo. But it's all right; we can stay here quietly until your nanomeds fix you."

I closed my eyes. The nanomeds were already releasing painkillers, and the hurting receded. Sedatives took me. My last thought was gratitude that ^17843 had no predators. No, that was my second-last thought. The last was a memory, confused and frightened, from the moment before I crashed: a flash of light bright enough to temporarily blind me, light as silent and deadly as a distant nova.

Then I slept.

◆◆◆

"You're back," Bej said. "Akilo, you're back."

A campfire burned beside me. My body, wrapped in two of the superthin blankets from our toolbelts, was warm on the fire side, slightly chilled on the other. A strange odor floated from the fire. I sat up.

"How long have I—"

"Three days," Bej said. "We've made quite a little camp. Here, drink this."

She held out to me a cup of the odd-smelling liquid. It tasted worse than it smelled, and I made a face.

"At least it's not poisonous," Bej said cheerfully. "Local flora. We're trying to conserve the food pellets as long as we can. How do you feel?"

"All right." I flexed my leg; it was fine. Thanks to the nanomeds that Haradil had to do without.

"Seliku and Camy are out gathering more food. We had to do something while you were out, so we gathered leaves, tested them with our nanomeds for biocompatability, and boiled them down to make that drink."

"Boiled them in what?" I finished the drink and stood, working my muscles. Without the blankets, the air was cold.

"That," Bej said, pointing at a rickety arrangement of bent wood and huge leaves. "It's remarkably effective, but ready to fall apart, so it's a good thing you're ready to travel. You can eat those same leaves raw, too, but they taste even worse that way."

"Travel to where?" I said. Bej seemed too cheerful. Didn't she realize that we might all die here? Of course she did. Her cheerfulness was a kind of bravery, sparing me not only her fear but also her share of the intense shame we all felt over Haradil's crime.

"We haven't seen any prisoners yet," Bej said, "but Seliku came across a campsite—old ashes, that sort of thing. The scent is long gone but Camy thinks we can track them. Do you think we can?"

"Bej," I said irritably, "I'm an adjustment biologist. Of course I can track, probably much better than Camy can."

"That's good, because she said you're going to do it. Jump around a bit. It gets much warmer here when the star is higher."

In the dim filtered green of dense forest, I hadn't realized it was early morning.

Seliku and Camy returned. Seen together, I became aware of the changes that three "days" (how long was each?) had made in my sister-selves. Their dung-colored fur was matted and dirty, especially Camy's, who didn't smile at me as she walked into camp. For the first time, she and comparatively cheerful Bej, standing side by side, did not look alike. It was unsettling.

They packed up our few bits of equipment: blankets, boiled-down food wrapped in more leaves, ceramic knives. Seliku lead me to the abandoned camp. Following the trail from there was easy compared to the seedings I had tracked on other worlds. These prisoners had nothing to hide and no predators to confuse, and they'd left a blindingly obvious trail of broken ferns, missing edible leaves, and old shit. A child could have found the settlement.

^17843 proved to have stretches of open ground within the fern forests. But even these low-lying "meadows" were overgrown with pulpy green, so that everywhere our feet sunk onto squishy vegetation and stagnant water. The green was unrelieved by any color of fruit or flower. In the sky the gas giant loomed oppressively, blocking the sun. The only sound was a low, unceasing hum from insect-analogues, monotonous and dulling. I hated the place.

At midday, which seemed to come very quickly on this small world, we reached the top of a fern-crested hill, and suddenly before us, down a steeper slope, was the welcome blue of the sea.

"Wait," I said, when Bej would have rushed down the hill toward huts built on the seashore.

"Wait for what? Haradil's down there!"

I pulled her back into the thick fronds. Seliku and Camy, dirty and sweaty, watched us. "Bej, listen to me. These people have been sent here by the Mori for crimes. Some of them may have only violated some idiotic Mori custom, but some might be truly dangerous. They may have destroyed or killed."

As Haradil had.

Seliku said, "Alo is right." She drew her ceramic knife and looked at us.

Camy stared back in disbelief. "The knives are for work, not . . . you can't expect me to . . . Sel, I don't want to!"

"None of us want to," I said. I shared Camy's distaste, shared Seliku's reluctant foresight, shared Bej's eagerness to see Haradil. These were my sister-selves. After a moment, Camy, Bej, and I drew our knives.

Together, with me in the lead, we started toward the settlement.

As we got closer, details emerged, all of them sickening. The flimsy huts, which looked as if a good wind would blow them over, were built of woody fern trunks topped with broad fronds. Among them burned two or three open fires ringed with stones and topped with leaf cauldrons. People, including some children, skittered around frantically as soon as they glimpsed us.

We halted halfway down the hill, smiling painfully, and waited.

Eventually two prisoners started toward us. Seliku glanced at me, and I gestured helplessly. I had guessed as well as I could without data. Still, I'd gotten the bodies wrong.

The two coming toward us were even smaller and lighter than we, which on reflection made sense: less mass to support with food gathering. Fragile, tailless, thickly furred to conserve heat and discourage insect bites, they walked on two legs but had only two thick tentacles, which ended in clumsy opposable digits. But the faces were human. One of the prisoners had been infected with some sort of local fungus that covered its head and part of its back. I saw Camy gaze at it in horror. The other had a scar along the left side of its face. I don't think I'd ever seen uglier sentients, or more pathetic ones.

Silently, simultaneously, we put our knives back into our toolbelts. Any one of us could have smashed both of these sad people into jelly.

Then came the worst.

Seliku said, "Hello. We are looking for our sister-self, Jiuinip Haradil Sister-Self 7664-3. Is she here?"

Both creatures stared at us. Then one chattered incomprehensibly. Bej gasped. "They don't have translation capability!"

Of course not. Translations went through QUENTIAM by implant, so simultaneously that hardly anyone noticed it happening. These poor beings had no implants. And neither did we. So they lived here, unable to talk even to the other pathetic prisoners, deprived even of the solace of words to share the unendurable. It seemed the worst cruelty yet. Wouldn't death have been better than this?

Camy took a step backward and brought up her tentacles to cover her face. Seliku pressed on, her voice quavering slightly, in several other languages; I hadn't realized she'd learned so many. No response.

Finally I said, very slowly and with a variety of pitches and inflections, "Haradil? Har . . . a . . . dil? HARadil? HaraDIL? HarAdil? Haarrrraaadddiiilll? $^{Har}ad_{il?\ Ha}ra^{dil}$?"

One of them worked. The prisoner with fungus made a quick snapping gesture with his digits, a gesture I didn't understand, as he repeated "Haradil" in a guttural tone with a rising inflection. The other prisoner watched dully. I nodded and smiled, and the first man pointed toward the forest we'd just left. I made helpless gestures and he rose to his full stunted height, scowled fiercely, and gestured for us to follow. The four of us trailed behind him laterally along the edge of the forest until, about half a blinu from the settlement, he turned into the ferns.

We seemed to walk a long way into the forest. Finally, in a small hacked-out clearing, in front of the flimsiest hut yet, crouched another of the ugly creatures. As we approached, it raised its eyes to us and they were filled with despair and anguish and, then, recognition.

Haradil.

Bej burst into tears. But Camy rushed forward and with all the strength of her superior body, slammed a fisted tentacle into Haradil's weeping face. "How could you, Hari? How *could* you do it, to all of us?"

◦◦◦

I understood Camy's fury, Bej's sorrow, Seliku's distaste. I shared all three. But I was the biologist. After Seliku had pulled Camy off Haradil, I knelt beside her to examine her wounds. Our prisoner-guide had oozed back into the forest. The light bones of Haradil's face didn't seem broken, but she was obviously in pain, and my anger turned from her to Camy.

"You could have killed her! This body is really fragile!"

"I'm sorry," Camy choked out. She didn't cry. We were not easy criers.

Haradil said nothing, and that was at first oddly reassuring because it was the way she'd been ever since her merger with QUEN-TIAM, was at least a token of the Haradil we'd known.

"Haradil," I said as calmly as I could manage, "I'm going to give you nanomeds."

She shrank back under my hands. Seliku said, too harshly, "Hari, the Mori won't know, nor QUENTIAM. It has no sensors here. No one will know what we do in this place."

"No nanomeds!" Haradil cried, and somehow her voice was still her own, horrifying in that awful body.

"Why not?" I said, but I already knew. Holding her delicate, filthy face between my hands, I saw the start of the same fungal infection that the other prisoner had, and I shuddered.

"Nanomeds will keep me alive!"

"And you want to die," Seliku said, still in that same harsh voice. "Burn that, Haradil. You live. You owe us that, and a lot more."

"No!" Haradil cried, and then she was gone, squirming out from under my gentle clasp. Bej caught her with a flying tackle that might, all by itself, have broken bones. Haradil screamed and flailed ineffectually.

Horrified, furious, and determined, we set on her. Bej and Camy held her legs and the one set of arms. Seliku unwound a long superfine rope from her toolbelt and we tied Haradil. The others looked at me; I was the biologist. I drew my knife, sliced into Haradil's arm and then my own, and pressed them firmly together. Nanomeds flowed from me to her. Haradil began a low, keening sound, like a trapped animal.

It took a long time for enough nanomeds to replicate within Haradil to achieve sedation. Until nightfall we had to listen to that terrible sound. Finally she fell asleep, and we carried her into the forest and lay down under our blankets.

We didn't need much sleep, but there wasn't anything else to do. I had never known such blackness. No starlight penetrated the overhang of fronds. My infrared vision was, except for my sister-selves, a uniform and low-key haze of plant and insect life. We didn't build a fire for the same reason we'd left Haradil's hut. Not all the prisoners on ^17843 might be as scowlingly cooperative as the one that had brought us to Haradil. Some of these people had killed.

As she had.

"I'm sorry I hit you," I heard Camy whisper in the dark to Haradil's sedated form, and I knew that Camy both was and was not sorry.

But the strangest thing in that dark night was the absence of QUENTIAM. I hadn't expected to feel so completely bereft. My sister-selves lay so close to me that their breathing was mine, the scent of their bodies filled my mouth, their tentacles clutched patches of my fur. Yet it was QUENTIAM I missed. That voice in my head, always there, knowing what I was doing without being told, knowing what I wanted next. Support and companion and fellow biologist. I missed It so fiercely that my throat closed and my body shuddered.

"Are you cold, Alo?" Seliku whispered. In the dark she pushed more of her own blanket onto me. But it brought no warmth, brought no comfort, was not—shockingly, horrifyingly—what I needed, not at all.

∞∞∞

Haradil slept for days, during which we did nothing except move farther inland, gather leaves, and consume them to supplement and conserve our pellets of concentrated food. It was an exhausting, endless, boring process. The bodies I had asked for were too big for the available nourishment, with too little storage capacity. We all lost weight, and each time it was my turn to carry the sedated Haradil, she seemed heavier on my back. Despite our efforts, we had to use some of the food pellets, and our supply diminished steadily.

The farther we moved away from the other prisoners, the more I could see why they'd camped on the shore. There may have been some edibles, plankton or small marine worms, in the sea; that would be compatible with Level 4 fauna. More important, on the beach it would have been possible to see the sky, hear the waves. Under the fern cover we saw nothing but pulpy green in half-light, alien and silent. The only sound was the high-pitched drone of insects that stung constantly. Occasionally, when the wind was right, a stench of rotting plants blew toward us, fetid and overpowering. I had been on many ugly worlds, but none I hated as much as this one.

On the sixth day, we camped just past noon in a small, relatively dry clearing. We were so tired, and even the huge blob of the gas giant overhead was better than yet more oppressive green. Bej and Seliku made a fire, despite the risk of smoke rising above the ferns and giving away our positions. We sat around it and ate, by unspoken agreement, twice our usual ration of food pellets, washed down with water from a muddy stream.

"What's that?" Seliku asked Camy.

Camy held up a particularly thick section of woody fern trunk, which she was carving with her ceramic knife. She'd sculpted a pattern of beads along its length, smooth ovals gracefully separated in the CeeHee intervals, loveliest of proportions in both art and mathematics. Even here, Camy had to be an artist.

The sight inexplicably cheered me. "Camy—" I began, and the sky exploded.

Some of us screamed. There was no noise, but the sky opposite to the gas giant grew bright, then even brighter. Bej threw herself across Camy, I did the same with Haradil, and Seliku fell to the ground. In a moment it was over. Seliku gazed upward.

"What . . . what was that?" Camy, but it might have been any of us.

"I don't know," Seliku said, and her voice held even more strain than Camy's. "But I think the station just blew up."

"The station?" Bej said. "The Mori station? *QUENTIAM's* station?" All the stations were, in one sense, QUENTIAM's. It created and maintained and ran them. "How could that be?"

"I don't know," Seliku said. "It can't be. Unless QUENTIAM did it."

"*Why?*"

"I said I don't know!"

"Sel," I said, "I saw something like that when we landed, just before I fell into that giant fern, only not as bright. A flash of light. Could that have been the shuttle blowing up, too?

No, I know you don't *know*, but did you see a flash then as well?"

"No. But we all landed before you, and we were below the fronds—that first flash wasn't as bright as this?"

"No, not as bright. But I saw it."

Seliku said, with a reluctance I didn't understand, "If that big flash was the station, then I suppose what you saw could have been the shuttle. But there's no reason for QUENTIAM to blow up either of them."

"Maybe It didn't," Camy said.

We all looked at Haradil, still deeply sedated. If there were answers, they must come from her. But if the shuttle and station really had blown up—

"I think," Camy began, "that we better—" Men burst from the dense pulpy foliage.

Twelve prisoners, all armed with longer, thicker, sharper versions of Camy's carved wood. *Spears*—my mouth tasted the archaic, slimy word. So the exiles had known all along where we were. They had experience in tracking, just as I had, and they'd stayed upwind of us.

I said quietly, "Draw your knives and make a circle facing outward around Haradil."

We did, four comparatively large women against a dozen frail pygmies. Only then did I see that the tip of the spear closest to me was sticky with something thick and green.

These people had had years of exile to learn about the flora here, as well as to develop warfare unrestrained by QUENTIAM's parameters. The spear could easily be tipped with some local poison. Our nanos could handle it, but while the nanos worked we would probably be automatically sedated, completely vulnerable.

A sense of reality swept over me. I stood here—I, Jiuinip Akilo Sister-Self 7664-3, who had adjusted sentient seedings not dissimilar to these on scores of worlds—facing an enemy armed with spears, while I myself held only a ceramic knife. And the most unreal part was that these people, too, at least the ones not born here, had come from my same universe of nano, of abundance, of peace. Of QUENTIAM, who would never have permitted this.

Seliku said in a voice I didn't recognize, "Do . . . do any of you speak Standard?"

To my surprise, the closest prisoner answered, in a strange whining accent. "You do this! You and your magic! You destroy clouds and now we never have no rain!"

Magic. Five little girls, playing at "magic" and "death" and "nova." Knowing, secure in QUENTIAM, that for us such things did not exist.

I said to the pygmy, who must be third- or fourth-generation to be so ignorant, "The clouds will return. But we did not destroy them. We are not destroyers."

He waved his spear at Haradil. "She is. She say it."

O, what had Haradil said? That she was a destroyer, perhaps that she wanted to die. She might have been trying to make them kill her. Suicide by fellow outcast.

Camy said, "But you did not kill her. You knew that if you killed her, all her bad magic would come to you."

I saw on his face, on all their diseased and debased faces, that it was true. They feared Haradil's powers of destruction too much to kill her. So what were they doing here now?

I said, "You want us to go far away."

"Yes! Go!"

That was why Haradil had lived apart from what could have been the comfort of shared misery. But, of course, she hadn't wanted comfort. She wanted death and suffering, as atonement for what she'd done.

Seliku said, "It could be a trick, to make us put down our knives."

I looked again at the pathetic creatures before us. Two, I saw now, had legs actually shivering with fear. I said quietly, "It's not a trick. Bej, carry Haradil. We'll move even farther inland. Move slowly but purposefully . . . now."

The prisoners watched us go. In just a few moments the sight of them was blocked by the everlasting spongy green.

❧❧❧

So again we walked, all the rest of that day and the next, taking turns carrying Haradil. We saved the last of our concentrated nutrients for Haradil and ate only a safe kind of raw leaf snatched from plants as we marched. The leaf tasted vile. Nanomeds help with neither taste nor hunger; in any civilized place, both are enjoyable human sensations. I could feel my body shift into energy-conservation mode, which made it harder to keep going but easier to not think. That, now, was my hope. To not think.

Finally, as darkness fell, we made camp in another small clearing. A fire, the blankets from our belts, stars overhead but not, I saw with exhausted gratitude, the gas giant. And as we sat around the fire, too dispirited to talk, Haradil awoke.

"What—"

"You're with us. You've had nanomeds. Sit up," Camy ordered.

Haradil did. She looked around, and then at us. Maybe Camy and Bej, the artists, could have imagined such a tormented expression, but I could not have.

Seliku said, neither gently nor harshly, "Haradil, we've forced our way onto this planet, and now we—"

"QUENTIAM let you come? The Mori let you come?"

"No," Camy grated. "Sel just told you—we forced our way down. And now it looks as if our way home has just closed for good."

"What do you mean!" Haradil cried. At least she was talking.

I said, from sudden pity, "Camy, don't. QUENTIAM will rebuild the shuttle, you know that."

"We don't know anything!" Camy said.

Seliku said, still in that carefully neutral voice, as if she were addressing a skittish child, "Haradil, we'll talk about getting home in a moment. Right now, we're saying that we came all this way, with all this danger—we don't have implants now, you know, none of us—to find out what happened. Why you destroyed that inhabited star system."

Haradil looked at us hopelessly, her gaze moving from one face to another around the fire. In its flickering light, her gaunt face in its pygmy body looked older than QUENTIAM Itself.

Bej said, "Was it the Great Mission, Hari? Did you become an Arlbenist, and did that system include a planet with non-DNA life on it? There's documentation now, you know, the Arlbenists were wrong, the galaxy wasn't empty before humans began to fill it. If you became an Arlbenist—"

"I don't know whether any planet in the system had non-DNA life," Haradil said bleakly.

"So you—"

"I wasn't an Arlbenist."

Camy said, "Then *why?*" I saw her ferocity drive Haradil back into silence.

Seliku broke it. "And *how?* How could you turn an asteroid into a missile powerful enough to blow up a star? Even QUENTIAM said It didn't know how to do that!"

"It didn't," Haradil said.

I burst out, "Then what *happened?*"

"Light happened," Haradil said. "Pieces of light."

"Pieces of what?" Camy demanded angrily. "What are you talking about?"

"Photons," Seliku said. "Is that right, Haradil? You mean photons?"

"Yes." She looked down at her ugly hands, the digits so thick that even in her thinness, firelight did not shine through them. "I was transforming an asteroid, more of a planetoid, in orbit around the star. I was—"

"You couldn't have been," Seliku said. "I've seen the Morit data on the explosion. That asteroid was in a deeply eccentric orbit—it had been captured by the star's gravity only about a half million years ago and was spiraling in to the stellar disk. Just before the explosion, the asteroid was very close to the star, getting a slingshot gravity assist. There's no way even a machine body could have survived on it."

"I know," Haradil said. "I wasn't on the asteroid."

Seliku said, "Where were you?"

Instead of answering, Haradil said, "I was transforming the asteroid—trying to transform the asteroid—into a work of art. Light art. To be an artist like you, Bej. Like you, Camy. All four of you have . . . have things you do. I only had QUENTIAM."

Bej said, "That's where you were. Not on the star, but in upload with QUENTIAM. Directing the artwork through It. We've done that."

Haradil didn't look at Bej, and all at once I knew that she hadn't been in upload, either. Haradil said, "The art was merged photons. You know, to create increased energy."

"Yes," Seliku said, but she looked a little startled. The rest of us must have looked blank because she said, "It's how QUENTIAM operates, in part. It merges photons with atoms to create a temporary blend of matter and energy. It also forces shared photons between quantum states, to create entanglement. It's how QUENTIAM makes the t-holes, how It moves around information—how it exists, actually. The whole process is the basis for QUENTIAM's being woven into spacetime. That's just basic knowledge."

Not to me, it wasn't, and from Bej and Camy's faces, not to them, either. But Haradil had apparently learned enough about it.

I said, trying to keep my voice soft enough not to push Haradil into more opposition, "Is that what happened, Hari? You were directing QUENTIAM to create this 'art' and somehow you massed enough photon energy or something to blow up the star?"

"QUENTIAM wouldn't permit that to happen," Seliku said. "Anyway, the energy you'd need would be huge, more than you'd get from any light sculpture."

Bej said, "Was it a sculpture, Hari?"

"No. It was . . . was going to be . . . what does it matter what I was making! I couldn't make it and I killed a star system!"

I said gently, "The sculpture doesn't matter if you don't think it does, my sister-self. What matters is how the system blew up. What happened?"

"I don't know!" Haradil cried. "I was there, working on the art, and all at once the asteroid slipped away from my control and sped toward the star, and I don't know how!"

"That doesn't make sense," Bej said. "If you were in upload with QUENTIAM and that happened, then It would tell you what happened the moment you asked."

Seliku said, "Did you ask?"

Haradil was silent. Camy rose to her feet and uncoiled her tentacles. Lit from the firelight below, she suddenly looked terrible, avenging. "Didn't you ask, Haradil? You blew up a star system and you *didn't ask what happened*?"

"Of course she did," Bej said. "Hari?"

"I asked later," Haradil said. I had seen that posture on primitive mammals on other worlds. Haradil cringed, from fear of her pack. It turned my stomach sick.

"I asked later and QUENTIAM said . . . said It didn't know what I'd done."

"That's not possible!" Camy said angrily. "If you were in upload with QUENTIAM, it would know exactly what you'd done and so would you! You're lying!"

The two words hung in the firelit air. Insects whined, unseen, in the unfriendly dark. We never lied to each other. Sister-selves did not lie to each other. Your sister-selves were the only ones in the universe that you could say anything to, confess anything to, because the capacity for the same action lay in each of them. A sister-self always accepted everything about you, as no lover ever did, no friend, no one else but QUENTIAM.

"She's not lying," I said.

Camy turned on me. "But if she was in upload and did something to—"

"She wasn't in upload," I said slowly. "Were you, Haradil? You weren't in upload state, you were in merged state. You'd merged a second time with QUENTIAM."

Haradil turned her eyes to me, and in the relief mirrored in them, I knew that I'd been right. She was relieved that now we knew.

Bej burst out, "O, Hari! Why? The first time you did that you came back so . . . so . . . merging reduces people, destroys them! You left parts of yourself behind in QUENTIAM, or something—you know you were never the same after that!"

"I know," Hari said, so simply that my heart turned over. Haradil, knowing herself to be incomplete, fragmented, had gone back into merged state to find the lost pieces of herself. Or maybe just to redeem what she saw as a wasted life ("All four of you have . . . have things you do") by creating this one stupendous, innovative piece of art. Which of us hasn't dreamed of that kind of glory and fame for our work? Only Seliku had attained it.

It was Seliku who moved the discussion back from Haradil's state to what Seliku saw as the more important state: QUENTIAM's. She said quietly, "If Haradil is not lying, then QUENTIAM is."

We gaped at her. Seliku was a cosmologist; she knew QUEN-TIAM as well as any human could. She knew that QUENTIAM could not lie.

"That's impossible!" Bej said.

"Yes, it's impossible," Seliku agreed, and the four of us stared at each other across the low fire.

Haradil said despairingly, "Don't you see that it doesn't matter whether QUENTIAM's lying or not? It only matters that even if I don't know why, I destroyed *life*. A whole worldful of life. My art, my action. And nothing I can do—nothing anyone can do, not even QUENTIAM—can ever change even one tiny piece of that guilt and shame."

I think I knew then, in that moment, what would happen to Haradil. But my attention was on Seliku. She and I were the only sci-entists. I said to her, "If QUENTIAM can't lie, and if It *is* lying, what does that mean?"

She answered obliquely, her tentacles quiet in her lap, her voice just low enough to reach the four of us sealed in our circle of wavering firelight amid the dark. "I know none of you understand my work, the algorithms that won me the Zeotripab Prize. You'd have to understand how the universe itself works.

"Spacetime vibrates, you know, in its most minute particles. They vibrate through space. Gravitons—one of the particles, the ones that create the force of gravity—are the only particles that also oscillate minutely in time. That's what makes them the only particles—I don't know how to say this without the math—the only particles that 'leak' out of the universe, affecting its mass. That's why the universe keeps expanding. That loss of gravitons is what makes spacetime possible at all, which in turn makes everything else possible."

Bej said naively, "You proved all that?"

Seliku smiled. "No. Only a tiny part of it. It's old knowledge. QUENTIAM functions by manipulating those minute time oscillations, in even more minute ways. But it means that It cannot lie. It's bound by the physical constants of the universe. If It said that It doesn't know how Haradil blew up the star system, then It doesn't know."

"But," I said, "could It and Haradil together—they were merged, remember—have done it? Could It have used Haradil to do that? In fact, did anyone ask QUENTIAM if *It* had blown up the system?"

Camy gasped. "QUENTIAM?"

"It can't lie," I said, staring at Seliku, "but It can destroy, right? It destroyed the shuttle and the station. There might have been Mori on that station, we don't know. Within all those physical constants you mentioned, are there any that could absolutely keep QUENTIAM from destroying a star system with life on it?"

"Physical constants?" Seliku said. "No."

Bej said, "But there are QUENTIAM's own parameters! It preserves, not destroys! Everyone knows that! Everyone knows that!"

"Seliku," I said, "are QUENTIAM's moral parameters as woven into spacetime as Its inability to lie?"

"Yes. Its moral parameters are programming, but inviolable programming, core programming. Redundancy doesn't even begin to describe how deeply those parameters are a part of QUENTIAM. They can't be touched, not even by It."

"Nonetheless," I said, "if It can't lie, and if Haradil blew up the star system while she was merged with QUENTIAM, then It blew up the system. It destroyed life. Not you, Hari—" I turned to her, beseeching, "—*not you*. QUENTIAM."

"I don't believe it!" Camy said. "QUENTIAM can't do that! It can't destroy . . ." She fell silent, and I knew she remembered the shuttle, the station.

Haradil had not moved. She sat looking down at her tentacles in her lap, an unconscious mirror of Seliku's pose, although Hari's shoulders slumped forward.

"Haradil," I repeated, "you didn't do it. QUENTIAM did."

Finally she raised her eyes to mine. "It doesn't matter, Alo. There's no difference. I was in the merged state. At that time, I *was* QUENTIAM."

We all stared at her. None of us knew what to say to that. None of us but her had been there.

"I think," Bej finally said, "that it's time for us to go home."

●●●

We couldn't leave until morning. The engineered spores stored in our cloth belts, the same spores that had created the biological floaters that brought us downstairs, needed sunlight to feed on for both growth and inflation. We could only leave the surface on a clear, sunny day. We could only leave from a large open space among the huge ferns.

And, of course, once we'd floated to the upper atmosphere, we could only survive if QUENTIAM had created another shuttle to pick us up.

Nobody mentioned this. We talked very little as we wrapped ourselves in blankets near the fire. I couldn't get to sleep, and I doubted the others could, either.

Seliku would be thinking about the paradox of QUENTIAM. It couldn't destroy, and It had destroyed. She would be going over the mathematics, the spacetime logic, trying to find a way out.

Bej and Camy would be wrestling with the moral problem. Haradil had been QUENTIAM; It had killed; had Haradil therefore really killed? Could you commit genocide without knowing it, and if you did, was it still genocide?

Haradil—I didn't know what Haradil was thinking. "I *was* QUENTIAM," she'd said. I didn't know, couldn't imagine, what that actually meant. But she was right, in one sense—she hadn't been Haradil for a long time now.

It seemed millennia before I fell asleep.

When I woke, as the first dismal light was filtering through the pulpy ferns, Haradil was gone.

◦◦◦

"Burn her in hell forever!" Camy cried. I didn't know what "hell" was; Camy liked to poke around in QUENTIAM's archaic deebees. Had liked to.

Seliku said, "Alo, can you track her?"

"Yes."

Hastily we packed. The morning was overcast and drizzly; we couldn't have left ^17843 that day even if Haradil hadn't run away. At first I scented her easily. After following for half the morning, I was sure. "She's heading back to the beach," I said. "To the settlements."

Bej, her dirty face set hard to avoid tears, said, "She wants them to kill her. She still thinks she was responsible for . . . for the genocide."

"Maybe she was," Camy said bitterly. I felt that bitterness echo in myself. Didn't Haradil realize we would follow her—and thereby risk our own lives? She knew we planned on leaving ^17843 today. She, one-fifth of a sister-self, was endangering the whole. At what point did moral atonement turn into selfishness?

And if our circumstances were reversed, would I have done the same thing?

I might have. The realization only worsened my bitterness.

We were taking a different, more direct route toward the coast than the one we'd arrived by. The ground sloped downward and became much more marshy. The flora changed, too. As the ground became wetter, the huge, looming ferns were replaced by smaller, sedge-like plants farther apart.

"Wait," Seliku called from the rear of our dismal procession. "Akilo, these plants here are the ones we've been eating and I don't see any ahead of us. I think we should stop and eat here, while we can."

"That's a good idea."

We stuffed handfuls of the vile things into our mouths and chewed. These small, light bodies packed very little extra fat; my tentacles had the thinned, bluish look of rapid weight loss. But at least the leaves temporarily stopped the ache in my stomach.

After eating, we slogged forward. In the marshland, walking was much harder. Each footstep made a quiet spurgling sound. The ground grew steadily wetter and muddier, broken by small hillocks that offered better footing but also swarmed with small pale worms. The sun, behind thick gray clouds, did little to warm my fur, and nothing could warm my heart.

"Alo . . . stop a minute . . ."

I turned in time to see Camy vomit. A moment later the cramps hit me. All the leaves I'd eaten came back up in a disgusting green mass. And then another. And then I felt it at the other end of my body.

When it was over, I moved away, toward a hillock of mossy sedge, and lay down. The nanomeds were efficient; I would feel better in just a few moments, and there would be no lingering toxins in my body. But that wasn't what bothered me.

"That takes care of lunch," Seliku said, flopping down beside me. Worms crawled toward her tail. "O, I hate this place."

Bej said passionately, "We weren't meant for this life. This is how animals live, not people!"

I took this as a moral statement, not a biological one. Anyway, I didn't have the heart to argue.

Camy, always the most fastidious of us, said, "There's sand over there. I'm going to scrub my disgusting ass."

Seliku rolled onto her side to face me. "Alo, those were the same leaves we've been eating all along. Exactly the same. You said so."

"Yes. The only thing I can figure out is that they were enantiomorphs."

Seliku said, "Mirror images."

"Yes. Some molecules, especially but not exclusively crystals, are right-handed and some are left-handed—they're called enantiomorphs of each other. Biologicals can usually digest only one or the other."

Bej said, "Mirror images of each other. Like us."

I smiled at her. "I sense an artwork coming on."

"Maybe." She smiled back, and I thought: *This is the only good moment we've had on this foul satellite.*

Camy screamed.

The three of us jumped up. Bej raced toward Camy and I yelled, "No, Bej! Stop!"

"She's sinking!"

"Stop! You'll go, too! I've seen this, I can help her! Camy, don't struggle! Arch backwards and lie slowly—slowly—onto your back and spread your arms and legs as wide as you can. *Slowly.*"

She had only sunk into the quicksand a little above her ankles. She arched backward and spread her four tentacles. I could see them tremble. Her feet didn't come up from the sand but she sank no further, bent backwards like a bow, her eyes and mouth just above the sand. "Please . . . O, please . . ."

Arlbenists prayed. We did not. I yanked the rope from my belt and threw it toward Camy. It wasn't long enough and fell short. Before I could even ask, Bej had her rope out and was knotting the two together, her digits trembling. I talked to Camy, anything that came into my mind: "Camy it's going to be all right I've seen this on ^3982 and ^12983, it's just ordinary sand mixed with upswelling water and so it behaves like a liquid, it will buoy you up just like any water—" On ^3982 I had seen a small biological sucked down by quicksand in the time it took me to open my pack. "We'll get you out it's going to be fine, remember when we were children, we played at rescuing each other on quiet planets and—" What was I saying? This was no game. Fear makes idiots of us all.

The rope reached her on my second throw. Slowly, carefully, we pulled her out. The four of us collapsed in a heap on the dry hillock. No one spoke; we just clutched each other hard enough to bruise.

Nanomeds would fix the bruises.

It was Seliku who pulled away first. "Sister-selves—it's time to go home."

Bej said, shocked, "Without Haradil?"

"Without Haradil. Bejers, she's dead. She wanted to die. This is the trail she was following. She came to this . . . this 'quicksand,' just as we did. And she wanted to die."

Bej's head whipped around to stare at the quicksand. I saw the moment she rejected Seliku's logic. "You don't know that!"

"But it's almost certainly true," I said. "Seliku's right. There's nothing more we can do here."

"We can find Haradil again!" Camy, surprising me. But I shouldn't have been surprised; she and Bej nearly always thought as one. "Akilo can go on tracking her!"

"No, I can't. Not through this."

"You mean you won't! How can you even think of leaving a sister-self? Especially *here*, in this place—"

Covered with wet sand, smelling of vomit and diarrhea, Camy took a step back from me. Bej went with her. Bej said, "We won't go back without Haradil. How can you even think about it? We came here to get her and to find out what happened and we haven't accomplished either one. Yet you want us to go back to Calyx, with everyone knowing that our sister-self, that we . . . that she destroyed a *planetful of sentients* and you just—"

"Which are you really terrified of, losing Haradil or your own shame?" I demanded, out of my own shame, my own loss. "Is Haradil the only one being selfish here?"

They flew at me, simultaneously, as if it were choreographed. Bej's fist hit me in the mouth. Camy punched me in the stomach and I went down. I couldn't see, couldn't breathe. When I could, they had Seliku down, too. We would have been evenly matched, Seliku and I against the two of them, but they'd struck first. My nanomeds began working and I tried to get up, but my feet and tentacles were tangled in the long rope we had used to rescue Camy.

"I'm sorry, I'm sorry, it's Haradil," I heard Bej say. By the time Seliku and I had recovered our breath and untied the vine, Bej and Camy were running back the way we had come, toward the fern forest.

❦

We could have followed them. Their fresh scent would have made it easy. But Seliku and I were equal in strength and stamina to them—*were* them. Sister-selves. They could probably stay as just ahead of us as they were now. And if we did catch them, then what? Another fight? Another unthinkable severing of self from self?

I had thought before that I knew what it was like to be alone. I had been wrong.

Seliku and I gazed at each other. Finally she nodded.

"Yes," I answered.

She gazed bleakly at the gray sky. "Not today, there's not enough sunlight. We'll need to spend the night here."

Silently we took out our blankets and spread them on the mossy hillock. It seemed to take forever for darkness to fall. Neither of us mentioned making a fire. It occurred to me then that Bej and Camy could have tied us up, cut off our cloth belts and taken not only our blankets but the spores of the floaters, thus ensuring that all four of us would stay here. Perhaps they hadn't had time, or hadn't thought of it. Perhaps it was something they wouldn't have done.

I no longer knew.

Toward morning the clouds blew over and the sky turned clear and starlit. The gas giant was just setting. I lay on my back, having slept not at all, and looked for a long time at the unfamiliar constellations. QUENTIAM was up there, among the cold stars.

"Seliku," I said softly, "are you awake?"

"Yes."

I groped for the way to phrase such an unfamiliar question. "When the gravitons you talked about 'leak' from the universe— where do they go?"

"The math says they go into other universes."

"Right beside ours?"

" 'Beside' isn't the right concept. Other universes coexist with ours. It's called a multiverse."

"Do the other universes have their own spacetime?"

"Presumably."

"Is it like ours? Four-dimensional?"

"We don't know."

"Do these other universes—could they—have life?"

"Presumably," Seliku said. I heard her shift in the darkness.

"Could life there have created their own membranes, woven into the fabric of their spacetime?"

She said, "And could that universe be an enantiomorph of our own? Is that what you're asking?"

I raised myself on one elbow to gaze at her, but could only make out her blanketed profile. "You knew."

"No, of course not. But I guessed, after you described the enantiomorph flora. And right after that, Camy—"

"Yes. Sel, is another universe somehow contacting ours? Through QUENTIAM?"

" 'Contacting' may be the wrong word," Seliku said, and I recognized the scientist's caution. "It's more like . . . the two universes bump into each other. A lot of energy would be released from even a small bump. In fact, one theory about the origin of matter is that it resulted from a huge collision between universes. There's so much we don't know, Alo. Technology has gone so far ahead of basic theory. It couldn't always have been this way, or QUENTIAM wouldn't know as much as It does."

"But if two universes bump and energy is released, a lot of energy, wouldn't QUENTIAM absorb it?"

"As much as It could. Think of it this way: You drop a stone in a pond. It creates ripples. Then the pond settles back down. Drop a bigger stone, and you create bigger ripples. Afterward, the pond is subtly changed. The water level is a bit higher, the topography of the pond bottom a little different."

"Don't talk down to me, Sel."

"Sorry. I find it hard to talk to nonscientists about my field."

As did I. My irritation dissolved.

She continued, "To take the metaphor just a bit farther, hurl a big asteroid at a planet. Depending on where it hits, you get a huge crater, a tsunami, an axial wobble, climate changes, biological die-offs. Everything reconfigures. If QUENTIAM is getting hit with some sort of enantiomorph of energy or matter—maybe some version of gravitons—It's being forced to reconfigure spacetime. That's been theoretically possible forever, in small dimensions: it's called a flop transition. We understand the mathematics. QUENTIAM might be doing that in our universal dimensions. And if parts of QUENTIAM Itself are being destroyed either by bumping the other universe or by the reconfiguration, It might not even know that was happening."

"Haradil—"

"She was merged with QUENTIAM. She wouldn't know, either. And a star system died."

All at once I remembered the machine body on the shuttle to Calyx. It had momentarily gone rigid, refused to function. I had said then, even knowing how ridiculous the statement was, that the machine body had "fainted." Machine states were intricately linked with QUENTIAM.

I said, with the numb calm of shock, "You have to tell QUENTIAM. Have to tell everybody. Maybe that's even why there was no record of the first seeding of that planet that Haradil destroyed . . . QUENTIAM's *records* . . . you have to tell—"

"Don't you think I know that?" Seliku's irritation was back. "That's why we're leaving our sister-selves here tomorrow."

Was that why? Or was it because we had finally come to some mental and moral place where our sisters were no longer ourselves? Or was it just because we could no longer stand this cursed moon one more minute?

I could no longer tell my reasons—our reasons—apart.

I could no longer be sure of anything.

❦❦❦

Dawn came clear and warm. Seliku and I tore open our cloth belts and dumped the spores on the mossy ground. Carefully—so carefully— we sopped up a little water from the squishy edge of the quicksand and wrung it over them. In just a few minivals, the spores opened and the floaters began to form around us.

"Seliku, what if QUENTIAM hasn't recreated the shuttle or the station? What if It couldn't? If there's nothing there . . ." I had to ask, even though I already knew the answer.

"Then we die." A moment later she added, "I don't have enough information to do the math, Alo. I'm sorry."

All five of us take on more accountability than should properly be ours.

The floaters sealed and began to rise. I had engineered this group for a gravity greater than this one, and they would just rise until they ran out of air and died. Still, the trip upstairs, going against gravity, would be longer than the one going down. We drifted out over the quicksand, and I tried not to think of Haradil, possibly sunk somewhere beneath that gritty alien lake. The tough, thick membrane around me magnified the sunlight and I grew uncomfortably, but not dangerously, warm. I lay cradled in the sag of floater created by my weight. Maybe it was the warmth but, incredibly, I fell asleep. When I woke, the shuttle was in view, a dark speck growing larger against the pale-slug color of the gas giant.

We had no way to steer. I couldn't see Seliku's floater; winds had carried us apart. Already the membrane that was my floater had thinned, weakened by the less concentrated sunlight and fewer atmospheric molecules at this altitude.

QUENTIAM, come through for us . . .

The shuttle turned and started toward me.

I barely made it into the airlock, holding my breath and enduring the bodily shock while the airlock pressurized. The capillaries in my eyeballs popped and my eyes filled with blood. Then Seliku was pulling me into the shuttle and my nanomeds were going to work.

"Alo! Are you—"

"F-fine," I gasped.

"Rest here, sister." She stretched me out on the deck.

QUENTIAM said on the shuttle's system, "You two went downstairs to a quiet planet."

"It's been scolding me since I got aboard," Seliku said grimly.

"Going downstairs to a quiet planet is forbidden."

"S-Sel . . . did you . . ."

"I've been trying to tell It," she snapped. "QUENTIAM, *listen to me*. We found Haradil. When she destroyed that star system, she was merged with you, and it was *you* who destroyed it. One theory is—"

"I did not destroy the star system containing ^5387. I would remember."

"You don't remember because it wasn't a decision you actually made. Spacetime may have been reconfigured in a giant flop transition after another universe in the multiverse bumped into this universe—"

"I remember everything. I did not destroy the star system containing ^5387."

"—and huge amounts of energy were released. Haradil's art project with the asteroid must have been near the impact point. So—"

Lying on the floor, listening, an irrelevant part of my mind wondered at the ease with which Seliku spoke in whole universes.

"—your memory of the event was reconfigured when spacetime was. You lost a nanosecond of time. The energy—"

"I have lost no time. I cannot lose time. Oscillations of gravitons through time are part of my functioning."

"I'm not talking about gravitons, QUENTIAM. Listen—"

She launched into complicated explanations, with terms and principles I could not follow. What was clear to me was QUENTIAM's utter refusal of her reasoning. And in one sense Its refusal *was* more reasonable than her wild statements. QUENTIAM wanted proof, physical or experimental or mathematical. She had none.

My nanomeds repaired my body and I stood. The meal created by the food-synthesizer was the best I have ever tasted. I made Seliku eat. She didn't want to. She sat in the front seat of the shuttle, no longer arguing with QUENTIAM, but instead asking for equations on the display, staring at them, asking QUENTIAM to perform various complex mathematical processes. I knew better than to interrupt for long. After she ate a few bites, I left them alone.

"The shuttle has reached the t-hole," QUENTIAM said to me. "Where do you wish to go?"

I hesitated, for more reasons than one.

"Seliku . . . Sel?"

I don't think she even heard me.

"Seliku!"

"What? I'm working!"

"We're at the t-hole. Where are we going? And is it safe to go through? If your parallel universe bumps while we're—"

"It's not 'my' parallel universe." Then her irritation vanished and she gave me her full attention. "I know what you're asking, Alo. It might not be safe. But if this goes on, if I'm right about the multiverse, and if this series of bumps and spacetime reconfigurations doesn't end soon, then nothing is going to be safe ever again."

"You are talking nonsense," QUENTIAM said.

I said, "Where do you need to go to make this . . . your theory known? To warn everyone?"

As soon as I said it, I knew how stupid it was. The way to warn everyone, the way to disseminate any kind of information throughout the galaxy, was through QUENTIAM. And QUENTIAM did not believe us.

I saw that Seliku was thinking the same thing. Slowly she said, "We should go back to Calyx, I guess. The Communion of Cosmology is there. It's something, anyway."

"QUENTIAM," I said, "We're going to Calyx."

The shuttle slipped through the t-hole. I would have held my breath, but of course I couldn't tell exactly when it happened until it was over and the stars changed configuration. Calyx rotated just below us. The city-continent came into view and the blue sea gave way to the riot of colors that was Bej and Camy's flower art. For the first time since Seliku had first told me about Haradil, my eyes filled with tears. We are not easy criers.

"I want a new body," Seliku said. "No matter what the risk. I won't stay in this one a minival longer than I have to. Not one minival."

Her tone was violent. I knew, without turning around, that she was crying, too.

❧❧❧

The first thing I did on Calyx was get a new body from QUENTIAM. Burn the risk; I could not stay a minival longer in this ugly, ineffective shell whose every pore breathed ^17843.

"You know it's a risk," Seliku said. She had barely paused long enough to clean herself before hurrying off to the Communion of Cosmologists. "If QUENTIAM takes a bump near here while you're in the nanomachinery . . ."

"I'll take the chance," I said, and then added, "and so will you. You'll make your initial impact on all those unsuspecting cosmologists and then just work on in upload state while QUENTIAM makes you a body."

She did need to answer. "What body are you choosing?"

"The one we use in bond time."

She nodded sadly and left, dragging her body through the gravity it had not been designed for.

On my way to a vat room, I took the short walk to the sea. A fresh wind stirred up small waves and blew toward me the fragrance of blossoms. So much color: magenta and cerulean, scarlet and damson, rose and crimson and delphinium. I rolled the words in my mind. This, then, was how my remote ancestors had lived, wondering if each moment might be their last. They must have had unimaginable courage. Either that or they were all crazy all the time.

I went to the vat room, climbed into an available vat, and uploaded into QUENTIAM.

Are you sure, Akilo, that you don't want implants in the new body? It asked.

I'm sure. No implants.

Is this because of the nonsense Seliku has been saying?

No implants, QUENTIAM. That's my choice.

Yes, it is.

The human mind does not do well in upload without visual simulations. I considered my standard sim, a forested bedroom copied from ^894, and rejected it. Nor did I want our childhood home, or Calyx. Too many memories. Instead I created an austere room with a simple table, single chair and display screen. An open window looked out on a bare rocky plain. It was a room for thinking, for concentration.

Seliku would have known what to look for in QUENTIAM, what data or processes, to see if It was fundamentally different. I did not. Instead I asked questions, an endless stream of questions, about the multiverse and spacetime. Some of the answers I didn't understand. Some seemed contradictory. Since I didn't know whether this was inherent in the science or represented a flaw in QUENTIAM, I gave up on the whole thing, created a door in my room, and went for a walk on the soothingly blank plain. No pulpy green, no looming fronds, no treacherous sand. Firm ground underneath my "feet," and a horizon I could scan in all directions.

The Arlbenists are wrong to think that filling the universe is a divine mission. Sometimes the best healer is emptiness.

I was examining some old, round rocks of my own imagining when QUENTIAM suddenly said, *Akilo. Magnitude one news message.*

What?

The Mori Core has been destroyed.

Destroyed?

Yes. There was an explosion and the entire structure crumpled from within.

Do you . . . do you have visuals?

Yes.

And then I was back in my austere room, watching the huge Mori Core cease to exist. The visuals were from the outside and slightly above, perhaps from a very low orbital. The Core, a huge precise structure of concentric rings, covered half a subcontinent.

The Mori, in direct opposition to the Arlbenists, have over time made themselves more and more biologically similar, while the Arlbenists became more and more diverse in order to seed strange worlds. Mori favor substantial, heavily furred biologicals and cold worlds. The Core stood frosted with icicles, while the winter gardens between the concentric rings bloomed with low, lacy plants in alabaster, ivory, silver, very pale blue. People with white fur walked in the gardens.

The next moment the entire huge structure was gone and a blinding flash of light filled my screen.

Was the First Mori in residence?

Yes.

I tried to sort out my feelings. The Mori had claimed more and more worlds, had imposed their own ideas of order and justice on them, had sent Haradil to ^17843 for a monstrosity she did not commit. But the Mori were not fundamentally evil—and they were *people*.

How many . . . how many sentients died?

19,865,842 humans, 15,980 androids, 598,654 enhanced dokins.

I braced myself. *What caused the explosion, QUENTIAM?*

Quark release seems to best fit the data.

Who used a quark-release device?

Unknown.

QUENTIAM—

Akilo, I cannot monitor humans without implants if there are no sensors in their immediate indoor environments. You and your sister-selves demonstrated that already. I don't know what human had a quark-release device inside the Core, or why, or what motive existed for the sabotage. I have reported that to the new First Mori, on ^10236.

Are you sure the . . . the saboteur was human?

Androids are not created to cause any damage without direct human instruction, and dokins do not have the intellectual capacity to detonate, let alone create, a quark-release device. Therefore, by simple logic, the destroyer was human.

In upload—but not in merger—my thoughts are a separate program, hidden from QUENTIAM unless I choose to address It.

Is my new body almost done?

No.

Get me a link to Seliku.

She looked at me from the display screen, still in her ^17843 body. She must have been standing in some great hall of the Communion of Cosmologists. Behind her rose tall pillars covered with flowers. "I heard, Akilo. And no, I can't tell one way or the other, not for certain. There are a lot of people who hate the Mori, for religious or personal reasons. It could have been a human or . . . or not."

"Your best guess."

"Not."

That is nonsense. QUENTIAM said. *Seliku, I wish you would stop disseminating this misinformation.*

In Seliku's eyes, an exact image of the real Seliku, I saw fear.

QUENTIAM's parameters protect you from any retaliation by It, I wanted to say to her. But she already knew that. And she knew, too, that Its parameters could be the next thing to change.

"Does the Communion have data on the explosion?" I asked her.

"Yes, we have all QUENTIAM's measurements. We're sorting the data now. Alo, come home."

She knew I couldn't hurry the creation of my body. Her plea had nothing to do with logic.

"I'm coming," I said, "as fast as I can."

196

Nothing else happened before my body was done, except for one thing: I dreamed.

This was the second time I had dreamed in upload, supposedly an impossibility. To shorten the unbearable time waiting for my biological, I had put myself in down-program mode within QUENTIAM. There should have been no thoughts, no sensation, no anything. But a sort of sudden current ran through me and then I had the dream, the same one as before: Something menacing and ill-defined chased me through a shifting landscape, something unknowably vast, coming closer and closer, its terrifying breath on my back, its—

Your body is ready.

I downloaded into the body, climbed from the vat, and looked in the mirror.

It was us, the body my sister-selves and I always used for bond time. A female all-human with pale brown skin, head hair in a dark green crest, black eyes. Four coiled tentacles, each a meter long, the digits slim and graceful—the body we would have grown up with had our creation occurred on a quiet planet. Nothing seemed amiss with the body. QUENTIAM had had the nanos make it perfectly.

I let out a long breath.

"I can still add an implant, you know. Not a full one, now that the brain is grown, but still very functional."

"No, thank you, QUENTIAM."

"It makes communication so much fuller."

"No, thank you."

"As you choose."

"Please tell Seliku that I'm done."

"She knows."

She came through the door a few minivals later, dragging her heavy small body, looking as exhausted as she had on ^17843. I was over twice as tall as she, probably three times as strong. I picked her up and carried her, unprotesting, to the beach. We sat at the very edge of the land, our feet in the warm sea, away from any of QUENTIAM's sensors.

"Anything, Sel?"

"No. I can't even convince most of the Communion. They're good cosmologists, but they weren't there. They didn't see the shuttle go, the station go. They still think that Haradil destroyed that star system, and they probably think my demented theory is a mind-defense to keep from acknowledging that. The only thing I've got on my side is my reputation, and I'm straining that."

I nodded. "Sel, while I was in upload, I dreamed."

She didn't tell me that was impossible. She closed her eyes, as if absorbing a blow. I described the dream, adding, "I think it wasn't my dream. I think it was QUENTIAM's. Upload is supposed to be a separate subprogram within It, but I think I was—in some very tiny, tiny way—beyond upload into merged state. Sel, I don't think you should get another body."

Her eyes remained closed, and her face grimaced in pain.

"I'm not saying that nanomachinery and even t-holes aren't safe. Or if they're not, it will be one finite explosion, like Haradil's system or the Mori Core, and we'll be dead before we even realize it. But the upload state, even the machine state . . ." I remembered Haradil saying *I was QUENTIAM*.

"Yes," Seliku said. "You're right."

"Once before I dreamed in upload, the same dream. It was the day you first told me about Haradil. So even then . . . even then."

"Yes. You were just lucky about your body." She opened her eyes and looked at it longingly.

"I'm sorry," I said, inadequately.

"Not your fault. Will you carry me to the Communion hall? I'm very tired."

"Of course I will."

Tenderly I carried my sister-self back to her work. It was almost like cradling a child. I saw that there must come a new relationship between me and my one remaining sister-self, physically frail on this planet but mentally leading a crusade to convince the galaxy of cataclysmic danger. I would be her protector, caretaker, aide. The change between us was permanent. Nothing would ever be the same again.

●●●

I was wrong. Many things are the same.

Seliku has been unable to convince the galaxy of her theory. She has won a few adherents among cosmologists, but for most people, the idea that QUENTIAM might be decaying, might be unreliable, is impossible to even consider. It's like saying gravity is unreliable. Which, I suppose, might happen next. *That* would convince everybody, or at least everybody who survived it.

Meanwhile, some do not survive. There have been mistakes in vat nanos, creating bodies other than ordered, or killing the bodies before they were done. No one knows how many mistakes; I no longer trust QUENTIAM's records.

A new quasar has appeared in the sky, and six supernovas, all outside our galaxy. They filled the sky, night after night, with brilliant light. Seliku says that is too many supernovas to be statistically random, but not even her colleagues all believe her. She works night and day to find the evidence, physical or experimental or mathematical, that may convince them. Her big question is this: Is the unseen other universe just brushing ours in passing, creating supernovas and quasars and small reconfigurations of spacetime that also change and reconfigure QUENTIAM? Or are the two universes set for a full collision, from which neither will emerge without changes so fundamental that basic particles themselves are affected, and all life ceases?

The Arlbenists were wrong, in ways they could never have foreseen when Arlbeni created his Divine Mission over a hundred thousand years ago. We were never alone in the galaxy, and not only because spores have drifted in from beyond its edges and seeded non-DNA-based life here. Even without that panspermia, we were not alone. Humans were already everywhere because QUENTIAM, our collective and historical selves, filled spacetime. And we weren't alone in a much more profound sense.

I have suggested another question to Seliku, as well. Is it possible that the other universe, too, has a membrane like QUENTIAM, but more advanced? And that It knows what It's doing in probing ours? On ^17843, Seliku likened our brushes with the other universe to stones dropping in a pond. Dropped stones sometimes have droppers.

Seliku dismisses this question, not because it's completely stupid but because for that there really is no evidence. But I know she can imagine it. She is my sister-self, still, and sister-self to artists as well. She can imagine a Dropper of stones into the cosmic well between universes.

What is It, or Them, like? Do they guess what effects their experiments have on us?

None of this speculation reaches the Arlbenists, who still blithely seed worlds in the egocentric belief that only humans can create life. I, however, no longer correct and adjust Arlbenist seedings on other worlds. I won't risk the vat rooms necessary for that. And I have my own work here, now, both in aiding Seliku in her all-important fight and in caring for her. Her nanomeds keep her healthy, but her body is not meant for this planet and is not doing well here. It doesn't, surprisingly, bother me that I never leave Calyx. This is, finally, home, here with my new work and my sister-self. I am learning to grow a garden of edible plants, without nanos and without QUENTIAM, just in case. In a weird way, I'm not uncontent.

Not that Calyx looks the same, either. A new artist received the design privilege when Bej and Camy's franchise ended. His name is Kiibceroti, and he has made of Calyx a serene, spare city. Gone are the gorgeous lush flowers, replaced by gentle curves of sand in soft pastels, with perhaps one dark rock placed precisely at the edge of the curve and a single tall fern. I don't much like the ferns, or the overall design. But I admit that it's beautiful in its own way. There is something melancholy about it, something of grief. Someone told me that Kiibceroti lost a brother-self in the Mori Core, but I don't know if that's true. I could ask QUENTIAM, but I ask QUENTIAM very little these days.

One good thing about Kiibceroti's city: All that low-key tranquility is good for dreaming. I dream now, nearly every night. Last night I dreamed of Bej and Camy.

I dreamed they had joined the settlement of prisoners on ^17843, somehow making peace with them, finding companionship and working together to create whatever good exists on that pulpy moon. Bej and Camy cut their arms and shared the nanomeds from their bodies, and the fungi disappeared from everyone's heads and feet. None of them would die.

Then I saw Bej and Camy walking on a seashore with their friends, all approaching some large object in the distance. In the dream, I walked with them. As we neared the object, I saw that it was a great boulder thrown up by the sea millennia ago. Camy and Bej had painstakingly chipped away at it over vast amounts of time, using other sharp stones and their own artistic talent. They had polished the stone with sand and the statue shone in the sunlight with bits of mica and quartz. It was Haradil, smiling and happy, solid by the blue sea for as long as the waves permitted the sculpture to last.

"Alo?" Seliku said sleepily beside me.

I laid my tentacles protectively across her body and moved slightly to nestle closer to her. "I'm here, sister-self. Go back to sleep. We're still here."

THOUSANDTH NIGHT

Alastair Reynolds

Alastair Reynolds is a frequent contributor to Interzone, *and has also sold to* Asimov's Science Fiction, Spectrum SF, *and elsewhere. His first novel,* Revelation Space, *was widely hailed as one of the major SF books of the year; it was quickly followed by* Chasm City, Redemption Ark, Absolution Gap, *and* Century Rain, *all big books that were big sellers as well, establishing Reynolds as one of the best and most popular new SF writers to enter the field in many years. His most recent book is a novella collection,* Diamond Dogs, Turquoise Days. *Coming up is a new novel,* Chasing Janus. *A professional scientist with a Ph.D. in astronomy, he comes from Wales, but lives in the Netherlands, where he works for the European Space Agency.*

Here he takes us to a distant future where our remote descendants have become immortal supermen who possess the powers of gods, for a riveting tale of murder and intrigue that proves that even for those who have everything, there's always a little bit more *to reach for that's hanging just out of reach . . .*

It was the afternoon before my threading, and stomach butterflies were doing their best to unsettle me. I had little appetite and less small talk. All I wanted was for the next twenty-four hours to slip by so that it could be someone else's turn to sweat. Etiquette forbade it, but there was nothing I'd have preferred than to flee back to my ship and put myself to sleep until morning. Instead I had to grin and bear it, just as everyone else had to when their night came around.

Waves crashed a kilometre below, dashing against the bone-white cliffs, the spray cutting through one of the elegant suspension bridges that linked the main island to the smaller ones surrounding it. Beyond the islands, the humped form of an aquatic crested the waves. I made out the tiny dots of people frolicking on the bridge, dancing in the spray. It had been my turn to design the venue for this carnival, and I thought I'd made a tolerable job of it.

A pity none of it would last.

In little over a year machines would pulverise the islands, turning their spired buildings into powdery rubble. The sea would have pulled them under by the time the last of our ships had left the system. But even the sea would only last a few thousand years after that. I'd steered water-ice comets onto this arid world just to make its oceans. The atmosphere itself was dynamically unstable. We could breathe it now, but there was no biomass elsewhere on Reunion to replenish the oxygen we were turning into carbon dioxide. In twenty thousand years the world would be uninhabitable to all but the hardiest micro-organisms. It would stay like that for the better part of another hundred and eighty thousand years, until our return.

By then the scenery would be someone else's problem, not mine. On Thousandth Night—the final evening of the reunion—the person who had threaded the most acclaimed strand would be charged with designing the venue for the next gathering. Depending on their plans, they'd arrive between one thousand and ten thousand years before the official opening of the next gathering.

My hand tightened on the rail at the edge of the high balcony as I heard urgent footsteps approach from behind. High hard heels on marble, the swish of an evening gown.

"Don't tell me, Campion. Nerves."

I turned around, greeting Purslane—beautiful, regal Purslane—with a stiff smile and a grunt of acknowledgement. "Mm. How did you guess?"

"Intuition," she said. "Actually, I'm surprised you're here at all."

"Why's that?"

"When it's my turn I'm sure I'll still be on my ship, furiously re-editing until the last possible moment."

"That's the problem," I said. "I've done all the editing I need. There's nothing *to* edit. Nothing of any consequence has happened to me since the last time."

Purslane fixed me with a knowing smile. Her hair was bunched and high, sculpted like a fairytale palace with spires and turrets. "Typical false modesty." She pushed a glass of red wine into my hand before I could refuse.

"Well, this time there's nothing false about it. My thread is going to be a crashing anticlimax. The sooner we get over it, the better."

"It's going to be that dull?"

I sipped at the wine. "The very exemplar of dullness. I've had a spectacularly uneventful two hundred thousand years."

"You said exactly the same thing last time, Campion. Then you showed us wonders and miracles. You were the hit of the reunion."

"Maybe I'm getting old," I said, "but this time I felt like taking things a little bit easier. I made a conscious effort to keep away from inhabited worlds; anywhere there was the least chance of something exciting happening. I watched a lot of sunsets."

"Sunsets," she said.

"Mainly solar-type stars. Under certain conditions of atmospheric calm and viewing elevation you can sometimes see a flash of green just before the star slips below the horizon . . ." I trailed off lamely, detesting the sound of my own voice. "All right. It's just scenery."

"Two hundred thousand years of it?"

"I'm not repentant. I enjoyed every minute of it."

Purslane sighed and shook her head: I was her hopeless case, and she didn't mind if I knew it. "I didn't see you at the orgy this morning. I was going to ask what you thought of Tormentil's strand."

Tormentil's memories, burned into my mind overnight, still had an electric brightness about them. "The usual self-serving stuff," I said. "Ever noticed that all the adventures he embroils himself in always end up making him look wonderful, and everyone else a bit thick?"

"True. This time even his usual admirers have been tut-tutting behind his back."

"Serves him right."

Purslane looked out to sea, through the thicket of hovering ships parked around the tight little archipelago. A layer of cloud had formed during the afternoon, with the ships—most of them stationed nose down—piercing it like daggers. There were nearly a thousand of them. The view resembled an inverted landscape: a sea of fog, interrupted by the sleek, luminous spires of tall buildings.

"Asphodel's ship still hasn't been sighted," Purslane said. "It's looking as if she won't make it."

"Do you think she's dead?"

Purslane dipped her head. "I think it's a possibility. That last strand of hers . . . a lot of risk-taking."

Asphodel's strand, delivered during the last reunion, had been full of death-defying sweeps past lethal phenomena. What had seemed beautiful then—a whiplashing binary star, or a detonating nova—must have finally reached out and killed her. Killed one of *us*.

"I liked Asphodel," I said absently. "I'll be sorry if she doesn't make it. Maybe she's just delayed."

"Why don't you come inside and stop moping?" Purslane said, edging me away from the balcony. "It's not good for you."

"I'm not really in the mood."

"Honestly, Campion. I'm sure you're going to startle us tonight."

"That depends," I said, "on how much you like sunsets."

That night my memories were threaded into the dreams of the other guests. Come morning most of them managed to say something vaguely complimentary about my strand, but beneath the surface politeness their bemused disappointment was all too obvious. It wasn't just that my memories had added nothing startling to the whole. What really annoyed them was that I'd apparently gone out of my way to have as dull a time as possible. The implication was that I'd let the side down by looking for pointless green flashes rather than adventure; that I'd deliberately sought to add nothing useful to the tapestry of our collective knowledge.

By the afternoon, my patience was wearing perilously thin.

"Well, at least you won't be on the edge of your seat come Thousandth Night," said Samphire, an old acquaintance in the line. "That *was* the idea, wasn't it?"

"I'm sorry?"

"Deliberate dullness, to take you out of the running for best strand."

"That wasn't the idea at all," I said testily. "Still, if you think it was dull . . . that's your prerogative. When's your strand, Samphire? I'll be sure to offer my heartfelt congratulations when everyone else is sticking the boot in."

"Day eight hundred," he said easily. "Plenty of time to study the opposition and make a few judicious alterations." Samphire sidled a bit too close for comfort. I had always found Samphire cloying, but I tolerated his company because his strands were usually memorable. He had a penchant for digging through the ruins of ancient human cultures, looting their tombs for quaint technologies, grisly weapons, and machine minds driven psychotic by two million of isolation. "So anyway," he said, conspiratorially. "Thousandth Night. *Thousandth Night.* Can't wait to see what you've got lined up for us."

"Nor can I."

"What's it going to be? You can't do a Cloud Opera, if that's what you've planned. We had one of those last time."

"Not a very good one though."

"And the time before that—what was it?"

"A re-creation of a major space battle, I think. Effective, if a little on the brash side."

"Yes, I remember now. Didn't Fescue's ship mistake it for a real battle? Dug a ten kilometre wide crater into the crust when his screens went up. The silly fool had his defence thresholds turned down too low." Unfortunately, Fescue was in earshot. He looked at us over the shoulder of the line member he was talking to, shot me a warning glance then returned to his conversation. "Anyway," Samphire continued, oblivious. "What do you mean, you can't wait? It's your show, Campion. Either you've planned something or you haven't."

I looked at him pityingly. "You've never actually won best strand, have you?"

"Come close, though . . . my strand on the Homunculus Wars . . ." He shook his head. "Never mind. What's your point?"

"My point is that sometimes the winner elects to suppress their memories of exactly what form the Thousandth Night celebrations will take."

Samphire touched a finger to his nose. "I know you, Campion. It'll be tastefully restrained . . . and very, very dull."

"Good luck with your strand," I said icily.

Samphire left me. I thought I'd have a few moments alone, but no sooner had I turned to admire the view than Fescue leaned against the balustrade next to me, swilling a glass of wine. He held the glass by the stem, in jewelled and ringed fingers.

"Enjoying yourself, Campion?" he asked, in his usual deep-voiced, paternalistic, faintly disapproving way. The wind flicked iron-grey hair from his aristocratic brow.

"Yes, actually. Aren't you?"

"It's not a matter of enjoyment. Not for some of us, at any rate. There's work to be done during these reunions—serious business, of great importance to the future status of the line."

"Lighten up," I said under my breath.

Fescue and I had never seen eye to eye. Among the nine hundred and ninety-three surviving members of the line, there were two or three dozen who exerted special influence. Though we had all been created at the same time, these figures had cultured a quiet superiority, distancing themselves from the more frivolous aspects of a reunion. Their body plans and clothes were studiedly formal. They spent a lot of time standing around in grave huddles, shaking their heads at the rest of us. They had the strongest ties to external lines. Many of them were Advocates, like Fescue himself.

If Fescue had heard my whispered remark, he kept it to himself. "I saw you with Purslane earlier," he said.

"It's not against the law."

"You spend a lot of time with her."

"Again . . . whose business is it? Just because she turned her nose up at your elitist little club."

"Careful, Campion. You've done well with this venue, but don't overestimate your standing. Purslane is a troublemaker—a thorn in the line."

"She's my friend."

"That's clear enough."

I bristled. "Meaning what?"

"I didn't see either of you at the orgy this morning. You spend a lot of time together, just the two of you. You sleep together, yet you disdain sexual relationships with the rest of your fellows. That isn't how we like to do things in Gentian Line."

"You Advocates keep yourselves to yourselves."

"That's different. We have duties . . . obligations. Purslane wouldn't understand that. She had her chance to join us."

"If you've got something to say, why not say it to her face?"

He looked away, to the brush-thin line of the horizon. "You did well with the aquatics," he said absently. "Nice touch. Mammals. They're from . . . *the old place*, aren't they?"

"I forget. What is this little pep talk about, Fescue? Are you telling me to keep away from Purslane?"

"I'm telling you to buck up your ideas. Start showing some *spine*, Campion. Turbulent times are coming. Admiring sunsets is all very well, but what we need now is hard data on emergent cultures across the entire Galaxy. We need to know who's with us and who isn't. There'll be all the time in the world for lolling around on beaches after we've completed the Great Work." Fescue poured the remains of his wine into my ocean. "Until then we need a degree of focus."

"Focus yourself," I said, turning away.

Things began to improve in the afternoon, when interest shifted to the next evening's strand. Purslane found me again, attending to a whimsical redesign of one of the outlying towers. She told me that she had heard about an orgy on the fiftieth level of the main spire, very exclusive, and that I should join her there in an hour. Still stinging from Fescue's criticism, I told her that I was in no mood for it, but Purslane won me over and I agreed to meet when I was done with the tower.

When I arrived, the only other person there was Purslane.

"Wrong floor, I take it?"

"No," she said, standing on the perfectly transparent floor of an out-flung balcony, so that she appeared to float two kilometres above the sea. "Right floor, right time. I told you it was exclusive."

"But you didn't tell me it was *this* exclusive," I said.

Purslane disrobed. As they stepped away, her clothes assumed the texture of weathered stone and froze into sculptural forms from deep antiquity. "Are you complaining?" she asked.

My own clothes broke up into a cloud of cherry blossom petals and scudded away across the floor. "Not exactly, no."

Purslane looked on approvingly. "I can tell."

We rolled around on the glass floor, which softened and hardened itself in perfect consideration of our needs. As we made love, I tried to remember whether I'd designed the glass floor to be transparent in both directions—and if so what kind of entertainment we were providing to the line members who might be looking up to the fiftieth floor from below. Then I decided that I didn't care. If we outraged them, so be it.

"You were right," Purslane said, when we were lying together afterwards.

"Right about what?"

"The sunsets. Every bit as . . . challenging . . . as you said."

"Go on. Kick a man when he's down."

"Actually I admire your nerve," she said. "You had a plan and you stuck with it. And some of the sunsets were actually quite nice."

She'd meant it as a compliment, but I couldn't help looking wounded. "Quite nice."

Purslane conjured a grape and popped it into my mouth. "Sorry, Campion."

"It's all right," I said. "At least I won't have people pestering me for the rest of the carnival, trying to get at the memories I edited out of the strand. At least they'll know that's precisely as exciting as it gets."

It was true: the pressure was off, and to my surprise, I actually started relaxing and enjoying the remaining days and nights. The last time, my submitted strand had been so well received that there'd been mutterings that I must have spiced things up for effect. I hadn't—those things really had happened to me—but I'd still spent the rest of the reunion in a state of prickly self-defence.

It was better now. I enjoyed feeling my mind filling with bright new experience; multiple snapshots of a dizzying complex and teeming Galaxy. It was the euphoria of drunkenness combined with an absolute, crystalline clarity of mind. It was glorious and overwhelming: an avalanche of history.

At the last count there were ten million settled solar systems out there. Fifty million planet-class worlds. Entire upstart civilisations had risen and fallen since the last reunion, several times over. With the passing of every reunion it seemed impossible that the wilder fringes of humanity could become any stranger, any less recognisable. Yet they always contrived to do so; oozing into every cosmic niche like molten lava, and then carving out new niches that no one had dared dreamed of before.

Two million years of bioengineering and cyborg reshaping had equipped humankind for any possible physical environment. Twenty thousand distinct branches of humanity had returned to alien seas, each adopting a different solution to the problem of aquatic life. Some were still more or less humanoid, but others had sculpted themselves into sleek sharklike things, or dextrous multi-limbed molluscs or hard-shelled arthropods. There were thirteen hundred distinct human cultures in the atmospheres of gas giants. Ninety that swam in the metallic hydrogen oceans under those atmospheres. There were vacuum dwellers and star dwellers. There were people who lived in trees, and people who had, by some definition, become trees themselves. There were people as large as small moons, which fostered entire swarming communities within their bodies. There were people who had encoded themselves into the nuclear structure of neutron stars, although no one had heard much from *them* lately. Against all this change, the nine hundred and ninety-three members of the Gentian Line must have appeared laughably quaint and antique, with our stolid adherence to traditional anatomy. But all this was just convention. Prior to arrival on the planet, we were free to adopt whatever forms we chose. The only rule was that when we emerged from our ships we must assume the forms of adult humans, and that we must bring our minds with us. Minor matters such as gender, build, pigmentation and sexual orientation were left to our discretion, but we were all obliged to carry the facial characteristics of Abigail Gentian: her high cheekbones, her strong jaw and the fact that her left eye was green and the other a wintery, jackdaw blue.

Everything else was up for grabs.

Perhaps it was the stirring up of the past as each new thread was added, but we all felt Abigail Gentian's base memories looming large in our thoughts as Thousandth Night approached. We remembered how it had felt to be just one individual, in the centuries before Abigail shattered herself into pieces and sent them roaming the Galaxy. We all remembered being Abigail.

Somewhere near the seven-hundredth threading, I was again approached by Purslane. Her hair was styled in stiff spiral arms, like the structure of our galaxy. They twinkled with embedded gems: reds, yellows and hard blue-whites for different stellar populations.

"Campion?" she asked cautiously.

I turned from the balcony. I was repairing one of the bridges after a storm, knitting it back together with wizardlike hand movements, making the invisibly small machines that composed the bridge dance to my commands. Matter flowed like milk, and then hardened magically.

"Come to torment me about sunsets?"

"Not exactly. You and I need to talk."

"We could always go to one of those exclusive orgies," I said teasingly.

"I mean somewhere private. *Very* private." She seemed distracted, quite unlike her usual self. "Did you create a Secure on this island?"

"I didn't see the need. I can create one, if you think it's worth it."

"No: that'll just draw too much attention. We'll have to make do with my ship."

"I really need to finish this bridge."

"Finish it. I'll be on my ship whenever you're ready."

"What is this about, Purslane?"

"Be on my ship."

She turned away. A few moments later a square glass pane tumbled out of the sky and lowered itself to the ground. Purslane stepped onto the pane. Its edges expanded and then angled upward to form a box. The box rose into the air, carrying Purslane, and then suddenly accelerated away from the island. I watched it speed into the distance, the grey light occasionally flaring off one of its flat sides. The box became tiny and then just a twinkling dot. It vanished into the scarred, mountainous hull of an enormous waiting ship.

I returned to my bridge-repair work, wondering.

"What is all this about?"

"It's about your thread, among other things." She looked at me astutely, reclining in the lounge chair that her ship had provided. "You told us all the truth, didn't you? You really did spend two hundred thousand years watching sunsets?"

"If I wanted to make something up, don't you think I would have made it a tiny bit more exciting?"

"That's what I thought."

"Besides," I said. "I didn't *want* to win this time. Creating this venue was a major headache. You've no idea how much I agonised about the placement of these islands, let alone whatever I've cooked up for Thousandth Night."

"No, I can believe it. And I believe *you*. I just had to ask." She tugged down one of the spiral arms in her hair and bit on it nervously. "Though you could still be lying, I suppose."

"I'm not. Are you going to get to the point?"

My travel box had brought me into Purslane's hovering ship an hour after her departure. My ship was modestly sized for an interstellar craft; only three kilometres long, but Purslane's was enormous. It was two hundred kilometres from nose to tail, with a maximum width of twenty. The tail parts of her ship projected above the atmosphere, into the vacuum of space. By night they sparkled as anticollision fields intercepted and vaporised meteorites. Auroral patterns played around the upper extremities like a lapping tide.

There were many reasons why someone might need a ship this big. It might have been constructed around some antique but valuable moon-sized engine, or some huge, fabulously efficient prototype drive that no one else possessed. Any advance that could get you slightly closer to the speed of light was to be treasured. Or it might be that her ship carried some vast, secret cargo, like the entire sentient population of an evacuated planet. Or it might be that the ship had been made this big in a gesture of mad exuberance, simply because it was possible to do so. Or it might be—and here my thoughts choked on bitter alienness—that the ship had to be this big to contain its one living passenger. Purslane was human-sized now, but who was to say what her true form was like between our visits to Reunion?

I didn't want to know, and I didn't ask.

"The point is delicate," Purslane said. "I could be wrong about it. I almost certainly am. After all, no one else seems to have noticed anything unusual . . ."

"Anything unusual about what?"

"Do you remember Burdock's thread?"

"Burdock? Yes, of course." It was a silly, if understandable question. None of us were capable of forgetting any of the threaded strands unless we made a conscious effort to delete them. "Not that there was much about it *worth* remembering." Burdock was a quiet, low-profile line member who never went out of his way to make a show of himself. He'd threaded his strand a few weeks earlier. It had been uneventful, and I hadn't paid much attention to it. "It was almost as if he was trying to upstage me in the dullness stakes."

"I think he lied," Purslane said. "I think Burdock's thread was deliberately altered."

"By Burdock himself?"

"Yes."

"Why would he do that, though? The strand still wasn't very interesting."

"I think that was the point. I think he wanted to conceal something that did happen. He used dullness as a deliberate camouflage."

"Wait," I said. "How can you be sure things just weren't that dull?"

"Because of a contradiction," Purslane said. "Look, when the last reunion ended we all of us hared off into the Galaxy in different directions. As far as I'm aware, none of us swapped plans or itineraries."

"Forbidden, anyway," I said.

"Yes. And the chances of any of us bumping into each other between then and now were tiny."

"But it happened?"

"Not exactly. But I think *something* happened to Burdock: something that had him doctoring his thread to create a false alibi."

I shifted in my seat. These were serious allegations, far above the usual bitchy speculation that attended any private discussion about other members of the Gentian Line. "How can you know?"

"Because his memories contradict yours. I know: I've checked. According to your mutual strands, the two of you should have both been in the same system at the same time."

"Which system?"

She told me. It was an unremarkable place: just another star dipping into an alien sea, as far as I was concerned. "I was there," I said. "But I definitely didn't bump into Burdock." I rummaged through my memories, digging through mnemonic headers to those specific events. "He didn't come nearby either. No interstellar traffic came close to that world during my entire stay. His ship might have been stealthed . . ."

"I don't think it was. Anyway, he doesn't mention you either. Was your ship stealthed?"

"No."

"Then he'd have seen you arriving or departing. The interstellar medium's pretty thick near there. Relativistic ships can't help but carve a wake through it. He'd surely have made some mention of that if the strand was real."

She was right. Accidental encounters were always celebrated: a triumph of coincidence over the inhuman scale of the Galaxy.

"What do you think happened?"

"I think Burdock was unlucky," Purslane said. "I think he picked that world out of a hat, never imagining you'd visit it just when he claimed to be there."

"But his strand was threaded after mine. If he was going to lie . . ."

"I don't think he paid enough attention to your catalogue of sunsets," Purslane said. "Can't blame him, though, can you?"

"It could be me that's lying," I said.

"My money's still on Burdock. Anyway, that's not the only problem with his story. There are a couple of other glitches: nothing quite so egregious, but enough to make me pick through the whole thing looking for anomalies. That's when I spotted the contradiction."

I looked at her wonderingly. "This is serious."

"It could be."

"It must be. Harmless exaggeration is one thing. Even outright lying is understandable. But why would you replace the truth with something less interesting, unless you had something to hide?"

"That's what I thought as well."

"Why would he go to the trouble of creating an alibi, when he could just as easily delete the offending memories from his strand?"

"Risky," Purslane said. "Safer to swap the system he did visit with one in the same neck of the woods, so that it didn't throw his timings too far out, in case anyone dug too deeply into his strand."

"That doesn't help us work out where he was, though—the same neck of the woods still means hundreds of light years, thousands of possible systems."

"It's a big galaxy," Purslane.

There was an uneasy silence. Far above us, beyond layers of armoured metal, I heard the seismic groan as something colossal shifted and settled like a sleeping baby.

"Have you spoken to Burdock?"

"Not about this."

"Anyone else?"

"Just you," Purslane said. "I'm worried, Campion. What if Burdock did something?"

"A crime?"

"It's not unthinkable."

But unthinkable was precisely what it was. Gentian Line was not the only one of its kind. When Abigail shattered herself, others had done likewise. Some of those lines had died out over the intervening time, but most had endured in some shape or form. Although customs varied, most of those lines had something similar to Reunion: a place where they convened and re-threaded memories.

In the last two million years, there had been many instances of contact between those lines. Until recently, Gentian Line had been isolationist, but some of the others had formed loose associations. There had been treaties and feuds. One entire line had been murdered, when a rival line booby-trapped its equivalent of Reunion with an antimatter device left over from the War of the Local Bubble. Nowadays we were all a lot more careful. There were formal ties between many of the lines. There were agreed rules of behaviour. Feuds were out, marriages were in. There were plans for future collaboration, like the Great Work.

The Great Work was a project—not yet initiated—which would require the active cooperation of many lines. Whatever it was was *big*. Beyond that I knew nothing about it. I wasn't alone in my ignorance. Officially, no members of Gentian Line were privy to detailed knowledge about the Great Work. That information was held by an alliance of lines to which we hadn't yet been granted full membership. The expectation, however, was that it wouldn't be long before we were invited into the club. Among the guests on Reunion were ambassadors from other lines—some of which were in on the big secret. They were keeping an eye on us, sampling our strands, judging our wisdom and readiness.

Unofficially, there were also Gentian members who seemed to know something. I remembered Fescue's criticism of my strand: how there were turbulent times coming and how I'd have all the time in the world to loll around on beaches after the Great Work had been completed. Fescue—and a handful of other line members—had almost certainly been tipped off.

We called them the Advocates.

But while it seemed likely that we'd be invited to participate in the project before very long, we were also now at our most vulnerable. A single error could jeopardize our standing with the other lines. We'd all been mindful of this as we prepared our strands.

But what if one of us had done something truly awful? A crime committed by one Gentian Line member would reflect badly upon all of us. Technically, we were different manifestations of the same individual. If one Gentian member had it in them to do something bad, then it could be presumed that we all did.

If Burdock had indeed committed a crime, and if that crime came to light, then we might well be excluded from the Great Work.

"This could be bad," I said.

It was very hard to behave normally in the days and weeks that followed. No matter where I went, I bumped into Burdock with unerring regularity. Our paths had hardly crossed during this latest carnival, but now he and I seemed doomed to meet each other every day. During these awkward encounters I kept fumbling for the right tone, hoping that I never gave away any hint of the suspicion Purslane and I felt. At the same time, my mind spun out of control with imagined crimes. Like any members of a starfaring society, those of Gentian Line had terrible powers at their disposal. One of our ships, used carelessly, could easily incinerate a world. Deliberate action was even more chilling to contemplate. Members of other lines *had* committed atrocities in the remote past. History was paved with genocides.

But nothing about Burdock suggested a criminal streak. He wasn't ambitious. His strands had always been unmemorable. He'd never attempted to influence Gentian policy. He had no obvious enemies.

"Do you think anyone else knows?" I asked Purslane, during another covert meeting aboard her ship. "After all, the evidence is all out there in the public realm. Anyone else could spot those discrepancies if they paid enough attention."

"That's the point, though: I don't think anyone else will. You and I are friends. I probably paid more attention to your sunsets than anyone else did. And I'm a stickler for detail. I've been looking out for false threads during every carnival."

"Because you suspected one of us might lie?"

"Because it made it more interesting."

"Maybe we're making too much of this," I said. "Maybe he just did something embarrassing that he wanted to cover up. Not a crime, but just something that would have made him look foolish."

"We've all done foolish things. That hasn't stopped any of us including them in our strands when the mood suits us. Remember Orpine, during the third carnival?"

Orpine had made a fool of herself near the Whipping Star, SS433, nearly crashing her ship in the process. But her honesty had endeared her to the rest of us. She had been chosen to forge the venue for the fourth carnival. Ever since then, including an embarrassing anecdote in a strand had almost become *de rigueur*.

"Maybe we should talk to Burdock," I said.

"What if we're wrong? If Burdock felt aggrieved, we could be ostracized by the entire line."

"It's a risk," I admitted. "But if he has done something bad, the line has to know about it. It would look very bad if one of the other lines discovered the truth before we did."

"Maybe we're making a mountain out of a molehill."

"Or maybe we're not. Could we force the issue out into the open somehow? What if you publicly accuse *me* of lying?"

"Risky, Campion. What if they believe me?"

"They won't be able to find any chinks in my story because there aren't any. After due process, the attention will shift to Burdock. If, as you said, there are other things in his strand that don't check out . . ."

"I don't like it."

"Me neither. But it's not as if I can think of any other way of pursuing this."

"There might be one," Purslane said, eyeing me cautiously. "You built these islands, after all."

"Yes," I allowed.

"Presumably it wouldn't stretch your talents to spy on Burdock."

"Oh, no," I said, shaking my head.

She raised a calming hand. "I don't mean putting a bug on him, following him to his ship, or anything like that. I just mean keeping a record of anything he does or says in public. Is your environment sophisticated enough to allow that?"

I couldn't lie. "Of course. It's constantly monitoring everything we do in public anyway, for our own protection. If someone has an accident . . ."

"So what's the problem?"

"The environment doesn't report to me. It keeps this kind of thing to itself."

"But it could be programmed to report to you," Purslane said.

I squirmed. "Yes."

"I realise this is unorthodox, Campion. But I think we have to do it, given all that could be at stake."

"Burdock may say nothing."

"We won't know unless we try. How long would it take you to arrange this?"

"It's trivial," I admitted.

"Then do it. Last night was the eight hundred and third threading. There are less than two hundred days before we all leave Reunion. If we don't find out what Burdock's up to now, we may never have another chance." Purslane's eyes gleamed thrillingly. "We haven't a moment to lose."

Purslane and I agreed that we should keep our meetings to a minimum from then on, in case we began to draw attention to ourselves. Liaisons between line members were normal enough—even long-term relationships—but the fact that we insisted on meeting out of the public eye was bound to raise eyebrows. Even given the absence of a single Secure anywhere in the venue, there were plenty of places that were private enough for innocent assignations.

But our assignation was anything but innocent.

It wasn't difficult to keep in touch, once we'd agreed a scheme. Since I had designed and constructed the venue, the machinery that handled the threading of the strands into our nightly dreams lay under my control. Each evening, I took the environment's covert observations of Burdock over the last day, and ran a simple program to isolate those instances where Burdock was talking to someone else or accessing data from one of the public nodes I'd dotted around the venue. I then took those isolated sequences and slipped them into Purslane's dreams, along with the allotted strand for that night. I did the same for myself: it meant that we had more to dream than everyone else, but that was a small price to pay.

By day, as we fulfilled our social obligations, we reviewed the Burdock data independently. The agreement was that if either of us noticed something unusual, we should leave a signal for the other party. Since I ran the venue, my signal consisted of a change to the patterning of the floor tiles on the thirtieth-level terrazzo, cunningly encoding the time of the unusual event in the Burdock data. I'd been fiddling around with the patterns long before the Burdock affair, so there was nothing odd about my actions as far as anyone else was concerned. As for Purslane, she'd agreed to stand at noon at a certain position on one of my spray-lashed suspension bridges. By counting the number of wires between her and land, I could isolate the anomaly to within a few tens of minutes.

We'd agreed that we wouldn't meet in person until we'd had time to review each other's observations. If we agreed that there was something worth talking about, then we'd "accidentally" meet each other within the next few days. Then we'd judge the right moment to slip away to Purslane's ship. In practise, days and weeks would go by without Burdock doing anything that we both agreed was noteworthy or odd. Now and then he'd do or say something that hinted at a dark personal secret—but under that level of scrutiny, it was difficult to think of anyone who wouldn't. And who among us didn't have some secrets, anyway?

But by turns we noticed something that we couldn't dismiss.

"This is the third time that he's fished for information about the Great Work," Purslane said.

I nodded. On three occasions, Burdock had steered his conversations with other line members around to the subject of the Great Work. "He's very discreet about it," I said. "But you can tell he's itching to know more about it. But don't we all?"

"Not to that degree," she said. "I'm curious. I'd like to know what it is that has the lines so stirred up. But at the same time it doesn't keep me awake at night. I know that the secret will eventually be revealed. I'm patient enough to wait until then."

"Really?" I asked.

"Yes. And besides—I've heard enough rumours to think that I know half the answer already."

That was news to me. "Go on."

"It's about knitting the worlds of the lines into a cohesive entity— a Galactic Empire, if you like. At the moment such a thing clearly isn't practical. It takes us two hundred thousand years just to make one sweep through the Galaxy. That's much too long on a human scale. We might not experience much time passing in our ships, but that doesn't apply to the people living on planets. Entire cultures wax and wane while we're making course adjustments. Some of the people down on those planets have various forms of immortality, but that doesn't make history pass any less quickly. And it's history that keeps destroying things. It's history that stops us reaching our full potential."

"I'm not sure I follow you," I said.

"Think of all those myriad human cultures," Purslane said. "To all extents and purposes, they exist independently of each other. Those within a few light years of each other can exchange ideas and perhaps even enjoy a degree of trade. Most are too far apart from that: at best they might have some vague knowledge of each other's existence, based on transmissions and data passed on by the likes of you and me. But what can two cultures on either side of the Galaxy know of each other? By the time one gets to hear about the other, the other probably doesn't exist any more. There's no possibility of mutual cooperation; the sharing of intellectual resources and knowledge." Purslane shrugged. "So those cultures stumble through the dark, making the same mistakes over and over again, constantly reinventing the wheel. At best they have some knowledge of galactic history, so they can avoid repeating the worst mistakes. At worst they're evolving in near-total ignorance. Some of them don't even remember how they got where they are."

I echoed Purslane's shrug. "But that's the way things must be. It's human nature for us to keep changing, to keep experimenting with new societies, new technologies, new modes of thought . . ."

"The very experiments that rip societies apart, and keep the wheel of history turning."

"But if we weren't like that, we wouldn't be human. Every culture in the Galaxy has the means to engineer itself into social stasis tomorrow, if the will were there. Some of them have probably tried it. But what's the point? We might stop the wheel of history turning, but we wouldn't be human anymore."

"I agree," Purslane said. "Meddling in human nature isn't the solution. But imagine if the intellectual capacity of the entire human Diaspora could somehow be tapped. At the moment those cultures are bumping around like random atoms in a gas. What if they could be brought into a state of coherence, like the atoms in a laser? Then there'd be real progress, with each achievement leading to the next. Then we could really start *doing* something."

I almost laughed. "We're immortal superbeings who've lived longer than some starfaring civilisations, including many Priors. If we choose, we can cross the Galaxy in the gap between thoughts. We can make worlds and shatter suns for our amusement. We can sip from the dreams and nightmares of fifty million billion sentient beings. Isn't that enough for you?"

"It might be enough for you and I, Campion. But then we've always had modest ambitions."

"But what about Burdock?" I asked. "He isn't linked to the Advocates, as far as I'm aware. I don't think he's been actively frozen out, but he certainly hasn't spent any time cultivating the right connections."

"I'll have to review the recordings again," Purslane said. "But I'm pretty sure none of his enquiries were directed at known Advocates. He was targeting people on the fringe: line members who might know something, without being directly privy to the big secret."

"Why wouldn't he just ask the Advocates directly?"

"Good question," Purslane said. "Of course, we could always ask *him*."

"Not until we know a bit more about what he's involved in."

"You know," Purslane said. "There's something else we could consider."

The tone of her voice prickled the hairs on the back of my neck. "I'm not going to like this, am I?"

"We could examine the records on his ship and find out what he was really up to."

"He's hardly likely to give us permission to do that."

"I wasn't talking about asking his permission." Purslane's smile was wicked and thrilling: she was actually enjoying our little adventure. "I was talking about going aboard and finding out for ourselves."

"Just like that, without so much as a by-your-leave?"

"I'm not saying it would be easy. But you did make this venue, Campion. Surely it isn't beyond your immense capabilities to engineer a distraction."

"Flattery," I said, "will get you almost anywhere. But what about breaking into his ship? That won't exactly be child's play."

Purslane pressed a dainty finger to my lip. "I'll worry about the ship. You worry about the distraction."

We maintained our vigil on Burdock over the coming weeks, as our dangerous, delicious plan slowly came together. Burdock kept up the pattern of behaviour we had already noted, asking questions that probed the nature of the Great Work, but never directing his queries to known Advocates. More and more it seemed to us that there was something about the Work that had alarmed him; something too sensitive to bring to the attention of those who had a vested interest in the thing itself. But since Purslane and I were none the wiser about what the Great Work actually entailed, we could only guess about what it was that had unnerved Burdock. We both agreed that we needed to know more, but our suspicions about Burdock (and, by implication,

Burdock's own suspicions) meant that we were just as incapable of putting direct questions to the Advocates. Day by day, therefore, I found myself making surreptitious enquires much like those made by Burdock himself. I endeavoured to target my questioning at different people than the ones Burdock had buttonholed, not wanting to spark anyone else's curiosity. Purslane did likewise, and—even as we planned our utterly illegal raid on Burdock's ship—we pieced together the tidbits of information we had gathered.

None of it was very illuminating, but by the same token little of it contradicted Purslane's conviction that the Great Work was related to the emergence of a single, Galaxy-spanning Supercivilisation. There were dark, glamorous rumours concerning the covert development of technologies that would bring this state of affairs into being.

"It must be related to the slowness of interstellar communication," I mused. "That's the fundamental objection, no matter which way you look at it. No signals or ships can cross the Galaxy quickly enough to make any kind of orthodox political system possible. And the lines are too independent to tolerate the kind of social engineering we talked about before. They won't accept any kind of system that imposes limits on human creativity."

"No one takes faster than light travel seriously, Campion."

"It doesn't have to involve travel. A signalling mechanism would be just as useful. We could all stay at home, and communicate via clones or robots. Instead of sending my body to another planet, I'd piggyback a host body that was already there." I shrugged. "Or use sensory stimulation to create a perfect simulation of the other planet and all its inhabitants. Either way, I wouldn't be able to tell the difference. Why would I care?"

"But in two million years," Purslane said, "no culture in the Galaxy has come close to developing faster-than-light communication or travel."

"Lots of people have tried, though. What if some of them succeeded, but kept their breakthrough secret?"

"Or were wiped out to protect the status quo? We can play this game forever. The fact is, faster than light travel—or signalling, for that matter, looks even less likely now than it did a million years ago.

The universe simply isn't wired to permit it. It's like trying to play chequers on a chess board."

"You're right of course," I said, sighing. "I studied the mathematics once, for a century. It looks pretty watertight, once you get your head around it. But if that's not the answer . . ."

"I don't think it is. We should keep open minds, of course . . . but I think the Great Work has to be something else. What, though, I can't imagine."

"That's as far as you've got?"

"I'm afraid so. But don't look so disappointed, Campion. It really doesn't become you."

Then something odd happened to Burdock. The first hint of it was his flawless navigation of the Mood Maze.

It was customary to sprinkle harmless entertainments and diversions through the nights of the Reunion. On the afternoon of the eight hundred and seventieth night, I opened the maze on one of the high balconies, with a modest prize for the line member who found their way through it the fastest. The maze would remain in existence until the nine hundredth night; time enough for everyone to have a try at it.

But the Mood Maze was no ordinary labyrinth. Based on a game I had discovered during my travels, a Mood Maze was sensitive to emotional states, which the maze detected using a variety of subtle cues and mildly invasive sensors. As long as one remained perfectly calm, a Mood Maze held a fixed geometry. But as soon as the walls detected the slightest suggestion of frustration, the geometry of the maze underwent a sly modification: walls and gaps moving to block one route and open up another. The more frustrated one became, the more tortuous the labyrinth made itself. Extremes of anger could even cause the maze to form a closed-loop around the hapless player, so that they had no choice to wander in circles until they calmed down. Needless to say, it was considered very bad form to enter a Mood Maze with anything other than baseline human intelligence. Extreme faculties of memory or spatial positioning had to be turned off before participation.

The Mood Maze was a pleasant enough diversion, and popular

with most of those who took a chance on it. But I'd had more than that in mind when I set it up. I'd hoped that the maze would tell me something about Burdock's state of mind, if only he would participate. Since it was voluntary, I couldn't be accused of violating his mental privacy.

But when I ran the maze, Burdock sailed through it, with the walls registering hardly any change to his emotional state. Cheating could not be ruled out, though it was unlikely: a Mood Maze was designed to detect most forms of subterfuge and punish them accordingly. And if he had that much to hide, it would not have been hard to avoid the maze entirely.

What surprised me was the degree of frustration I saw in some of the other participants. When a group of Advocates wagered among themselves as to who would beat the maze the quickest, it was Fescue who ended up with the humiliation of being trapped in a closed-loop. His rage built to a crescendo until I tactfully intervened and allowed him an exit.

I greeted him as he left the maze. "Challenging little devil," I said lightly, trying to calm things down.

"A childish little prank," he said, spitting fury. "But then I shouldn't have expected any better from you."

"It's just a game. You didn't have to take part."

"That's all anything is to you, isn't it? Just a game with no consequences." He glanced at the other Advocates, who were looking on with amused expressions. "You have no idea what's at stake here. Even if you did, you'd shrivel from any hint of responsibility."

"All right," I said, holding up my hands in defeat. "I'll forbid you from taking part in any of my games. Will that make you happy?"

"What would make me happy . . ." Fescue began, before scowling and making to turn away.

"It's Purslane, isn't it," I said.

He lowered his voice to a hiss. "I've given you fair warning. But to what purpose? You continue to associate with her to the exclusion of others. Your sexual relations verge on the monogamous. You spit on the traditions of the line."

I kept my voice level, refusing to rise to his bait. "All this because of a maze, Fescue? I never had you down as quite that bad a loser."

"You have no idea what is at stake," he repeated. "Change is coming, Campion—violent, sudden change. The only thing that will hold the line together is self-sacrifice."

"Is this about the Great Work?" I asked.

"It's about duty," he said. "Something you seem incapable of grasping." He looked back at my maze, as it willing it to crumble to dust. "Keep playing with your toys, Campion. Fritter away your days in idleness and dissipation. Leave the important things to the rest of us."

Fescue stalked off. I stood blinking, regretting the fact that I had mentioned the Great Work. Now my interest in it was known to at least one Advocate.

A hand touched my shoulder. "I see the old fart's giving you a hard time again."

It was Samphire, pushing into my personal space. Normally I would have edged away, but for once I relaxed in his presence, glad to unburden myself.

"I don't think he was thrilled about the Mood Maze," I said.

"Don't take it personally. He's been acting odd for weeks, giving everyone hard stares. What's his problem?"

"Fescue doesn't like me spending time with Purslane."

"Only because the craggy bastard couldn't get a shag out of her."

"I think there's a bit more to it than that. Fescue's mixed up in something. You know what I mean, don't you."

Samphire kept his voice low. "No idea at all. Other than that it's a *work* and it's *great*. Are you any more clued up about it than me?"

"I doubt it," I said. "But whatever it is, Fescue think it's a lot more important than the kind of lazy, self-indulgent things Purslane and I tend to get up to."

"Has he tried to rope you in?"

"Not sure. I can't work out whether he totally disapproves of me on every level, or whether he's just bitterly disappointed that I waste so much potential talent."

"Well, I wouldn't lose any sleep over it. Fescue's just a wasted old bore. His strand didn't exactly set the island ringing, did it?"

"Nor did mine."

"Difference is Fescue obviously expected more. Between you and me . . ." Samphire hesitated and looked around. "I think he was just a tiny bit economical with the facts."

I frowned. "You're saying he fiddled his strand?"

"A few details here and there. We came close to meeting around the Hesperus Veil: near enough to exchange recognition protocols."

I nodded. There'd been a supernova near the Hesperus Veil, and a number of us had planned close approaches to it. "That's not enough to prove that he lied, though."

"No," Samphire said. "But according to his strand he skipped the Veil altogether. Why lie about that? Because either before or after that he was somewhere else he didn't want us to know about. Probably somewhere a lot less exciting than the places that showed up in his strand."

I felt a tingling sensation, wondering if Fescue might also be implicated in the Burdock business. Could the two of them be accomplices?

"That's a pretty heavy accusation," I said, my mind reeling.

"Oh, I'm not going to make anything of it. I've already edited down my own strand so as not to embarrass him. Let him trip himself up. He's bound to do it one of these days."

"I suppose you're right," I said, not quite able to suppress my disappointment. The idea of seeing Fescue publicly humiliated—revealed as fabricating chunks of his strand—tasted shamefully delicious.

"Don't let him get to you too much," Samphire said. "He's just a sad old man with too much time on his hands."

"The funny thing," I said, "is that he's no older than the rest of us."

"He *acts* old. That's all that matters."

Samphire's revelation improved my mood, and I took great delight in telling Purslane what I had learned. Robbed of their sting, Fescue's warnings only emboldened the two of us. Time and again, as covertly as we dared, we met aboard her ship and discussed what we had learned.

It was there that I mentioned Burdock's swift passage through the maze.

"He could have been cheating," I said. "His emotional registers were all very flat, according to the maze."

"I don't see why he'd cheat," Purslane answered. "Admittedly, he doesn't have much prestige in the line—but there are other ways he could have won it by now, if it mattered to him that much. It's almost as if he did the maze because he felt obliged to do so . . . but that it just wasn't difficult for him."

"There's something else, too," I said. "I'm not sure if I'd have noticed it were it not for the whole business with the maze . . . but ever since then, I've been watching for anything even more out of the ordinary than normal."

"You've seen something?"

"More a case of what he hasn't been doing, rather than what he has been doing, if that makes any sense."

Purslane nodded sagely. "I noticed too—if we're talking about the same thing. It's been going on for at least a week now."

"Then it isn't just me," I said, relieved that she had shared my observation.

"I wasn't sure whether to say anything. It's not that there's been any dramatic change in his behaviour, just that . . ."

I completed her sentence for her: an annoying habit I'd spent the last million years trying to break. ". . . he isn't poking around the Great Work any more."

Purslane's eyes gleamed confirmation. "Exactly."

"Unless I've missed something, he's given up trying to find what it's all about."

"Which tells us one of two possibilities," Purslane said. "Either he thinks he knows enough by now . . ."

"Or someone has scared him off."

"We really need to take a look at that ship of his," she said. "Now more than ever."

Purslane had done her homework. During one of Burdock's visits to his ship, she had shadowed him with a drone, a glassy dragonfly small and transparent enough to slip undetected into his travel box. The drone had eavesdropped on the exchange of recognition protocols between the box and the hovering ship. A second visit confirmed that the protocol had not changed since the last time: Burdock wasn't using some randomly varying key. There was nothing too surprising about that: we were all meant to be family, after all, and many of the parked ships probably had no security measures at all. It was simply not the done thing to go snooping around without permission.

That was one half of the problem cracked, at least. We could get aboard Burdock's ship, but we would still need to camouflage our departure and absence from the island.

"I hope you've given some thought to this," Purslane said.

Well, I had: but I didn't think she was going to like my suggestion overmuch.

"Here's one idea," I said. "I have the entire island under surveillance, so I always know where Burdock is at a given moment, and what he's doing."

"Go on."

"We wait until my systems pick an interval when Burdock's otherwise engaged. An orgy, a game, or a long, distracting conversation . . ."

Purslane nodded provisionally. "And if he bores of this orgy, or game, or conversation, and extricates himself prematurely?"

"That'll be trickier to handle," I admitted. "But the island is still mine. With some deft intervention I might be able to hold him on the ground for an hour or two before he gets too suspicious."

"That might not be long enough. You can't very well make him a prisoner."

"No, I can't."

"And even if you did manage to keep Burdock occupied for as long as we need, there's the small problem of everyone else. What if someone sees us entering or leaving his ship?"

"That's also a problem," I said. "Which is why that was only suggestion number one. I didn't really think you'd go for it. Are you ready for number two?"

"Yes," she said, with the tone of someone half aware that they were walking into a trap.

"We need a better distraction: one Burdock can't walk away from after an hour or two. We also need one that will keep everyone else tied up—and where *our* absences won't be noticed."

"You've thought of something, haven't you?"

"In ten days you deliver your strand, Purslane." I saw a flicker of concern in her face, but I continued, knowing she would see the sense in my proposal. "This is our only chance. By Gentian rules, every person on this island is required to receive your strand. With, of course, one exception."

"Me," she said, with a slow, dawning nod. "I don't have to be physically present, since I already know my own memories. But what about . . ."

"Me? Well, that isn't a problem either. Since I control the apparatus anyway, no one else need know that I wasn't on the island when your strand was threaded."

I watched Purslane's expression as she considered my idea. It was workable: I was convinced of that. I had examined the problem from every conceivable angle, looking for a hairline flaw—and I had found nothing. Well, nothing I could do anything about, anyway.

"But you won't know my strand," Purslane said. "What if someone asks . . ."

"That isn't a problem, either. Once we've agreed on the strand, I can receive it immediately. I just won't tell anyone until the day after your threading. It'll be just as if I received it the same way as everyone else."

"Wait," Purslane said, raising a hand. "What you just said . . . about us 'agreeing' on the strand."

"Um, yes?"

"Am I missing something? There isn't anything *to* agree on. I've already prepared and edited my strand to my complete satisfaction. There isn't a single memory I haven't already agonised over a thousand times: putting it in, taking it out again."

"I'm sure you're right," I said, knowing how much of a perfectionist Purslane was. "But unfortunately, we need to make this a tiny bit more of an event."

"I'm not following you, Campion."

"It has to be an effective distraction. Your memories have to be electrifying—the talk of the island for days afterwards. We have to talk them up before the thread, so that everyone is in a state of appropriate expectation. Obviously, there's only one person who can do that beforehand. You'll have to drop hints. You'll have to look smug and self-satisfied. You'll have to pour lukewarm praise on someone else's strand."

"Oh, God preserve us from lukewarm praise."

"Trust me," I said. "I know all about that."

She shook her head. "I can't do this, Campion. It isn't me. I don't boast."

"Breaking into ships isn't you either. The rules have changed. We have to be flexible."

"It's all very well you saying that. It's me who's being asked to lie here . . . and anyway, why do I have to lie in the first place? Are you actually saying you don't think my real strand would be interesting enough?"

"Tell you what," I said, as if the idea had just occurred to me. "Why don't you let me have a look at your strand tonight? I'll speed-dream the scheduled strand to make room for yours."

"And then what?"

"Then we meet and discuss the material we have to work with. We'll make a few tweaks here and there—heighten this memory, downplay that one. Perhaps exercise a smidgeon of economy with regard to the strict veracity of the events portrayed . . ."

"Make things up, you mean."

"We need a distraction," I said. "This is the only way, Purslane. If it helps . . . don't think of it as lying. Think of it as creating a small untruth in order to set free a larger truth. How does that sound?"

"It sounds very dangerous, Campion."

We did it anyway.

Ten days was nowhere as much time as I would have liked, but if we had been given any longer the utter incaution of what we were doing would have had time to gnaw away at my better judgement. It was a false strand that had set this entire enterprise in motion, I had to remind myself. Burdock had perpetrated a lie, and now we were perpetrating another because of it. Unfortunately, I saw no practical alternative.

Purslane's original strand wasn't as bad as I had feared: there was actually some promising material in it, if only it could be brought out more effectively. It was certainly a lot more dramatic and exciting than my essay on sunsets. Nonetheless, there was plenty of scope for some judicious fiddling with the facts: nothing outrageous, nothing that would have people looking for flaws in Purslane's strand, but enough to justify the anticipation she had begun to stoke. And in that respect she excelled herself: without actually saying anything, she managed to whip everyone into a state of heady expectation. It was all in the haughtiness of her walk, the guarded confidence of her looks, the sympathetic, slightly pitying smile with which she greeted everyone else's efforts. I know she hated every minute of that performance, but to her credit she threw herself into it with giddy abandon. By the time the evening of her threading came around, the atmosphere tingled with excitement. Her strand would be the subject of so much discussion tomorrow that no one could possibly take the risk of not dreaming it tonight, even if my apparatus had permitted such evasion. It would be the most exquisite of embarrassments not to be able to hold a view on Purslane's strand.

At midnight, the line members and their guests dispersed to sleep and dream. Surveillance confirmed that they were all safely under: including, Burdock. The strand was threading into their collective memories. There had been no traffic to and from the island and the ships for an hour. A warm breeze rolled in from the west, but the sea was tranquil, save for the occasional breaching aquatic.

Purslane and I made our move. Two travel boxes folded around us and pulled us away from the island, through the thicket of hanging vessels, out to the ship belonging to Burdock. A kilometre long, it was a modest craft by Gentian standards: neither modern nor fast, but rugged and dependable for all that. Its armoured green hull had something of the same semi-translucence as polished turtleshell. Its drive was a veined green bulb, flung out from the stern on a barbed stalk: it hung nose-down from the bulb, swaying gently in the late evening breeze.

Purslane's box led the way. She curved under the froglike bow of the ship, then rose up on the other side. Halfway up the hull, between a pair of bottle-green hull plates, lay a wrinkled airlock. Her box transmitted recognition protocols and the airlock opened like a gummed eye. There was room inside for both boxes. They opened and allowed us to disembark.

Nothing about Burdock's outward appearance had suggested that the air aboard his ship would be anything but a standard oxygen-nitrogen mix. It was still a relief when I gulped down a lungful and found it palatable. It would have been a chore to have to return to the island and remake my lungs to cope with something poisonous.

"I recognise this design of ship," Purslane said, whispering. We were inside a red-lined antechamber, like a blocked throat. "It's Third Intercessionary. I owned one like it once. I should be able to find my way around it quite easily, provided he hasn't altered too many of the fittings."

"Does the ship know we're here?"

"Oh, yes. But it should regard us as friendly, once we're inside."

"Suddenly this doesn't seem like quite the excellent idea it did ten days ago."

"We're committed now, Campion. Back on the island they're dreaming my strand and wondering what the hell turned me into such an adventuress. I didn't go to all that trouble to have you back out now."

"All right," I said. "Consider me suitably emboldened."

But though I strove for a note of easy-going jocularity, I could not shake the sense that our adventure had taken a turn into something far more serious. Until this evening all we had done was indulge in harmless surveillance: an indulgence that had added spice to our days. Now we had falsified a strand and were trespassing on someone else's ship. Both deeds were as close to crimes as anything perpetrated within the history of the Gentian Line. Discovery could easily mean expulsion from the line, or something worse.

This was not a game any more.

As we approached the end of the chamber, the constriction at the end eased open with an obscene sucking sound. It admitted warm, wet, pungent air.

We stooped through the low overhang into a much larger room. Like the airlock chamber, it was lit by randomly spaced light nodes, embedded in the fleshy walls like nuts wedged into the bark of a tree. Half a dozen corridors fed off in different directions, labelled with symbols in an obsolete language. I paused a moment while my brain retrieved the necessary reading skills from deep recall.

"This one is supposed to lead the command deck," I said, as the symbols became suddenly meaningful. "Do you agree?"

"Yes," Purslane said, but with the tiniest note of hesitation in her voice.

"Something wrong?"

"Maybe you're right. Maybe this isn't such a good idea after all."

"What's got you afraid all of a sudden?"

"This is too easy," Purslane said.

"I thought it was meant to be easy. I thought that was the point of going to all that trouble with the access protocol."

"I know," she said. "But it just seems . . . I was expecting something to slow us down. Now I'm worried that we're walking into a trap."

"Burdock has no reason to set a trap," I said. But I could not deny that I felt the same unease. "Burdock isn't expecting us to visit. He isn't aware that we're onto him."

"Let's check out the command deck," she said. "But let's be quick about it, all right? The sooner we're back on the island, the happier I'll be."

We took the corridor, following its rising, curving ramp through several rotations, obeying signs for the deck all the while. Around us the ship breathed and gurgled like a sleeping monster, digesting its last big meal. Biomechanical constructs were typical products of the Third Intercessionary period, but I had never taken to them myself. I preferred my machines hard-edged, the way nature intended.

But nothing impeded our progress to the command deck. The deck was spaciously laid-out, with a crescent window let into one curve of wall. It looked back across the sea, to the island. A spray of golden lights betrayed the darkening sliver of the main spire. I thought of the dreamers ranged throughout that tower, and of the lies we were peddling them.

Mushroom-shaped consoles studded the floor, rising to waist height. Purslane moved from one to the next, conjuring a status readout with a pass of her hand.

"This all looks good so far," she said. "Control architecture is much as I remember it from my ship. The navigations logs should be about . . . here." She halted at one of the mushrooms and flexed her hands in the stiffly formal manner of a dancer. Text and graphics cascaded through the air in a flicker of primary colours. "No time to go through it all now," she said. "I'll just commit it to eidetic memory and review it later." She increased the flow of data, until it blurred into whiteness.

I paced nervously up and down the crescent window. "Fine by me. Just out of interest, what are the chances we'll find anything incriminating anyway?"

Purslane's attention snapped onto me for a second. "Why not? We know for a fact that he lied."

"But couldn't he have doctored those logs as well? If he had something to hide . . . why leave the evidence aboard his ship?"

But Purslane did not answer me. She was looking beyond me, to the door where we had entered. Her mouth formed a silent exclamation of horror and surprise.

"Stop, please," said a voice.

I looked around, all my fears confirmed. But I recognised neither the voice nor the person who had spoken.

It was a man, baseline human in morphology. Nothing about his face marked him as Gentian Line. His rounded skull lacked Abigail's prominent cheekbones, and his eyes were pure matched blue of a deep shade, piercing even in the subdued light of the command deck.

"Who are you?" I asked. "You're not one of us, and you don't look like one of the guests."

"He isn't," Purslane said.

"Step away from the console, please," the man said. His voice was soft, unhurried. The device he held in his fist was all the encouragement we needed. It was a weapon: something unspeakably ancient and nasty. Its barrel glittered with inlaid treasure. His gloved finger caressed the delicate little trigger. Above the grip, defined by swirls of ruby, was the ammonite spiral of a miniature cyclotron. The weapon was a particle gun.

Its beam would slice through us as cleanly as it sliced through the hull of Burdock's ship.

"I will use this," the man said, "so please do as I say. Move to the middle of the room, away from any instruments."

Purslane and I did as he said, joining each other side by side. I looked at the man, trying to fit him into the Burdock puzzle. By baseline standards his physiological age was mature. His face was lined, especially around the eyes, with flecks of grey in his hair and beard. Something about the way he deported himself led me to believe that he was just as old as he looked. He wore a costume of stiff, skin-tight fabric in a shade of fawn, interrupted here and there by metal plugs and sockets. A curious metal ring encircled his neck.

"We don't know who you are," I said. "But we haven't come to do you any harm."

"Interfering with this ship doesn't count as doing harm?" He spoke the Gentian tongue with scholarly precision, as if he had learned it for this occasion.

"We were just after information," Purslane said.

"Were you, now? What kind?"

Purslane flashed me a sidelong glance. "We may as well tell the truth, Campion," she said quietly. "We won't have very much to lose."

"We wanted to know where this ship had been," I said, knowing she was right but not liking it either.

The man jabbed the barrel of the particle gun in my direction. "Why? Why would you care?"

"We care very much. Burdock—the rightful owner of this ship— seems not to have told the truth about what he was up to since the last reunion."

"That's Burdock's business, not yours."

"Do you know Burdock?" I asked, pushing my luck.

"I know him very well," the man told me. "Better than you, I reckon."

"I doubt it. He's one of us. He's Gentian flesh."

"That's nothing to be proud of," the man said. "Not where I come from. If Abigail Gentian was here now, I'd put a hole in her you could piss through."

The dead calm with which he made this statement erased any doubt that he meant exactly what he said. I felt an existential chill. The man would have gladly erased not just Abigail but her entire line.

It was a strange thing to feel despised.

"Who are you?" Purslane asked. "And how do you know Burdock?"

"I'm Grisha," the man said. "I'm a survivor."

"A survivor of what?" I asked. "And how did you come to be aboard Burdock's ship?"

The man looked at me, little in the way of expression troubling his rounded face. Then by some hidden process he seemed to arrive at a decision.

"Wait here," he said. "I'll be back in a moment."

He let go of the particle gun. Instead of dropping to the floor the weapon simply hung exactly where he had left it, with its barrel still aimed in our general direction. Grisha stepped through the door and left the command deck.

"I knew this was a mistake," Purslane whispered. "Do you think that thing is really . . ."

I moved a tiny distance away from Purslane and the gun flicked its attention onto me. I drew breath and returned to my former spot, the gun following my motion.

"Yes," I said.

"I thought so."

Grisha returned soon enough. He closed his hand around the gun and lowered it a little. It was no longer trained on us, but we were still in Grisha's power.

"Come with me," he said. "There's someone you need to meet."

A windowless room lay near the core of the ship. It was, I realised, the sleeping chamber: the place where the ship's occupants (even if they only amounted to a single person) would have entered metabolic stasis for the long hops between stars. Some craft had engines powerful enough to push them so close to the speed of light that time dilation squeezed all journeys into arbitrarily short intervals of subjective time, but this was not one of those. At the very least Burdock would have had to spend years between stars. For that reason the room was equipped with the medical systems needed to maintain, modify and rejuvenate a body many times over.

And there *was* a body. A pale form, half eaten by some form of brittle, silvery calcification—a plaque that consumed his lower body to the waist, and which had begun to envelope the side of his chest, right shoulder and the right side of his face. A bustle of ivory machines attended the body, which trembled behind the distorting effect of a containment bubble.

"You can look," Grisha said.

We looked. Purslane and I let out a joint gasp of disbelief. The body on the couch belonged to Burdock.

"It doesn't make any sense," I said, studying the recumbent, damaged form. "The body he has on the island is intact. Why keep this failing one alive?"

"That isn't a duplicate body," Grisha said, nodding at the half-consumed form. "That's his only one. That *is* Burdock."

"No," I said. "Burdock was still on the island when we left."

"That wasn't Burdock," Grisha said, with a weary sigh. He pointed the gun at a pair of seats next to the bed. "Sit down, and I'll try and explain."

"What's wrong with him?" Purslane asked, as we followed Grisha's instruction.

"He's been poisoned. It's some kind of assassination weapon: very subtle, very slow, very deadly." Grisha leaned over and stroked the containment bubble, his fingertips pushing flickering pink dimples into the field. "This is more for your benefit than mine. If his contagion touched me, all I'd have to show for it is a nasty rash. It would kill you the same way it's killing him."

"No," I said. "He's Gentian. We can't be killed by an infection."

"It's a line weapon. It's made to kill the likes of you."

"Who did this to him?" Purslane asked. "You, Grisha?"

The question seemed not to offend him. "No, I didn't do this. It was one of *you*—an Advocate, he thought."

I frowned at the silver-ridden corpse. "Burdock told you who did it?"

"Burdock had his suspicions. He couldn't be sure who exactly had poisoned him."

"I don't understand. What exactly happened? How can Burdock be sick here, if we've seen him running around on the island only a couple of hours ago?"

Grisha smiled narrowly: the first hint of emotion to have troubled his face since our introduction. "That wasn't Burdock that you saw. It was a construct, a mimic, created by his enemies. It replaced the real Burdock nearly three weeks ago. They poisoned him before he returned to his ship."

I looked at Purslane and nodded. "If Grisha's telling the truth, that at least explains the change in Burdock's behaviour. We thought he'd been scared off asking any more questions about the Great Work. Instead he'd been supplanted."

"So he did ask too many questions," Purslane said. She creased her forehead prettily. "Wait, though. If he knew he'd been poisoned, why didn't he tell the rest of us? And why did he stay aboard the ship, out of sight, when his impostor was running around on the island?"

"He had no choice," Grisha answered. "When he arrived here, the ship detected the contagion and refused to let him leave."

"Noble of it," I said.

"He'd programmed it that way. I think he had a suspicion his enemies might try something like this. If he was infected, he didn't want to be allowed to return and spread it around. He was thinking of the rest of you."

Purslane and I were quiet for a few moments. I think we were both thinking the same rueful thoughts. We had never considered the possibility that Burdock might be acting honourably, even heroically. No matter what else I learned that evening, I knew that I had already misjudged someone who deserved better.

"All the same," I said, "that still doesn't explain why he didn't alert the rest of us. If he knew he'd been poisoned, and if he had half an idea as to who might have been behind it, there'd have been hell to pay."

"Doubtless there would have been," Grisha said. "But Burdock knew the risk was too great."

"Risk of what?" asked Purslane.

"My existence coming to light. If his enemies learned of my existence, learned of what I know, they'd do all in their power to silence me."

"You mean they'd kill you as well?" I asked.

Grisha gave off a quick, henlike cluck of amusement. "Yes, they'd certainly kill me. But not *just* me. That wouldn't be thorough enough. They wouldn't stop at this ship, either. They'd destroy every ship parked around the island, and then the island, and then perhaps the world."

I absorbed what he had said with quiet horror. Again, there was no doubt as to the truth of his words.

"You mean they'd murder all of us?"

"This is about more than just Gentian Line," Grisha said. "The loss of a single line would be a setback, but not a crippling one. The other lines would take up the slack. It wouldn't stop the Great Work."

I looked at him. "What do you know about the Great Work?"

"Everything," he said.

"Are you going to tell us?" Purslane asked.

"No," he said. "I'll leave that to Burdock. He still has several minutes of effective consciousness left, and I think he'd rather tell you in person. Before I wake him, though, it might not hurt if I told you a thing or two about myself, and how I came to be here."

"We've got all evening," I said.

Grisha's people were archaeologists. They had been living in the same system for two million years, ever since settling it by generation ark. They had no interest in wider galactic affairs, and seemed perfectly content with a mortal lifespan of a mere two hundred years. They occupied their days in the diligent, monkish study of the Prior culture that had inhabited their system before their own arrival, in the time when humanity was still a gleam in evolution's eye.

The Priors had no name for themselves except the Watchers. They had been hard-shelled, multi-limbed creatures that spent half their lives beneath water. Their biology and culture was alien enough for a lifetime of study: even a modern one. But although they differed from Grisha's people in every superficial respect, there were points of similarity between the two cultures. They too were archaeologists, of a kind.

The Watchers had chosen to focus on a single, simple question. The universe had already been in existence for more than eleven billion years by the time the Watchers learned its age. And yet the study of the stellar populations in spiral galaxies at different redshifts established that the preconditions for the emergence of intelligent life had been in place for several billion years before the Watchers had evolved, even in the most conservative of scenarios.

Were they therefore the first intelligent culture in the universe, or had sentience already arisen in one of those distant spirals?

To answer this question, the Watchers had taken one of their worlds and shattered it to molecular rubble. With the materials thus liberated, they had constructed a swarm of miraculous eyes: a fleet of telescopes that outnumbered the stars in the sky. They had wrapped this fleet around their system and quickened it to a kind of slow, single-minded intelligence. The telescopes peered through the hail of local stars out into intergalactic space. They shared data across a baseline of tens of light hours, sharpening their acuity to the point where they approximated a single all-seeing eye as wide as a solar system.

It took time for light to reach the Eye from distant galaxies. The further out the Eye looked, the further it looked back into the history of the universe. Galaxies ten million light years away were glimpsed as they were ten million years earlier; those a billion light years away offered a window into the universe when it was a billion years younger than the present epoch.

The Eye looked at a huge sample of spiral galaxies, scrutinising them for signs of intelligent activity. It looked for signals across the entire electromagnetic spectrum; it sifted the parallel data streams of neutrino and gravity waves. It hunted for evidence of stellar engineering, of the kind that other Priors had already indulged in: planets remade to increase their surface area, stars sheathed in energy-trapping shells, entire star systems relocated from one galactic region to another.

One day it found what it was looking for.

At a surprisingly high redshift, the Eye detected a single spiral galaxy that was alive with intelligence. Judging by the signals emerging from the galaxy—accidental or otherwise—the ancient spiral was home to a single starfaring culture two or three million years into its dominion. The culture might have begun life as several distinct emergent intelligences that had amalgamated into one, or it might have arisen on a single world. At this distance in time and space, it hardly mattered.

What was clear was that the culture had reached a plateau of social and technological development. They had colonised every useful rock in their galaxy, to the point where their collective biomass exceeded that of a large gas giant. They became expert in the art of stellar husbandry: tampering in the nuclear burning processes of stars to prolong their lifetime, or to fan them to hotter temperatures. They shattered worlds and remade them into artful, energy-trapping forms.

They played with matter and elemental force the way a child might play with sand and water. There was nothing they couldn't conquer, except time and distance and the iron barrier of the speed of light.

At this point in Grisha's story, Purslane and I looked at each other in a moment of dawning recognition.

"Like us," we both said.

Grisha favoured this assessment with a nod. "They were like you in so very many ways. They desired absolute omniscience. But the sheer scale of the galaxy always crushed them. They could never know everything: only out of date snapshots. Entire histories slipped through their fingers, unwitnessed, unmourned. Like you, they evolved something like the great lines: flocks of cloned individuals to serve as independent observers, gathering information and experience that would later be merged into the collective whole. And like you, they discovered that it was only half a victory."

"And then?" I asked.

"Then . . . they did something about it." Grisha opened his mouth as if to speak more on the matter, then seemed to think better of it. "The Watchers continued to study the spiral culture. They gathered data, and when the Watchers passed away, that same data was entombed on the first world that my people settled. In the course of our study, we found this data and eventually we learned how to understand it. And for hundreds of thousands of years we thought no more of it: just one observational curiosity among the many gathered by our Priors."

"What did the spiral culture do?" I asked.

"Burdock can tell you that. It'll be better coming from him."

"You were going to tell us how you ended up on his ship," Purslane prompted.

Grisha looked at the recumbent figure, trapped within those trembling fields. "I'm here because Burdock saved me," he said. "Our culture was murdered. Genocide machines took apart our solar system world by world. We made evacuation plans, of course; built ships so that some of us might cross space to another system. We still knew nothing of relativistic starflight, so those ships were necessarily slow and vulnerable. That was our one error. If there was one piece of knowledge we should have allowed ourselves, it was how to build faster ships. Then perhaps, I wouldn't be speaking to you now. Too many of us would have reached other systems for there to be any need for this subterfuge. But as it is, I'm the only survivor."

His ship had crawled away from the butchered system with tens of thousands of refugees aboard. They had stealthed the ship to the best of their ability, and for a little while it looked as if they might make it into interstellar space unmolested. Then an instability in their narrow, shielded fusion flame had sent a clarion across tens of light hours.

The machines were soon on them.

Most had died immediately, but there had been enough warning for a handful of people to abandon the ship in smaller vehicles. Most of those had been picked off, as well. But Grisha had made it. He had fallen out of his system, engines dead, systems powered down to a trickle of life-support. And still he hadn't been dark or silent enough to avoid detection.

But this time it wasn't the machines that found him. It was another ship—a Gentian Line vessel that just happened to be passing by.

Burdock had pulled him out of the escape craft, warmed him from the emergency hibernation, and cracked the labyrinth of his ancient language.

Then Burdock taught Grisha how to speak his own tongue.

"He saved my life," Grisha said. "We fled the system at maximum thrust, outracing the machines. They tried to chase us, and for a little while it seemed that they had the edge. But eventually we made it."

Even as I framed the question, I think I already had an inkling of the answer. "These machines . . . the ones that murdered your people?"

"Yes," Grisha said.

"Who sent them?"

He looked at both of us and said, very quietly, "You did."

We woke Burdock.

The assassination toxin was eating him at a measurable rate; cubic centimetres per hour at normal body temperatures. With Burdock cooled below consciousness, the consumption was retarded to a glacially slow attack. But he would have to be warmed to talk to us, and so his remaining allowance of conscious life could be defined in a window of minutes, with the quality of that consciousness degrading as the weapon gorged itself on his mind.

"I was hoping someone would make it this far," Burdock said, opening his eyes. He didn't turn his head to greet us—the consuming plaque would have made that all but impossible even if he had the will—but I assumed that he had some other means of identifying us. His lips barely moved, but something was amplifying his words, or his intention to speak. "I know how you broke into my ship," he said, "and I presume Grisha's told you something of his place in this whole mess."

"A bit," I said.

"That's good—no need to go over that again." The words had their own erratic rhythm, like slowly dripping water. "But what made you come out here in the first place?"

"There was a discrepancy in your strand," Purslane said, approaching uncomfortably close to the bedside screen. "It conflicted with Campion's version of events. One of you had to be lying."

"You said you'd been somewhere you hadn't," I said. "I happened to be there at the same time, or else no one would ever have known."

"Yes," he said. "I lied; submitted a false strand. Most of it was true—you probably guessed that much—but I had to cover up my visit to Grisha's system."

I nodded. "Because you knew who had destroyed Grisha's people?"

"The weapons were old: million-year-old relics from some ancient war. That should have made them untraceable. But I found one of the weapons, adrift and deactivated. New control systems had been grafted over the old machinery. These control systems used line protocols."

"Gentian?"

"Gentian, or one of our allies. I had witnessed a terrible crime, a genocide worse than anything recorded in our history."

"Why did you cover it up?" Purslane asked.

"The knowledge frightened me. But that wasn't the reason I altered my strand. I did it because I needed time: time to identify those responsible, and protect Grisha from them until I had enough evidence to bring them to justice. If the perpetrators were among us—and I had reason to think they were—they would have killed Grisha to silence him. And if killing Grisha meant killing the rest of us, I don't think they'd have blinked at that." He managed a despairing laugh. "When you've just wiped out a two-million-year-old civilisation, what do a thousand clones matter?"

I tried not to sound too disbelieving. "The murder of an entire line? You think they'd go that far, just to cover up an earlier crime?"

"And more," Burdock said gravely. "This is about more than our piddling little line, Campion."

"The Great Work," Purslane said, voicing my own thoughts. "A project bigger than any single line. That's what they killed for, isn't it. And that's what they'll kill for again."

"You're good," Burdock said. "I couldn't have asked for a better pair of amateur sleuths."

"We still don't know anything about the Great Work itself," I told him. "Or why Grisha's people had to die."

"I'll tell you about the Work in good time. First we need to talk about the people who want Grisha dead."

Purslane looked at the other man, and then returned her attention to Burdock. "Do you know their names?"

"It was names I was after," he said. "I had a suspicion—little more than a hunch—that the genocide had something to do with the Work."

"Quite a hunch," I commented.

"Not really. Whoever was behind this had murdered those people because of something big, and the only big thing I could think of was the Work. What else do the Advocates talk about, Campion—other than their own inflated sense of self-worth?"

"You have a point."

"Anyway, the more I dug, the more it looked like I was right about that hunch. It did tie in with the Work. But I still didn't have any names. I thought if I could at least isolate the line members who had the strongest ties to the Work, then I could start looking for flaws in their strands . . ."

"Flaws?" Purslane asked.

"Yes. At least one of them had to have been near Grisha's system at the same time as me. They won't have used intermediaries for that kind of thing."

But it was only good luck that we had found the flaw in Burdock's strand in the first place, I thought. Even if someone else had fabricated all or part of their strand, there was no reason to assume they had made the same kind of mistake.

"Did you narrow it down to anyone?" Purslane asked.

"A handful of plausible suspects . . . conspicuous Advocates, for the most part. I'm sure you could draw up the same shortlist with little effort."

I thought of the Advocates I knew, and the one in particular I had never liked. "Was Fescue among them?"

"Yes," Burdock said. "He was one of them. No love lost there, I see."

"Fescue is a senior Advocate," Purslane said. "He's tried to keep Campion and I apart. It could easily be that he knows we're onto something. If anyone has the means . . ."

"There are others besides Fescue. I needed to know who it was. That was why I started asking questions, nosing around, trying to goad someone into an indiscretion."

"We noticed," I said.

"Obviously my idea of subtle wasn't *their* idea of subtle. Well, it proves I was onto something, I suppose. At least one of our line has to be involved."

I tapped a finger against my nose. "Why didn't they just kill you on the island, and be done with it?"

"It was *your* island, Campion. How would they have killed me without you noticing it? Administering a poisonous agent was simpler—at least that way they didn't have a body to dispose of."

"Do you know about the impostor?" I asked.

"My ship kept a watch on the island. More than once I saw myself strolling on the high promenades."

"You could have signalled us," Purslane said. "Made your ship malfunction, or something like that."

"No. I thought of that, of course. But if my enemies had the slightest suspicion I was still alive, they might have attacked the ship. Remember: they poisoned me not because I knew what had happened, but simply because I was asking too many questions. It's entirely possible that they've done this to other line members in the past. There might be other impostors on your island, Campion."

"I'd know," I said automatically.

"Would you? Would you really?"

When he put it like that, I wasn't sure. I wasn't in the habit of looking inside the skulls of other line members, just to make sure they were really who I assumed them to be. Mental architecture was a private thing at the best of times. And a strand was a strand, whether it was delivered by a thinking person or a mindless duplicate.

"You could have sent a message to one of us," Purslane said.

"How would I have known you were to be trusted? From where I was sitting, hardly anyone wasn't a possible suspect."

"Do you trust us now?" I asked.

"I suppose so," Burdock said, with not quite the conviction I might have hoped for. "Does it look like I have a great deal of choice?"

"We're not implicated," Purslane said soothingly. "But we are concerned to expose the truth."

"It's dangerous. Everything I said still holds. They'll take this world apart to safeguard the Great Work. Unless you can organise a significant number of allies and move against them quickly . . . I fear they'll gain the upper hand."

"Then we'll just have to outplay them, so that they never get a chance." Easier said than done, I thought. We had no more idea who we could trust than Burdock himself.

"Whatever we do," Purslane said, "it'll have to happen before Thousandth Night. If there's any evidence pointing to a crime now, it'll be lost forever by the time we return here."

"She's right," I said. "If Gentian Line is implicated, then whoever's involved is on the island now. That gives us something. We've at least got them in one place."

"Thousandth Night would be a good time to move," Purslane mused. "If we leave it until then—the last possible moment—they'll probably have assumed nothing's going to happen."

"Risky," I said.

"It's all risky. At least that way we stand a chance of catching them off guard. There's only one thing anyone ever thinks about on Thousandth Night."

"Purslane may have a point," Burdock said. "Whoever the perpetrators are, they're still part of the line. They'll be waiting to see who wins best strand, just like the rest of you."

I noticed that he said "you" rather than "us." On his deathbed, Burdock had already begun the process of abdication from Gentian affairs. Knowing he would not see Thousandth Night, let alone another reunion, he was turning away from the line.

Abigail valued death as much as she valued life. Though we were all technically immortal, that immortality only extended to our cellular processes. If we destroyed our bodies, we died. Gentian protocol forbade backups, or last minute neural scans. She wanted her memories to burn bright with the knowledge that life—even a life spanning hundreds of thousands of years—was only a sliver of light between two immensities of darkness.

Burdock would die. Nothing in the universe could stop that now.

"When you witnessed the crime," I said, "did you see anything that could tell us who was responsible?"

"I've been through my memories of my passage through Grisha's system thousand times," he said. "After I rescued Grisha, I caught a trace of a drive flame exiting the system in the opposite direction. Presumably whoever deployed the machines was still around until then, making sure that the job was done."

"We should be able to match the drive signature to one of the ships parked here," I said.

"I've tried, but the detection was too faint. There's nothing that narrows down my list of suspects."

"Maybe a fresh pair of eyes might help, though," Purslane said. "Or even two pairs."

"Direct exchange of memories is forbidden outside of threading," Burdock said heavily.

"Add it to the list of Gentian rules we've already broken tonight," I said. "Falsification of Purslane's strand, absence from the island during a threading, breaking into someone else's ship . . . why don't you let *me* worry about the rules, Burdock? My neck's already on the line."

"I suppose one more wrong won't make much difference," he said, resignedly. "The sensor records of my passage through Grisha's system are still in my ship files—will they be enough?"

"You had no other means of witnessing events?"

"No. Everything I saw came through the ship's eyes and ears in one form or another."

"That should be good enough Can you pass those records to my ship?"

"Mine as well," Purslane said.

Burdock waited a moment. "It's done. I'm afraid you'll still have some compatibility issues to deal with."

A coded memory flash—a bee landing on a flower—told me that my ship had just received a transmission from another craft, in an unfamiliar file format. I sent another command to my ship to tell it to start working on the format conversion. I had faith that it would get there in the end: I often set it the task of interpreting Prior languages, just to keep its mental muscles in shape.

"Thank you," I said.

"Make what you will of it. I'm afraid there are many gaps in the sensor data. You'll just have to fill in the holes."

"We'll do what we can," Purslane said. "But if we're to bring anyone to justice, we have to know what this is all about. You must tell us what you've learned of the Great Work."

"I only know parts. I've guessed most of it."

"That's still more than Campion and I know."

"All right," he said, with something like relief. "I'll tell you. But there isn't time to do this the civilised way. Will you give me permission to push imagery into your heads?"

Purslane and I looked at each other uneasily. Rationally, we had nothing to fear: if Burdock had the means to tamper with our heads, he could have already forced hallucinations on us by now, or killed us effortlessly. We willingly opened our memories during each threading, but that was within the solemn parameters of age-old ceremony, when we were all equally vulnerable. We already knew Burdock had lied once. What if the rest of his story was a lie as well? We had no evidence that Grisha was authentic, and not just a figment created by the ship.

"You have to trust me," Burdock pleaded. "There isn't much time left."

"He's right," Purslane said, gripping my hand. "There's a risk, but there's also a risk in doing nothing. We have to do this."

I nodded at Burdock. "Tell us."

"Prepare," he whispered.

An instant later I felt a kind of mental prickle as something touched my brain, groping its way in like an octopus seeking a way into a shell. Purslane tightened her hold, anchoring herself to me. There was a moment of resistance and then the intrusive thing was ensconced.

My sense of being present in the room became attenuated, as if my body was suddenly at the far end of a long thread of nerve fibres, with my brain somewhere else entirely. I didn't know how Burdock was doing it, but I could see at least two possibilities. The air in his ship might have been thick with machines, able to swim into neural spaces and tap into direct mental processes. Or the ship itself might been generating external magnetic fields of great precision, steering the foci into my skull and stimulating microscopic areas of my mind. I was only dimly aware of Grisha and Burdock looking on, half a universe away.

Coldness seized me, electric with the crackle and fizz of sub-atomic radiation. I was somewhere dark beyond imagination. My point of view shifted and something awesome hoed into view. As my disembodied eyes adjusted to the darkness, the thing brightened and grew layers of dizzying detail.

It was a spiral galaxy.

I recognised it instantly as the Milky Way. I had crossed it enough times to know the kinked architecture of its stellar arms and dust lanes, a whorl as familiar and idiosyncratic as a fingerprint. The hundreds of billions of stars formed a blizzard of light, but through some trick of perception I felt that I recognised all the systems I had visited during my travels, as well as all those I had come to know through the shared memories of the Gentian Line. I made out the little yellow sun which we now orbited, and felt both inconsequential and godlike as I imagined myself on a watery world circling that star, a thing tiny beyond measure, yet with an entire galaxy wheeling inside my head.

"You know this place, of course," said Burdock's disembodied voice. "As one facet of Abigail, you've crossed it ten or twelve times;

tasted the air of a few hundred worlds. Enough for one lifetime, perhaps. But that was never enough for Abigail, for us. As Abigail's shattered self, we've crossed it ten thousand times; known a million worlds. We've seen wonder and terror; heaven and hell. We've seen empires and dynasties pass like seasons. And still that isn't enough. We're still monkeys, you know. In terms of the deep structure of our minds, we've barely left the trees. There's always a shinier, juicier piece of fruit just out of reach. We've reached for it across two million years and it's brought to us this place, this moment. And now we reach again. We embark on our grandest scheme to date: the Great Work."

The view of the Milky Way did not change in any perceptible way, but I was suddenly aware of human traffic crossing between the stars. Ships much like those of the Gentian Line fanned out from points of reunion, made vast circuits across enormous swathes of the Galaxy, and converged back again two or three hundred thousand years later, ready to merge experiences. Cocooned in relativistic time, the journeys did not seem horrendously long for the pilots: mere years or decades of flight, with the rest of time (which might equal many centuries) spent soaking up planetary experience, harvesting memory and wisdom. But the true picture was of crushing slowness, even though the ships moved at the keen, sharp edge of lightspeed. Interesting star systems were thousands or tens of thousands of years of flight time apart. Planetary time moved much faster than that. Human events outpaced the voyagers, so that what they experienced was only glimpses of history, infuriatingly incomplete. Brief, bittersweet golden ages flourished for a handful of centuries while the ships were still moving between stars. Glories went unrecorded, unremembered.

Something had to be done.

"The lines have been gnawing at the lightspeed problem for half a million years," Burdock said. "It won't crack. It's just the way the universe is. Faced with that, you have two other possibilities. You can reengineer human nature to slow history to a crawl, so that starfarers can keep pace with planetary time. Or you can consider the alternative. You can reengineer the Galaxy itself, to shrink it to a human scale."

In an eye blink of comprehension we understood the Great Work, and why it had been necessary for Grisha's people to die. The Great

Work concerned nothing less than the relocation of entire stars and all the worlds that orbited them.

Moving stars was not actually as difficult as it sounded. The Priors had moved stars around many times, using many different methods. It had even taken place in the human era: demonstration projects designed to boost the prestige of whichever culture or line happened to be sponsoring it. But the Great Work was not about moving one or two stars a few light years, impressive as such a feat undoubtedly was. The Great Work was about the herding of stars in numbers too large to comprehend: the movement of hundreds of millions of stars across distances of tens of thousand of light years. The Advocates dreamed of nothing less than compactifying the Milky Way; taking nature's work and remaking it into something more useful for human occupation. For quick-witted monkeys, it was no different than clearing a forest, or draining a swamp.

Burdock told us that the Advocates had been covertly resurrecting Prior methods of stellar engineering, contesting them against each other to find the most efficient processes. The methods that worked best seemed to be those that employed some of the star's own fusion power as the prime mover. They used mirrors to direct the star's energy output in a single direction, in the manner of a rocket motor. If the star's acceleration were sufficiently gentle, it would carry its entire family of worlds and rubble and dust with it.

Of all the Prior methods tested so far, none were able to accelerate a sunlike star to anything faster that one percent of the speed of light. This was laughably slow compared to our oldest ships, but it didn't matter to the Advocates. Even if it took two or three more million years to move all their target stars, this was still a price worth paying. Everything that had happened to date, they liked to say, was just a *prologue to history*. Real human affairs would not begin in earnest until the last star was dropped into its designed Galactic orbit. Set against the billions of years ahead of us (before the Galaxy itself began to wither, or suffered a damaging encounter with Andromeda) what was a mere handful of millions of years?

It was like delaying a great voyage by a few hours.

When they were done, the Galaxy would look very different. All life-bearing stars (cool and long-lived suns, for the most part) would have been shunted much closer to the core, until they fell within a volume only five thousand light years across. Superhot blue stars—primed to explode as supernovae in mere millions of years—would be prematurely triggered, or shoved out of harm's way. Unstable binaries would be dismantled like delicate time bombs. The unwieldy clockwork of the central black hole would be tamed and harnessed for human consumption. Stars that were already on the point of falling into the central engine would be mined for raw materials. New worlds would be forged, vast as stars themselves: the golden palaces and senates of this new galactic empire. With a light-crossing time of only fifty centuries, something like an empire was indeed possible. History would no longer outpace starfarers like Purslane and I. If we learned of something magical on the other side of human space, there would be every hope that it would still be there when we arrived. And most of humanity would be packed into a light-crossing time much less than fifty centuries.

This was the Great Work. It was the culminative project of two million years of human advancement: the enterprise that would tax the ingenuity and resourcefulness of the most powerful lines. Where the lines squabbled now, they would come together in peaceful cooperation. And at the end of it (if any of us lived that long), we would have something wonderful to show for it. It would be the ultimate human achievement, a spectacle of engineering visible across cosmological distance. A beacon to our bright monkey cleverness.

It could not be allowed to happen.

That was the message Grisha's people had uncovered, in their archaeological enquiries into their planet's Prior culture. It transpired that the Watchers had witnessed something like the Great Work once already, in the distant spiral galaxy that they had been monitoring. Perhaps it was a kind of recurrent pathology, destined to afflict civilisations once they reached a certain evolutionary state. They grew weary of the scale of their galaxy and sought to shrink it.

In doing so they created the preconditions for their own extinction. Where once they had moved too slowly to threaten more than a handful of neighbouring systems, the compactification allowed war and disease to spread like wildfire. The inhuman scale of the colonised Galaxy was its strength as well as its weakness: time and distance were buffers against catastrophe. Spread out across tens of thousands of light years, we were immune to extinction, at least by our own hands.

Compactified, death could touch us all in less than five thousand years.

"The Advocates knew this, I think," Burdock said. "But they considered it to be a theoretical problem they would deal with when the time came. Surely, they rationalised, we would be wise enough to avoid such foolishness. But then they learned of the discovery made by the Watchers, and rediscovered by Grisha's people. Another spiral culture that had gone down the same path—and ended up extinct; wiped out in a cosmological instant. Perhaps the fate was not so avoidable after all, no matter how wise you became. By rights, they should have viewed this data as an awful warning, and acted accordingly: abandoning the Great Work before a single star had moved an inch."

But it was never going to happen like that. The lines had already invested too much of themselves in the future success of the Work. Alliances had already been forged; hierarchies of influence and responsibility agreed upon. To back down now would involve crushing loss of face to the senior lines. Old wounds would be reopened; old rivalries would simmer to the fore. If the Great Work was the project that would bind the lines, its abandonment could very easily push some of them to war. That was why Grisha's people had to be silenced, even if it meant their genocide. For what was the loss of one culture, against something so huge? If we were still living in the prologue to history, they would be doing well to merit a footnote.

The vision ended then, and I felt my mind being sucked back to the body I had left (and nearly forgotten) aboard Burdock's ship. There was a moment of unpleasant confinement, as if I was a being squeezed into a too-small bottle, and then I was back, still holding hands with Purslane, the two of us reeling as our inner ears adjusted to the return of gravity.

Grisha stood by the couch, his gun still in his hand. "Did you learn all that you needed to know?" he asked.

"I think so," I started to say.

"Good," he said. "Because Burdock's dead. He gave you the last minute of his life."

Purslane and I returned to the island as the sky lightened in anticipation of dawn. It was still midnight blue overhead, but the horizon was tinged with the softest tangerine orange, cut through by ribbons of cloud. As the box wheeled through the thicket of hanging ships toward the island, I began to see the crests of waves, stippled in brightening gold.

I had seen many dawns, but in all my travels I had never tired of them. Even now, with the weight of all that had happened and all that we had learned, some part of me stood aside from the moment to acknowledge the simple beauty of sunrise on another world. I wondered what Burdock would have made of it. Would it have touched him with the same alchemical force, bypassing the rational mind to speak to that animal part from which we were separated by only an evolutionary heartbeat? Perhaps I'd find a clue in all the strands Burdock had submitted during his time among us. Now there would be no more.

A death among the line was a terrible and rare thing. When it happened, one of us would be tasked to create a suitable memorial somewhere out in the stars. Such a memorial could take many forms. Long ago, the death of one of our number had been commemorated by the seeding of ferrite dust into the atmosphere of a dying star, just before the star expelled its outer envelope to create a nebula in the shape of a human head, sketched in lacy curves of blue green oxygen and red hydrogen, racing outward at sixty kilometres a second. Another memorial, no less heartfelt, had taken the form of a single stone kiln on an airless moon. Both had been appropriate.

Burdock would surely receive his due, but his death had to remain a secret until Thousandth Night. Until then Purslane and I would have to walk among our fellow line members with that knowledge in our hearts, and not betray the slightest hint of it.

We owed it to Burdock.

"We're in time," I said, as the box neared the island. "That took longer than I'd hoped, but the threading is still taking place. No one will have missed us yet."

Purslane pressed a hand to her brow. "God, the threading. I'd forgotten all about that. Now I'll have to spend all day telling lies. Please tell me this was a good idea, Campion."

"Wasn't it? We know what happened to Burdock now. We know about Grisha and the Great Work. *Of course* it was worth it."

"Are you so sure? All we know now is that asking questions could get us into serious trouble. We're still none the wiser about who's actually behind this. I'm not sure I wasn't happier in blissful ignorance."

"We have the data from Burdock's ship," I reminded her.

"Have you looked at it yet, Campion?" I could tell from her tone that she wasn't impressed. "My ship's already sent me back a preliminary analysis. Burdock's data is riddled with gaps."

"He warned us there were a few holes."

"What he didn't say was that thirty percent of his records were missing. There may be something useful in the remaining data, but there's still a good chance that the clues fell into the gaps."

"Why the gaps in the first place? Do you think he edited out something he didn't want us to see?"

Purslane shook her head. "Don't think so. The gaps seem to be caused by his anticollision screens going up, blinding his sensors. You saw how old that ship was: it probably has pretty ancient screen generators, or pretty ancient sensors, or both."

"Why the anticollision screens?"

"Debris," Purslane said. "Grisha's system had been turned into a cloud of radioactive rubble. Burdock's approach never took him all that close to the main action, but there must still have been a lot of debris flying around. If he'd thought to turn up his triggering threshold, he might have given us more to work with . . ."

I tried to sound optimistic. "We'll just to have make the best of what's left."

"My ship's already made the obvious checks. I've seen the flame Burdock mentioned, but it really is too faint for an accurate match. If the murderers were hanging around the system before then, they must have been very well camouflaged."

"We can't just . . . give up," I said, thinking of the man we had left behind on Burdock's ship. "We owe it to Burdock, and Grisha, and Grisha's people."

"If there's nothing there, there's nothing there," Purslane said.

She was right. But it wasn't what I wanted to hear.

We landed on the island and reset our body clocks so that—to first approximation—we looked and felt as if we had just passed a restful, dream-filled night. That was the idea, at least. But when I conjured a mirror and examined my face in it I saw a quivering, tic-like tightness around the mouth. I tried a kinesic reset but it didn't go away. When Purslane and I met alone on one of the high balconies, after breakfasting with a few other line members, I swear I saw the same tightness.

"How did it go?" I asked.

She kept her voice low. "It was as bad as I feared. They thought my strand was *wonderful, darling*. They won't stop asking me about it. They hate me."

"That's sort of the reaction we were hoping for. The one thing no one will be wondering about is what you were up to last night. And we can be sure no one ducked out of the strand."

"What about Burdock's impostor? We didn't know about him when we hatched this plan."

"He still had to act like Burdock," I said. "That means he'll have needed to dream your strand."

"I hope you're right."

"You only have to get through this one day. It's Squill's strand tonight. He always gives good dream."

Purslane looked at me pityingly. "Keep up, Campion. Squill's been off-form for half a million years."

Unfortunately, she was right about Squill. His strand consisted of endless visits to planets and artefacts left over from the Interstitial Uprising, overlaid with tedious, self-serving monologues of historical analysis. It was not the hit of the reunion, and it did little to take the heat off Purslane. The next night wasn't much better: Mullein's strand was a workmanlike trudge through thirty cultures that had collapsed back to pre-industrial feudalism. "Mud," I heard someone say dispiritedly, the day after. "Lots of . . . mud."

The third night was a washout as well. That was when Asphodel would have delivered her strand, had she made it back to the reunion. As was our custom, her contribution took the form of a compilation from her previous strands. It was all very worthy, but not enough to stop people talking about Purslane's exploits.

Thankfully, things picked up for her on the fourth night. Borage's strand detailed his heroic exploits in rescuing an entire planet's worth of people following the close approach of a star to their Oort cloud. Borage dropped replicators on their nearest moon and converted part of it into a toroidal defence screen, shielding their planet from the infall of dislodged comets. Then he put the moon back together again and (this was a touch of genius, we had to admit) he *wrote his signature* on the back of the tide-locked moon in a chain of craters. It was flashy, completely contrary to any number of Line strictures, but it got people talking about Borage, not Purslane.

I could have kissed the egomaniacal bastard.

"I think we got away with that one," I told Purslane, when she was finally able to move through the island without being pestered by an entourage of hangers-on.

"Good," she said. "But that doesn't mean we're any closer to finding out who killed Grisha's people."

"Actually," I said, "I've been thinking about that. Maybe there's something in that data after all."

"We've been through it with a fine-toothed comb."

"But looking for the obvious signatures," I said.

"There are too many gaps."

"But maybe the gaps are telling us something. What caused the gaps?"

"Burdock being too cautious, throwing up his screens every time a speck of dust came within a light-second of his ship. His screens are sensor-opaque, at least in all the useful bands."

"Correct. But some of those activations were probably necessary: there *was* a lot of rubble, after all."

"Go on," she said.

"Well, if there was a lot of debris that far out, there must have been even more closer to the action. Enough to trigger the screens of the other ship."

"I hadn't thought of that."

"Me neither, until now. And the type of search we've been doing wouldn't have picked up screen signatures. We need to slice the data up into short time windows and filter on narrow-band graviton pulses. *Then* we might find something."

"I'm already on it," Purslane said.

I closed my eyes and directed a command at my own ship. "Me too. Want to take a bet on who finds something first?"

"No point, Campion. I'd thrash you."

She did, too. Her ship found something almost immediately, now that it had been given the right search criteria. "It's still at the limits of detection," she said. "They must have had their screens tuned right down, for just this reason. But they couldn't run with them turned off."

"Is this enough to narrow it down?"

"Enough to improve matters. The resonant frequency of the graviton pulse is at the low end: that means whoever's doing this was throwing up a big screen."

Like blowing a low note in a big bottle, rather than a high note in a small bottle.

"Meaning big ship," I said.

"I'm guessing fifty or sixty kilometres at the minimum." She looked at the parade of hanging ships. "That already narrows it down to less than a hundred."

My ship pushed a memory into my head: a girl seated in the lotus position, with a golden, glowing cube rotating above her cupped palms. It meant that the ship had a result.

"Mine's in," I said, requesting a full summary. "My ship says seventy kilometres at the low end, with a central estimate around ninety. See: slow, but she gets there in the end."

"My ship's refined its analysis and come to more or less the same conclusion," Purslane said. "That narrows it down even more. We're talking about maybe twenty ships."

"Still not good enough," I said ruefully. "We can't point fingers unless we have a better idea than that."

"Agreed. But we have the drive flame as an additional constraint. Not all of those twenty ships even use visible thrust. And we also know who Burdock spoke to about the Great Work."

I paused and let those numbers crunch against each other. "Better. Now we're down to . . . what? Seven or eight ships, depending on where you draw the cut-off for the size estimate. Seven or eight names. One of which happens to be Fescue."

"Still not good enough, though."

I thought for a moment. "If we could narrow it down to one ship . . . then we'd be sure, wouldn't we?"

"That's the problem, Campion. We can't narrow it down. Not unless we saw what those anticollision fields looked like."

"Exactly," I said. "If we could get them to put up their screens . . . all we'd need to do is find the ship with the closest resonance to the one in Grisha's system."

"Wherever you're taking this line of thought . . ." Purslane's eyes flashed a warning at me.

"All I need to do is find a way to get them to trigger their shields. Full ship screens, of course."

"It won't work. If they get an inkling of what you're up to, they'll tune to a different resonance."

"Then I'd better not give them much warning," I said. "We'll do it on Thousandth Night, just the way we said we would. They'll be too distracted to plan anything in advance, and they won't be expecting a last-minute surprise."

"I like the way you say 'we'."

"We're in this together now," I said. "All the way. Even if we take the line with us."

Purslane sniffed her wineglass. "How are you going to get everyone to turn on their shields?"

I squinted against the sun. "I'm sure I'll think of something."

Because I was dreading its arrival, Thousandth Night was suddenly upon us. Since Purslane's discovery that Burdock had lied, the reunion had passed by in a blur. For nine hundred and ninety-nine nights we had dreamed of suns and worlds, miracles and wonders, and perhaps a little mud along the way. Our knowledge of the galaxy we called home had accreted yet another layer of detail, even as the endless transformations of history rendered much of that knowledge obsolete. For most of us, it was of no concern. The innate fascination of the strands, the spectacle, intrigue, and glamour of this final evening together was all that mattered. Not the Advocates, though. Though they did their best to hide it, they itched with impatience. For two million years, they had accepted the crushing scale of the galaxy and their own fixed relationship to that immensity. When Abigail Gentian shattered herself into nine hundred and ninety-nine gemlike pieces, she had hoped to conquer space and time. Instead, she had only come to a deeper understanding of her own microscopic insignificance. The Advocates could not tolerate that any longer.

I kept a stiff, strained smile on my face as I made my rounds of the Thousandth Night revellers, accepting compliments. Although my strand had not set the world on fire, no one had any serious complaints about the venue. The island was just the right size: small enough to feel intimate, but with enough curious little byways and quirks of design not to become boring. Every now and then I had introduced some minor change—moving a passage here, or a staircase there, and my efforts were generally deemed to have been worthwhile. The white terraces, balconies and bridges of the island had a charm of their own, but they had not detracted from the strands, and the threadings had gone flawlessly. Time and again, people squeezed my sleeve and asked me what I had lined up for the final night, and time and again, I confessed that I couldn't even be sure that I *had* lined anything up at all.

Of course, I knew I must have planned something.

Evening turned to night. Floating paper lanterns glowed in the warm air, casting lozenges of pastel colour on the revellers. As was Gentian custom, everyone wore a costume that, subtly or otherwise, reflected the content of their dream. We wore carnival masks, the game being to match the dreamer to the dream before the masks were ripped away. I wore a moon mask and a simple outfit patterned in sunset shades, with a repeating motif of half-swallowed suns. Purslane wore a fox mask and a harlequin costume, in which each square detailed one of her legendary adventures. It didn't take very long for people to work out who she was. Once again, she was tormented by questions about the false strand, but she only had to keep up the pretence for a few more hours. Soon our deception would be revealed, and we would beg forgiveness for weaving a lie.

"Look," I heard someone say, pointing to the zenith. "A shooting star!"

I looked up sharply enough to catch the etched trail before it faded from sight. A shooting star, I thought: a good omen, perhaps. Except I didn't believe in omens, especially not when they were signified by pieces of cosmic grit slamming into our planet's atmosphere.

Purslane sidled up to me a few minutes later. "Are you sure you want to go through with this?"

"Yes. In less than a day, every ship you see here will be on its way out of the system. We do it now or we forget about it forever."

"Maybe that would be easier."

"Easier, yes. The right thing—no."

Another shooting star slashed the sky.

"I agree," she said.

Upon midnight, the revellers assembled on a high balcony flung out from the side of the main tower on an arm of curved ivory. They had all cast their votes and my system had tallied the winning strand. Shortly it would push the information into my head, and I would deliver the much-anticipated announcement. One of us would leave the system heady with the knowledge their dream had moved us like no other, and that they had been honoured with the design of the next venue. Whoever it was, I wished them well. As I had discovered, the praise burned off very quickly, and what was left was a dark, ominous clinker of responsibility.

I looked down on the assembled gathering from a much higher balcony, watching the masked and costumed figures slow in their orbits. The atmosphere of the revellers became perceptibly tense, as my announcement drew nearer. There was a palpable sadness amongst all the gaiety. Friendships made here must be put on hold until the next reunion, two hundred thousand years in the future. Time and space would change some of us. We would not all be the same people, and not all of those friendships would endure.

It was time.

I stepped from the side of my balcony, into open space. There was a collective gasp from the revellers, even though no one seriously expected me to come to harm. As my left foot pushed down into thin air, a sheet of white marble whisked under it to provide support. As my right foot stepped below my left, another sheet whisked under that one. I took weight from my left foot and stepped down again, and the first sheet curved back under me to meet my falling foot. Stepping between these two sheets, I walked calmly down to the lower balcony. The effect was everything I could have wished for, and I tried to look as quietly pleased with myself as I ought to have been.

But not all the eyes were upon me. Masked and unmasked faces were caught by something above. I followed their gaze to see another slashing shooting star, and then another. In quick succession, six more cut the sky from zenith to horizon. Then more. A dozen in the first minute, and then two dozen in the second. I smiled, realising that this must be the surprise I had arranged for Thousandth Night. A meteor shower!

Easily done, I thought. All I would have needed to do is shove a comet onto the right orbit, shatter it and let its dusty tail intersect the orbit of my planet at the right point in space and time . . . here, to-night. Now that I thought of that, there was a twinge of familiarity about it . . . the memory of doing so not completely erased.

By the standards of some, it was very low-key, and for a moment I wondered if I had misjudged the effect . . . but just as I was begin-ning to worry about that, people started clapping. It was polite at first, but soon it built in enthusiasm, even as the stars quickened their dis-play, flashing overhead too quickly to count.

They liked it.

"Bravo, Campion!" I heard someone say. "Tasteful restraint . . . beautifully simple!"

I stepped onto a low plinth, so that I was head and shoulders above the crowd. I forced a smile and waved down the applause. "Thank you everyone," I said. "I'm glad things have gone so well. If this reunion has been a success, it has far more to do with the people than the venue." I looked over my shoulder, at the central spire rising behind me. "Al-though the venue isn't half bad, is it?" They laughed and applauded, and I smiled again, hoping I looked and sounded genuine. It was hard, but it was vital that no one suspect I had anything else up my sleeve.

"Every strand is to be treasured," I said, injecting a note of solem-nity into my voice. "Every experience, every memory, is sacred. On this Thousandth Night, we gather to select one strand in particular that has touched us more than others. That is our custom. But in doing so, we do not denigrate any other strands. In the totality of experience, they are all equally vital, and all equally cherished." I singled out Mullein, and smiled sympathetically. "Even the ones with an unusu-ally high mud content."

Mullein laughed good-naturedly, and, for a moment, he was the star of the show again. The gentle mocking of one of our number was also part of tradition. Of all us, Mullein could relax now.

"In a little while, we will return to our ships," I continued. "We will travel back out into the Galaxy and seek new experiences; new strands to be woven into the greater tapestry of the Gentian collective memory. None of us will leave here the same person he or she was a thousand days ago, and when we return, we will have changed again. That is part of the wonder of what Abigail made of herself. Other Lines favour rigid regimentation: a thousand identical clones, each programmed to respond to the same stimulus in exactly the same way. You might as well send out robots. That wasn't how Abigail wanted to do things. She wanted to gorge on reality. She wanted to feed her face with it, drunk on curiosity. In our bickering diversity, we honour that impulse." I paused and laced my hands, nodding at the nearest faces. "And now the time has come. The system has informed me of the winner . . . the name I am about to reveal." I pulled a face that suggested amused surprise. "The name is . . ."

And then I paused again, and frowned. The crowd tensed.

"Wait a moment," I said. "I'm sorry, but . . . something's wrong. I'm receiving an emergency message from my ship." I raised my voice over the people who had started talking. "This is . . . unfortunate. My ship has a technical problem with drive containment. There's a small but non-negligible risk of detonation." I tried to sound panicked, but still in some kind of control. "Please, remain calm. I'm ordering my ship to move to a safe distance . . ." I looked over the heads, beyond the island to the forest of parked ships, and counted to five in my head. "No response . . . I'm trying again, but . . ." The heads started moving, their voices threatening to drown me out. "Still no response," I said, tightening my face to a grimace. "I don't seem to be able to get a command through." I raised my voice, until I was almost shouting. "We're safe here: in a few seconds, I'll screen the island. Before I do that, I recommend that you order your ships to protect themselves."

Some of them already had. Their ships trembled within the vague, wobbling shapes of anticollision screens, like insects in spit. After a few seconds, the screens locked into stable forms and became harder to see. I allowed myself a glance in Purslane's direction. She responded with the tiniest encouraging nod.

It was working.

"Please," I urged. "Hurry. I'll raise the island's own screen in ten seconds. You may not be able to get a message through once that happens."

More and more ships wobbled as their screens flicked on. Peals of thunder, distant and low, signalled the activations. Doubtless many of the people were wondering what was going on: how it just happened that it was my ship that was threatening to blow up, when I was already the centre of attention. I just hoped that they would have the sense to put up their screens first and worry about the coincidence later.

But some of the largest ships were still not screened. I could not delay the screening of the island any longer. I would just have to hope that the necessary commands had already been sent, and that those ships were just a bit slow to respond.

But even as the island's own screen flickered on—blurring the view all around us, as if smeared glass had dropped into place—I knew that my plan was coming adrift.

Fescue spoke, his deep voice commanding instant attention. "The danger is passed," he said. "My own ship has projected a secondary screen around yours, Campion. You may lower the island's shield."

My answer caught in my throat. "My ship may blow at any moment. Are you sure that secondary screen is going to be good enough?"

"Yes," Fescue said, with withering authority. "I'm more than sure."

The gathered revellers looked out to my ship, which remained stubbornly intact within the envelope Fescue had projected around it.

"Lower the island screen, Campion." And even as he spoke, Fescue's ship pushed mine up and away, into the high atmosphere, until it was lost among the stars.

The meteor shower was over, I noticed.

"The screen," Fescue said.

I gave the necessary commands, lowering the screen. "Thank you," I said, breathless and distraught. "That was . . . quick thinking, Fescue."

"It must have been a false alarm after all," he said, his unmasked eyes piercing mine. "Or a mistake."

"I thought my ship was going to blow up."

"Of course you did. Why else would you have told us?" He made a growl-like sound. "You were about to announce the winner, Campion. Perhaps you ought to continue."

There was a murmur of approval. If I'd had the sympathy of the crowd five minutes ago, I had lost it completely now. My throat was dry. I saw Purslane, the fox mask tugged down, and something like horror on her face.

"Campion," Fescue pushed. "The winner . . . if it isn't too much trouble."

But I didn't know the winner. The system wasn't due to inform me for another hour. I had delayed my receipt of the announcement, not wishing to be distracted from the main business.

"I . . . the winner. Yes. The winner of the strand . . . the best strand winner . . . is . . . the winner. And the winner is . . ." I fell silent for ten or twenty seconds, frozen in the gaze of nearly a thousand mortified onlookers. Then my thoughts suddenly quietened, as if I'd found an epicentre of mental calm. I seemed to stand outside myself.

"There is no winner," I said softly. "Not yet."

"Perhaps you ought to stand down," Fescue said. "You've arranged a fine reunion; we all agree on that. It would be a shame to ruin it now."

Fescue took a step toward me, presumably intending to help me from the plinth.

"Wait," I said, with all the dignity I could muster. "Wait and hear me out. All of you."

"You have an explanation for this travesty?" Fescue asked.

"Yes," I said. "I do."

He stopped in his tracks and folded his arms. "Then let's hear it. Part of me would love to think that this is all part of your Thousandth Night plans, Campion."

"Something awful has happened," I said. "There has been a conspiracy . . . a murder. One of us has been killed."

Fescue cocked his head. "One of us?"

I scanned the crowd and pointed to Burdock's duplicate. "That's not Burdock," I said. "That's an impostor. The real Burdock is dead."

The duplicate Burdock pulled a startled face. He looked at the people surrounding him, and then back at me, aghast. He said something and the onlookers laughed.

"The real Burdock is dead?" Fescue asked. "Are you quite sure of this, Campion?"

"Yes. I know because I've seen his body. When we broke into his ship . . ."

"When 'we' broke into his ship," Fescue repeated, silencing me. "You mean there was someone else involved?"

Purslane's voice rang out clear and true. "It was me. Campion and I broke into the ship. Everything he's told you is the truth. Burdock was murdered by proponents of the Great Work, because Burdock knew what they had done."

Fescue looked intrigued. "Which was?"

"They destroyed an entire culture . . . Grisha's people . . . a culture that had uncovered Prior data damaging to the Great Work. Wiped them out with Homunculus weapons. Burdock tried to cover up his discovery, for fear of what the Advocates would do to him. There was a discrepancy in Burdock's dreams . . . an error." Purslane's control began to falter. "He said he'd been somewhere he hadn't . . . somewhere Campion had been."

"So it was Burdock's word against Campion?" Fescue turned to the impostor. "Does this make the slightest sense to you?"

The impostor shrugged and looked at me with something between pity and spite.

"Hear us out," Purslane insisted. "All Campion was hoping to do was provoke the raising of anticollision shields. The ship that destroyed Grisha's people . . . we had data on its field resonance, but we needed to see our own fields before we could establish a match." Purslane swallowed and regained some measure of calm. "I'm broadcasting the resonance data to all ships. See it for yourselves. See what those bastards did to Grisha's people."

There was a moment, a lull, while the crowd assessed the data Purslane had just made public. She had taken a frightful risk in revealing the information, for now our enemies had every incentive to move against us, even if that meant killing everyone else on the island. But I agreed with what she had done. We were out of options.

Except one.

"Very impressive," Fescue admitted. "But we've no evidence that you didn't forge this data."

"The authentication stamp ties it to Burdock," Purslane said.

Fescue looked regretful. "Authentication can always be faked, with sufficient ingenuity. You've already admitted that you broke into his ship, after all. Disavow your involvement in this, Purslane, before it's too late."

"No," she said. "I won't."

Fescue nodded at a number of the people around him, including a handful of senior Advocates.

"Restrain the two of them," he said.

I fingered the metal shape under my flame-coloured costume. My hand closed on the haft and removed Grisha's particle gun. The crowd silenced as the evil little thing glinted in the lantern light. Earlier, un-witnessed, I had primed the weapon onto Burdock. I squeezed a jew-elled button and the gun moved as if in an invisible grip, nearly dragging itself from my fist. It swivelled onto Burdock and locked steady as a snake. Even if I released my hold on the gun, it would keep tracking its designated target.

"Stand aside, please," I said.

"Don't do anything silly," Fescue said, even as the crowd parted around Burdock's impostor.

The moment closed around me like a vice. I had seen the real, dy-ing Burdock aboard his ship—at least, I believed I had. When I squeezed the trigger, I would be killing a mindless automaton, a bio-mechanical construct programmed to duplicate Burdock's responses with a high degree of accuracy . . . but not a living thing. Nothing with a sense of self.

But what if the dying figure on the ship was the impostor, and this was still the real Burdock? What if the whole story about Grisha and the assassination agent had been the lie, and the real Burdock was standing in front of me? I had no idea why such an elaborate charade might have been staged . . . but I couldn't rule it out, either. And there was one possibility that sprang to mind. What if Burdock had enemies among the line, and they wanted him dead, with someone else to pin the blame on? Suddenly I felt dizzy, lost in mazelike permutations of bluff and double bluff. I had to make a simple choice. I had to trust my intuitive sense of what was true and what was false.

"If this is a mistake," I said, "forgive me."

I squeezed the trigger. The particle beam sliced its way across space, piercing the figure in the chest.

Burdock's impostor touched a hand to the smoking wound, opened its mouth as it speak, and fell lifeless to the floor. The crowd screamed their horror, revolted at the idea that a member of the Gentian Line had murdered another.

My work done, I let go of the particle gun. It remained floating before me, as if inviting me to take another shot. Burdock's impostor lay on its side, with one dry hand open to the sky. He had touched the wound and there had been no blood. I allowed myself a moment of relief. The others would see that the thing I had killed was not a man, but a bloodless construct. But even as these thoughts formed, the body retched and coughed a mouthful of dark blood onto the perfect white marble of the terrace. Its face was a mask of fear and incomprehension. Then it was still.

The crowd surged. They were on me in seconds, swatting aside the gun. They pulled me from the plinth and smothered me to the ground. The breath was knocked out of me. They began to pull at my clothing with animal fury. I heard shouts as some of the revellers tried to pull the others off me, but the collective anger—the collective repulsion—was too great to be resisted. I felt something crack in my chest, tasted my own blood as someone smashed a fist into my jaw. I thrashed out, survival instincts kicking in, but there were too many of them. Most of them were still wearing carnival masks.

Then something happened. Just before I was about to go under, the attack calmed. Someone landed a final punch in my chest, sending a bolt of pain up my spine, and then pulled away. I received a desultory kick, and then they left me there, sprawled on the ground, my mouth wet, my body bruised. I knew they hadn't finished with me. They were just leaving me alone while something else attracted their attention.

In their hundreds, they were pressing against the low railing that encircled the balcony. They were looking out to sea, drawn by some-thing going on beyond the island. I pushed myself to my feet and stumbled to the slumped form of Purslane. They had not hurt her as badly as me, but there was still a cut on her lip where someone had slapped her.

"Are you all right?" I said, my mouth thick with blood.

"Better than you," she said.

"I don't think they're done with us. There's a distraction now . . . maybe we could reach our ships?"

She shook her head and used her finger to wipe blood from my chin. "We started this, Campion. Let's finish it."

"It's Fescue," I said. "He's the one."

We followed the onlookers to the balcony. No one gave us a sec-ond glance, even as we pushed forward to the front. All round us the revellers were looking at the sea. Sleek dark forms were surfacing from the midnight waters, black as night themselves. They lolled and bellied in the waves, pushing great flukes and flippers into the sky, jet-ting white spouts of water from blowholes.

Purslane asked me what was happening.

"I don't know," I said truthfully.

"You planned this, Campion. This has to be something to do with Thousandth Night."

"I know." I winced at the pain in my chest, certain that the mob had broken a rib. "But I don't remember what I planned. I thought the meteor shower was an end to it."

They were everywhere now, surfacing in multitudes. "It's as if they're gathering in readiness for something," Purslane said. "Like the start of a migration."

"To where?"

"You tell me, Campion."

But I didn't have to tell her. It was soon obvious. In ones and twos they started leaving the ocean, rising into the air. Curtains of water drained off their flanks as they parted company with the sea. Ones and twos at first, then whole schools of them, rising into the sky between the hovering cliffs of our ships, as if they were born to fly.

"This is . . . impossible," I said. "They're aquatics. They don't . . . fly."

"Unless you made them that way. Unless you always planned this."

Pink-tinged aurorae flickered around the rising forms, hinting at the fields that allowed them to fly, and which would—I presumed—sustain them when the air thinned out, high above us. Some ghost of a memory now pushed its way into my consciousness. Had I truly engineered these aquatics for flight, equipping them with implanted field generators, and enough animal wisdom to use them? The memory beckoned, and then shrivelled under my attention.

"Maybe," I said.

"Good," Purslane said. "But now the next question: why?"

But we didn't have long to wonder about that. Suddenly the sky was cut in two by a brighter meteor than any we had seen during the earlier display. It boomed, reverberating down to the horizon and left a greenish aftertinge.

Another followed it: brighter now.

As if the meteor had triggered something, the sea erupted with a vast wave of departing aquatics. Thousands of them now, packed into huge and ponderous shoals or flocks, each aggregation moving with its own dim identity. The seas were emptying of life. Another meteor slashed the sky, bringing a temporary daylight to the scene. Over the horizon, an ominous false dawn signalled some terrible impact. Something large had smashed into my world. As more trails of light split the sky, I sensed that it would not be the last.

The island shook beneath our feet. That made no sense at all: there surely hadn't been enough time for shockwaves to reach us yet, but none of us had imagined the vibration. I steadied myself on the handrail.

"What . . ." Purslane began.

The island shook again. That was a cue for the crowd to renew their interest in me, tearing their attention away from the departing aquatics. Purslane squeezed closer to me. I tightened my hold on her, while she redoubled her hold on me.

The crowd advanced.

"Stop," boomed out a voice.

Everyone halted and turned to look at the speaker. It was Fescue, and he was kneeling by the figure I had shot. He had a hand in the wound I had bored through the body, plunged deep to the wrist. Slowly he withdrew his hand, slick to the cuff with blood, but holding something between his fingers, something that wriggled in them like a little silver starfish.

"This wasn't Burdock," he said, standing to his feet, while still holding the obscene, wriggling thing. "It was . . . a thing. Just like Campion and Purslane told us." Fescue turned to look at me, his expression grave and forgiving. "You told the truth."

"Yes," I said, with all the breath I could muster. I realised that I had been wrong about Fescue: utterly, utterly wrong.

"Then it's true," he said. "One of us has committed a crime."

"Burdock's body is still on his ship," I said. "All of this can be proved . . . if you allow us."

The ground shook again. Overhead, the meteor assault had become continuous, and the horizon was aglow with fire. I had no sooner registered this than a small shard slammed out of the sky no more than fifteen kilometres from the island, punching a bright frothing wound into the sea. Sensing danger, the island's screen came on, muting the impact blast to a salty roar. Another trail lanced down fifty kilometres away, raising a huge plume of superheated steam.

The impacts were increasing in severity.

Fescue spoke again. "We've all seen the evidence Purslane submitted. Given the truth about Burdock . . . I believe we should take the rest of the story seriously. Including the part about the murder of an entire culture." He looked at the two of us. "You wanted to see our anticollision fields, I believe."

"That'll tell us who did it," Purslane said.

"I think you may shortly have your wish."

He was right. All around the island, the ships were raising their screens again, as protection against the bombardment. The smaller ships at first, then the larger ones—all the way up to the biggest craft of all, those that were already poking into space. The screens quivered and stabilised, and a hail of minor impacts glittered off them.

"Well," Fescue said, addressing Purslane. "Do you see a match?"

"Yes," she said. "I do."

Fescue nodded grimly. "Would you care to tell us who it is?"

Purslane blinked, paralysed by the enormity of what she had to reveal. I held her hand, willing her to find the strength. "I thought it might be you," she told Fescue. "Your ship matched the size profile . . . and when you ruined Campion's ploy . . ."

"I don't think he meant to," I said.

"No, he didn't," Purslane said. "That's obvious now. And in any case, his ship isn't the best match. Samphire's ship, on the other hand . . ."

As one, the crowd's attention locked onto Samphire. "No," he said. "There's been a mistake."

"Perhaps," Fescue said. "But there is the matter of the weapons Purslane mentioned: the ones used against Grisha's people. You've always had an interest in ancient weapons, Samphire . . . especially the weapons of the Homunculus wars."

Samphire looked astonished. "That was over a million years ago. It's ancient history!"

"But what's a million years to the Gentian Line? You knew where those weapons were to be found, and you probably had more than an inkling of how they worked."

"No," Samphire said. "This is preposterous."

"It may well be," Fescue allowed. "In which case, you'll be allowed all the time you need to make your case, before a jury of your peers. If you are innocent, we'll prove it and ask your forgiveness—just as we did with Betony, all those years ago. If you are guilty, we will prove that instead—and uncover the rest of your collaborators. You've never struck me as the calculating kind, Samphire: I doubt that you put this together without assistance."

A wave of change overcame Samphire: his expression hardening. "You can prove what you like," he said. "It will change nothing."

"That sounds suspiciously like an admission of guilt," Fescue said. "Is it true? Did you really murder an entire culture, just to protect the Great Work?"

Now his expression was full of disdain. There was an authority in his voice I had never heard before. "One culture," Samphire said. "One pebble on the beach, against an ocean of possibility! Do you honestly think they mattered? Do you honestly think we'll remember them, in a billion years?"

Fescue turned to his Advocate friends. "Restrain him."

Three of the Advocates took purposeful steps toward Samphire. But they had only taken three or four paces when Samphire shook his head, more in sorrow than anger, and ripped open his tunic, exposing his smooth and hairless chest to the waist. He plunged his fingers into his own skin and pulled it aside like two theatrical curtains, showing no pain. Instead of muscle and bone, we saw only an oozing clockwork of translucent pink machines, layered around a glowing blue core.

"Homunculus machinery," Fescue said, with an awesome calm. "He's a weapon."

Samphire smiled. A white light curdled in his open chest. It brightened to hellfire, ramming from his mouth and eyes. The construct body writhed as the detonating weapon consumed its nervous system from within. The outer layers crisped and collapsed.

But something was containing the blast. The white light—almost too bright to look at now—could not escape. It was being held back by a man-sized containment bubble, locked around Samphire.

I looked at Fescue. He stood with his arms outstretched, like a sculptor visualising a composition. Thick metal jewellery glinted on his fingers. Not jewellery, I realised now, but miniature field generators. Fescue was holding the containment bubble around Samphire, preventing the blast from escaping and destroying us all. His face was etched with the strain of controlling the generators.

"I'm not sure of the yield," Fescue said to me, forcing each word out. "Sub-kilotonne range, I think, or else your systems would have detected the homunculus machinery. But it will still be enough to destroy this balcony. Can the island lock a screen around him?"

"No," I said. "I never allowed for . . . this."

"That's as I thought. I can't hold it much longer . . . twenty-five, thirty seconds." Fescue's eyes bored into me with iron determination. "You have complete control of the structure, Campion? You can reshape it according to your requirements?"

"Yes," I said, faltering.

"Then you must drop the two of us through the floor."

They were standing only a few metres apart. It would only cost me a moment's concentration to order that part of the floor to detach itself, falling free. But if I did that, I would be sending Fescue to his death.

"Do it!" he hissed.

"I can't," I said.

"Campion," he said. "I know you and I have had our differences. I have always criticised you for lacking spine. Well, now is your chance to prove me wrong. *Do this.*"

"I . . ."

"Do it! For the sake of the line!"

I looked at the faces of the other line members. I saw their pain, but also their solemn consent. They were telling me that I had no choice. They were telling me to kill Fescue, and save us all.

I did it.

I willed the floor around the two figures to detach itself from the rest of the balcony. The tiny machines forming the fabric of the floor followed my will with dumb obedience, severing the molecular bonds that linked each machine to its neighbour.

For a heart-rending moment, the floor seemed to hover in place.

The field around Samphire quivered, beginning to lose integrity. Fescue's generators were running out of power, Fescue running out of concentration . . .

He looked at me and nodded. "Good work, Campion."

Then they dropped.

It was a long way down, and they were still falling when the revellers surged to the edge of the balcony to look down. The light from the explosion momentarily eclipsed the brightest impacts still raining down on the planet. I nodded at Fescue's assessment: kilotonne range, easily. He had been right. It would have killed us all, and snapped the spire in two had the balcony not been flung so far out in space. It had been an accidental whim of design, but it had saved us all.

So had Fescue.

There was a great space battle that night, but this time it was for real, not staged in memory of some ancient, time-fogged conflict. The real Samphire had been on his ship, and when the construct failed to destroy the island, he made a run for orbit. From orbit, he must have planned to turn the ship's own armaments on Reunion. But Fescue's allies had anticipated him, and when his ship moved, so did a dozen others. They made interception above the lacerated atmosphere of my dying world and lit the sky with obscene energies. Samphire died, or at least that version of Samphire that had been sent to infiltrate our gathering. It may or may not have been the final one. It may or may not have been the only impostor in our midst.

After the battle, Vetchling, one of the other Advocates, took me aside and told me what she knew.

"Fescue supported the Great Work," she said. "But not at any cost. When evidence reached him that an atrocity had been committed in the name of the Work . . . the murder of an entire human culture . . . he realised that not all of us shared his view."

"Then Fescue knew all along," I said, dismayed.

"No. He had shards of intelligence—hints, rumours, whisperings. He still had no idea who had committed the crime; how deeply they were tied to Gentian Line. He did not know whether the rest of the Advocates could be trusted." She paused. "He trusted me, and a handful of others. But not everyone."

"But Fescue spoke to me about the Great Work," I said. "Of how we all had to bind together to bring it into being."

"He believed it would be for the best. But more than likely he was sounding you out, seeing what you thought of it, goading you into an indiscretion." Vetchling looked to the simmering sea, punctured by hundreds of volcanic vents that had reopened in the planet's crust. We were looking down on the sea from a dizzy height now: the island had detached itself from Reunion, and was now climbing slowly into space, pushed by the vast motors I must have installed in its foundation rocks. The blast from Samphire's weapon had shattered the outlying islands, crumbling them back into the sea. The water had rushed into the fill the caldera left after the main island's departure, and now there was no trace that it had ever existed.

The party was over.

"He suspected Advocate involvement in the crime," Vetchling continued. "But he could not rule out someone else being implicated: a sleeper, an agent no one would suspect."

"He must have suspected Purslane and I," I said.

"That's possible. You did spend a lot of time associating, after all. If it's any consolation, the two of you wouldn't have been his only suspects. He may even have had his suspicions about Samphire."

"What will happen to the Great Work now?"

"That's not just a matter for Gentian Line," Vetchling said. "But my guess is there'll be pressure to put the whole thing on the back burner for a few hundred thousand years. A cooling-off period." She sounded sad. "Fescue was respected. He had a lot of friends beyond our line."

"I hated him," I said.

"He wouldn't have minded. All he really cared about was the line. You did the right thing, Campion."

"I killed him."

"You saved us all. You have Fescue's gratitude."

"How can you know?" I asked.

She touched a finger to her lips. "I know. Isn't that enough for you?"

A little later, Purslane and I stood alone on the highest balcony of the island's central spire. The island had climbed out of what would have been Reunion's atmosphere, had the atmosphere remained.

Far below, viewed through the flickering curtain of the containment bubble, my planet writhed in the agonies of its death by stoning. The impacting asteroids struck her like fists, bludgeoning her in furious quick-time. At least two, sometimes three or four, arrived within every minute. Their impact fireballs had dispersed most of the atmosphere by now, and had elevated a goodly fraction of the crust into parabolas of molten rock, tongues of flame that arced thousands of kilometres before splashing down. They reminded me of the coronal arcs near the surface of a late-type star. The ocean was a memory: boiled into a dust-choked vapour. Concussion from the multiple impacts was already unhinging the delicate clockwork of the planet's magnetohydrodynamic core. Had there been a spot on the planet where it was still night, the auroral storms would have been glorious. For a moment, I regretted that I had not arranged matters so that the aurorae had formed part of the show, somehow, someway.

But it was much too late for second thoughts now. It would be someone else's turn next time.

Purslane took my hand. "Don't look so sad, Campion. You did well. It was a fine end."

"You think so?"

"They'll be raving about this for a million years. What you did with those whales . . ." She shook her head in undisguised admiration.

"I couldn't very well let them stay in the ocean."

"It was lovely. Putting aside everyone else that happened . . . I think that was my favourite bit. Not that this is bad, either."

We paused a while to watch a succession of major impacts: a long, sequenced string of them. Continent-sized fissures were beginning to open up deep into the planet's mantle: wounds as bright as day.

"I created something and now I'm ruining it. Doesn't that strike you as just the tiniest bit . . . infantile? Fescue certainly wouldn't have approved."

"I don't know," she said. "It's not as if that world ever had any chance of outlasting us. It was created to endure for a specific moment in time. Like a sandcastle, or an ice sculpture. Here, and then gone. In a way, that's the beauty of it. Who'd marvel at a sandcastle, if sandcastles lasted forever?"

"Or sunsets, I suppose," I said.

"Oh, no," she said. "Don't start talking about sunsets again. I thought you got that safely out of your system last time."

"I have," I said. "Completely and utterly. I'm thinking of a radically different theme for my tour this time. Something as far removed from sunsets as possible."

"Oh, good."

"Something like . . . waterfalls."

"Waterfalls."

"They're pretty universal, you know. Any planet with some kind of atmosphere, and some kind of surface, usually ends up with something vaguely like a waterfall, somewhere. As long as you're not too fussy about the water part."

"Actually," Purslane said, "I quite like waterfalls. I remember one I encountered in my travels . . . ten vertical kilometres of it, pure methane. I stood under it, allowed myself to feel a little of the cold. Just enough to shiver at the wonder of it."

"It's probably gone now," I said sadly. "They don't last long, compared to us."

"But perhaps you'll find an even better one."

"I'll keep my eyes open. I mapped some promising rivers during my tour; places where the geology might have allowed waterfalls to form by now. I think I'll revisit some of those old places, for old time's sake."

"Bring me back a memory."

"I'll be sure to. It's just such a shame you won't ever see them with your own eyes . . ." I paused, aware that I stood on the thrilling, dangerous threshold of something. "I mean with me, the two of us."

"You know the line frowns upon planned associations," Purslane said, as if I needed to be reminded. "Such meetings erode the very spirit of chance and adventure Abigail sought to instil in us. If we meet between now and the next reunion, it must be by chance and chance alone."

"Then we'll never meet."

"No. Probably not."

"That's a silly rule, isn't it? I mean, given everything else that's happened here . . . why should we care?"

Purslane was a great while answering. "Because we're traditionalists, Campion. Line loyalists, to the marrow." She tightened her grip on the rail as something came streaking up from the molten world below: the last of my aquatics, lingering out of idleness or some instinctive curiosity. The huge field-encased creature was as sleek as night, its under parts highlit in brassy reds from the fires. It paused at the level of the balcony, long enough to scrutinise us with one small, wrinkled, distressingly human eye. Then with a powerful flick of its fluke it soared higher, to the orbital shallows where its fellow were already assembling.

"There is something, though," Purslane added.

"What?"

"I shouldn't even mention it . . . but I've been less than discreet about my flight plan. That trick I used to break into Burdock's ship? It worked equally well with yours."

"What did you do?"

"Nothing harmful. Just installed a copy of my flight plan on your ship . . . for your information. Just so you know where I am."

"You're right," I said, wonderingly. "That was spectacularly indiscreet."

"I couldn't help it."

"It would be completely improper for us to meet."

"Utterly," Purslane agreed, nodding emphatically.

"But you'll stick to that flight plan?"

"To the letter." She had finished her wine. She flung the empty glass into space. I watched it fall, waiting for the glint when it impacted the bubble. But before it hit, Purslane took my arm and turned me away from the view. "Come on, Campion. Let's go inside. They're still all waiting to hear who's won best strand."

"I can't believe anyone still cares about that, after all that's happened."

"Never underestimate the recuperative powers of human vanity," Purslane said sagely. "Besides: it isn't just the strand we have to think about. There are two memorials that need to be created. We'll need one for Burdock, and one for Fescue."

"One day we might need one for Samphire as well," I said.

"I think we'll do our best to forget all about him."

"He won't go away that easily. He may still be alive. Or it may be that he was murdered and replaced with an impostor, just like Burdock. Either way, I have a feeling we haven't finished with him. Or the Great Work."

"We've won this battle, though. That's enough for tonight, isn't it?"

"It'll have to be," I said.

"Something worries me, though," Purslane said. "We still haven't told anyone that my strand wasn't all it appears to be. They'll have to find out one of these days."

"Not tonight, though."

"Campion . . . if my name comes out of the hat . . . *what will I do?*"

I feigned concern, suppressing an amused smile. "Do what I'd do. Keep a very straight face."

"You mean . . . just accept it? That would be a little on the mischievous side, wouldn't it?"

"Very," I said. "But worth it, all the same."

Purslane tightened her grasp on my arm. Together we walked back toward the auditorium where the others waited. Under us, the fires of creation consumed my little world while, far above it, aquatics gathered in squadrons and schools, ready for their long migration.

MISSILE GAP

Charles Stross

Although he made his first sale back in 1987, it's only recently that British writer Charles Stross has begun to make a name for himself as a Writer to Watch in the new century ahead (in fact, as one of the key *Writers to Watch in the Oughts), with a sudden burst in the last few years of quirky, inventive, high-bit-rate stories such as "Antibodies," "A Colder War," "Bear Trap," "Dechlorinating the Moderator," "Toast: A Con Report," and others in markets such as* Interzone, Spectrum SF, Asimov's Science Fiction, Odyssey, Strange Plasma, *and* New Worlds. *Starting in a sequence of frenetic, densely packed stories in what's come to be known as his* Accelerado *series—"Lobsters," "Troubadour," "Tourist," "Halo," "Router," "Nightfall," "Curator," "Elector," and "Survivor," each story taking us a jump further into an acceleratingly strange future, and eventually* through *a Vingian Singularity and out the other side—really cranked up the buzz about him to high volume, as well as getting him on the Hugo Final Ballot several times. Taken together, the* Accelerado *stories represent one of the most dazzling feats of sustained imagination in science fiction history, and radically up the Imagination Ante for every* other *writer who wants to sit down at the Future History table and credibly deal themselves into the game.*

Recently, Stross has become prolific at novel length as well. He'd already "published" a novel online, Scratch Monkey, *available to be read on his Web site (www.*

*antipope.org/charlie/), and saw his first commercially pub-
lished novel,* Singularity Sky, *released in 2003, but he had*
three *novels come out in 2004,* The Iron Sunrise, A Family
Trade, *and* The Atrocity Archive *(formerly serialized in the
British magazine* Spectrum SF*), with another new novel,* The
Clan Corporate, *hard on their heels in early 2005. Coming up
is the long-awaited* Accelerando *novel, and a sequel to* A Family Trade *called* The Hidden Family. *His first collection,* Toast,
and Other Burned-Out Futures, *was released in 2002. He lives
with his wife in Edinburgh, Scotland.*

*In the sly and visionary story that follows, he takes us to a
world where absolutely* nothing *is as it seems, for a story that's*
not *going to go anywhere you* think *it's going to go, we guarantee it!*

BOMB SCARE

Gregor is feeding pigeons down in the park when the sirens go off.

A stoop-shouldered forty-something male in a dark suit, pale-
skinned and thin, he pays no attention at first: the birds hold his attention. He stands at the side of a tarmac path, surrounded by damp
grass that appears to have been sprayed with concrete dust, and digs
into the outer pocket of his raincoat for a final handful of stale bread-
crumbs. Filthy, soot-blackened city pigeons with malformed feet jostle with plump white-collared wood pigeons, pecking and lunging for
morsels. Gregor doesn't smile. What to him is a handful of stale
bread, is a deadly business for the birds: a matter of survival. The
avian struggle for survival runs parallel to the human condition, he
ponders. It's all a matter of limited resources and critical positioning.
Of intervention by agencies beyond their bird-brained understanding, dropping treats for them to fight over. Then the air raid sirens
start up.

The pigeons scatter for the treetops with a clatter of wings. Gregor
straightens and looks round. It's not just one siren, and not just a test:
a policeman is pedaling his bicycle along the path towards him, waving one-handed. "You there! Take cover!"

Gregor turns and presents his identity card. "Where is the nearest shelter?"

The constable points towards a public convenience thirty yards away. "The basement there. If you can't make it inside, you'll have to take cover behind the east wall—if you're caught in the open, just duck and cover in the nearest low spot. Now go!" The cop hops back on his black boneshaker and is off down the footpath before Gregor can frame a reply. Shaking his head, he walks towards the public toilet and goes inside.

It's early spring, a weekday morning, and the toilet attendant seems to be taking the emergency as a personal comment on the cleanliness of his porcelain. He jumps up and down agitatedly as he shoves Gregor down the spiral staircase into the shelter, like a short troll in a blue uniform stocking his larder. "Three minutes!" shouts the troll. "Hold fast in three minutes!" So many people in London are wearing uniforms these days, Gregor reflects; it's almost as if they believe that if they play their wartime role properly the ineffable will constrain itself to their expectations of a humanly comprehensible enemy.

A double-bang splits the air above the park and echoes down the stairwell. It'll be RAF or USAF interceptors outbound from the big fighter base near Hanworth. Gregor glances round: A couple of oafish gardeners sit on the wooden benches inside the concrete tunnel of the shelter, and a louche City type in a suit leans against the wall, irritably fiddling with an unlit cigarette and glaring at the NO SMOKING signs. "Bloody nuisance, eh?" he snarls in Gregor's direction.

Gregor composes his face in a thin smile. "I couldn't possibly comment," he says, his Hungarian accent betraying his status as a refugee. (Another sonic boom rattles the urinals, signaling the passage of yet more fighters.) The louche businessman will be his contact, Goldsmith. He glances at the shelter's counter. Its dial is twirling slowly, signaling the marked absence of radon and fallout. Time to make small-talk, verbal primate grooming: "Does it happen often?"

The corporate tough relaxes. He chuckles to himself. He'll have pegged Gregor as a visitor from stranger shores, the new NATO dominions overseas where they settled the latest wave of refugees ejected by the communists. Taking in the copy of *The Telegraph* and the pattern of stripes on Gregor's tie, he'll have realized what else Gregor is to him. "You should know, you took your time getting down here. Do you come here often to visit the front line, eh?"

· "I am here in this bunker with you," Gregor shrugs. "There is no front line on a circular surface." He sits down on the bench opposite the businessman gingerly. "Cigarette?"

"Don't mind if I do." The businessman borrows Gregor's cigarette case with a flourish: the symbolic peace-offering accepted, they sit in silence for a couple of minutes, waiting to find out if it's the curtain call for world war four, or just a trailer.

A different note drifts down the staircase, the warbling tone that indicates the all-clear these days. The Soviet bombers have turned for home, the ragged lion's stumpy tail tickled yet again. The toilet troll dashes down the staircase and windmills his arms at them: "No smoking in the nuclear bunker!" he screams. "*Get out!* Out, I say!"

Gregor walks back into Regent's Park, to finish disposing of his stale bread-crumbs and ferry the contents of his cigarette case back to the office. The businessman doesn't know it yet, but he's going to be arrested, and his English nationalist/neutralist cabal interned: meanwhile, Gregor is being recalled to Washington, D.C. This is his last visit, at least on this particular assignment. There are thin times ahead for the wood pigeons.

VOYAGE

It's a moonless night and the huge reddened whirlpool of the milky way lies below the horizon. With only the reddish-white pinprick glare of Lucifer for illumination, it's too dark to read a newspaper.

Maddy is old enough to remember a time when night was something else: when darkness stalked the heavens, the milky way a faded tatter spun across half the sky. A time when ominous Soviet spheres bleeped and hummed their way across a horizon that curved, when geometry was dominated by pi, astronomy made sense, and serious men with horn-rimmed glasses and German accents were going to the moon. October 2, 1962: that's when it all changed. That's when life stopped making sense. (Of course it first stopped making sense a few days earlier, with the U-2 flights over the concrete emplacements in Cuba, but there was a difference between the lunacy of brinksmanship—Khrushchev's shoe banging on the table at the UN as he shouted "We will bury you!"—and the flat-earth daydream that followed, shattering history and plunging them all into this nightmare of revisionist geography.)

But back to the here-and-now: she's sitting on the deck of an elderly ocean liner on her way from somewhere to nowhere, and she's annoyed because Bob is getting drunk with the F-deck boys again and eating into their precious grubstake. It's too dark to read the ship's daily news sheet (mimeographed blurry headlines from a world already fading into the ship's wake), it'll be at least two weeks before their next landfall (a refueling depot somewhere in what the National Oceanic and Atmospheric Administration surveyors—in a fit of uncharacteristic wit—named the Nether Ocean), and she's half out of her skull with boredom.

When they signed up for the Emigration Board tickets Bob had joked: "A six-month cruise? After a vacation like that we'll be happy to get back to work!"—but somehow the sheer immensity of it all didn't sink in until the fourth week out of sight of land. In those four weeks they'd crawled an expanse of ocean wider than the Pacific, pausing to refuel twice from huge rust-colored barges: and still they were only a sixth of the way to Continent F-204, New Iowa, immersed like the ultimate non sequitur in the ocean that replaced the world's horizons on October 2, 1962. Two weeks later, they passed The Radiators. The Radiators thrust from the oceanic depths to the stratosphere, Everest-high black fins finger-combing the watery currents. Beyond them the tropical heat of the Pacific gave way to the sub-arctic chill of the Nether Ocean. Sailing between them, the ship was reduced to the proportions of a cockroach crawling along a canyon between skyscrapers. Maddy had taken one look at these guardians of the interplanetary ocean, shuddered, and retreated into their cramped room for the two days it took to sail out from between the slabs.

Bob kept going on about how materials scientists from NOAA and the National Institutes were still trying to understand what they were made of, until Maddy snapped at him. He didn't seem to understand that they were the bars on a prison cell. He seemed to see a waterway as wide as the English Channel, and a gateway to the future: but Maddy saw them as a sign that her old life was over.

If only Bob and her father hadn't argued; or if mum hadn't tried to pick a fight with her over Bob—

Maddy leans on the railing and sighs, and a moment later nearly jumps out of her skin as a strange man clears his throat behind her.

"Excuse me, I didn't mean to disturb you."

"That's alright," Maddy replies, irritated and trying to conceal it. "I was just going in."

"A shame: it's a beautiful night," says the stranger. He turns and puts down a large briefcase next to the railing, fiddling with the latches. "Not a cloud in sight, just right for stargazing." She focuses on him, seeing short hair, small paunch, and a worried thirty-something face. He doesn't look back, being preoccupied with something that resembles a photographer's tripod.

"Is that a telescope?" she asks, eyeing the stubby cylindrical gadget in his case.

"Yes." An awkward pause. "Name's John Martin. Yourself?"

"Maddy Holbright." Something about his diffident manner puts her at ease. "Are you settling? I haven't seen you around."

He straightens up and tightens joints on the tripod's legs, screwing them into place. "I'm not a settler, I'm a researcher. Five years, all expenses paid, to go and explore a new continent." He carefully lifts the telescope body up and lowers it onto the platform, then begins tightening screws. "And I'm supposed to point this thing at the sky and make regular observations. I'm actually an entomologist, but there are so many things to do that they want me to be a jack of all trades, I guess."

"So they've got you to carry a telescope, huh? I don't think I've ever met an entomologist before."

"A bug-hunter with a telescope," he agrees: "kind of unexpected."

Intrigued, Maddy watches as he screws the viewfinder into place then pulls out a notebook and jots something down. "What are you looking at?"

He shrugs. "There's a good view of S-Doradus from here," he says. "You know, Satan? And his two little angels."

Maddy glances up at the violent pinprick of light, then looks away before it can burn her eyes. It's a star, but bright enough to cast shadows from half a light year's distance. "The disks?"

"Them." There's a camera body in his bag, a chunky old Bronica from back before the Soviets swallowed Switzerland and Germany whole. He carefully screws it onto the telescope's viewfinder. "The Institute wants me to take a series of photographs of them—nothing fancy, just the best this eight-inch reflector can do—over six months. Plot the ship's position on a map. There's a bigger telescope in the hold, for when I arrive, and they're talking about sending a real astronomer one of these days, but in the meantime they want photographs from sixty thousand miles out across the disk. For parallax, so they can work out how fast the disks are moving."

"Disks." They seem like distant abstractions to her, but John's enthusiasm is hard to ignore. "Do you suppose they're like, uh, here?" She doesn't say like *Earth*—everybody knows this isn't Earth any more. Not the way it used to be.

"Maybe." He busies himself for a minute with a chunky film cartridge. "They've got oxygen in their atmospheres, we know that. And they're big enough. But they're most of a light year away—far closer than the stars, but still too far for telescopes."

"Or moon rockets," she says, slightly wistfully. "Or sputniks."

"If those things worked any more." The film is in: he leans over the scope and brings it round to bear on the first of the disks, a couple of degrees off from Satan. (The disks are invisible to the naked eye; it takes a telescope to see their reflected light.) He glances up at her. "Do you remember the moon?"

Maddy shrugs. "I was just a kid when it happened. But I saw the moon, some nights. During the day, too."

He nods. "Not like some of the kids these days. Tell them we used to live on a big spinning sphere and they look at you like you're mad."

"What do they think the speed of the disks will tell them?" she asks.

"Whether they're all as massive as this one. What they could be made of. What that tells us about who it was that made them." He shrugs. "Don't ask me, I'm just a bug-hunter. This stuff is *big*, bigger than bugs." He chuckles. "It's a new world out here."

She nods very seriously, then actually sees him for the first time: "I guess it is."

BOLDLY GO

"So tell me, comrade colonel, how did it really feel?"

The comrade colonel laughs uneasily. He's forty-three and still slim and boyish-looking, but carries a quiet melancholy around with him like his own personal storm cloud. "I was very busy all the time," he says with a self-deprecating little shrug. "I didn't have time to pay attention to myself. One orbit, it only lasted ninety minutes, what did you expect? If you really want to know, Gherman's the man to ask. He had more time."

"Time." His interrogator sighs and leans his chair back on two legs. It's a horribly old, rather precious Queen Anne original, a gift to some Tsar or other many years before the October revolution. "What a joke. Ninety minutes, two days, that's all we got before they changed the rules on us."

" 'They,' comrade chairman?" The colonel looked puzzled.

"Whoever." The chairman's vague wave takes in half the horizon of the richly paneled Kremlin office. "What a joke. Whoever they were, at least they saved us from a pasting in Cuba because of that louse Nikita." He pauses for a moment, then toys with the wine glass that sits, half-empty, before him. The colonel has a glass too, but his is full of grape juice, out of consideration for his past difficulties. "The 'whoever' I speak of are of course the brother socialists from the stars who brought us here." He grins humorlessly, face creasing like the muzzle of a shark that smells blood in the water.

"Brother socialists." The colonel smiles hesitantly, wondering if it's a joke, and if so, whether he's allowed to share it. He's still un- sure why he's being interviewed by the premier—in his private office, at that. "Do we know anything of them, sir? That is, am I sup-posed to—"

"Never mind." Aleksey sniffs, dismissing the colonel's worries. "Yes, you're cleared to know everything on this topic. The trouble is, there is nothing to know, and this troubles me, Yuri Alexeyevich. We infer purpose, the engine of a greater history at work—but the dialec-tic is silent on this matter. I have consulted the experts, asked them to read the chicken entrails, but none of them can do anything other than parrot pre-event dogma: 'Any species advanced enough to do to us what happened that day must of course have evolved true Commu-nism, comrade premier! Look what they did for us!' (That was Shchlovskii, by the way.) And yes, I look and I see six cities that no-body can live in, space ships that refuse to stick to the sky, and a land-scape that Sakharov and that bunch of double-domes are at a loss to explain. There are fucking miracles and wonders and portents in the sky, like a galaxy we were supposed to be part of that is now a million years too old and shows extensive signs of construction. There's no room for miracles and wonders in our rational world, and it's giving the comrade general secretary, Yuri, the *comrade general secretary*, stomach ulcers; did you know that?"

The colonel sits up straight, anticipating the punch line: it's a well-known fact throughout the USSR that when Brezhnev says "frog," the premier croaks. And here he is in the premier's office, watching that very man, Aleksey Kosygin, chairman of the Council of Ministers, third most powerful man in the Soviet Union, taking a deep breath.

"Yuri Alexeyevich, I have brought you here today because I want you to help set Leonid Illich's stomach at rest. You're an aviator and a hero of the Soviet Union, and more importantly you're smart enough to do the job and young enough to see it through, not like the old farts cluttering up Stavka. (It's going to take most of a lifetime to sort out, you mark my words.) You're also, you will pardon the bluntness, about as much use as a fifth wheel in your current posting right now: we have to face facts, and the sad reality is that none of Korolev's birds will ever fly again, not even with the atomic bomb pusher-thing they've been working on." Kosygin sighs and shuffles upright in his chair. "There is simply no point in maintaining the Cosmonaut Training Centre. A decree has been drafted and will be approved next week: the manned rocket program is going to be wound up and the cosmonaut corps reassigned to other duties."

The colonel flinches. "Is that absolutely necessary, comrade chairman?"

Kosygin drains his wine glass, decides to ignore the implied criticism. "We don't have the resources to waste. But, Yuri Alexeyevich, all that training is not lost." He grins wolfishly. "I have new worlds for you to explore, and a new ship for you to do it in."

"A new ship." The colonel nods then does a double-take, punch-drunk. "A ship?"

"Well, it isn't a fucking horse," says Kosygin. He slides a big glossy photograph across his blotter towards the colonel. "Times have moved on." The colonel blinks in confusion as he tries to make sense of the thing at the centre of the photograph. The premier watches his face, secretly amused: confusion is *everybody's* first reaction to the thing in the photograph.

"I'm not sure I understand, sir—"

"It's quite simple: you trained to explore new worlds. You can't, not using the rockets. The rockets won't ever make orbit. I've had astronomers having nervous breakdowns trying to explain why, but they all agree on the key point: rockets won't do it for us here. Something wrong with the gravity, they say it even crushes falling starlight." The chairman taps a fat finger on the photograph. "But you can do it using *this*. We invented it and the bloody Americans didn't. It's called an ekranoplan, and you rocket boys are going to stop being grounded cosmonauts and learn how to fly it. What do you think, Colonel Gagarin?"

The colonel whistles tunelessly through his teeth: he's finally worked out the scale. It looks like a flying boat with clipped wings, jet engines clustered by the sides of its cockpit—but no flying boat ever carried a runway with a brace of MiG-21s on its back. "It's bigger than a cruiser! Is it nuclear powered?"

"Of course." The chairman's grin slips. "It cost as much as those moon rockets of Sergei's, *colonel-general*. Try not to drop it."

Gagarin glances up, surprise and awe visible on his face. "Sir, I'm honored, but—"

"Don't be." The chairman cuts him off. "The promotion was coming your way anyway. The posting that comes with it will earn you as much honor as that first orbit. A second chance at space, if you like. But you can't fail: the cost is unthinkable. It's not your skin that will pay the toll, it's our entire rationalist civilization." Kosygin leans forward intently.

"Somewhere out there are beings so advanced that they skinned the earth like a grape and plated it onto this disk—or worse, copied us all right down to the atomic level and duplicated us like one of those American xerox machines. It's not just us, though. You are aware of the other continents in the oceans. We think some of them may be inhabited, too—nothing else makes sense. Your task is to take the *Sergei Korolev*, the first ship of its class, on an historic five-year cruise. You will boldly go where no Soviet man has gone before, explore new worlds and look for new peoples, and to establish fraternal socialist relations with them. But your primary objective is to discover who built this giant mousetrap of a world, and why they brought us to it, and to report back to us—*before* the Americans find out."

COMMITTEE PROCESS

The cherry trees are in bloom in Washington, D.C., and Gregor perspires in the summer heat. He has grown used to the relative cool of London and this unaccustomed change of climate has disoriented him. Jet lag is a thing of the past—a small mercy—but there are still adjustments to make. Because the disk is flat, the daylight source—polar flares from an accretion disk inside the axial hole, the scientists call it, which signifies nothing to most people—grows and shrinks the same wherever you stand.

There's a concrete sixties-vintage office block with a conference suite furnished in burnt umber and orange, chromed chairs and Kandinsky prints on the walls: all very seventies. Gregor waits outside the suite until the buzzer sounds and the receptionist looks up from behind her IBM typewriter and says "You can go in now, they're expecting you."

Gregor goes in. It's an occupational hazard, but by no means the worst, in his line of work.

"Have a seat." It's Seth Brundle, Gregor's divisional head—a grey-looking functionary, more adept at office backstabbing than field-expedient assassinations. His cover, like Gregor's, is an innocuous-sounding post in the Office of Technology Assessment. In fact, both he and Gregor work for a different government agency, although the notional task is the same: identify technological threats and stamp on them before they emerge.

Brundle is not alone in the room. He proceeds with the introductions: "Greg Samsa is our London station chief and specialist in scientific intelligence. Greg, this is Marcus." The bald, thin-faced German in the smart suit bobs his head and smiles behind his horn-rimmed glasses. "Civilian consultant." Gregor mistrusts him on sight. Marcus is a defector—a former Stasi spook, from back before the Brezhnev purges of the mid-sixties. Which puts an interesting complexion on this meeting.

"Murray Fox, from Langley."

"Hi," says Gregor, wondering just what kind of insane political critical mass Brundle is trying to assemble: Langley and Brundle's parent outfit aren't even on speaking terms, to say the least.

"And another civilian specialist, Dr. Sagan." Greg nods at the doctor, a thin guy with sparkling brown eyes and hippyish long hair. "Greg's got something to tell us in person," says Brundle. "Something very interesting he picked up in London. No sources please, Greg."

"No sources," Gregor echoes. He pulls out a chair and sits down. Now he's here, he supposes he'll just have to play the role Brundle assigned to him in the confidential briefing he read on the long flight home. "We have word from an unimpeachable HUMINT resource that the Russians have—" he coughs into his fist. "Excuse me." He glances at Brundle. "Okay to talk about COLLECTION RUBY?"

"They're all cleared," Brundle says dryly. "That's why it says 'joint committee' on the letterhead."

"I see. My invitation was somewhat terse." Gregor stifles a sigh that seems to say, *all I get is a most urgent recall; how am I meant to know what's going on and who knows what*? "So why are we here?"

"Think of it as another collective analysis board," says Fox, the man from the CIA. He doesn't look enthused.

"We're here to find out what's going on, with the benefit of some intelligence resources from the other side of the curtain."

Dr. Sagan, who has been listening silently with his head cocked to one side like a very intelligent blackbird, raises an eyebrow.

"Yes?" asks Brundle.

"I, uh, would you mind explaining that to me? I haven't been on one of these committees before."

No indeed, thinks Gregor. It's a miracle Sagan ever passed his political vetting: he's too friendly by far with some of those Russian astronomer guys who are clearly under the thumb of the KGB's First Department. And he's expressed doubts—muted, of course—about the thrust of current foreign policy, which is a serious no-no under the McNamara administration.

"A CAB is a joint committee feeding into the Central Office of Information's external bureaux on behalf of a blue-ribbon panel of experts assembled from the intelligence community," Gregor recites in a bored tone of voice. "Stripped of the bullshit, we're a board of wise men who're meant to rise above narrow bureaucratic lines of engagement and prepare a report for the Office of Technology Assessment to pass on to the Director of Central Intelligence. It's not meant to reflect the agenda of any one department, but to be a Delphi board synergizing our lateralities. Set up after the Cuban fiasco to make sure that we never again get backed into that kind of corner by accidental groupthink. One of the rules of the CAB process is that it has to include at least one dissident: unlike the commies we know we're not perfect." Gregor glances pointedly at Fox, who has the good sense to stay silent.

"Oh, I see," Sagan says hesitantly. With more force: "So that's why I'm here? Is that the only reason you've dragged me away from Cornell?"

"Of course not, doctor," oozes Brundle, casting Gregor a dirty look. The East German defector, Wolf, maintains a smug silence: *I am above all this.* "We're here to come up with policy recommendations for dealing with the bigger picture. The *much* bigger picture."

"The Builders," says Fox. "We're here to determine what our options look like if and when they show up, and to make recommendations about the appropriate course of action. Your background in, uh, SETI recommended you."

Sagan looks at him in disbelief. "I'd have thought that was obvious," he says.

"Eh?"

"We won't have any choice," the young professor explains with a wry smile. "Does a termite mound negotiate with a nuclear superpower?"

Brundle leans forward. "That's rather a radical position, isn't it? Surely there'll be some room for maneuver? We know this is an artificial construct, but presumably the Builders are still living people. Even if they've got green skin and six eyes."

"Oh. My. God." Sagan leans forward, his face in his hands. After a moment Gregor realizes that he's laughing.

"Excuse me." Gregor glances round. It's the German defector, Wolff, or whatever he's called. "Herr professor, would you care to explain what you find so funny?"

After a moment Sagan leans back, looks at the ceiling, and sighs. "Imagine a single, a 45 rpm record with a centre hole punched out. The inner hole is half an astronomical unit—forty-six million miles— in radius. The outer edge is of unknown radius, but probably about two and a half AUs—two hundred and forty-five million miles. The disk's thickness is unknown—seismic waves are reflected off a mirror-like rigid layer eight hundred miles down—but we can estimate it at eight thousand miles, if its density averages out at the same as Earth's. Surface gravity is the same as our original planet, and since we've been transplanted here and survived we have learned that it's a remarkably hospitable environment for our kind of life; only on the large scale does it seem different."

The astronomer sits up. "Do any of you gentlemen have any idea just how preposterously powerful whoever built this structure is?"

"How do you mean, preposterously powerful?" asks Brundle, looking more interested than annoyed.

"A colleague of mine, Dan Alderson, did the first analysis. I think you might have done better to pull him in, frankly. Anyway, let me itemise: item number one is escape velocity." Sagan holds up a bony finger. "Gravity on a disk does not diminish in accordance with the inverse square law, the way it does on a spherical object like the planet we came from. We have roughly earthlike gravity, but to escape, or to reach orbit, takes tremendously more speed. Roughly two hundred times more, in fact. Rockets that from Earth could reach the moon just fall out of the sky after running out of fuel. Next item": another finger. "The area and mass of the disk. If it's double-sided it has a surface area equal to billions and billions of Earths. We're stuck in the middle of an ocean full of alien continents, but we have no guarantee that this hospitable environment is anything other than a tiny oasis in a world of strangeness."

The astronomer pauses to pour himself a glass of water, then glances round the table. "To put it in perspective, gentlemen, this world is so big that, if one in every hundred stars had an earthlike planet, this single structure could support the population of our *entire home galaxy*. As for the mass—this structure is as massive as fifty thousand suns. It is, quite bluntly, impossible: as-yet-unknown physical forces must be at work to keep it from rapidly collapsing in on itself and creating a black hole. The repulsive force, whatever it is, is strong enough to hold the weight of fifty thousand suns: think about that for a moment, gentlemen."

At that point, Sagan looks around and notices the blank stares. He chuckles ruefully.

"What I mean to say is, this structure is not permitted by the laws of physics as we understand them. Because it clearly *does* exist, we can draw some conclusions, starting with the fact that our understanding of physics is incomplete. Well, that isn't news: we know we don't have a unified theory of everything. Einstein spent thirty years looking for one, and didn't come up with it. But, secondly." He looks tired for a moment, aged beyond his years. "We used to think that any extraterrestrial beings we might communicate with would be fundamentally comprehensible: folks like us, albeit with better technology. I think that's the frame of mind you're still working in. Back in '61, we had a brainstorming session at a conference, trying to work out just how big an engineering project a space-faring civilization might come up with. Freeman Dyson, from Princeton, came up with about the biggest thing any of us could imagine: something that required us to imagine dismantling Jupiter and turning it into habitable real estate.

"This disk is about a hundred million times bigger than Dyson's sphere. And that's before we take into account the time factor."

"Time?" echoes Fox from Langley, sounding confused.

"Time." Sagan smiles in a vaguely disconnected way. "We're nowhere near our original galactic neighborhood and whoever moved us here, they didn't bend the laws of physics far enough to violate the speed limit. It takes light about one hundred sixty thousand years to cross the distance between where we used to live, and our new stellar neighborhood, the Lesser Magellanic Cloud. Which we have fixed, incidentally, by measuring the distance to known Cepheid variables, once we were able to take into account the measurable red shift of infalling light and the fact that some of them were changing frequency slowly and seem to have changed rather a lot. Our best estimate is eight hundred thousand years, plus or minus two hundred thousand. That's about four times as long as our species has *existed*, gentlemen. We're fossils, an archaeology experiment or something. Our relevance to our abductors is not as equals, but as subjects in some kind of vast experiment. And what the purpose of the experiment is, I can't tell you. I've got some guesses, but . . ."

Sagan shrugs, then lapses into silence. Gregor catches Brundle's eye and Brundle shakes his head, very slightly. *Don't spill the beans.* Gregor nods. Sagan may realize he's in a room with a CIA spook and an East German defector, but he doesn't need to know about the Alienation Service yet.

"Well that's as may be," says Fox, dropping words like stones into the hollow silence at the table. "But it begs the question, what are we going to tell the DCI?"

"I suggest," says Gregor, "that we start by reviewing COLLECTION RUBY." He nods at Sagan. "Then, maybe when we're all up to speed on *that*, we'll have a better idea of whether there's anything useful we can tell the DCI."

CANNON-FODDER

Madeleine and Robert Holbright are among the last of the immigrants to disembark on the new world. As she glances back at the brilliant white side of the liner, the horizon seems to roll around her head, settling into a strange new stasis that feels unnatural after almost six months at sea.

New Iowa isn't flat and it isn't new: rampart cliffs loom to either side of the unnaturally deep harbor (gouged out of bedrock courtesy of General Atomics). A cog-driven funicular railway hauls Maddy and Robert and their four shipping trunks up the thousand-foot climb to the plateau and the port city of Fort Eisenhower—and then to the arrival and orientation camp.

Maddy is quiet and withdrawn, but Bob, oblivious, natters constantly about opportunities and jobs and grabbing a plot of land to build a house on. "It's the new world," he says at one point: "why aren't you excited?"

"The new world," Maddy echoes, biting back the urge to say something cutting. She looks out the window as the train climbs the cliff-face and brings them into sight of the city. *City* is the wrong word: it implies solidity, permanence. Fort Eisenhower is less than five years old, a leukaemic gash inflicted on the landscape by the Corps of Engineers. The tallest building is the governor's mansion, at three stories. Architecturally, the town is all Wild West meets the Radar Age, raw pine houses contrasting with big grey concrete boxes full of seaward-pointing Patriot missiles to deter the inevitable encroachment of the communist hordes. "It's so *flat*."

"The nearest hills are two hundred miles away, past the coastal plain—didn't you read the map?"

She ignores his little dig as the train squeals and clanks up the side of the cliff. It wheezes asthmatically to a stop beside a wooden platform, and expires in a belch of saturated steam. An hour later, they're weary and sweated-up in the lobby of an unprepossessing barrack-hall made of plywood. There's a large hall and a row of tables and bunch of bored-looking colonial service types, and people are walking from one position to another with bundles of papers, answering questions in low voices and receiving official stamps. The would-be colonists mill around like disturbed livestock among the piles of luggage at the back of the room. Maddy and Robert queue uneasy in the damp afternoon heat, overhearing snippets of conversation. "Country of origin? Educational qualifications? Yes, but what was your last job?" Religion and race—almost a quarter of the people in the hall are refugees from India or Pakistan or somewhere lost to the mysterious east forever—seem to obsess the officials. "Robert?" she whispers.

"It'll be alright," he says with false certainty. Taking after his dad already, trying to pretend he's the solid family man. Her sidelong glance at him steals any residual confidence. Then it's their turn.

"Names, passports, country of origin?" The guy with the moustache is brusque and bored, irritated by the heat.

Robert smiles at him. "Robert and Madeleine Holbright, from Canada?" He offers their passports.

"Uh-huh." The official gives the documents a very American going-over. "What schooling have you done? What was your last job?"

"I've, uh, I was working part-time in a garage. On my way through college—I was final year at Toronto, studying structural engineering, but I haven't sat the finals. Maddy—Maddy's a qualified paramedic."

The officer fixes her with a stare. "Worked at it?"

"What? Uh, no—I'm freshly qualified." His abrupt questioning flusters her.

"Huh." He makes a cryptic notation against their names on a long list, a list that spills over the edge of his desk and trails towards the rough floor. "Next." He hands the passports back, and a couple of cards, and points them along to the row of desks.

Someone is already stepping up behind them when Maddy manages to read the tickets. Hers says TRAINEE NURSE. Robert is staring at his and saying "No, this is wrong."

"What is it, Bob?" She looks over his shoulder as someone jostles him sideways. His card reads LABOURER (unskilled); but she doesn't have time to read the rest.

CAPTAIN'S LOG

Yuri Gagarin kicks his shoes off, loosens his tie, and leans back in his chair. "It's hotter than fucking Cuba!" he complains.

"You visited Cuba, didn't you, boss?" His companion, still standing, pours a glass of iced tea and passes it to the young colonel-general before drawing one for himself.

"Yeah, thanks, Misha." The former first cosmonaut smiles tiredly. "Back before the invasion. Have a seat."

Misha Gorodin is the only man on the ship who doesn't have to give a shit whether the captain offers him a seat, but he's grateful all the same: a little respect goes a long way, and Gagarin's sunny disposition and friendly attitude is a far cry from some of the fuckheads Misha's been stuck with in the past. There's a class of officer who thinks that because you're a *zampolit* you're somehow below them, but Yuri doesn't do that: in some ways, he's the ideal New Soviet Man, progress personified. Which makes life a lot easier, because Yuri is one of the very few naval commanders who don't have to give a shit what their political officer thinks, and life would be an awful lot stickier without that grease of respect to make the wheels go round. Mind you, Yuri is also commander of the only Naval warship operated by the Cosmonaut Corps, which is a branch of the Strategic Rocket Forces, another howling exception to the usual military protocol. Somehow this posting seems to be breaking all the rules . . .

"What was it like, boss?"

"Hot as hell. Humid, like this. Beautiful women but lots of dark-skinned comrades who didn't bathe often enough—all very jolly, but you couldn't help looking out to sea, over your shoulder. You know there was an American base there, even then? Guantanamo. They don't have the base now, but they've got *all* the rubble." For a moment Gagarin looks morose. "Bastards."

"The Americans."

"Yes. Shitting on a small defenseless island like that, just because they couldn't get to us any more. You remember when they had to hand out iodine tablets to all the kids? That wasn't Leningrad or

Gorky, the fallout plume: it was Havana. I don't think they wanted to admit just how bad it was."

Misha sips his tea. "We had a lucky escape." Morale be damned, it's acceptable to admit at least that much in front of the CO, in private. Misha's seen some of the KGB reports on the U.S. nuclear capabilities back then, and his blood runs cold; while Nikita had been wildly bluffing about the Rodina's nuclear defenses, the Americans had been hiding the true scale of their own arsenal. From themselves as much as the rest of the world.

"Yes. Things were going to the devil back then, no question: if we hadn't woken up over here, who knows what would have happened? They out-gunned us back then. I don't think they realized." Gagarin's dark expression lifts: he glances out of the open porthole—the only one in a private cabin that opens—and smiles. "This isn't Cuba, though." The headland rising above the bay tells him that much: no tropical island on earth supported such weird vegetation. Or such ruins.

"Indeed not. But, what about the ruins?" asks Misha, putting his tea glass down on the map table.

"Yes." Gagarin leans forward: "I was meaning to talk to you about that. Exploration is certainly in line with our orders, but we are a trifle short of trained archaeologists, aren't we? Let's see: we're four hundred and seventy thousand kilometers from home, six major climactic zones, five continents—it'll be a long time before we get any settlers out here, won't it?" He pauses delicately. "Even if the rumors about reform of the penal system are true."

"It is certainly a dilemma," Misha agrees amiably, deliberately ignoring the skipper's last comment. "But we can take some time over it. There's nobody out here, at least not within range of yesterday's reconnaissance flight. I'll vouch for Lieutenant Chekhov's soundness: he has a solid attitude, that one."

"I don't see how we can leave without examining the ruins, but we've got limited resources and in any case I don't want to do anything that might get the Academy to slap our wrists. No digging for treasure until the egg-heads get here." Gagarin hums tunelessly for a moment, then slaps his hand on his thigh: "I think we'll shoot some film for the comrade general secretary's birthday party. First we'll secure a perimeter around the beach, give those damned spetsnaz a chance to earn all the vodka they've been drinking. Then you and I, we can take Primary Science Party Two into the nearest ruins with lights and cameras. Make a visual record, leave the double-domes back in Moscow to figure out what we're looking at and whether it's worth coming back later with a bunch of archaeologists. What do you say, Misha?"

"I say that's entirely logical, comrade general," says the political officer, nodding to himself.

"That's so ordered, then. We'll play it safe, though. Just because we haven't seen any active settlement patterns, doesn't mean there're no aborigines lurking in the forest."

"Like that last bunch of lizards." Misha frowns. "Little purple bastards!"

"We'll make good communists out of them eventually," Yuri insists. "A toast! To making good communists out of little purple lizard-bastards with blowpipes who shoot political officers in the arse!"

Gagarin grins wickedly and Gorodin knows when he's being wound up on purpose and summons a twinkle to his eye as he raises his glass: "And to poisons that don't work on human beings."

DISCOGRAPHY

Warning:
The following briefing film is classified COLLECTION RUBY. If you do not possess both COLLECTION and RUBY clearances, leave the auditorium and report to the screening security officer immediately. Disclosure to unauthorized personnel is a federal offense punishable by a fine of up to ten thousand dollars and/or imprisonment for up to twenty years. You have thirty seconds to clear the auditorium and report to the screening security officer.

Voice-over:
Ocean—the final frontier. For twelve years, since the momentous day when we discovered that we had been removed to this planar world,

we have been confronted by the immensity of an ocean that goes on as far as we can see. Confronted also by the prospect of the spread of Communism to uncharted strange lands, we have committed ourselves to a strategy of exploration and containment.

Film clip:
An Atlas rocket on the launch pad rises slowly, flames jetting from its tail: it surges past the gantry and disappears into the sky.

Cut to:
A camera mounted in the nose, pointing back along the flank of the rocket. The ground falls behind, blurring into blue distance. Slowly, the sky behind the rocket is turning black: but the land still occupies much of the fisheye view. The first stage engine ring tumbles away, leaving the core engine burning with a pale blue flame: now the outline of the California coastline is recognizable. North America shrinks visibly: eventually another, strange outline swims into view, like a cipher in an alien script. The booster burns out and falls behind, and the tumbling camera catches sunlight glinting off the upper-stage Centaur rocket as its engine ignites, thrusting it higher and faster.

Voice-over:
We cannot escape.

Cut to:
A meteor streaking across the empty blue bowl of the sky; slowing, deploying parachutes.

Voice-over:
In 1962, this rocket would have blasted a two-ton payload all the way into outer space. That was when we lived on a planet that was an oblate sphere. Life on a dinner plate seems to be different: while the gravitational attraction anywhere on the surface is a constant, we can't get away from it. In fact, anything we fire straight up will come back down again. Not even a nuclear rocket can escape: according to JPL scientist Dan Alderson, escape from a Magellanic disk would require a speed of over one thousand six hundred miles per second. That is be-

cause this disk masses many times more than a star—in fact, it has a mass fifty thousand times greater than our own sun.

What stops it collapsing into a sphere? Nobody knows. Physicists speculate that a fifth force that drove the early expansion of the universe—they call it "quintessence"—has been harnessed by the makers of the disk. But the blunt truth is, nobody knows for sure. Nor do we understand how we came here—how, in the blink of an eye, something beyond our comprehension peeled the earth's continents and oceans like a grape and plated them across this alien disk.

Cut to:
A map. The continents of earth are laid out—Americas at one side, Europe and Asia and Africa to their east. Beyond the Indonesian island chain, Australia and New Zealand hang lonely on the edge of an abyss of ocean.

The map pans right: strange new continents swim into view, ragged-edged and huge. A few of them are larger than Asia and Africa combined; most of them are smaller.

Voice-over:
Geopolitics was changed forever by the Move. While the surface topography of our continents was largely preserved, wedges of foreign material were introduced below the Mohorovicik discontinuity—below the crust—and in the deep ocean floor, to act as spacers. The distances between points separated by deep ocean were, of necessity, changed, and not in our geopolitical favor. While the tactical balance of power after the Move was much as it had been before, the great circle flight paths our strategic missiles were designed for—over the polar ice cap and down into the Communist empire—were distorted and stretched, placing the enemy targets outside their range. Meanwhile, although our manned bombers could still reach Moscow with in-flight refueling, the changed map would have forced them to traverse thousands of miles of hostile airspace en route. The Move rendered most of our strategic preparations useless. If the British had been willing to stand firm, we might have prevailed—but in retrospect, what went for us also went for the Soviets, and it is hard to condemn the British for being unwilling to take the full force of the inevitable Soviet bombardment alone.

In retrospect the only reason this was not a complete disaster for us is that the Soviets were caught in the same disarray as ourselves. But the specter of Communism now dominates western Europe: the supposedly independent nations of the European Union are as much in thrall to Moscow as the client states of the Warsaw Pact. Only the ongoing British State of Emergency offers us any residual geopolitical traction on the red continent, and in the long term we must anticipate that the British, too, will be driven to reach an accommodation with the Soviet Union.

Cut to:

A silvery delta-winged aircraft in flight. Stub wings, pointed nose, and a shortage of windows proclaim it to be an unmanned drone: a single large engine in its tail thrusts it along, exhaust nozzle glowing cherry-red. Trackless wastes unwind below it as the viewpoint—a chase plane—carefully climbs over the drone to capture a clear view of the upper fuselage.

Voice-over:

The disk is vast—so huge that it defies sanity. Some estimates give it the surface area of more than a billion earths. Exploration by conventional means is futile: hence the deployment of the NP-101 Persephone drone, here seen making a proving flight over land mass F-42. The NP-101 is a reconnaissance derivative of the nuclear-powered D-SLAM Pluto missile that forms the backbone of our post-Move deterrent force. It is slower than a strategic D-SLAM, but much more reliable: while D-SLAM is designed for a quick, fiery dash into Soviet territory, the NP-101 is designed to fly long duration missions that map entire continents. On a typical deployment, the NP-101 flies outward at thrice the speed of sound for nearly a month: traveling fifty thousand miles a day, it penetrates a million miles into the unknown before it turns and flies homeward. Its huge mapping cameras record two images every thousand seconds, and its sophisticated digital computer records a variety of data from its sensor suite, allowing us to build up a picture of parts of the disk that our ships would take years or decades to reach. With resolution down to the level of a single nautical mile, the NP-101 program has been a resounding success, allowing us to map whole new worlds that it would take us years to visit in person.

At the end of its mission, the NP-101 drops its final film capsule and flies out into the middle of an uninhabited ocean, to ditch its spent nuclear reactor safely far from home.

Cut to:
A bull's-eye diagram. The centre is a black circle with a star at its heart; around it is a circular platter, of roughly the same proportions as a 45 rpm single.

Voice-over:
A rough map of the disk. Here is the area we have explored to date, using the NP-101 program.

(A dot little larger than a sand grain lights up on the face of the single.)

That dot of light is a million kilometers in radius—five times the distance that used to separate our old Earth from its moon. (To cross the radius of the disk, an NP-101 would have to fly at Mach Three for almost ten years.) We aren't even sure exactly where the centre of that dot lies on the disk: our highest sounding rocket, the Nova-Orion block two, can barely rise two degrees above the plane of the disk before crashing back again. Here is the scope of our knowledge of our surroundings, derived from the continental-scale mapping cameras carried by Project Orion:

(A salmon pink area almost half an inch in diameter lights up around the red sand grain on the face of the single.)

Of course, cameras at an altitude of a hundred thousand miles can't look down on new continents and discern signs of Communist infiltration; at best they can listen for radio transmissions and perform spectroscopic analyses of the atmospheric gasses above distant lands, looking for gasses characteristic of industrial development such as chlorofluorocarbons and nitrogen oxides.

This leaves us vulnerable to unpleasant surprises. Our long-term strategic analyses imply that we are almost certainly not alone on the disk. In addition to the Communists, we must consider the possibility that whoever built this monstrous structure—clearly one of the wonders of the universe—might also live here. We must contemplate their motives for bringing us to this place. And then there are the aboriginal cultures discovered on continents F-29 and F-364, both now placed under quarantine. If some land masses bear aboriginal inhabitants, we may speculate that they, too, have been transported to the disk in the same manner as ourselves, for some as-yet unknown purpose. It is possible that they are genuine stone-age dwellers—or that they are the remnants of advanced civilizations that did not survive the transition to this environment. What is the possibility that there exists on the disk one or more advanced alien civilizations that are larger and more powerful than our own? And would we recognize them as such if we saw them? How can we go about estimating the risk of our encountering hostile Little Green Men—now that other worlds are in range of even a well-equipped sailboat, much less the *Savannah*-class nuclear powered exploration ships? Astronomers Carl Sagan and Daniel Drake estimate the probability as high—so high, in fact, that they believe there are several such civilizations out there.

We are not alone. We can only speculate about why we might have been brought here by the abductors, but we can be certain that it is only a matter of time before we encounter an advanced alien civilization, that may well be hostile to us. This briefing film will now continue with an overview of our strategic preparations for first contact, and the scenarios within which we envisage this contingency arising, with specific reference to the Soviet Union as an example of an unfriendly ideological superpower . . .

TENURE TRACK

After two weeks, Maddy is sure she's going mad.

She and Bob have been assigned a small prefabricated house (not much more than a shack, although it has electricity and running water) on the edge of town. He's been drafted into residential works, put to work erecting more buildings: and this is the nearest thing to a success they've had, because after a carefully controlled protest his status has been corrected, from just another set of unskilled hands to trainee surveyor. A promotion of which he is terribly proud, evidently taking it as confirmation that they've made the right move by coming here.

Maddy, meanwhile, has a harder time finding work. The district hospital is fully staffed. They don't need her, won't need her until the next shipload of settlers arrive, unless she wants to pack up her bags and go tramping around isolated ranch settlements in the outback. In a year's time the governor has decreed they'll establish another town-scale settlement, inland near the mining encampments on the edge of the Hoover Desert. Then they'll need medics to staff the new hospital: but for now, she's a spare wheel. Because Maddy is a city girl by upbringing and disposition, and not inclined to take a job tramping around the outback if she can avoid it.

She spends the first week and then much of the second mooching around town, trying to find out what she can do. She's not the only young woman in this predicament. While there's officially no unemployment, and the colony's dirigiste administration finds plenty of hard work for idle hands, there's also a lack of openings for ambulance crew, or indeed much of anything else she can do. Career-wise it's like a trip into the 1950s. Young, female, and ambitious? Lots of occupations simply don't exist out here on the fringe, and many others are closed or inaccessible. Everywhere she looks she sees mothers shepherding implausibly large flocks of toddlers with guardians pinch-faced from worry and exhaustion. Bob wants kids, but Maddy's not ready for that yet. But the alternatives on offer are limited.

Eventually Maddy takes to going through the "Help Wanted" ads on the bulletin board outside city hall. Some of them are legit: and at least a few are downright peculiar. One catches her eye: field assistant wanted for biological research. *I wonder?* she thinks, and goes in search of a door to bang on.

When she finds the door—raw wood, just beginning to bleach in the strong colonial sunlight—and bangs on it, John Martin opens it and blinks quizzically into the light. "Hello?" he asks.

"You were advertising for a field assistant?" She stares at him. *He's the entomologist*, right? She remembers his hands on the telescope on the deck of the ship. The voyage itself is already taking on the false patina of romance in her memories, compared to the dusty present it has delivered her to.

"I was? Oh—yes, yes. Do come in." He backs into the house—another of these identikit shacks, *colonial, family, for the use of*—and offers her a seat in what used to be the living room. It's almost completely filled by a work table and a desk and a tall wooden chest of sample drawers. There's an odd, musty smell, like old cobwebs and leaky demijohns of formalin. John shuffles around his den, vaguely disordered by the unexpected shock of company. There's something touchingly cute about him, like the subjects of his studies, Maddy thinks. "Sorry about the mess, I don't get many visitors. So, um, do you have any relevant experience?"

She doesn't hesitate: "None whatsoever, but I'd like to learn." She leans forward. "I qualified as a paramedic before we left. At college I was studying biology, but I had to drop out midway through my second year: I was thinking about going to medical school later, but I guess that's not going to happen here. Anyway, the hospital here has no vacancies, so I need to find something else to do. What exactly does a field assistant get up to?"

"Get sore feet." He grins lopsidedly. "Did you do any lab time? Field work?" Maddy nods hesitantly so he drags her meager college experiences out of her before he continues. "I've got a whole continent to explore and only one set of hands: we're spread thin out here. Luckily NSF budgeted to hire me an assistant. The assistant's job is to be my Man Friday; to help me cart equipment about, take samples, help with basic lab work—*very* basic—and so on. Oh, and if they're interested in entomology, botany, or anything else remotely relevant that's a plus. There aren't many unemployed life sciences people around here, funnily enough: have you had any chemistry?"

"Some," Maddy says cautiously; "I'm no biochemist." She glances round the crowded office curiously. "What are you meant to be doing?"

He sighs. "A primary survey of an entire continent. Nobody, but nobody, even bothered looking into the local insect ecology here. There're virtually no vertebrates, birds, lizards, what have you—but back home there are more species of beetle than everything else put together, and this place is no different. Did you know nobody has even sampled the outback fifty miles inland of here? We're doing nothing but throw up shacks along the coastline and open-cast quarries a few miles inland. There could be *anything* in the interior, absolutely anything." When he gets excited he starts gesticulating, Maddy notices, waving his hands around enthusiastically. She nods and smiles, trying to encourage him.

"A lot of what I'm doing is the sort of thing they were doing in the eighteenth and nineteenth century. Take samples, draw them, log their habitat and dietary habits, see if I can figure out their life cycle, try and work out who's kissing-cousins with what. Build a family tree. Oh, I also need to do the same with the vegetation, you know? And they want me to keep close watch on the other disks around Lucifer. 'Keep an eye out for signs of sapience,' whatever that means: I figure there's a bunch of leftovers in the astronomical community who feel down-right insulted that whoever built this disk and brought us here didn't land on the White House lawn and introduce themselves. I'd better tell you right now, there's enough work here to occupy an army of zoolo-gists and botanists for a century; you can get started on a PhD right here and now if you want. I'm only here for five years, but my succes-sor should be okay about taking on an experienced RA . . . the hard bit is going to be maintaining focus. Uh, I can sort you out a subsistence grant from the governor-general's discretionary fund and get NSF to reimburse him, but it won't be huge. Would twenty Truman dollars a week be enough?"

Maddy thinks for a moment. Truman dollars—the local scrip—aren't worth a whole lot, but there's not much to spend them on. And Rob's earning for both of them anyway. And a PhD . . . *that could be my ticket back to civilization, couldn't it*? "I guess so," she says, feel-ing a sense of vast relief: so there's something she's useful for besides raising the next generation, after all. She tries to set aside the visions of herself, distinguished and not too much older, gratefully accepting a professor's chair at an ivy league university. "When do I start?"

ON THE BEACH

Misha's first impressions of the disturbingly familiar alien continent are of an oppressively humid heat, and the stench of decaying jellyfish.

The *Sergei Korolev* floats at anchor in the river estuary, a huge streamlined visitor from another world. Stubby fins stick out near the waterline, like a seaplane with clipped wings: gigantic Kuznetsov atomic turbines in pods ride on booms to either side of its high-ridged back, either side of the launch/recovery catapults for its parasite MiG fighter-bombers, aft of the broad curve of the ekranoplan's bridge. Near the waterline, a boat bay is open: a naval spetsnaz team is busy loading their kit into the landing craft that will ferry them to the small camp on the beach. Misha, who stands just above the waterline, turns away from the giant ground effect ship and watches his commander, who is staring inland with a faint expression of worry. "Those trees— awfully close, aren't they?" Gagarin says, with the carefully studied stupidity that saw him through the first dangerous years after his patron Khrushchev's fall.

"That is indeed what Captain Kirov is taking care of," replies Gorodin, playing his role of foil to the colonel-general's sardonic humor. And indeed shadowy figures in olive-green battle dress are stalking in and out of the trees, carefully laying tripwires and screamers in an arc around the beachhead. He glances to the left, where a couple of sailors with assault rifles stand guard, eyes scanning the jungle. "I wouldn't worry unduly, sir."

"I'll still be happier when the outer perimeter is secure. And when I've got a sane explanation of this for the comrade General Secretary." Gagarin's humor evaporates: he turns and walks along the beach, towards the large tent that's already gone up to provide shelter from the heat of noon. The bar of solid sunlight—what passes for sunlight here—is already at maximum length, glaring like a rod of white-hot steel that impales the disk. (Some of the more superstitious call it the axle of heaven. Part of Gorodin's job is to discourage such non-materialist backsliding.)

The tent awing is pegged back: inside it, Gagarin and Misha find

Major Suvurov and Academician Borisovitch leaning over a map. Already the scientific film crew—a bunch of dubious civilians from the TASS agency—are busy in a corner, preparing cans for shooting. "Ah, Oleg, Mikhail." Gagarin summons up a professionally photogenic smile. "Getting anywhere?"

Borisovitch, a slight, stoop-shouldered type who looks more like a janitor than a world-famous scientist, shrugs. "We were just talking about going along to the archaeological site, General. Perhaps you'd like to come, too?"

Misha looks over his shoulder at the map: it's drawn in pencil, and there's an awful lot of white space on it, but what they've surveyed so far is disturbingly familiar in outline—familiar enough to have given them all a number of sleepless nights even before they came ashore. Someone has scribbled a dragon coiling in a particularly empty corner of the void.

"How large is the site?" asks Yuri.

"Don't know, sir." Major Suvurov grumps audibly, as if the lack of concrete intelligence on the alien ruins is a personal affront. "We haven't found the end of it yet. But it matches what we know already."

"The aerial survey—" Mikhail coughs, delicately. "If you'd let me have another flight I could tell you more, general. I believe it may be possible to define the city limits narrowly, but the trees make it hard to tell."

"I'd give you the flight if only I had the aviation fuel," Gagarin explains patiently. "A chopper can burn its own weight in fuel in a day of surveying, and we have to haul everything out here from Archangel. In fact, when we go home we're leaving most of our flight-ready aircraft behind, just so that on the next trip out we can carry more fuel."

"I understand." Mikhail doesn't look happy. "As Oleg Ivanovitch says, we don't know how far it reaches. But I think when you see the ruins you'll understand why we need to come back here. Nobody's found anything like this before."

"Old Capitalist Man." Misha smiles thinly. "I suppose."

"Presumably." Borisovitch shrugs. "Whatever, we needed to bring archaeologists. And a mass spectroscope for carbon dating. And other stuff." His face wrinkles unhappily. "They were here back when we would still have been living in caves!"

"Except we weren't," Gagarin says under his breath. Misha pretends not to notice.

By the time they leave the tent, the marines have got the *Korolev*'s two BRDMs ashore. The big balloon-tired armored cars sit on the beach like monstrous amphibians freshly emerged from some primeval sea. Gagarin and Gorodin sit in the back of the second vehicle with the academician and the film crew: the lead BRDM carries their spetsnaz escort team. They maintain a dignified silence as the convoy rumbles and squeaks across the beach, up the gently sloping hillside, and then down towards the valley with the ruins.

The armored cars stop and doors open. Everyone is relieved by the faint breeze that cracks the oven-heat of the interior. Gagarin walks over to the nearest ruin—remnants of a wall, waist-high—and stands, hands on hips, looking across the wasteland.

"Concrete," says Borisovitch, holding up a lump of crumbled notstone from the foot of the wall for Yuri to see.

"Indeed." Gagarin nods. "Any idea what this was?"

"Not yet." The camera crew is already filming, heading down a broad boulevard between rows of crumbling foundations. "Only the concrete has survived, and it's mostly turned to limestone. This is *old*."

"Hmm." The First Cosmonaut walks round the stump of wall and steps down to the foundation layer behind it, looking around with interest. "Interior column here, four walls—they're worn down, aren't they? This stuff that looks like a red stain. Rebar? Found any intact ones?"

"Again, not yet sir," says Borisovitch. "We haven't looked everywhere yet, but . . ."

"Indeed." Gagarin scratches his chin idly. "Am I imagining it or are the walls all lower on that side?" He points north, deeper into the sprawling maze of overgrown rubble.

"You're right, sir. No theory for it, though."

"You don't say." Gagarin walks north from the five-sided building's ruin, looks around. "This was a road?"

"Once, sir. It was nine meters wide—there seems to have been derelict ground between the houses, if that's what they were, and the road itself."

"Nine meters, you say." Gorodin and the academician hurry to follow him as he strikes off, up the road. "Interesting stonework here, don't you think, Misha?"

"Yessir. Interesting stonework."

Gagarin stops abruptly and kneels. "Why is it cracked like this? Hey, there's sand down there. And, um. Glass? Looks like it's melted. Ah, trinitite."

"Sir?"

Borisovitch leans forward. "That's odd."

"What is?" asks Misha, but before he gets a reply both Gagarin and the researcher are up again and off towards another building.

"Look. The north wall." Gagarin's found another chunk of wall, this one a worn stump that's more than a meter high: he looks unhappy.

"Sir? Are you alright?" Misha stares at him. Then he notices the academician is also silent, and looking deeply perturbed. "What's wrong?"

Gagarin extends a finger, points at the wall. "You can just see him if you look close enough. How long would it take to fade, Mikhail? How many years have we missed them by?"

The academician licks his lips: "At least two thousand years, sir. Concrete cures over time, but it takes a very long time indeed to turn all the way to limestone. And then there's the weathering process to take account of. But the surface erosion . . . yes, that could fix the image from the flash. Perhaps. I'd need to ask a few colleagues back home."

"What's wrong?" the political officer repeats, puzzled.

The first cosmonaut grins humorlessly. "Better get your Geiger counter, Misha, and see if the ruins are still hot. Looks like we're not the only people on the disk with a geopolitical problem . . ."

BEEN HERE BEFORE

Brundle has finally taken the time to pull Gregor aside and explain what's going on; Gregor is not amused.

"Sorry you walked into it cold," says Brundle. "But I figured it would be best for you to see for yourself." He speaks with a Midwestern twang, and a flatness of affect that his colleagues sometimes mistake for signs of an underlying psychopathology.

"See what, in particular?" Gregor asks sharply. "*What*, in particular?" Gregor tends to repeat himself, changing only the intonation, when he's disturbed. He's human enough to recognize it as a bad habit but still finds it difficult to suppress the reflex.

Brundle pauses on the footpath, looks around to make sure there's nobody within earshot. The Mall is nearly empty today, and only a humid breeze stirs the waters on the pool. "Tell me what you think."

Gregor thinks for a moment, then summons up his full command of the local language: it's good practice. "The boys in the big house are asking for a CAB. It means someone's pulled his head out of his ass for long enough to realize they've got worse things to worry about than being shafted by the Soviets. Something's happened to make them realize they need a policy for dealing with the abductors. This is against policy, we need to do something about it fast before they start asking the right questions. Something's shaken them up, something secret, some HUMINT source from the wrong side of the curtain, perhaps. Could it be that man Gordievsky? But they haven't quite figured out what being here means. Sagan—does his presence mean what I think it does?"

"Yes," Brundle says tersely.

"Oh dear." A reflex trips and Gregor takes off his spectacles and polishes them nervously on his tie before replacing them. "Is it just him, or does it go further?" He leaves the rest of the sentence unspoken by convention—*is it* just him *you think we'll have to silence?*

"Further." Brundle tends to talk out of the side of his mouth when he's agitated, and from his current expression Gregor figures he's really upset. "Sagan and his friends at Cornell have been using the Arecibo dish to listen to the neighbors. This wasn't anticipated. Now they're asking for permission to beam a signal at the nearest of the other disks. Straight up, more or less; 'Talk to us.' Unfortunately Sagan is well-known, which is why he caught the attention of our nominal superiors. Meanwhile, the Soviets have found something that scared them. CIA didn't hear about it through the usual assets—they contacted the State Department via the embassy, they're *that* scared." Brundle pauses a moment. "Sagan and his buddies don't know about that, of course."

"Why has nobody shot them already?" Gregor asks coldly.

Brundle shrugs. "We pulled the plug on their funding just in time. If we shot them as well someone might notice. Everything could go nonlinear while we were trying to cover it up. You know the problem; this is a semi-open society, inadequately controlled. A bunch of astronomers get together on their own initiative—academic conference, whatever—and decide to spend a couple of thousand bucks of research grant money from NIST to establish communications with the nearest disk. How are we supposed to police that kind of thing?"

"Shut down all their radio telescopes. At gunpoint, if necessary, but I figure a power cut or a congressional committee would be just as effective as leverage."

"Perhaps, but we don't have the Soviets' resources to work with. Anyway, that's why I dragged Sagan in for the CAB. It's a Potemkin village, you understand, to convince everybody he contacted that something is being done, but we're going to have to figure out how to shut him up."

"Sagan is the leader of the 'talk-to-us, alien gods' crowd, I take it."

"Yes."

"Well." Gregor considers his next words carefully. "Assuming he's still clean and uncontaminated, we can turn him or we can ice him. If we're going to turn him we need to do it convincingly—full Tellerization—and we'll need to come up with a convincing rationale. Use him to evangelize the astronomical community into shutting up or haring off in the wrong direction. Like Heisenberg and the Nazi nuclear weapons program." He snaps his fingers. "Why don't we tell him the truth? At least, something close enough to it to confuse the issue completely?"

"Because he's a member of the Federation of American Scientists and he won't believe anything we tell him without independent confirmation," Brundle mutters through one side of his mouth. "That's the trouble with using a government agency as our cover story."

They walk in silence for a minute. "I think it would be very dangerous to underestimate him," says Gregor. "He could be a real asset to us, but uncontrolled he's very dangerous. If we can't silence him we may have to resort to physical violence. And with the number of colonies they've already seeded, we can't be sure of getting them all."

"Itemize the state of their understanding," Brundle says abruptly.

"I want a reality check. I'll tell you what's new after you run down the checklist."

"Okay." Gregor thinks for a minute. "Let us see. What everyone knows is that between zero three fifteen and twelve seconds and thirteen seconds Zulu time, on October second, '62, all the clocks stopped, the satellites went away, the star map changed, nineteen airliners and forty-six ships in transit ended up in terminal trouble, and they found themselves transferred from a globe in the milky way galaxy to a disk which we figure is somewhere in the lesser Magellanic cloud. Meanwhile the Milky Way galaxy—we *assume* that's what it is—has changed visibly. Lots of metal-depleted stars, signs of macroscopic cosmic engineering, that sort of thing. The public explanation is that the visitors froze time, skinned the earth, and plated it over the disk. Luckily they're still bickering over whether the explanation is Minsky's copying, uh, hypothesis, or that guy Moravec with his digital simulation theory."

"Indeed." Brundle kicks at a paving stone idly. "Now. What is your forward analysis?"

"Well, sooner or later they're going to turn dangerous. They have the historic predisposition towards teleological errors, to belief in a giant omnipotent creator and a *purpose* to their existence. If they start speculating about the intentions of a transcendent intelligence, it's likely they'll eventually ask whether their presence here is symptomatic of God's desire to probe the circumstances of its own birth. After all, we have evidence of how many technological species on the disk, ten million, twelve? Replicated many times, in some cases. They might put it together with their concept of manifest destiny and conclude that they are, in fact, doomed to give birth to God. Which is an entirely undesirable conclusion for them to reach from our point of view. Teleologists being bad neighbors, so to speak."

"Yes indeed," Brundle says thoughtfully, then titters quietly to himself for a moment.

"This isn't the first time they've avoided throwing around H-bombs in bulk. That's unusual for primate civilizations. If they keep doing it, they could be dangerous."

"Dangerous is relative," says Brundle. He titters again. Things move inside his mouth.

"Don't *do* that!" Gregor snaps. He glances round instinctively, but nothing happens.

"You're jumpy." Brundle frowns. "Stop worrying so much. We don't have much longer here."

"Are we being ordered to move? Or to prepare a sterilization strike?"

"Not yet." Brundle shrugs. "We have further research to continue with before a decision is reached. The Soviets have made a discovery. Their crewed exploration program. The *Korolev* lucked out."

"They—" Gregor tenses. "What did they find?" He knows about the big nuclear-powered ekranoplan, the dragon of the Caspian, searching the seven oceans for new worlds to conquer. He even knows about the small fleet they're trying to build at Archangelsk, the ruinous expense of it. But this is new. "What did they *find*?"

Brundle grins humorlessly. "They found ruins. Then they spent another eight weeks mapping the coastline. They've confirmed what they found, they sent the State Department photographs, survey details—the lot." Brundle gestures at the Cuban War monument, the huge granite column dominating the Mall, its shadow pointing towards the Capitol. "They found Washington, D.C., in ruins. One hundred and forty thousand miles *that* way." He points due north. "They're not total idiots, and it's the first time they've found one of their own species-transfer cognates. They might be well on their way to understanding the truth, but luckily our comrades in Moscow have that side of the affair under control. But they communicated their discovery to the CIA before it could be suppressed, which raises certain headaches.

"We must make sure that nobody *here* asks *why*. So I want you to start by dealing with Sagan."

COLLECTING JAR

It's noon, and the rippling heat haze turns the horizon to fog in the distance. Maddy tries not to move too much: the cycads cast imperfect shadows, and she can feel the Venetian blinds of light burning into her pale skin. She sighs slightly as she hefts the heavy canvas sample bag out of the back of the Land Rover: John will be needing it soon, once he's finished photographing the mock-termite nests. It's their third field trip together, their furthest dash into the outback, and she's already getting used to working with John. He's surprisingly easy to get on with, because he's so absorbed in his work that he's refreshingly free of social expectations. If she didn't know better she could almost let her guard down and start thinking of him as a friend, not an employer.

The heat makes her mind drift: she tries to remember what sparked her most recent quarrel with Bob, but it seems so distant and irrelevant now—like home, like Bob arguing with her father, like their hurried registry-office wedding and furtive emigration board hearing. All that makes sense now is the stifling heat, the glare of not-sunlight, John working with his camera out in the noonday sun where only mad dogs and Englishmen dare go. Ah, *it was the washing.* Who was going to do the washing while Maddy was away on the two-day field trip? Bob seemed to think he was doing her a favor, cooking for himself and taking his clothes to the single over-used public laundry. (Some year real soon now they'd get washing machines, but not yet . . .) Bob seemed to think he was being big-hearted, not publicly getting jealous all over her having a job that took her away from home with a male superior who was notoriously single. Bob seemed to think he was some kind of progressive liberated man, for putting up with a wife who had read Betty Friedan and didn't shave her armpits. *Fuck you, Bob*, she thinks tiredly, and tugs the heavy strap of the sample case over her shoulder and turns to head in John's direction. There'll be time to sort things out with Bob later. For now, she's got a job to do.

John is leaning over the battered camera, peering through its viewfinder in search of . . . something. "What's up?" she asks.

"Mock-termites are up," he says, very seriously. "See the entrances?" The mock-termites are what they've come to take a look at—nobody's reported on them from close up, but they're very visible as soon as you venture into the dusty plain. She peers at the foot of the termite mound, a baked clay hump in the soil that seems to writhe with life. There are little pipe-like holes, tunnels almost, emerging from the base of the mound, and little black mock-termites dancing in and out of the holes in never-ending streams. *Little* is relative—they're almost as large as mice. "Don't touch them," he warns.

"Are they poisonous?" asks Maddy.

"Don't know, don't want to find out this far from the hospital. The fact that there are no vertebrates here—" he shrugs. "We know they're poisonous to other insectoida."

Maddy puts the sample case down. "But nobody's been bitten, or died, or anything."

"Not that we know of." He folds back the lid of the case and she shivers, abruptly cold, imagining bleached bones lying unburied in the long grass of the inland plain, where no humans will live for centuries to come. "It's essential to take care out here. We could be missing for days before anyone noticed, and a search party wouldn't necessarily find us, even with the journey plan we filed."

"Okay." She watches as he takes out an empty sample jar and a label and carefully notes down time and date, distance and direction from the milestone at the heart of Fort Eisenhower. *Thirty-six miles.* They might as well be on another planet. "You're taking samples?"

He glances round: "Of course." Then he reaches into the side pocket of the bag and removes a pair of heavy gloves, which he proceeds to put on, and a trowel. "If you could put the case down over there?"

Maddy glances inside the case as he kneels down by the mock-termite mound. It's full of jars with blank labels, neatly segregated, impassable quarantine zones for improbable species. She looks round. John is busy with the mock-termite mound. He's neatly lopped the top off it: inside, the earth is a squirming mass of—things. Black things, white things like bits of string, and a pulp of half-decayed vegetable matter that smells damply of humus. He probes the mound delicately with the trowel, seeking something. "Look," he calls over his shoulder. "It's a queen!"

Maddy hurries over. "Really?" she asks. Following his gloved finger, she sees something the size of her left forearm, white and glistening. It twitches, expelling something round, and she files her gorge rise. "Ugh!"

"It's just a happy mother," John says calmly. He lowers the trowel, works it in under the queen and lifts her—and a collection of hangers-on, courtiers, and bodyguards alike—over the jar. He tips, he shakes, and he twists the lid into place. Maddy stares at the chaos within.

What is it like to be a mock-termite, suddenly snatched up and transplanted to a mockery of home? What's it like to see the sun in an electric light bulb, to go about your business, blindly pumping out eggs and eating and foraging for leaves, under the eyes of inscrutable collectors? She wonders if Bob would understand if she tried to tell him. John stands up and lowers the glass jar into the sample case, then freezes. "Ouch," he says, and pulls his left glove off.

"Ouch." He says it again, more slowly. "I missed a small one. Maddy, medical kit, please. Atropine and neostigmine."

She sees his eyes, pinprick pupils in the noonday glare, and dashes to the Land Rover. The medical kit, olive green with a red cross on a white circle, seems to mock her: she rushes it over to John, who is now sitting calmly on the ground next to the sample case. "What do you need?" she asks.

John tries to point, but his gloved hand is shaking wildly. He tries to pull it off, but the swollen muscles resist attempts to loosen the glove. "Atropine—" A white cylinder, with a red arrow on one side: she quickly reads the label, then pushes it hard against his thigh, feels something spring-loaded explode inside it. John stiffens, then tries to stand up, the automatic syringe still handling from his leg. He staggers stiff-legged towards the Land Rover and slumps into the passenger seat.

"Wait!" she demands. Tries to feel his wrist: "Did one of them bite you?"

His eyes roll. "Silly of me. No vertebrates." Then he leans back. "I'm going to try and hold on. Your first-aid training."

Maddy gets the glove off, exposing fingers like angry red sausages: but she can't find the wound on his left hand, can't find anything to suck the poison out of. John's breathing is labored and he twitches: he needs the hospital but it's at least a four-hour drive away and she can't look after him while she drives. So she puts another syringe load of atropine into his leg and waits with him for five minutes while he struggles for breath hoarsely, then follows up with adrenalin and anything else she can think of that's good for handling anaphylactic shock. "Get us back," he manages to wheeze at her between emphysemic gasps. "Samples too."

After she gets him into the load bed of the truck, she dashes over to the mock-termite mound with the spare petrol can. She splashes the best part of a gallon of fuel over the heap, coughing with the stink: she caps the jerry can, drags it away from the mound, then strikes a match and throws it flickering at the disordered insect kingdom. There's a soft *whump* as the igniting gas sets the mound aflame: small shapes writhe and crisp beneath an empty blue sky pierced by the glaring pinprick of S Doradus. Maddy doesn't stay to watch. She hauls the heavy sample case back to the Land Rover, loads it into the trunk alongside John, and scurries back towards town as fast as she can.

She's almost ten miles away before she remembers the camera, left staring in cyclopean isolation at the scorched remains of the dead colony.

HOMEWARD BOUND

The big ground effect ship rumbles softly as it cruises across the endless expanse of the Dzerzhinsky Ocean at nearly three hundred knots, homeward bound at last. Misha sits in his cubby-hole—as shipboard political officer he rates an office of his own—and sweats over his report with the aid of a glass of Polish pear schnapps. Radio can't punch through more than a few thousand miles of air directly, however powerful the transmitters; on earth they used to bounce signals off the ionosphere or the moon, but that doesn't work here—the other disks are too far away to use as relays. There's a chain of transceiver buoys marching out across the ocean at two thousand kilometer intervals, but the equipment is a pig to maintain, very expensive to build, and nobody is even joking about stringing undersea cables across a million kilometers of sea floor. Misha's problem is that the expedition, himself included, is effectively stranded back in the eighteenth century, without even the telegraph to tie civilization together—which is a pretty pickle to find yourself in when you're the bearer of news that will make the Politburo shit a brick. He desperately wants to be able to boost this up the ladder a bit, but instead it's going to be his name and his alone on the masthead.

"Bastards. Why couldn't they give us a signal rocket or two?" He gulps back what's left of the schnapps and winds a fresh sandwich of paper and carbon into his top-secret-eyes-only typewriter.

"Because it would weigh too much, Misha," the captain says right behind his left shoulder, causing him to jump and bang his head on the overhead locker.

When Misha stops swearing and Gagarin stops chuckling, the Party man carefully turns his stack of typescript face down on the desk then politely gestures the captain into his office. "What can I do for you, boss? And what do you mean, they're too heavy?"

Gagarin shrugs. "We looked into it. Sure, we could put a tape recorder and a transmitter into an ICBM and shoot it up to twenty thousand kilometers. Trouble is, it'd fall down again in an hour or so. The fastest we could squirt the message, it would cost about ten rubles a character—more to the point, even a lightweight rocket would weigh as much as our entire payload. Maybe in ten years." He sits down. "How are you doing with that report?"

Misha sighs. "How am I going to explain to Brezhnev that the Americans aren't the only mad bastards with hydrogen bombs out here? That we've found the new world and the new world is just like the old world, except it glows in the dark? And the only communists we've found so far are termites with guns?" For a moment he looks haggard. "It's been nice knowing you, Yuri."

"Come on! It can't be that bad—" Gagarin's normally sunny disposition is clouded.

"*You* try and figure out how to break the news to them." After identifying the first set of ruins, they'd sent one of their MiGs out, loaded with camera pods and fuel: a thousand kilometers inland it had seen the same ominous story of nuclear annihilation visited on an alien civilization: ruins of airports, railroads, cities, factories. A familiar topography in unfamiliar form.

This was New York—once, thousands of years before a giant stamped the bottom of Manhattan island into the sea bed—and that was once Washington, D.C. Sure there'd been extra skyscrapers, but they'd hardly needed the subsequent coastal cruise to be sure that what they were looking at was the same continent as the old capitalist enemy, thousands of years and millions of kilometers beyond a nuclear war. "We're running for home like a dog that's seen the devil ride out, hoping that he doesn't see us and follow us home for a new winter hat."

Gagarin frowns. "Excuse me?" He points to the bottle of pear schnapps.

"You are my guest." Misha pours the First Cosmonaut a glass then tops up his own. "It opens certain ideological conflicts, Yuri. And nobody wants to be the bearer of bad news."

"Ideological—such as?"

"Ah." Misha takes a mouthful. "Well, we have so far avoided nuclear annihilation and invasion by the forces of reactionary terror during the Great Patriotic War, but only by the skin of our teeth. Now, doctrine has it that any alien species advanced enough to travel in space is almost certain to have discovered socialism, if not true communism, no? And that the enemies of socialism wish to destroy socialism, and take its resources for themselves. But what we've seen here is evidence of a different sort. This *was* America. It follows that somewhere nearby there is a continent that *was* home to another Soviet Union—two thousand years ago. But this America has been wiped out, and our elder Soviet brethren are not in evidence and they have not colonized this other-America—what can this mean?"

Gagarin's brow wrinkled. "They're dead too? I mean, that the alternate-Americans wiped them out in an act of colonialist imperialist aggression but did not survive their treachery," he adds hastily.

Misha's lips quirk in something approaching a grin: "Better work on getting your terminology right first time before you see Brezhnev, comrade," he says. "Yes, you are correct on the facts, but there are matters of *interpretation* to consider. No colonial exploitation has occurred. So either the perpetrators were also wiped out, or perhaps . . . well, it opens up several very dangerous avenues of thought. Because if New Soviet Man isn't home hereabouts, it implies that something happened to them, doesn't it? Where are all the true Communists? If it turns out that they ran into hostile aliens, then . . . well, theory says that aliens should be good brother socialists. Theory and ten rubles will buy you a bottle of vodka on this one. Something is badly wrong with our understanding of the direction of history."

"I suppose there's no question that there's something we don't know about," Gagarin adds in the ensuing silence, almost as an afterthought.

"Yes. And that's a fig leaf of uncertainty we can hide behind, I hope." Misha puts his glass down and stretches his arms behind his head, fingers interlaced until his knuckles crackle. "Before we left, our agents reported signals picked up in America from—damn, I should not be telling you this without authorization. Pretend I said nothing." His frown returns.

"You sound as if you're having dismal thoughts," Gagarin prods.

"I *am* having dismal thoughts, comrade colonel-general, very dismal thoughts indeed. We have been behaving as if this world we occupy is merely a new geopolitical game board, have we not? Secure in the knowledge that brother socialists from beyond the stars brought us here to save us from the folly of the imperialist aggressors, or that anyone else we meet will be either barbarians or good communists, we have fallen into the pattern of an earlier age—expanding in all directions, recognizing no limits, assuming our manifest destiny. But what if there are limits? Not a barbed-wire fence or a line in the sand, but something more subtle. Why does history demand success of *us*? What we know is the right way for humans on a human world, with an industrial society, to live. But this is not a human world. And what if it's a world where we're not destined to succeed? Or what if the very circumstances which gave rise to Marxism are themselves transient, in the broader scale? What if there is a—you'll pardon me—a materialist God? We know this is our own far future we are living in. *Why* would any power vast enough to build this disk bring us here?"

Gagarin shakes his head. "There are no limits, my friend," he says, a trifle condescendingly: "if there were, do you think we would have gotten this far?"

Misha thumps his desk angrily. "Why do you think they put us somewhere where your precious rockets don't work?" he demands. "Get up on high, one push of rocket exhaust and you could be halfway to anywhere! But down here we have to slog through the atmosphere. We can't get away! Does that sound like a gift from one friend to another?"

"The way you are thinking sounds paranoid to me," Gagarin insists. "I'm not saying you're wrong, mind you: only—could you be overwrought? Finding those bombed cities affected us all, I think."

Misha glances out of his airliner-sized porthole: "I fear there's more to it than that. We're not unique, comrade; we've been here before. *And we all died.* We're a fucking duplicate, Yuri Alexeyevich, there's a larger context to all this. And I'm scared by what the politburo will decide to do when they see the evidence. Or what the Americans will do . . ."

LAST SUPPER

Returning to Manhattan is a comfort of sorts for Gregor, after the exposed plazas and paranoid open vistas of the capital. Unfortunately he won't be here for long—he is, after all, on an assignment from Brundle—but he'll take what comfort he can from the deep stone canyons, the teeming millions scurrying purposefully about at ground level. The Big Apple is a hive of activity, as always, teeming purposeful trails of information leading the busy workers about their tasks. Gregor's nostrils flare as he stands on the sidewalk on Lexington and East 100th. There's an Italian restaurant Brundle recommended when he gave Gregor his briefing papers. "Their spaghetti al' polpette is to die for," Brundle told him. That's probably true, but what's inarguable is that it's only a couple of blocks away from the offices of the Exobiology Annex to Cornell's New York campus, where Sagan is head of department.

Gregor opens the door and glances around. A waiter makes eye contact. "Table for one?"

"Two. I'm meeting—ah." Gregor sees Sagan sitting in a booth at the back of the restaurant and waves hesitantly. "He's already here."

Gregor nods and smiles at Sagan as he sits down opposite the professor. The waiter drifts over and hands him a menu. "Have you ordered?"

"I just got here." Sagan smiles guardedly. "I'm not sure why you wanted this meeting, Mr., uh, Samsa, isn't it?" Clearly he thinks he gets the joke—a typical mistake for a brilliant man to make.

Gregor allows his lower lip to twitch. "Believe me, I'd rather it wasn't necessary," he says, entirely truthfully. "But the climate in D.C. isn't really conducive to clear thought or long-range planning—I mean, we operate under constraints established by the political process. We're given questions to answer, we're not encouraged to come up with new questions. So what I'd like to do is just have an open-ended informal chat about anything that you think is worth considering. About our situation, I mean. In case you can open up any avenues we ought to be investigating that aren't on the map right now."

Sagan leans forward. "That's all very well," he says agreeably, "but I'm a bit puzzled by the policy process itself. We haven't yet made contact with any nonhuman sapients. I thought your committee was supposed to be assessing our policy options for when contact finally occurs. It sounds to me as if you're telling me that we already have a policy, and you're looking to find out if it's actually a viable one. Is that right?"

Gregor stares at him. "I can neither confirm nor deny that," he says evenly. Which is the truth. "But if you want to take some guesses I can either discuss things or clam up when you get too close," he adds, the muscles around his eyes crinkling conspiratorially.

"Aha." Sagan grins back at him boyishly. "I get it." His smile vanishes abruptly. "Let me guess. The policy is predicated on MAD, isn't it?"

Gregor shrugs then glances sideways, warningly: the waiter is approaching. "I'll have a glass of the house red," he says, sending the fellow away as fast as possible. "Deterrence presupposes communication, don't you think?" Gregor asks.

"True." Sagan picks up his bread knife and absentmindedly twirls it between finger and thumb. "But it's how the idiots—excuse me, our elected leaders—treat threats, and I can't see them responding to tool-using nonhumans as anything else." He stares at Gregor. "Let me see if I've got this right. Your committee pulled me in because there has, in fact, been a contact between humans and nonhuman intelligences—or at least some sign that there are NHIs out there. The existing policy for dealing with it was drafted some time in the sixties under the influence of the hangover left by the Cuban war, and it basically makes the *conservative* assumption that any aliens are green-skinned Soviets and the only language they talk is nuclear annihilation. This policy is now seen to be every bit as bankrupt as it sounds but nobody knows what to replace it with because there's no data on the NHIs. Am I right?"

"I can neither confirm nor deny that," says Gregor.

Sagan sighs. "Okay, play it your way." He closes his menu. "Ready to order?"

"I believe so." Gregor looks at him. "The spaghetti al' polpette is really good here," he adds.

"Really?" Sagan smiles. "Then I'll try it."

They order, and Gregor waits for the waiter to depart before he continues. "Suppose there's an alien race out there. More than one. You know about the multiple copies of Earth. The uninhabited ones. We've been here before. Now let's see . . . suppose the aliens aren't like us. Some of them are recognizable, tribal primates who use tools made out of metal, sea-dwelling ensemble entities who communicate by ultrasound. But others—most of them—are social insects who use amazingly advanced biological engineering to grow what they need. There's some evidence that they've colonized some of the empty Earths. They're aggressive and territorial and they're so different that . . . well, for one thing we think they don't actually have conscious minds except when they need them. They control their own genetic code and build living organisms tailored to whatever tasks they want carrying out. There's no evidence that they want to talk to us, and some evidence that they may have emptied some of those empty Earths of their human population. And because of their, um, decentralized ecosystem and biological engineering, conventional policy solutions won't work. The military ones, I mean."

Gregor watches Sagan's face intently as he describes the scenario. There is a slight cooling of the exobiologist's cheeks as his peripheral arteries contract with shock: his pupils dilate and his respiration rate increases. Sour pheromones begin to diffuse from his sweat ducts and organs in Gregor's nasal sinuses respond to them.

"You're kidding?" Sagan half-asks. He sounds disappointed about something.

"I wish I was." Gregor generates a faint smile and exhales breath laden with oxytocin and other peptide messengers fine-tuned to human metabolism. In the kitchen, the temporary chef who is standing in for the regular one—off sick, due to a bout of food poisoning—will be preparing Sagan's dish. Humans are creatures of habit: once his meal arrives the astronomer will eat it, taking solace in good food. (Such a shame about the chef.) "They're not like us. SETI assumes that NHIs are conscious and welcome communication with humans and, in fact, that humans aren't atypical. But let's suppose that humans *are* atypical. The human species has only been around for about a third of a million years, and has only been making metal tools and building settlements for ten thousand. What if the default for sapient species is measured in the millions of years? And they develop strong defense mechanisms to prevent other species moving into their territory?"

"That's incredibly depressing," Sagan admits after a minute's contemplation. "I'm not sure I believe it without seeing some more evidence. That's why we wanted to use the Arecibo dish to send a message, you know. The other disks are far enough away that we're safe, whatever they send back: they can't possibly throw missiles at us, not with a surface escape velocity of twenty thousand miles per second, and if they send unpleasant messages we can stick our fingers in our ears."

The waiter arrives, and slides his entree in front of Sagan.

"Why do you say that?" asks Gregor.

"Well, for one thing, it doesn't explain the disk. We couldn't make anything like it—I suppose I was hoping we'd have some idea of who did? But from what you're telling me, insect hives with advanced biotechnology . . . that doesn't sound plausible."

"We have some information on that." Gregor smiles reassuringly. "For the time being, the important thing to recognize is that the species who are on the disk are roughly equivalent to ourselves in technological and scientific understanding. Give or take a couple of hundred years."

"Oh." Sagan perks up a bit.

"Yes," Gregor continues. "We have some information—I can describe our sources—but anyway. You've seen the changes to the structure of the galaxy we remember. How would you characterize that?"

"Hmm." Sagan is busy with a mouthful of delicious tetrodotoxin-laced meatballs. "It's clearly a Kardashev type-III civilization, harnessing the energy of an entire galaxy. What else?"

Gregor smiles. "Ah, those Russians, obsessed with coal and steel production! This is the information age, Dr. Sagan. What would the informational resources of a galaxy look like, if they were put to use? And to what use would an unimaginably advanced civilization put them?"

Sagan looks blank for a moment, his fork pausing halfway to his mouth, laden with a deadly promise. "I don't see—ah!" He smiles, finishes his forkful, and nods. "Do I take it that we're living in a nature reserve? Or perhaps an archaeology experiment?"

Gregor shrugs. "Humans are time-binding animals," he explains. "So are all the other tool-using sentient species we have been able to characterize; it appears to be the one common factor, they like to understand their past as a guide to their future. We have sources that have . . . think of a game of Chinese whispers? The belief that is most widely held is that the disk was made by the agencies we see at work restructuring the galaxy, to house their, ah, experiments in ontology. To view their own deep past, before they became whatever they are, and to decide whether the path through which they emerged was inevitable or a low probability outcome. The reverse face of the Drake equation, if you like."

Sagan shivers. "Are you telling me we're just . . . memories? Echoes from the past, reconstituted and replayed some unimaginable time in the future? That this entire monstrous joke of a cosmological experiment is just a sideshow?"

"Yes, Dr. Sagan," Gregor says soothingly. "After all, the disk is not so large compared to an entire galaxy, don't you think? And I would not say the sideshow is unimportant. Do you ever think about your own childhood? And wonder whether the you that sits here in front of me today was the inevitable product of your upbringing? Or could you have become someone completely different—an airline pilot, for example, or a banker? Alternatively, could *someone else* have become *you*? What set of circumstances combine to produce an astronomer and exobiologist? Why should a God not harbour the same curiosity?"

"So you're saying it's introspection, with a purpose. The galactic civilization wants to see its own birth."

"The galactic hive mind," Gregor soothes, amused at how easy it is to deal with Sagan. "Remember, information is key. Why should human-level intelligences be the highest level?" All the while he continues to breathe oxytocin and other peptide neurotransmitters across the table towards Sagan. "Don't let such speculations ruin your meal," he adds, phrasing it as an observation rather than an implicit command.

Sagan nods and returns to using his utensils. "That's very thought-provoking," he says, as he gratefully raises the first mouthful to his lips. "If this is based on hard intelligence it . . . well, I'm worried. Even if it's inference, I have to do some thinking about this. I hadn't really been thinking along these lines."

"I'm sure if there's an alien menace we'll defeat it," Gregor assures him as he masticates and swallows the neurotoxin-laced meatball in tomato sauce. And just for the moment, he is content to relax in the luxury of truth: "Just leave everything to me and I'll see that your concerns are communicated to the right people. Then we'll do something about your dish and everything will work out for the best."

POOR PROGNOSIS

Maddy visits John regularly in hospital. At first it's a combination of natural compassion and edgy guilt; John is pretty much alone on this continent of lies, being both socially and occupationally isolated, and Maddy can convince herself that she's helping him feel in touch, motivating him to recover. Later on it's a necessity of work—she's keeping the lab going, even feeding the squirming white horror in the earth-filled glass jar, in John's absence—and partly boredom. It's not as if Bob's at home much. His work assignments frequently take him to new construction sites up and down the coast. When he is home they frequently argue into the small hours, picking at the scabs on their relationship with the sullen pinch-faced resentment of a couple fifty years gone in despair at the wrongness of their shared direction. So she escapes by visiting John and tells herself that she's doing it to keep his spirits up as he learns to use his prostheses.

"You shouldn't blame yourself," he tells her one afternoon when he notices her staring. "If you hadn't been around I'd be dead. Neither of us was to know."

"Well." Maddy winces as he sits up, then raises the tongs to his face to nudge the grippers apart before reaching for the water glass. "That won't"—she changes direction in mid-sentence—"make it easier to cope."

"We're all going to have to cope," he says gnomically, before re-laxing back against the stack of pillows. He's a lot better now than he was when he first arrived, delirious with his hand swollen and blacken-ing, but the after-effects of the mock-termite venom have weakened him in other ways. "I want to know why those things don't live closer to the coast. I mean, if they did we'd never have bothered with the place. After the first landing, that is." He frowns. "If you can ask at the crown surveyor's office if there are any relevant records, that would help."

"The crown surveyor's not very helpful." That's an understate-ment. The crown surveyor is some kind of throwback; last time she went in to his office to ask about maps of the north-east plateau he'd asked her whether her husband approved of her running around like this. "Maybe when you're out of here." She moves her chair closer to the side of the bed.

"Doctor Smythe says next week, possibly Monday or Tuesday." John sounds frustrated. "The pins and needles are still there." It's not just his right hand, lopped off below the elbow and replaced with a crude affair of padding and spring steel; the venom spread and some of his toes had to be amputated. He was fitting when Maddy reached the hospital, two hours after he was bitten. She knows she saved his life, that if he'd gone out alone he'd almost certainly have been killed, so why does she feel so bad about it?

"You're getting better," Maddy insists, covering his left hand with her own. "You'll see." She smiles encouragingly.

"I wish—" For a moment John looks at her; then he shakes his head minutely and sighs. He grips her hand with his fingers. They feel weak, and she can feel them trembling with the effort. "Leave Johnson"—the surveyor—"to me. I need to prepare an urgent report on the mock-termites before anyone else goes poking them."

"How much of a problem do you think they're going to be?"

"Deadly." He closes his eyes for a few seconds, then opens them again. "We've got to map their population distribution. And tell the governor-general's office. I counted twelve of them in roughly an acre, but that was a rough sample and you can't extrapolate from it. We also need to learn whether they've got any unusual swarming behaviors—like army ants, for example, or bees. Then we can start investigating whether any of our insecticides work on them. If the governor wants to start spinning out satellite towns next year, he's going to need to know what to expect. Otherwise people are going to get hurt." *Or killed*, Maddy adds silently.

John is very lucky to be alive: Doctor Smythe compared his condition to a patient he'd once seen who'd been bitten by a rattler, and that was the result of a single bite by a small one. *If the continental interior is full of the things, what are we going to do?* Maddy wonders.

"Have you seen any sign of her majesty feeding?" John asks, breaking into her train of thought.

Maddy shivers. "Turtle tree leaves go down well," she says quietly. "And she's given birth to two workers since we've had her. They chew the leaves to mulch then regurgitate it for her."

"Oh, really? Do they deliver straight into her mandibles?"

Maddy squeezes her eyes tight. This is the bit she was really hoping John wouldn't ask her about. "No," she says faintly.

"Really?" He sounds curious.

"I think you'd better see for yourself." Because there's no way in hell that Maddy is going to tell him about the crude wooden spoons the mock-termite workers have been crafting from the turtle tree branches, or the feeding ritual, and what they did to the bumbler fly that got into the mock-termite pen through the chicken wire screen. He'll just have to see for himself.

RUSHMORE

The *Korolev* is huge for a flying machine but pretty small in nautical terms. Yuri is mostly happy about this. He's a fighter jock at heart and he can't stand Navy bullshit. Still, it's a far cry from the MiG-17s he qualified in. It doesn't have a cockpit, or even a flight deck—it has a *bridge*, like a ship, with the pilots, flight engineers, navigators, and observers sitting in a horseshoe around the captain's chair. When it's thumping across the sea barely ten meters above the wave-tops at nearly five hundred kilometers per hour, it rattles and shakes until the crew's

vision blurs. The big reactor-powered turbines in the tail pods roar and
the neutron detectors on the turquoise radiation bulkhead behind them
tick like demented death-watch beetles: the rest of the crew are huddled
down below in the nose, with as much shielding between them and the
engine rooms as possible. It's a white-knuckle ride, and Yuri has difficulty resisting the urge to curl his hands into fists because whenever he
loses concentration his gut instincts are telling him to grab the stick and
pull up. The ocean is no aviator's friend, and skimming across this infinite gray expanse between planet-sized land-masses forces Gagarin to
confront the fact that he is not, by instinct, a sailor.

They're two days outbound from the new-old North America,
forty thousand kilometers closer to home and still weeks away even
though they're cutting the corner on their parabolic exploration track.
The fatigue is getting to him as he takes his seat next to Misha—who
is visibly wilting from his twelve-hour shift at the con—and straps
himself in. "Anything to report?" he asks.

"I don't like the look of the ocean ahead," says Misha. He nods at
the navigation station to Gagarin's left: Shaw, the Irish ensign, sees
him and salutes.

"Permission to report, sir?" Gagarin nods. "We're coming up on a
thermocline boundary suggestive of another radiator wall, this time
surrounding uncharted seas. Dead reckoning says we're on course for
home but we haven't charted this route and the surface waters are getting much cooler. Any time now we should be spotting the radiators,
and then we're going to have to start keeping a weather eye out."

Gagarin sighs: exploring new uncharted oceans seemed almost
romantic at first, but now it's a dangerous but routine task. "You have
kept the towed array at altitude?" he asks.

"Yes sir," Misha responds. The towed array is basically a kite-
born radar, tugged along behind the *Korolev* on the end of a kilometer
of steel cable to give them some warning of obstacles ahead. "Nothing
showing—"

Right on cue, one of the radar operators raises a hand and waves
three fingers.

"—Correction, radiators ahoy, range three hundred, bearing . . .
okay, let's see it."

"Maintain course," Gagarin announces. "Let's throttle back to two hundred once we clear the radiators, until we know what we're running into." He leans over to his left, watching over Shaw's shoulder.

The next hour is unpleasantly interesting. As they near the radiator fins, the water and the air above it cool down. The denser air helps the *Korolev* generate lift, which is good, but they need it, which is bad. The sky turns gray and murky and rain falls in continuous sheets that hammer across the armored bridge windows like machine-gun fire. The ride becomes gusty as well as bumpy, until Gagarin orders two of the nose turbines started just in case they hit a down-draft. The big jet engines guzzle fuel and are usually shut down in cruise flight, used only for take-off runs and extraordinary situations. But punching through a cold front and a winter storm isn't flying as usual as far as Gagarin's concerned, and the one nightmare all ekranoplan drivers face is running into a monster ocean wave nose-first at cruise speed.

Presently the navigators identify a path between two radiator fins, and Gagarin authorizes it. He's beginning to relax as the huge monoliths loom out of the gray clouds ahead when one of the sharp-eyed pilots shouts: "Icebergs!"

"*Fucking* hell." Gagarin sits bolt-upright. "Start all boost engines! Bring up full power on both reactors! Lower flaps to nine degrees and get us the hell out of this!" He turns to Shaw, his face gray. "Bring the towed array aboard, *now*."

"Shit." Misha starts flipping switches on his console, which doubles as damage control central. "*Icebergs*?"

The huge ground-effect ship lurches and roars as the third pilot starts bleeding hot exhaust gasses from the running turbines to start the other twelve engines. They've probably got less than six hours' fuel left, and it takes fifteen minutes on all engines to get off the water, but Gagarin's not going to risk meeting an iceberg head-on in ground-effect. The ekranoplan can function as a huge, lumbering, ungainly sea-plane if it has to; but it doesn't have the engine power to do so on reactors alone, or to leap-frog floating mountains of ice. And hitting an iceberg isn't on Gagarin's to-do list.

The rain sluices across the roof of the bridge and now the sky is louring and dark, the huge walls of the radiator slabs bulking in twilight to either side. The rain is freezing, supercooled droplets that smear the Korolev's wings with a lethal sheen of ice. "Where are the leading edge heaters?" Gagarin asks. "Come on!"

"Working, sir," calls the number four pilot. Moments later the treacherous rain turns to hailstones, rattling and booming but fundamentally unlikely to stick to the flight surfaces and build up weight until it flips the ship over. "I think we're going to—"

A white and ghostly wall comes into view in the distance, hammering towards the bridge windows like a runaway freight train. Gagarin's stomach lurches. "Pull up, pull up!" The first and second pilots are struggling with the hydraulically boosted controls as the *Korolev*'s nose pitches up almost ten degrees, right out of ground effect. "Come on!"

They make it.

The iceberg slams out of the darkness of the storm and the sea like the edge of the world; fifty meters high and as massive as mountains, it has lodged against the aperture between the radiator fins. Billions of tons of pack-ice has stopped dead in the water, creaking and groaning with the strain as it butts up against the infinite. The *Korolev* skids over the leading edge of the iceberg, her keel barely clearing it by ten meters, and continues to climb laboriously into the darkening sky. The blazing twin eyes of her reactors burn slick scars into the ice below. Then they're into the open water beyond the radiator fins, and although the sea below them is an expanse of whiteness they are also clear of icy mountains.

"Shut down engines three through fourteen," Gagarin orders once he regains enough control to keep the shakes out of his voice. "Take us back down to thirty meters, lieutenant. Meteorology, what's our situation like?"

"Arctic or worse, comrade general." The meteorologist, a hatchet-faced woman from Minsk, shakes her head. "Air temperature outside is thirty below, pressure is high." The rain and hail has vanished along with the radiators and the clear seas—and the light, for it is now fading towards nightfall.

"Hah. Misha, what do you think?"

"I think we've found our way into the freezer, sir. Permission to put the towed array back up?"

Gagarin squints into the darkness. "Lieutenant, keep us at two hundred steady. Misha, yes, get the towed array back out again. We need to see where we're going."

The next three hours are simultaneously boring and fraught. It's darker and colder than a Moscow apartment in winter during a power cut; the sea below is ice from horizon to horizon, cracking and groaning and splintering in a vast expanding V-shape behind the *Korolev*'s pressure wake. The spectral ruins of the Milky Way galaxy stretch overhead, reddened and stirred by alien influences. Misha supervises the relaunch of the towed array, then hands over to Major Suvurov before stiffly standing and going below to the unquiet bunk room. Gagarin sticks to a quarter-hourly routine of reports, making sure that he knows what everyone is doing. Bridge crew come and go for their regular station changes. It is routine, and deadly with it. Then:

"Sir, I have a return. Permission to report?"

"Go ahead." Gagarin nods to the navigator. "Where?"

"Bearing zero—it's horizon to horizon—there's a crest rising up to ten meters above the surface. Looks like landfall, range one sixty and closing. Uh, there's a gap and a more distant landfall at thirty-five degrees, peak rising to two hundred meters."

"That's some cliff." Gagarin frowns. He feels drained, his brain hazy with the effort of making continual decisions after six hours in the hot seat and more than two days of this thumping roaring progression. He glances round. Major? Please summon Colonel Gorodin. Helm, come about to zero thirty-five. We'll take a look at the gap and see if it's a natural inlet. If this is a continental mass we might as well take a look before we press on for home."

For the next hour they drive onwards into the night, bleeding off speed and painting in the gaps in the radar map of the coastline. It's a bleak frontier, inhumanly cold, with a high interior plateau. There are indeed two headlands, promontories jutting into the coast from either side of a broad, deep bay. Hills rise from one of the promontories and across the bay. Something about it strikes Gagarin as strangely familiar, if only he could place it. Another echo of Earth? But it's too cold by far, a deep Antarctic chill. And he's not familiar with the coastline of Zemlya, the myriad inlets off the north-east passage, where the submarines cruise on eternal vigilant patrols to defend the frontier of the Rodina.

A thin pre-dawn light stains the icy hilltops gray as the *Korolev* cruises slowly between the headlands—several kilometers apart—and into the wide open bay beyond. Gagarin raises his binoculars and scans the distant coastline. There are structures, straight lines! "Another ruined civilization?" he asks quietly.

"Maybe, sir. Think anyone could survive in this weather?" The temperature has dropped another ten degrees in the pre-dawn chill, although the ekranoplan is kept warm by the outflow of its two Kuznetsov aviation reactors.

"Hah."

Gagarin begins to sweep the northern coast when Major Suvurov stands up. "Sir! Over there!"

"Where?" Gagarin glances at him. Suvurov is quivering with anger, or shock, or something else. He, too, has his binoculars out.

"Over there! On the southern hillside."

"Where—" He brings his binoculars to bear as the dawn light spills across the shattered stump of an immense skyscraper.

There is a hillside behind it, a jagged rift where the land has risen up a hundred meters. It reeks of antiquity, emphasized by the carvings in the headland. Here is what the expedition has been looking for all along, the evidence that they are not alone.

"My God," Misha swears, shocked into politically incorrect language.

"Marx," says Gagarin, studying the craggy features of the nearest head. "I've seen this before, this sort of thing. The Americans have a memorial like it. Mount Rushmore, they call it."

"Don't you mean Easter Island?" asks Misha. "Sculptures left by a vanished people . . ."

"Nonsense! Look there, isn't that Lenin? And Stalin, of course." Even though the famous moustache is cracked and half of it has fallen away from the cliff. "But who's that next to them?"

Gagarin brings his binoculars to focus on the fourth head. Somehow it looks far less weathered than the others, as if added as an afterthought, perhaps some kind of insane statement about the mental health of its vanished builders. Both antennae have long since broken off, and one of the mandibles is damaged, but the eyeless face is still recognizably unhuman. The insectile head stares eyelessly out across

the frozen ocean, an enigma on the edge of a devastated island continent. "I think we've found the brother socialists," he mutters to Misha,
his voice pitched low so that it won't carry over the background noise
on the flight deck. "And you know what? Something tells me they
didn't win."

ANTHROPIC ERROR

As the summer dry season grinds on, Maddy finds herself spending
more time at John's home-cum-laboratory, doing the cleaning and cooking for herself in addition to maintaining the lab books and feeding the
live specimens. During her afternoons visiting in the hospital she helps
him write up his reports. Losing his right hand has hit John hard: he's
teaching himself to write again but his handwriting is slow and childish.

She finds putting in extra hours at the lab preferable to the empty
and uncomfortable silences back in the two-bedroom prefab she
shares with Bob. Bob is away on field trips to outlying ranches and
quarries half the time and working late the other half. At least, he says
he's working late. Maddy has her suspicions. He gets angry if she isn't
around to cook, and she gets angry right back at him when he expects
her to clean, and they've stopped having sex. Their relationship is in
fact going downhill rapidly, drying up and withering away in the arid
continental heat, until going to work in John's living room, among the
cages and glass vivaria and books feels like taking refuge. She took to
spending more time there, working late for real, and when Bob is
away she sleeps on the wicker settee in the dining room.

One day, more than a month later than expected, Dr. Smythe finally decides that John is well enough to go home. Embarrassingly,
she's not there on the afternoon when he's finally discharged. Instead,
she's in the living room, typing up a report on a sub-species of the turtle tree and its known parasites, when the screen door bangs and the
front door opens. "Maddy?"

She squeaks before she can stop herself. "John?" She's out of the
chair to help him with the battered suitcase the cabbie half-helpfully
left on the front stoop.

"Maddy." He smiles tiredly. "I've missed being home."

"Come on in." She closes the screen door and carries the suitcase over to the stairs. He's painfully thin now, a far cry from the slightly too plump entomologist she'd met on the colony liner. "I've got lots of stuff for you to read—but not until you're stronger. Don't want you over-working and putting yourself back in hospital!"

"You're an angel." He stands uncertainly in his own living room, looking around as if he hadn't quite expected to see it again. "I'm looking forward to seeing the termites."

She shivers abruptly. "I'm not. Come on." She climbs the stairs with the suitcase, not looking back. She pushes through the door into the one bedroom that's habitable—he's been using the other one to store samples—and dumps the case on the rough dressing table. She's been up here before, first to collect his clothing while he was in hospital and later to clean and make sure there are no poisonous spiders lurking in the corners. It smells of camphor and dusty memories. She turns to face him. "Welcome home." She smiles experimentally.

He looks around. "You've been cleaning."

"Not much." She feels her face heat.

He shakes his head. "Thank you."

She can't decide what to say. "No, no, it's not like that. If I wasn't here I'd be . . ."

John shuffles. She blinks at him, feeling stupid and foolish. "Do you have room for a lodger?" she asks.

He looks at her and she can't maintain eye contact. It's all going wrong, not what she wanted.

"Things going badly?" he asks, cocking his head on one side and staring at her. "Forgive me, I don't mean to pry—"

"No, no, it's quite alright." She sniffs. Takes a breath. "This continent breaks things. Bob hasn't been the same since we arrived, or I, I haven't. I need to put some space between us, for a bit."

"Oh."

"Oh." She's silent for a while. "I can pay rent—"

This is an excuse, a transparent rationalization, and not entirely true, but she's saved from digging herself deeper into a lie because John manages to stumble and reaches out to steady himself with his right arm, which is still not entirely healed, and Maddy finds herself with his weight on her shoulder as he hisses in pain. "Ow! Ow!"

"I'm sorry! I'm sorry!"

"It wasn't you—" They make it to the bed and she sits him down beside her. "I nearly blacked out then. I feel useless. I'm not half the man I was."

"I don't know about that," she says absently, not quite registering his meaning. She strokes his cheek, feeling it slick with sweat. The pulse in his neck is strong. "You're still recovering. I think they sent you home too early. Let's get you into bed and rest up for a couple of hours, then see about something to eat. What do you say to that?"

"I shouldn't need nursing," he protests faintly as she bends down and unties his shoelaces. "I don't need . . . nursing." He runs his fingers through her hair.

"This isn't about nursing."

Two hours later, the patient is drifting on the edge of sleep, clearly tired out by his physical therapy and the strain of homecoming. Maddy lies curled up against his shoulder, staring at the ceiling. She feels calm and at peace for the first time since she arrived here. *It's not about Bob any more, is it*? she asks herself. *It's not about what anybody expects of me. It's about what I want, about finding my place in the universe.* She feels her face relaxing into a smile. Truly, for a moment, it feels as if the entire universe is revolving around her in stately synchrony.

John snuffles slightly then startles and tenses. She can tell he's come to wakefulness. "Funny," he says quietly, then clears his throat.

"What is?" *Please don't spoil this*, she prays.

"I wasn't expecting this." He moves beside her. "Wasn't expecting much of anything."

"Was it good?" She tenses.

"Do you still want to stay?" he asks hesitantly. "Damn, I didn't mean to sound as if—"

"No, I don't mind—" She rolls towards him, then is brought up short by a quiet, insistent tapping that travels up through the inner wall of the house. "Damn," she says quietly.

"What's that?" He begins to sit up.

"It's the termites."

John listens intently. The tapping continues erratically, on-again, off-again, bursts of clattering noise. "What is she doing?"

"They do it about twice a day," Maddy confesses. "I put her in the number two aquarium with a load of soil and leaves and a mesh lid on top. When they start making a racket I feed them."

He looks surprised. "This I've got to see."

The walls are coming back up again. Maddy stifles a sigh: it's not about her any more, it's about the goddamn mock-termites. Anyone would think they were the center of the universe and she was just here to feed them. "Let's go look, then." John is already standing up, trying to pick up his discarded shirt with his prosthesis. "Don't bother," she tells him. "Who's going to notice, the insects?"

"I thought"—he glances at her, taken aback—"sorry, forget it."

She pads downstairs, pausing momentarily to make sure he's following her safely. The tapping continues, startlingly loud. She opens the door to the utility room in the back and turns on the light. "Look," she says.

The big glass-walled aquarium sits on the worktop. It's lined with rough-tamped earth and on top, there are piles of denuded branches and wood shavings. It's near dusk, and by the light filtering through the windows she can see mock-termites moving across the surface of the muddy dome that bulges above the queen's chamber. A group of them have gathered around a curiously straight branch: as she watches, they throw it against the glass like a battering ram against a castle wall. A pause, then they pick it up and pull back, and throw it again. They're huge for insects, almost two inches long: much bigger than the ones thronging the mounds in the outback. "That's odd." Maddy peers at them. "They've grown since yesterday."

"They? Hang on, did you take workers, or . . . ?"

"No, just the queen. None of these bugs are more than a month old."

The termites have stopped banging on the glass. They form two rows on either side of the stick, pointing their heads up at the huge, monadic mammals beyond the alien barrier. Looking at them closely Maddy notices other signs of morphological change: the increasing complexity of their digits, the bulges at the back of their heads. *Is the queen's changing, too?* she asks herself, briefly troubled by visions of a malignant intelligence rapidly swelling beneath the surface of the vivarium, plotting its escape by moonlight.

John stands behind Maddy and folds his arms around her. She shivers. "I feel as if they're *watching* us."

"But to them it's not about us, is it?" he whispers in her ear. "Come on. All that's happening is you've trained them to ring a bell so the experimenters give them a snack. They think the universe was made for their convenience. Dumb insects, just a bundle of reflexes really. Let's feed them and go back to bed."

The two humans leave and climb the stairs together, arm in arm, leaving the angry aboriginal hive to plot its escape unnoticed.

IT'S ALWAYS OCTOBER THE FIRST

Gregor sits on a bench on the Esplanade, looking out across the river towards the Statue of Liberty. He's got a bag of stale bread-crumbs and he's ministering to the flock of pigeons that scuttle and peck around his feet. The time is six minutes to three on the afternoon of October the First, and the year is irrelevant. In fact, it's too late. This is how it always ends, although the onshore breeze and the sunlight are unexpected bonus payments.

The pigeons jostle and chase one another as he drops another piece of crust on the pavement. For once, he hasn't bothered to soak them overnight in 5 percent warfarin solution. There *is* such a thing as a free lunch, if you're a pigeon in the wrong place at the wrong time. He's going to be dead soon, and if any of the pigeons survive they're welcome to the wreckage.

There aren't many people about, so when the puffing middle-aged guy in the suit comes into view, jogging along as if he's chasing his stolen wallet, Gregor spots him instantly. It's Brundle, looking slightly pathetic when removed from his man-hive. Gregor waves hesitantly, and Brundle alters course.

"Running late," he pants, kicking at the pigeons until they flap away to make space for him at the other end of the bench.

"Really?"

Brundle nods. "They should be coming over the horizon in another five minutes."

"How did you engineer it?" Gregor isn't particularly interested but technical chitchat serves to pass the remaining seconds.

"Man-in-the-middle, ramified by all their intelligence assessments." Brundle looks self-satisfied. "Understanding their caste specialization makes it easier. Two weeks ago we told the GRU that Kennedy was using the NP-101 program as cover for a preemptive D-SLAM strike. At the same time we got the NOAA to increase their mapping launch frequency, and pointed the increased level of Soviet activity out to our sources in SAC. It doesn't take much to get the human hives buzzing with positive feedback."

Of course, Brundle and Gregor aren't using words for this incriminating exchange. Their phenotypically human bodies conceal some useful modifications, knobby encapsulated tumors of neuroectoderm that shield the delicate tissues of their designers, neural circuits that have capabilities human geneticists haven't even imagined. A visitor from a more advanced human society might start excitedly chattering about wet-phase nanomachines and neural-directed broadband packet radio, but nobody in New York on a sunny day in 1979 plus one million is thinking in those terms. They still think the universe belongs to their own kind, skull-locked social—but not eusocial—primates. Brundle and Gregor know better. They're workers of a higher order, carefully tailored to the task in hand, and although they *look* human there's less to their humanity than meets the eye. Even Gagarin can probably guess better, an individualist trapped in the machinery of a utopian political hive. The termites of New Iowa and a host of other Galapagos continents on the disk are not the future, but they're a superior approximation to anything humans have achieved, even those planetary instantiations that have doctored their own genome in order to successfully implement true eusocial societies. Group minds aren't prone to anthropic errors.

"So it's over, is it?" Gregor asks aloud, in the stilted serial speech to which humans are constrained.

"Yep. Any minute now—"

The air raid sirens begin to wail. Pigeons spook, exploding outward in a cloud of white panic.

"Oh, look."

The entity behind Gregor's eyes stares out across the river, marking time while his cancers call home. He's always vague about these last hours before the end of a mission—a destructive time, in which information is lost—but at least he remembers the rest. As do the hyphae of the huge rhizome network spreading deep beneath the park, thinking slow vegetable thoughts and relaying his sparky monadic flashes back to his mother by way of the engineered fungal strands that thread the deep ocean floors. The next version of him will be created knowing almost everything: the struggle to contain the annoying, hard-to-domesticate primates with their insistent paranoid individualism, the dismay of having to carefully sterilize the few enlightened ones like Sagan . . .

Humans are not useful. The future belongs to ensemble intelligences, hive minds. Even the mock-termite aboriginals have more to contribute. And Gregor, with his teratomas and his shortage of limbs, has more to contribute than most. The culture that sent him, and a million other anthropomorphic infiltrators, understands this well: he will be rewarded and propagated, his genome and memeome preserved by the collective even as it systematically eliminates yet another outbreak of humanity. The collective is well on its way towards occupying a tenth of the disk, or at least of sweeping it clean of competing life forms. Eventually it will open negotiations with its neighbors on the other disks, joining the process of forming a distributed consciousness that is a primitive echo of the vast ramified intelligence wheeling across the sky so far away. And this time round, knowing *why* it is being birthed, the new God will have a level of self-understanding denied to its parent.

Gregor anticipates being one of the overmind's memories: it is a fate none of these humans will know save at second-hand, filtered through his eusocial sensibilities. To the extent that he bothers to consider the subject, he thinks it is a disappointment. He may be here to help exterminate them, but it's not a personal grudge: it's more like pouring gasoline on a troublesome ant heap that's settled in the wrong back yard. The necessity irritates him, and he grumbles aloud in Brundle's direction: "If they realized how thoroughly they'd been infiltrated, or how badly their own individuality lets them down—"

Flashes far out over the ocean, ruby glare reflected from the thin tatters of stratospheric cloud.

"—They might learn to cooperate some day. Like us."

More flashes, moving closer now as the nuclear battlefront evolves.

Brundle nods. "But then, they wouldn't be human any more. And in any case, they're much too late. A million years too late."

A flicker too bright to see, propagating faster than the signaling speed of nerves, punctuates their conversation. Seconds later, the mach wave flushes their cinders from the bleached concrete of the bench. Far out across the disk, the game of ape and ant continues; but in this place and for the present time, the question has been settled. And there are no human winners.

RIDING THE CROCODILE
Greg Egan

*Looking back at the century that's just ended, it's obvious that
Australian writer Greg Egan was one of the Big New Names to
emerge in SF in the '90s, and is probably one of the most significant talents to enter the field in the last several decades. Already one of the most widely known of all Australian genre
writers, Egan may well be the best new "hard-science" writer
to enter the field since Greg Bear, and is still growing in range,
power, and sophistication. In the last few years, he has become
a frequent contributor to* Interzone *and* Asimov's Science Fiction, *and has made sales as well as to* Pulphouse, Analog, Au-
realis, Eidolon, *and elsewhere; many of his stories have also
appeared in various "Best of the Year" series, and he was on
the Hugo Final Ballot in 1995 for his story "Cocoon," which
won the Ditmar Award and the Asimov's Readers Award. He
won the Hugo Award in 1999 for his novella "Oceanic." His
first novel,* Quarantine, *appeared in 1992; his second novel,*
Permutation City, *won the John W. Campbell Memorial Award
in 1994. His other books include the novels* Distress, Diaspora,
and Teranesia, *and three collections of his short fiction,* Ax-
iomatic, Luminous, *and* Our Lady of Chernobyl. *His most recent book is a new novel,* Schild's Ladder. *He has a Web site at
www.netspace.netau/^crgregegan/.*

*Egan's furthest penetration into the far future until now
was probably to be found in his story "Border Guards." Here
he takes us a good deal further into the future of an enhanced*

*and transmogrified human race to pose a profound and basic
question: is it possible to live too long? To succeed too well?
To have achieved everything you ever wanted to achieve? To
have reached a point where there's nothing worthwhile left to
do, and where the universe has run out of surprises for you?
And if you say "Yes," and mean it, what happens when that
universe suddenly comes up with a* brand-new *batch of surprises for you, and a whole new group of mysteries to be
solved?*

1

In their ten thousand, three hundred and ninth year of marriage, Leila
and Jasim began contemplating death. They had known love, raised
children, and witnessed the flourishing generations of their offspring.
They had traveled to a dozen worlds and lived among a thousand cultures. They had educated themselves many times over, proved theo-
rems, and acquired and abandoned artistic sensibilities and skills. They
had not lived in every conceivable manner, far from it, but what room
would there be for the multitude if each individual tried to exhaust the
permutations of existence? There were some experiences, they agreed,
that everyone should try, and others that only a handful of people in all
of time need bother with. They had no wish to give up their idiosyn-
crasies, no wish to uproot their personalities from the niches they had
settled in long ago, let alone start cranking mechanically through some
tedious enumeration of all the other people they might have been. They
had been themselves, and for that they had done, more or less, enough.

Before dying, though, they wanted to attempt something grand and
audacious. It was not that their lives were incomplete, in need of some
final flourish of affirmation. If some unlikely calamity had robbed
them of the chance to orchestrate this finale, the closest of their friends
would never have remarked upon, let alone mourned, its absence.
There was no esthetic compulsion to be satisfied, no aching existential
void to be filled. Nevertheless, it was what they both wanted, and once
they had acknowledged this to each other their hearts were set on it.

Choosing the project was not a great burden; that task required nothing but patience. They knew they'd recognize it when it came to them. Every night before sleeping, Jasim would ask Leila, "Did you see it yet?"

"No. Did you?"

"Not yet."

Sometimes Leila would dream that she'd found it in her dreams, but the transcripts proved otherwise. Sometimes Jasim felt sure that it was lurking just below the surface of his thoughts, but when he dived down to check it was nothing but a trick of the light.

Years passed. They occupied themselves with simple pleasures: gardening, swimming in the surf, talking with their friends, catching up with their descendants. They had grown skilled at finding pastimes that could bear repetition. Still, were it not for the nameless adventure that awaited them they would have thrown a pair of dice each evening and agreed that two sixes would end it all.

One night, Leila stood alone in the garden, watching the sky. From their home world, Najib, they had traveled only to the nearest stars with inhabited worlds, each time losing just a few decades to the journey. They had chosen those limits so as not to alienate themselves from friends and family, and it had never felt like much of a constraint. True, the civilization of the Amalgam wrapped the galaxy, and a committed traveler could spend two hundred thousand years circling back home, but what was to be gained by such an overblown odyssey? The dozen worlds of their neighborhood held enough variety for any traveler, and whether more distant realms were filled with fresh novelties or endless repetition hardly seemed to matter. To have a goal, a destination, would be one thing, but to drown in the sheer plenitude of worlds for its own sake seemed utterly pointless.

A destination? Leila overlaid the sky with information, most of it by necessity millennia out of date. There were worlds with spectacular views of nebulas and star clusters, views that could be guaranteed still to be in existence if they traveled to see them, but would taking in such sights firsthand be so much better than immersion in the flawless images already available in Najib's library? To blink away ten thousand years just to wake beneath a cloud of green and violet gas, however lovely, seemed like a terrible anticlimax.

The stars tingled with self-aggrandisement, plaintively tugging at her attention. The architecture here, the rivers, the festivals! Even if these tourist attractions could survive the millennia, even if some were literally unique, there was nothing that struck her as a fitting prelude to death. If she and Jasim had formed some whimsical attachment, centuries before, to a world on the other side of the galaxy rumoured to hold great beauty or interest, and if they had talked long enough about chasing it down when they had nothing better to do, then keeping that promise might have been worth it, even if the journey led them to a world in ruins. They had no such cherished destination, though, and it was too late to cultivate one now.

Leila's gaze followed a thinning in the advertising, taking her to the bulge of stars surrounding the galaxy's center. The disk of the Milky Way belonged to the Amalgam, whose various ancestral species had effectively merged into a single civilization, but the central bulge was inhabited by beings who had declined to do so much as communicate with those around them. All attempts to send probes into the bulge—let alone the kind of engineering spores needed to create the infrastructure for travel—had been gently but firmly rebuffed, with the intruders swatted straight back out again. The Aloof had maintained their silence and isolation since before the Amalgam itself had even existed.

The latest news on this subject was twenty thousand years old, but the status quo had held for close to a million years. If she and Jasim traveled to the innermost edge of the Amalgam's domain, the chances were exceptionally good that the Aloof would not have changed their ways in the meantime. In fact, it would be no disappointment at all if the Aloof had suddenly thrown open their borders: that unheralded thaw would itself be an extraordinary thing to witness. If the challenge remained, though, all the better.

She called Jasim to the garden and pointed out the richness of stars, unadorned with potted histories.

"We go where?" he asked.

"As close to the Aloof as we're able."

"And do what?"

"Try to observe them," she said. "Try to learn something about them. Try to make contact, in whatever way we can."

"You don't think that's been tried before?"

"A million times. Not so much lately, though. Maybe while the interest on our side has ebbed, they've been changing, growing more receptive."

"Or maybe not." Jasim smiled. He had appeared a little stunned by her proposal at first, but the idea seemed to be growing on him. "It's a hard, hard problem to throw ourselves against. But it's not futile. Not quite." He wrapped her hands in his. "Let's see how we feel in the morning."

In the morning, they were both convinced. They would camp at the gates of these elusive strangers, and try to rouse them from their indifference.

They summoned the family from every corner of Najib. There were some grandchildren and more distant descendants who had settled in other star systems, decades away at lightspeed, but they chose not to wait to call them home for this final farewell.

Two hundred people crowded the physical house and garden, while two hundred more confined themselves to the virtual wing. There was talk and food and music, like any other celebration, and Leila tried to undercut any edge of solemnity that she felt creeping in. As the night wore on, though, each time she kissed a child or grandchild, each time she embraced an old friend, she thought: this could be the last time, ever. There had to be a last time, she couldn't face ten thousand more years, but a part of her spat and struggled like a cornered animal at the thought of each warm touch fading to nothing.

As dawn approached, the party shifted entirely into the acorporeal. People took on fancy dress from myth or xenology, or just joked and played with their illusory bodies. It was all very calm and gentle, nothing like the surreal excesses she remembered from her youth, but Leila still felt a tinge of vertigo. When her son Khalid made his ears grow and spin, this amiable silliness carried a hard message: the machinery of the house had ripped her mind from her body, as seamlessly as ever, but this time she would never be returning to the same flesh.

Sunrise brought the first of the goodbyes. Leila forced herself to release each proffered hand, to unwrap her arms from around each nonexistent body. She whispered to Jasim, "Are you going mad, too?"

"Of course."

353

Gradually the crowd thinned out. The wing grew quiet. Leila found herself pacing from room to room, as if she might yet chance upon someone who'd stayed behind, then she remembered urging the last of them to go, her children and friends tearfully retreating down the hall. She skirted inconsolable sadness, then lifted herself above it and went looking for Jasim.

He was waiting for her outside their room.

"Are you ready to sleep?" he asked her gently.

She said, "For an eon."

2

Leila woke in the same bed as she'd lain down in. Jasim was still sleeping beside her. The window showed dawn, but it was not the usual view of the cliffs and the ocean.

Leila had the house brief her. After twenty thousand years—traveling more or less at lightspeed, pausing only for a microsecond or two at various way-stations to be cleaned up and amplified—the package of information bearing the two of them had arrived safely at Nazdeek-be-Beegane. This world was not crowded, and it had been tweaked to render it compatible with a range of metabolic styles. The house had negotiated a site where they could live embodied in comfort if they wished.

Jasim stirred and opened his eyes. "Good morning. How are you feeling?"

"Older."

"Really?"

Leila paused to consider this seriously. "No. Not even slightly. How about you?"

"I'm fine. I'm just wondering what's out there." He raised himself up to peer through the window. The house had been instantiated on a wide, empty plain, covered with low stalks of green and yellow vegetation. They could eat these plants, and the house had already started a spice garden while they slept. He stretched his shoulders. "Let's go and make breakfast."

They went downstairs, stepping into freshly minted bodies, then out into the garden. The air was still, the sun already warm. The house had tools prepared to help them with the harvest. It was the nature of travel that they had come empty-handed, and they had no relatives here, no fifteenth cousins, no friends of friends. It was the nature of the Amalgam that they were welcome nonetheless, and the machines that supervised this world on behalf of its inhabitants had done their best to provide for them.

"So this is the afterlife," Jasim mused, scything the yellow stalks. "Very rustic."

"Speak for yourself," Leila retorted. "I'm not dead yet." She put down her own scythe and bent to pluck one of the plants out by its roots.

The meal they made was filling but bland. Leila resisted the urge to tweak her perceptions of it; she preferred to face the challenge of working out decent recipes, which would make a useful counterpoint to the more daunting task they'd come here to attempt.

They spent the rest of the day just tramping around, exploring their immediate surroundings. The house had tapped into a nearby stream for water, and sunlight, stored, would provide all the power they needed. From some hills about an hour's walk away they could see into a field with another building, but they decided to wait a little longer before introducing themselves to their neighbors. The air had a slightly odd smell, due to the range of components needed to support other metabolic styles, but it wasn't too intrusive.

The onset of night took them by surprise. Even before the sun had set a smattering of stars began appearing in the east, and for a moment Leila thought that these white specks against the fading blue were some kind of exotic atmospheric phenomenon, perhaps small clouds forming in the stratosphere as the temperature dropped. When it became clear what was happening, she beckoned to Jasim to sit beside her on the bank of the stream and watch the stars of the bulge come out.

They'd come at a time when Nazdeek lay between its sun and the galactic center. At dusk one half of the Aloof's dazzling territory stretched from the eastern horizon to the zenith, with the stars' slow march westward against a darkening sky only revealing more of their splendor.

"You think that was to die for?" Jasim joked as they walked back to the house.

"We could end this now, if you're feeling unambitious."

He squeezed her hand. "If this takes ten thousand years, I'm ready."

It was a mild night, they could have slept outdoors, but the spectacle was too distracting. They stayed downstairs, in the physical wing. Leila watched the strange thicket of shadows cast by the furniture sliding across the walls. These neighbors never sleep, she thought. When we come knocking, they'll ask what took us so long.

3

Hundreds of observatories circled Nazdeek, built then abandoned by others who'd come on the same quest. When Leila saw the band of pristine space junk mapped out before her—orbits scrupulously maintained and swept clean by robot sentinels for eons—she felt as if she'd found the graves of their predecessors, stretching out in the field behind the house as far as the eye could see.

Nazdeek was prepared to offer them the resources to loft another package of instruments into the vacuum if they wished, but many of the abandoned observatories were perfectly functional, and most had been left in a compliant state, willing to take instructions from anyone.

Leila and Jasim sat in their living room and woke machine after machine from millennia of hibernation. Some, it turned out, had not been sleeping at all, but had been carrying on systematic observations, accumulating data long after their owners had lost interest.

In the crowded stellar precincts of the bulge, disruptive gravitational effects made planet formation rarer than it was in the disk, and orbits less stable. Nevertheless, planets had been found. A few thousand could be tracked from Nazdeek, and one observatory had been monitoring their atmospheric spectra for the last twelve millennia. In all of those worlds for all of those years, there were no signs of atmospheric composition departing from plausible, purely geochemical models. That meant no wild life, and no crude industries. It didn't prove that these worlds were uninhabited, but it suggested either that the Aloof went to great lengths to avoid leaving chemical fingerprints, or they lived in an entirely different fashion to any of the civilizations that had formed the Amalgam.

Of the eleven forms of biochemistry that had been found scattered around the galactic disk, all had given rise eventually to hundreds of species with general intelligence. Of the multitude of civilizations that had emerged from those roots, all contained cultures that had granted themselves the flexibility of living as software, but they also all contained cultures that persisted with corporeal existence. Leila would never have willingly given up either mode, herself, but while it was easy to imagine a subculture doing so, for a whole species it seemed extraordinary. In a sense, the intertwined civilization of the Amalgam owed its existence to the fact that there was as much cultural variation within every species as there was between one species and another. In that explosion of diversity, overlapping interests were inevitable.

If the Aloof were the exception, and their material culture had shrunk to nothing but a few discreet processors—each with the energy needs of a gnat, scattered throughout a trillion cubic light years of dust and blazing stars—then finding them would be impossible.

Of course, that worst-case scenario couldn't quite be true. The sole reason the Aloof were assumed to exist at all was the fact that some component of their material culture was tossing back every probe that was sent into the bulge. However discreet that machinery was, it certainly couldn't be sparse: given that it had managed to track, intercept and reverse the trajectories of billions of individual probes that had been sent in along thousands of different routes, relativistic constraints on the information flow implied that the Aloof had some kind of presence at more or less every star at the edge of the bulge.

Leila and Jasim had Nazdeek brief them on the most recent attempts to enter the bulge, but even after forty thousand years the basic facts hadn't changed. There was no crisply delineated barrier marking the Aloof's territory, but at some point within a border region about fifty light years wide, every single probe that was sent in ceased to function. The signals from those carrying in-flight beacons or transmitters went dead without warning. A century or so later, they would appear again at almost the same point, traveling in the opposite direction: back to where they'd come from. Those that were retrieved and examined were found to be unharmed, but their data logs contained nothing from the missing decades.

Jasim said, "The Aloof could be dead and gone. They built the perfect fence, but now it's outlasted them. It's just guarding their ruins."

Leila rejected this emphatically. "No civilization that's spread to more than one star system has ever vanished completely. Sometimes they've changed beyond recognition, but not one has ever died without descendants."

"That's a fact of history, but it's not a universal law," Jasim persisted. "If we're going to argue from the Amalgam all the time, we'll get nowhere. If the Aloof weren't exceptional, we wouldn't be here."

"That's true. But I won't accept that they're dead until I see some evidence."

"What would count as evidence? Apart from a million years of silence?"

Leila said, "Silence could mean anything. If they're really dead, we'll find something more, something definite."

"Such as?"

"If we see it, we'll know."

They began the project in earnest, reviewing data from the ancient observatories, stopping only to gather food, eat and sleep. They had resisted making detailed plans back on Najib, reasoning that any approach they mapped out in advance was likely to be rendered obsolete once they learned about the latest investigations. Now that they'd arrived and found the state of play utterly unchanged, Leila wished that they'd come armed with some clear options for dealing with the one situation they could have prepared for before they'd left.

In fact, though they might have felt like out-of-touch amateurs back on Najib, now that the Aloof had become their entire *raison d'être* it was far harder to relax and indulge in the kind of speculation that might actually bear fruit, given that every systematic approach had failed. Having come twenty thousand light years for this, they couldn't spend their time day-dreaming, turning the problem over in the backs of their minds while they surrendered to the rhythms of Nazdeek's rural idyll. So they studied everything that had been tried before, searching methodically for a new approach, hoping to see the old ideas with fresh eyes, hoping that—by chance if for no other reason—they might lack some crucial blind spot that had afflicted all of their predecessors.

After seven months without results or inspiration, it was Jasim who finally dragged them out of the rut. "We're getting nowhere," he said. "It's time to accept that, put all this aside, and go visit the neighbors."

Leila stared at him as if he'd lost his mind. "Go visit them? How? What makes you think that they're suddenly going to let us in?"

He said, "The neighbors. Remember? Over the hill. The ones who might actually want to talk to us."

4

Their neighbors had published a précis stating that they welcomed social contact in principle, but might take a while to respond. Jasim sent them an invitation, asking if they'd like to join them in their house, and waited.

After just three days, a reply came back. The neighbors did not want to put them to the trouble of altering their own house physically, and preferred not to become acorporeal at present. Given the less stringent requirements of Leila and Jasim's own species when embodied, might they wish to come instead to the neighbors' house?

Leila said, "Why not?" They set a date and time.

The neighbors' précis included all the biological and sociological details needed to prepare for the encounter. Their biochemistry was carbon-based and oxygen-breathing, but employed a different replicator to Leila and Jasim's DNA. Their ancestral phenotype resembled a large furred snake, and when embodied they generally lived in nests of a hundred or so. The minds of the individuals were perfectly autonomous, but solitude was an alien and unsettling concept for them.

Leila and Jasim set out late in the morning, in order to arrive early in the afternoon. There were some low, heavy clouds in the sky, but it was not completely overcast, and Leila noticed that when the sun passed behind the clouds, she could discern some of the brightest stars from the edge of the bulge.

Jasim admonished her sternly, "Stop looking. This is our day off."

The Snakes' building was a large squat cylinder resembling a water tank, which turned out to be packed with something mossy and pungent. When they arrived at the entrance, three of their hosts were waiting to greet them, coiled on the ground near the mouth of a large tunnel emerging from the moss. Their bodies were almost as wide as their guests', and some eight or ten meters long. Their heads bore two front-facing eyes, but their other sense organs were not prominent. Leila could make out their mouths, and knew from the briefing how many rows of teeth lay behind them, but the wide pink gashes stayed closed, almost lost in the gray fur.

The Snakes communicated with a low-frequency thumping, and their system of nomenclature was complex, so Leila just mentally tagged the three of them with randomly chosen, slightly exotic names—Tim, John and Sarah—and tweaked her translator so she'd recognize intuitively who was who, who was addressing her, and the significance of their gestures.

"Welcome to our home," said Tim enthusiastically.

"Thank you for inviting us," Jasim replied.

"We've had no visitors for quite some time," explained Sarah. "So we really are delighted to meet you."

"How long has it been?" Leila asked.

"Twenty years," said Sarah.

"But we came here for the quiet life," John added. "So we expected it would be a while."

Leila pondered the idea of a clan of one hundred ever finding a quiet life, but then, perhaps unwelcome intrusions from outsiders were of a different nature to family dramas.

"Will you come into the nest?" Tim asked. "If you don't wish to enter we won't take offense, but everyone would like to see you, and some of us aren't comfortable coming out into the open."

Leila glanced at Jasim. He said privately, "We can push our vision to IR. And tweak ourselves to tolerate the smell."

Leila agreed.

"Okay," Jasim told Tim.

Tim slithered into the tunnel and vanished in a quick, elegant motion, then John motioned with his head for the guests to follow. Leila went first, propelling herself up the gentle slope with her knees and elbows. The plant the Snakes' cultivated for the nest formed a cool, dry, resilient surface. She could see Tim ten meters or so ahead, like a giant glowworm shining with body heat, slowing down now to let her catch up. She glanced back at Jasim, who looked even weirder than the Snakes now, his face and arms blotched with strange bands of radiance from the exertion.

After a few minutes, they came to a large chamber. The air was humid, but after the confines of the tunnel it felt cool and fresh. Tim led them toward the center, where about a dozen other Snakes were already waiting to greet them. They circled the guests excitedly, thumping out a delighted welcome. Leila felt a surge of adrenaline; she knew that she and Jasim were in no danger, but the sheer size and energy of the creatures was overwhelming.

"Can you tell us why you've come to Nazdeek?" asked Sarah.

"Of course." For a second or two Leila tried to maintain eye contact with her, but like all the other Snakes she kept moving restlessly, a gesture that Leila's translator imbued with a sense of warmth and enthusiasm. As for lack of eye contact, the Snakes' own translators would understand perfectly that some aspects of ordinary, polite human behavior became impractical under the circumstances, and would not mislabel her actions. "We're here to learn about the Aloof," she said.

"The Aloof?" At first Sarah just seemed perplexed, then Leila's translator hinted at a touch of irony. "But they offer us nothing."

Leila was tongue-tied for a moment. The implication was subtle but unmistakable. Citizens of the Amalgam had a protocol for dealing with each other's curiosity: they published a précis, which spelled out clearly any information that they wished people in general to know about them, and also specified what, if any, further inquiries would be welcome. However, a citizen was perfectly entitled to publish no précis at all and have that decision respected. When no information was published, and no invitation offered, you simply had no choice but to mind your own business.

"They offer us nothing as far as we can tell," she said, "but that might be a misunderstanding, a failure to communicate."

"They send back all the probes," Tim replied. "Do you really think we've misunderstood what that means?"

Jasim said, "It means that they don't want us physically intruding on their territory, putting our machines right next to their homes, but I'm not convinced that it proves that they have no desire to communicate whatsoever."

"We should leave them in peace," Tim insisted. "They've seen the probes, so they know we're here. If they want to make contact, they'll do it in their own time."

"Leave them in peace," echoed another Snake. A chorus of affirmation followed from others in the chamber.

Leila stood her ground. "We have no idea how many different species and cultures might be living in the bulge. *One of them* sends back the probes, but for all we know there could be a thousand others who don't yet even know that the Amalgam has tried to make contact."

This suggestion set off a series of arguments, some between guests and hosts, some between the Snakes themselves. All the while, the Snakes kept circling excitedly, while new ones entered the chamber to witness the novel sight of these strangers.

When the clamor about the Aloof had quietened down enough for her to change the subject, Leila asked Sarah, "Why have you come to Nazdeek yourself?"

"It's out of the way, off the main routes. We can think things over here, undisturbed."

"But you could have the same amount of privacy anywhere. It's all a matter of what you put in your précis."

Sarah's response was imbued with a tinge of amusement. "For us, it would be unimaginably rude to cut off all contact explicitly, by decree. Especially with others from our own ancestral species. To live a quiet life, we had to reduce the likelihood of encountering anyone who would seek us out. We had to make the effort of rendering ourselves physically remote, in order to reap the benefits."

"Yet you've made Jasim and myself very welcome."

"Of course. But that will be enough for the next twenty years."

So much for resurrecting their social life. "What exactly is it that you're pondering in this state of solitude?"

"The nature of reality. The uses of existence. The reasons to live, and the reasons not to."

Leila felt the skin on her forearms tingle. She'd almost forgotten that she'd made an appointment with death, however uncertain the timing.

She explained how she and Jasim had made their decision to embark on a grand project before dying.

"That's an interesting approach," Sarah said. "I'll have to give it some thought." She paused, then added, "Though I'm not sure that you've solved the problem."

"What do you mean?"

"Will it really be easier now to choose the right moment to give up your life? Haven't you merely replaced one delicate judgment with an even more difficult one: deciding when you've exhausted the possibilities for contacting the Aloof?"

"You make it sound as if we have no chance of succeeding." Leila was not afraid of the prospect of failure, but the suggestion that it was inevitable was something else entirely.

Sarah said, "We've been here on Nazdeek for fifteen thousand years. We don't pay much attention to the world outside the nest, but even from this cloistered state we've seen many people break their backs against this rock."

"So when will you accept that your own project is finished?" Leila countered. "If you still don't have what you're looking for after fifteen thousand years, when will you admit defeat?"

"I have no idea," Sarah confessed. "I have no idea, any more than you do."

5

When the way forward first appeared, there was nothing to set it apart from a thousand false alarms that had come before it.

It was their seventeenth year on Nazdeek. They had launched their own observatory—armed with the latest refinements culled from around the galaxy—fifteen years before, and it had been confirming the null results of its predecessors ever since.

They had settled into an unhurried routine, systematically exploring the possibilities that observation hadn't yet ruled out. Between the scenarios that were obviously stone cold dead—the presence of an energy-rich, risk-taking, extroverted civilization in the bulge actively seeking contact by every means at its disposal—and the infinite number of possibilities that could never be distinguished at this distance from the absence of all life, and the absence of all machinery save one dumb but efficient gatekeeper, tantalizing clues would bubble up out of the data now and then, only to fade into statistical insignificance in the face of continued scrutiny.

Tens of billions of stars lying within the Aloof's territory could be discerned from Nazdeek, some of them evolving or violently interacting on a time scale of years or months. Black holes were flaying and swallowing their companions. Neutron stars and white dwarfs were stealing fresh fuel and flaring into novas. Star clusters were colliding and tearing each other apart. If you gathered data on this whole menagerie for long enough, you could expect to see almost anything. Leila would not have been surprised to wander into the garden at night and find a great welcome sign spelled out in the sky, before the fortuitous pattern of novas faded and the message dissolved into randomness again.

When their gamma ray telescope caught a glimmer of something odd—the nuclei of a certain isotope of fluorine decaying from an excited state, when there was no nearby source of the kind of radiation that could have put the nuclei into that state in the first place—it might have been just another random, unexplained fact to add to a vast pile. When the same glimmer was seen again, not far away, Leila reasoned that if a gas cloud enriched with fluorine could be affected at one location by an unseen radiation source, it should not be surprising if the same thing happened elsewhere in the same cloud.

It happened again. The three events lined up in space and time in a manner suggesting a short pulse of gamma rays in the form of a tightly focused beam, striking three different points in the gas cloud. Still, in the mountains of data they had acquired from their predecessors, coincidences far more compelling than this had occurred hundreds of thousands of times.

With the fourth flash, the balance of the numbers began to tip. The secondary gamma rays reaching Nazdeek gave only a weak and distorted impression of the original radiation, but all four flashes were consistent with a single, narrow beam. There were thousands of known gamma ray sources in the bulge, but the frequency of the radiation, the direction of the beam, and the time profile of the pulse did not fit with any of them.

The archives revealed a few dozen occasions when the same kind of emissions had been seen from fluorine nuclei under similar conditions. There had never been more than three connected events before, but one sequence had occurred along a path not far from the present one.

Leila sat by the stream and modeled the possibilities. If the beam was linking two objects in powered flight, prediction was impossible. If receiver and transmitter were mostly in free-fall, though, and only made corrections occasionally, the past and present data combined gave her a plausible forecast for the beam's future orientation.

Jasim looked into her simulation, a thought-bubble of stars and equations hovering above the water. "The whole path will lie out of bounds," he said.

"No kidding." The Aloof's territory was more or less spherical, which made it a convex set: you couldn't get between any two points that lay inside it without entering the territory itself. "But look how much the beam spreads out. From the fluorine data, I'd say it could be tens of kilometers wide by the time it reaches the receiver."

"So they might not catch it all? They might let some of the beam escape into the disk?" He sounded unpersuaded.

Leila said, "Look, if they really were doing everything possible to hide this, we would never have seen these blips in the first place."

"Gas clouds with this much fluorine are extremely rare. They obviously picked a frequency that wouldn't be scattered under ordinary circumstances."

"Yes, but that's just a matter of getting the signal through the local environment. We choose frequencies ourselves that won't interact with any substance that's likely to be present along the route, but no choice is perfect, and we just live with that. It seems to me that they've done the same thing. If they were fanatical purists, they'd communicate by completely different methods."

"All right." Jasim reached into the model. "So where can we go that's in the line of sight?"

The short answer was: nowhere. If the beam was not blocked completely by its intended target it would spread out considerably as it made its way through the galactic disk, but it would not grow so wide that it would sweep across a single point where the Amalgam had any kind of outpost.

Leila said, "This is too good to miss. We need to get a decent observatory into its path."

Jasim agreed. "And we need to do it before these nodes decide they've drifted too close to something dangerous, and switch on their engines for a course correction."

They crunched through the possibilities. Wherever the Amalgam had an established presence, the infrastructure already on the ground could convert data into any kind of material object. Transmitting yourself to such a place, along with whatever you needed, was simplicity itself: lightspeed was the only real constraint. Excessive demands on the local resources might be denied, but modest requests were rarely rejected.

Far more difficult was building something new at a site with raw materials but no existing receiver; in that case, instead of pure data, you needed to send an engineering spore of some kind. If you were in a hurry, not only did you need to spend energy boosting the spore to relativistic velocities—a cost that snowballed due to the mass of protective shielding—you then had to waste much of the time you gained on a lengthy braking phase, or the spore would hit its target with enough energy to turn it into plasma. Interactions with the interstellar medium could be used to slow down the spore, avoiding the need to carry yet more mass to act as a propellant for braking, but the whole business was disgustingly inefficient.

Harder still was getting anything substantial to a given point in the vast empty space between the stars. With no raw materials to hand at the destination, everything had to be moved from somewhere else. The best starting point was usually to send an engineering spore into a cometary cloud, loosely bound gravitationally to its associated star, but not every such cloud was open to plunder, and everything took time, and obscene amounts of energy.

To arrange for an observatory to be delivered to the most accessible point along the beam's line of sight, traveling at the correct velocity, would take about fifteen thousand years all told. That assumed that the local cultures who owned the nearest facilities, and who had a right to veto the use of the raw materials, acceded immediately to their request.

"How long between course corrections?" Leila wondered. If the builders of this hypothetical network were efficient, the nodes could drift for a while in interstellar space without any problems, but in the bulge everything happened faster than in the disk, and the need to counter gravitational effects would come much sooner. There was no way to make a firm prediction, but they could easily have as little as eight or ten thousand years.

Leila struggled to reconcile herself to the reality. "We'll try at this location, and if we're lucky we might still catch something. If not, we'll try again after the beam shifts." Sending the first observatory chasing after the beam would be futile; even with the present free-fall motion of the nodes, the observation point would be moving at a substantial fraction of lightspeed relative to the local stars. Magnified by the enormous distances involved, a small change in direction down in the bulge could see the beam lurch thousands of light years sideways by the time it reached the disk.

Jasim said, "Wait." He magnified the region around the projected path of the beam.

"What are you looking for?"

He asked the map, "Are there two outposts of the Amalgam lying on a straight line that intersects the beam?"

The map replied in a tone of mild incredulity. "No."

"That was too much to hope for. Are there three lying on a plane that intersects the beam?"

The map said, "There are about ten-to-the-eighteen triples that meet that condition."

Leila suddenly realized what it was he had in mind. She laughed and squeezed his arm. "You are completely insane!"

Jasim said, "Let me get the numbers right first, then you can mock me." He rephrased his question to the map. "For how many of those triples would the beam pass between them, intersecting the triangle whose vertices they lie on?"

"About ten-to-the-sixth."

"How close to us is the closest point of intersection of the beam with any of those triangles—if the distance in each case is measured via the worst of the three outposts, the one that makes the total path longest."

"Seven thousand four hundred and twenty-six light years."

Leila said, "Collision braking. With three components?"

"Do you have a better idea?"

Better than twice as fast as the fastest conventional method? "Nothing comes to mind. Let me think about it."

Braking against the flimsy interstellar medium was a slow process. If you wanted to deliver a payload rapidly to a point that fortuitously lay somewhere on a straight line between two existing outposts, you could fire two separate packages from the two locations and let them "collide" when they met—or rather, let them brake against each other magnetically. If you arranged for the packages to have equal and opposite momenta, they would come to a halt without any need to throw away reaction mass or clutch at passing molecules, and some of their kinetic energy could be recovered as electricity and stored for later use.

The aim and the timing had to be perfect. Relativistic packages did not make in-flight course corrections, and the data available at each launch site about the other's precise location was always a potentially imperfect prediction, not a rock-solid statement of fact. Even with the Amalgam's prodigious astrometric and computing resources, achieving millimeter alignments at thousand-light-year distances could not be guaranteed.

Now Jasim wanted to make three of these bullets meet, perform an elaborate electromagnetic dance, and end up with just the right velocity needed to keep tracking the moving target of the beam.

In the evening, back in the house, they sat together working through simulations. It was easy to find designs that would work if everything went perfectly, but they kept hunting for the most robust variation, the one that was most tolerant of small misalignments. With standard two-body collision braking, the usual solution was to have the first package, shaped like a cylinder, pass right through a hole in the second package. As it emerged from the other side and the two moved apart again, the magnetic fields were switched from repulsive to attractive. Several "bounces" followed, and in the process as much of the kinetic energy as possible was gradually converted into super-conducting currents for storage, while the rest was dissipated as electromagnetic radiation. Having three objects meeting at an angle would not only make the timing and positioning more critical, it would destroy the simple, axial symmetry and introduce a greater risk of instability.

It was dawn before they settled on the optimal design, which effectively split the problem in two. First, package one, a sphere, would meet package two, a torus, threading the gap in the middle, then bouncing back and forth through it seventeen times. The plane of the torus would lie at an angle to its direction of flight, allowing the sphere to approach it head-on. When the two finally came to rest with respect to each other, they would still have a component of their velocity carrying them straight toward package three, a cylinder with an axial borehole.

Because the electromagnetic interactions were the same as the two-body case—self-centring, intrinsically stable—a small amount of misalignment at each of these encounters would not be fatal. The usual two-body case, though, didn't require the combined package, after all the bouncing and energy dissipation was completed, to be moving on a path so precisely determined that it could pass through yet another narrow hoop.

There were no guarantees, and in the end the result would be in other people's hands. They could send requests to the three outposts, asking for these objects to be launched at the necessary times on the necessary trajectories. The energy needs hovered on the edge of politeness, though, and it was possible that one or more of the requests would simply be refused.

Jasim waved the models away, and they stretched out on the carpet, side by side.

He said, "I never thought we'd get this far. Even if this is only a mirage, I never thought we'd find one worth chasing."

Leila said, "I don't know what I expected. Some kind of great folly: some long, exhausting, exhilarating struggle that felt like wandering through a jungle for years and ending up utterly lost."

"And then what?"

"Surrender."

Jasim was silent for a while. Leila could sense that he was brooding over something, but she didn't press him.

He said, "Should we travel to this observatory ourselves, or wait here for the results?"

"We should go. Definitely! I don't want to hang around here for fifteen thousand years, waiting. We can leave the Nazdeek observatories hunting for more beam fluorescence and broadcasting the results, so we'll hear about them wherever we end up."

"That makes sense." Jasim hesitated, then added, "When we go, I don't want to leave a back-up."

"Ah." They'd traveled from Najib leaving nothing of themselves behind: if their transmission had somehow failed to make it to Nazdeek, no stored copy of the data would ever have woken to resume their truncated lives. Travel within the Amalgam's established network carried negligible risks, though. If they flung themselves toward the hypothetical location of this yet-to-be-assembled station in the middle of nowhere, it was entirely possible that they'd sail off to infinity without ever being instantiated again.

Leila said, "Are you tired of what we're doing? Of what we've become?"

"It's not that."

"This one chance isn't the be-all and end-all. Now that we know how to hunt for the beams, I'm sure we'll find this one again after its shifts. We could find a thousand others, if we're persistent."

"I know that," he said. "I don't want to stop, I don't want to end this. But I want to *risk* ending it. Just once. While that still means something."

Leila sat up and rested her head on her knees. She could understand what he was feeling, but it still disturbed her.

Jasim said, "We've already achieved something extraordinary. No one's found a clue like this in a million years. If we leave that to prosperity, it will be pursued to the end, we can be sure of that. But I desperately want to pursue it myself. With you."

"And because you want that so badly, you need to face the chance of losing it?"

"Yes."

It was one thing they had never tried. In their youth, they would never have knowingly risked death. They'd been too much in love, too eager for the life they'd yet to live; the stakes would have been unbearably high. In the twilight years, back on Najib, it would have been an easy thing to do, but an utterly insipid pleasure.

Jasim sat up and took her hand. "Have I hurt you with this?"

"No, no." She shook her head pensively, trying to gather her thoughts. She didn't want to hide her feelings, but she wanted to express them precisely, not blurt them out in a confusing rush. "I always thought we'd reach the end together, though. We'd come to some point in the jungle, look around, exchange a glance, and know that we'd arrived. Without even needing to say it aloud."

Jasim drew her to him and held her. "All right, I'm sorry. Forget everything I said."

Leila pushed him away, annoyed. "This isn't something you can take back. If it's the truth, it's the truth. Just give me some time to decide what I want."

They put it aside, and buried themselves in work: polishing the design for the new observatory, preparing the requests to send to the three outposts. One of the planets they would be petitioning belonged to the Snakes, so Leila and Jasim went to visit the nest for a second time, to seek advice on the best way to beg for this favor. Their neighbors seemed more excited just to see them again than they were at the news that a tiny rent had appeared in the Aloof's million-year-old cloak of discretion. When Leila gently pushed her on this point, Sarah said, "You're here, here and now, our guests in flesh and blood. I'm sure I'll be dead long before the Aloof are willing to do the same."

Leila thought: What kind of strange greed is it that I'm suffering from? I can be feted by creatures who rose up from the dust through a completely different molecule than my own ancestors. I can sit among them and discuss the philosophy of life and death. The Amalgam has already joined every willing participant in the galaxy into one vast conversation. And I want to go and eavesdrop on the Aloof? Just because they've played hard-to-get for a million years?

They dispatched requests for the three modules to be built and launched by their three as-yet unwitting collaborators, specifying the final countdown to the nanosecond but providing a ten-year period for the project to be debated. Leila felt optimistic; however blasé the Nazdeek nest had been, she suspected that no space-faring culture really could resist the chance to peek behind the veil.

They had thirty-six years to wait before they followed in the wake of their petitions; on top of the ten-year delay, the new observatory's modules would be traveling at a fraction of a percent below lightspeed, so they needed a head start.

No more telltale gamma ray flashes appeared from the bulge, but Leila hadn't expected any so soon. They had sent the news of their discovery to other worlds close to the Aloof's territory, so eventually a thousand other groups with different vantage points would be searching for the same kind of evidence and finding their own ways to interpret and exploit it. It hurt a little, scattering their hard-won revelation to the wind for anyone to use—perhaps even to beat them to some far greater prize—but they'd relied on the generosity of their predecessors from the moment they'd arrived on Nazdeek, and the sheer scale of the overall problem made it utterly perverse to cling selfishly to their own small triumph.

As the day of their departure finally arrived, Leila came to a decision. She understood Jasim's need to put everything at risk, and in a sense she shared it. If she had always imagined the two of them ending this together—struggling on, side by side, until the way forward was lost and the undergrowth closed in on them—then *that* was what she'd risk. She would take the flip side to his own wager.

When the house took their minds apart and sent them off to chase the beam, Leila left a copy of herself frozen on Nazdeek. If no word of their safe arrival reached it by the expected time, it would wake and carry on the search.

Alone.

6

"Welcome to Trident. We're honored by the presence of our most distinguished guest."

Jasim stood beside the bed, waving a triangular flag. Red, green and blue in the corners merged to white in the center.

"How long have you been up?"

"About an hour," he said. Leila frowned, and he added apologetically, "You were sleeping very deeply, I didn't want to disturb you."

"I should be the one giving the welcome," she said. "You're the one who might never have woken."

The bedroom window looked out into a dazzling field of stars. It was not a view facing the bulge—by now Leila could recognize the distinctive spectra of the region's stars with ease—but even these disk stars were so crisp and bright that this was like no sky she had ever seen.

"Have you been downstairs?" she said.

"Not yet. I wanted us to decide on that together." The house had no physical wing here; the tiny observatory had no spare mass for such frivolities as embodying them, let alone constructing architectural follies in the middle of interstellar space. "Downstairs" would be nothing but a scape that they were free to design at will.

"Everything worked," she said, not quite believing it.

Jasim spread his arms. "We're here, aren't we."

They watched a reconstruction of the first two modules coming together. The timing and the trajectories were as near to perfect as they could have hoped for, and the superconducting magnets had been constructed to a standard of purity and homogeneity that made the magnetic embrace look like an idealized simulation. By the time the two had locked together, the third module was just minutes away. Some untraceable discrepancy between reality and prediction in the transfer of momentum to radiation had the composite moving at a tiny angle away from its expected course, but when it met the third module the magnetic fields still meshed in a stable configuration, and there was energy to spare to nudge the final assembly precisely into step with the predicted swinging of the Aloof's beam.

The Amalgam had lived up to its promise: three worlds full of beings they had never met, who owed them nothing, who did not even share their molecular ancestry, had each diverted enough energy to light up all their cities for a decade, and followed the instructions of strangers down to the atom, down to the nanosecond, in order to make this work.

What happened now was entirely in the hands of the Aloof.

Trident had been functioning for about a month before its designers had arrived to take up occupancy. So far, it had not yet observed any gamma ray signals spilling out of the bulge. The particular pulse that Leila and Jasim had seen triggering fluorescence would be long gone, of course, but the usefulness of their present location was predicated on three assumptions: the Aloof would use the same route for many other bursts of data; some of the radiation carrying that data would slip past the intended receiver; and the two nodes of the network would have continued in free fall long enough for the spilt data to be arriving here still, along the same predictable path.

Without those three extra components, delivered by their least reliable partners, Trident would be worthless.

"Downstairs," Leila said. "Maybe a kind of porch with glass walls?"

"Sounds fine to me."

She conjured up a plan of the house and sketched some ideas, then they went down to try them out at full scale.

●●●

They had been into orbit around Najib, and they had traveled embodied to its three beautiful, barren sibling worlds, but they had never been in interstellar space before. Or at least, they had never been conscious of it.

They were still not truly embodied, but you didn't need flesh and blood to feel the vacuum around you; to be awake and plugged-in to an honest depiction of your surroundings was enough. The nearest of Trident's contributor worlds was six hundred light years away. The distance to Najib was unthinkable. Leila paced around the porch, looking out at the stars, vertiginous in her virtual body, unsteady in the phoney gravity.

It had been twenty-eight thousand years since they'd left Najib. All her children and grandchildren had almost certainly chosen death, long ago. No messages had been sent after them to Nazdeek; Leila had asked for that silence, fearing that it would be unbearably painful to hear news, day after day, to which she could give no meaningful reply, about events in which she could never participate. Now she regretted that. She wanted to read the lives of her grandchildren, as she might the biography of an ancestor. She wanted to know how things had ended up, like the time traveler she was.

A second month of observation passed, with nothing. A data feed reaching them from Nazdeek was equally silent. For any new hint of the beam's location to reach Nazdeek, and then the report of that to reach Trident, would take thousands of years longer than the direct passage of the beam itself, so if Nazdeek saw evidence that the beam was "still" on course, that would be old news about a pulse they had not been here to intercept. However, if Nazdeek reported that the beam had shifted, at least that would put them out of their misery immediately, and tell them that Trident had been built too late.

Jasim made a vegetable garden on the porch and grew exotic food in the starlight. Leila played along, and ate beside him; it was a harmless game. They could have painted anything at all around the house: any planet they'd visited, drawn from their memories, any imaginary world. If this small pretense was enough to keep them sane and anchored to reality, so be it.

Now and then, Leila felt the strangest of the many pangs of isolation Trident induced: here, the knowledge of the galaxy was no longer at her fingertips. Their descriptions as travelers had encoded their vast personal memories, declarative and episodic, and their luggage had included prodigious libraries, but she was used to having so much more. Every civilized planet held a storehouse of information that was simply too bulky to fit into Trident, along with a constant feed of exabytes of news flooding in from other worlds. Wherever you were in the galaxy, some news was old news, some cherished theories long discredited, some facts hopelessly out of date. Here, though, Leila knew, there were billions of rigourously established truths—the results of hundreds of millennia of thought, experiment and observation—that had slipped out of her reach. Questions that any other child of the Amalgam could expect to have answered instantly would take twelve hundred years to receive a reply.

No such questions actually came into her mind, but there were still moments when the mere fact of it was enough to make her feel unbearably rootless, cut adrift not only from her past and her people, but from civilization itself.

●●●

Trident shouted: "Data!"

Leila was halfway through recording a postcard to the Nazdeek Snakes. Jasim was on the porch watering his plants. Leila turned to see him walking through the wall, commanding the bricks to part like a gauze curtain.

They stood side by side, watching the analysis emerge.

A pulse of gamma rays of the expected frequency, from precisely the right location, had just washed over Trident. The beam was greatly attenuated by distance, not to mention having had most of its energy intercepted by its rightful owner, but more than enough had slipped past and reached them for Trident to make sense of the nature of the pulse.

It was, unmistakably, modulated with information. There were precisely repeated phase shifts in the radiation that were unimaginable in any natural gamma ray source, and which would have been pointless in any artificial beam produced for any purpose besides communication.

The pulse had been three seconds long, carrying about ten-to-the-twenty-fourth bits of data. The bulk of this appeared to be random, but that did not rule out meaningful content, it simply implied efficient encryption. The Amalgam's network sent encrypted data via robust classical channels like this, while sending the keys needed to decode it by a second, quantum channel. Leila had never expected to get hold of unencrypted data, laying bare the secrets of the Aloof in an instant. To have clear evidence that someone in the bulge was talking to someone else, and to have pinned down part of the pathway connecting them, was vindication enough.

There was more, though. Between the messages themselves, Trident had identified brief, orderly, unencrypted sequences. Everything was guesswork to a degree, but with such a huge slab of data statistical measures were powerful indicators. Part of the data looked like routing information, addresses for the messages as they were carried through the network. Another part looked like information about the nodes'

376

current and future trajectories. If Trident really had cracked that, they could work out where to position its successor. In fact, if they placed the successor close enough to the bulge, they could probably keep that one observatory constantly inside the spill from the beam.

Jasim couldn't resist playing devil's advocate. "You know, this could just be one part of whatever throws the probes back in our faces, talking to another part. The Aloof themselves could still be dead, while their security system keeps humming with paranoid gossip."

Leila said blithely, "Hypothesize away. I'm not taking the bait."

She turned to embrace him, and they kissed. She said, "I've forgotten how to celebrate. What happens now?"

He moved his fingertips gently along her arm. Leila opened up the scape, creating a fourth spatial dimension. She took his hand, kissed it, and placed it against her beating heart. Their bodies reconfigured, nerve-endings crowding every surface, inside and out.

Jasim climbed inside her, and she inside him, the topology of the scape changing to wrap them together in a mutual embrace. Everything vanished from their lives but pleasure, triumph and each other's presence, as close as it could ever be.

7

"Are you here for the Listening Party?"

The chitinous heptapod, who'd been wandering the crowded street with a food cart dispensing largesse at random, offered Leila a plate of snacks tailored to her and Jasim's preferences. She accepted it, then paused to let Tassef, the planet they'd just set foot on, brief her as to the meaning of this phrase. People, Tassef explained, had traveled to this world from throughout the region in order to witness a special event. Some fifteen thousand years before, a burst of data from the Aloof's network had been picked up by a nearby observatory. In isolation, these bursts meant very little; however, the locals were hopeful that at least one of several proposed observatories near Massa, on the opposite side of the bulge, would have seen spillage including many of the same data packets, forty thousand years before. If any such observations had in fact taken place, news of their precise contents should now, finally, be about to reach Tassef by the longer, disk-based routes of the Amalgam's own network. Once the two observations could be compared, it would become clear which messages from the earlier Eavesdropping session had made their way to the part of the Aloof's network that could be sampled from Tassef. The comparison would advance the project of mapping all the symbolic addresses seen in the data onto actual physical locations.

Leila said, "That's not why we came, but now we know, we're even more pleased to be here."

The heptapod emitted a chirp that Leila understood as a gracious welcome, then pushed its way back into the throng.

Jasim said, "Remember when you told me that everyone would get bored with the Aloof while we were still in transit?"

"I said that would happen eventually. If not this trip, the next one."

"Yes, but you said it five journeys ago."

Leila scowled, preparing to correct him, but then she checked and he was right.

They hadn't expected Tassef to be so crowded when they'd chosen it as their destination, some ten thousand years before. The planet had given them a small room in this city, Shalouf, and imposed a thousand-year limit on their presence if they wished to remain embodied without adopting local citizenship. More than a billion visitors had arrived over the last fifty years, anticipating the news of the observations from Massa, but unable to predict the precise time it would reach Tassef because the details of the observatories' trajectories had still been in transit.

She confessed, "I never thought a billion people would arrange their travel plans around this jigsaw puzzle."

"Travel plans?" Jasim laughed. "We chose to have our own deaths revolve around the very same thing."

"Yes, but we're just weird."

Jasim gestured at the crowded street. "I don't think we can compete on that score."

They wandered through the city, drinking in the decades-long-carnival atmosphere. There were people of every phenotype Leila had encountered before, and more: bipeds, quadrupeds, hexapods, heptapods, walking, shuffling, crawling, scuttling, or soaring high above the street on feathered, scaled or membranous wings. Some were encased in their preferred atmospheres; others, like Leila and Jasim, had chosen instead to be embodied in ersatz flesh that didn't follow every ancestral chemical dictate. Physics and geometry tied evolution's hands, and many attempts to solve the same problems had converged on similar answers, but the galaxy's different replicators still managed their idiosyncratic twists. When Leila let her translator sample the cacophony of voices and signals at random, she felt as if the whole disk, the whole Amalgam, had converged on this tiny metropolis.

In fact, most of the travelers had come just a few hundred light years to be here. She and Jasim had chosen to keep their role in the history of Eavesdropping out of their précis, and Leila caught herself with a rather smug sense of walking among the crowd like some unacknowledged sage, bemused by the late-blooming, and no doubt superficial, interest of the masses. On reflection, though, any sense of superior knowledge was hard to justify, when most of these people would have grown up steeped in developments that she was only belatedly catching up with. A new generation of observatories had been designed while she and Jasim were in transit, based on "strong bullets": specially designed femtomachines, clusters of protons and neutrons stable only for trillionths of a second, launched at ultra-relativistic speeds so great that time dilation enabled them to survive long enough to collide with other components and merge into tiny, short-lived gamma-ray observatories. The basic trick that had built Trident had gone from a one-off gamble into a miniaturized, mass-produced phenomenon, with literally billions of strong bullets being fired continuously from thousands of planets around the inner disk.

Femtomachines themselves were old hat, but it had taken the technical challenges of Eavesdropping to motivate someone into squeezing a few more tricks out of them. Historians had always understood that in the long run, technological progress was a horizontal asymptote: once people had more or less everything they wanted that was physically possible, every incremental change would take exponentially longer to achieve, with diminishing returns and ever less reason to bother. The Amalgam would probably spend an eon inching its way closer to the flatline, but this was proof that shifts of circumstance alone could still trigger a modest renaissance or two, without the need for any radical scientific discovery or even a genuinely new technology.

They stopped to rest in a square, beside a small fountain gushing aromatic hydrocarbons. The Tassef locals, quadrupeds with slick, rubbery hides, played in the sticky black spray then licked each other clean.

Jasim shaded his eyes from the sun. He said, "We've had our autumn child, and we've seen its grandchildren prosper. I'm not sure what's left."

"No." Leila was in no rush to die, but they'd sampled fifty thousand years of their discovery's consequences. They'd followed in the wake of the news of the gamma ray signals as it circled the inner disk, spending less than a century conscious as they sped from world to world. At first they'd been hunting for some vital new role to play, but they'd slowly come to accept that the avalanche they'd triggered had out-raced them. Physical and logical maps of the Aloof's network were being constructed, as fast as the laws of physics allowed. Billions of people on thousands of planets, scattered around the inner rim of the Amalgam's territory, were sharing their observations to help piece together the living skeleton of their elusive neighbors. When that project was complete it would not be the end of anything, but it could mark the start of a long hiatus. The encrypted, classical data would never yield anything more than traffic routes; no amount of ingenuity could extract its content. The quantum keys that could unlock it, assuming the Aloof even used such things, would be absolutely immune to theft, duplication, or surreptitious sampling. One day, there would be another breakthrough, and everything would change again, but did they want to wait a hundred thousand years, a million, just to see what came next?

The solicitous heptapods—not locals, but visitors from a world thirty light years away who had nonetheless taken on some kind of innate duty of hospitality—seemed to show up whenever anyone was hungry. Leila tried to draw this second one into conversation, but it politely excused itself to rush off and feed someone else.

Leila said, "Maybe this is it. We'll wait for the news from Massa, then celebrate for a while, then finish it."

Jasim took her hand. "That feels right to me. I'm not certain, but I don't think I'll ever be."

"Are you tired?" she said. "Bored?"

"Not at all," he replied. "I feel *satisfied*. With what we've done, what we've seen. And I don't want to dilute that. I don't want to hang around forever, watching it fade, until we start to feel the way we did on Najib all over again."

"No."

They sat in the square until dusk, and watched the stars of the bulge come out. They'd seen this dazzling jewelled hub from every possible angle now, but Leila never grew tired of the sight.

Jasim gave an amused, exasperated sigh. "That beautiful, maddening, unreachable place. I think the whole Amalgam will be dead and gone without anyone setting foot inside it."

Leila felt a sudden surge of irritation, which deepened into a sense of revulsion. "It's a place, like any other place! Stars, gas, dust, planets. It's not some metaphysical realm. It's not even far away. Our own home world is twenty times more distant."

"Our own home world doesn't have an impregnable fence around it. If we really wanted to, we could go back there."

Leila was defiant. "If we really wanted to, we could enter the bulge."

Jasim laughed. "Have you read something in those messages that you didn't tell me about? How to say 'open sesame' to the gatekeepers?"

Leila stood, and summoned a map of the Aloof's network to superimpose across their vision, crisscrossing the sky with slender cones of violet light. One cone appeared head-on, as a tiny circle: the beam whose spillage came close to Tassef. She put her hand on Jasim's shoulder, and zoomed in on that circle. It opened up before them like a beckoning tunnel.

She said, "We know where this beam is coming from. We don't know for certain that the traffic between these particular nodes runs in both directions, but we've found plenty of examples where it does. If we aim a signal from here, back along the path of the spillage, and we make it wide enough, then we won't just hit the sending node. We'll hit the receiver as well."

Jasim was silent.

"We know the data format," she continued. "We know the routing information. We can address the data packets to a node on the other side of the bulge, one where the spillage comes out at Massa."

Jasim said, "What makes you think they'll accept the packets?"

"There's nothing in the format we don't understand, nothing we can't write for ourselves."

"Nothing in the unencrypted part. If there's an authorization, even a checksum, in the encrypted part, then any packet without that will be tossed away as noise."

"That's true," she conceded.

"Do you really want to do this?" he said. Her hand was still on his shoulder, she could feel his body growing tense.

"Absolutely."

"We mail ourselves from here to Massa, as unencrypted, classical data that anyone can read, anyone can copy, anyone can alter or corrupt?"

"A moment ago you said they'd throw us away as noise."

"That's the least of our worries."

"Maybe."

Jasim shuddered, his body almost convulsing. He let out a string of obscenities, then made a choking sound. "What's wrong with you? Is this some kind of test? If I call your bluff, will you admit that you're joking."

Leila shook her head. "And no, it's not revenge for what you did on the way to Trident. This is our chance. *This* is what we were waiting to do—not the Eavesdropping, that's nothing! The bulge is right here in front of us. The Aloof are in there, somewhere. We can't force them to engage with us, but we can get closer to them than anyone has ever been before."

"If we go in this way, they could do anything to us."

"They're not barbarians. They haven't made war on us. Even the engineering spores come back unharmed."

"If we infest their network, that's worse than an engineering spore."

" 'Infest'! None of these routes are crowded. A few exabytes passing through is nothing."

"You have no idea how they'll react."

"No," she confessed. "I don't. But I'm ready to find out."

Jasim stood. "We could send a test message first. Then go to Massa and see if it arrived safely."

"We could do that," Leila conceded. "That would be a sensible plan."

"So you agree?" Jasim gave her a wary, frozen smile. "We'll send a test message. Send an encyclopedia. Send greetings in some universal language."

"Fine. We'll send all of those things first. But I'm not waiting more than one day after that. I'm not going to Massa the long way. I'm taking the short-cut, I'm going through the bulge."

8

The Amalgam had been so generous to Leila, and local interest in the Aloof so intense, that she had almost forgotten that she was not, in fact, entitled to a limitless and unconditional flow of resources, to be employed to any end that involved her obsession.

When she asked Tassef for the means to build a high-powered gamma-ray transmitter to aim into the bulge, it interrogated her for an hour, then replied that the matter would require a prolonged and extensive consultation. It was, she realized, no use protesting that compared to hosting a billion guests for a couple of centuries, the cost of this was nothing. The sticking point was not the energy use, or any other equally microscopic consequence for the comfort and amenity of the Tassef locals. The issue was whether her proposed actions might be seen as unwelcome and offensive by the Aloof, and whether that affront might in turn provoke some kind of retribution.

Countless probes and spores had been gently and patiently returned from the bulge unharmed, but they'd come blundering in at less than lightspeed. A flash of gamma rays could not be intercepted and returned before it struck its chosen target. Though it seemed to Leila that it would be a trivial matter for the network to choose to reject the data, it was not unreasonable to suppose that the Aloof's sensibilities might differ on this point from her own.

Jasim had left Shalouf for a city on the other side of the planet. Leila's feelings about this were mixed; it was always painful when they separated, but the reminder that they were not irrevocably welded together also brought an undeniable sense of space and freedom. She loved him beyond measure, but that was not the final word on every question. She was not certain that she would not relent in the end, and die quietly beside him when the news came through from Massa; there were moments when it seemed utterly perverse, masochistic and self-aggrandising to flee from that calm, dignified end for the sake of trying to cap their modest revolution with a new and spectacularly dangerous folly. Nor though, was she certain that Jasim would not change his own mind, and take her hand while they plunged off this cliff together.

When the months dragged on with no decision on her request, no news from Massa and no overtures from her husband, Leila became an orator, traveling from city to city promoting her scheme to blaze a trail through the heart of the bulge. Her words and image were conveyed into virtual fora, but her physical presence was a way to draw attention to her cause, and Listening Party pilgrims and Tassefi alike packed the meeting places when she came. She mastered the locals' language and style, but left it inflected with some suitably alien mannerisms. The fact that a rumor had arisen that she was one of the First Eavesdroppers did no harm to her attendance figures.

When she reached the city of Jasim's self-imposed exile, she searched the audience for him in vain. As she walked out into the night a sense of panic gripped her. She felt no fear for herself, but the thought of him dying here alone was unbearable.

She sat in the street, weeping. How had it come to this? They had been prepared for a glorious failure, prepared to be broken by the Aloof's unyielding silence, and instead the fruits of their labor had swept through the disk, reinvigorating a thousand cultures. How could the taste of success be so bitter?

Leila imagined calling out to Jasim, finding him, holding him again, repairing their wounds.

A splinter of steel remained inside her, though. She looked up into the blazing sky. The Aloof were there, waiting, daring her to stand before them. To come this far, then step back from the edge for the comfort of a familiar embrace, would diminish her. She would not retreat.

●●●

The news arrived from Massa: forty thousand years before, the spillage from the far side of the bulge had been caught in time. Vast swathes of the data matched the observations that Tassef had been holding in anticipation of this moment, for the last fifteen thousand years.

There was more: reports of other correlations from other observatories followed within minutes. As the message from Massa had been relayed around the inner disk, a cascade of similar matches with other stores of data had been found.

By seeing where packets dropped out of the stream, their abstract addresses became concrete, physical locations within the bulge. As Leila stood in Shalouf's main square in the dusk, absorbing the reports, the Aloof's network was growing more solid, less ethereal, by the minute.

The streets around her were erupting with signs of elation: polyglot shouts, chirps and buzzes, celebratory scents and vivid pigmentation changes. Bursts of luminescence spread across the square. Even the relentlessly sober heptapods had abandoned their food carts to lie on their backs, spinning with delight. Leila wheeled around, drinking it in, commanding her translator to punch the meaning of every disparate gesture and sound deep into her brain, unifying the kaleidoscope into a single emotional charge.

As the stars of the bulge came out, Tassef offered an overlay for everyone to share, with the newly mapped routes shining like golden highways. From all around her, Leila picked up the signals of those who were joining the view: people of every civilization, every species, every replicator were seeing the Aloof's secret roads painted across the sky.

Leila walked through the streets of Shalouf, feeling Jasim's absence sharply, but too familiar with that pain to be overcome by it. If the joy of this moment was muted, every celebration would be blighted in the same way, now. She could not expect anything else. She would grow inured to it.

Tassef spoke to her.

"The citizens have reached a decision. They will grant your request."

"I'm grateful."

"There is a condition. The transmitter must be built at least twenty light years away, either in interstellar space, or in the circumstellar region of an uninhabited system."

"I understand." This way, in the event that the Aloof felt threatened to the point of provoking destructive retribution, Tassef would survive an act of violence, at least on a stellar scale, directed against the transmitter itself.

"We advise you to prepare your final plans for the hardware, and submit them when you're sure they will fulfill your purpose."

"Of course."

Leila went back to her room, and reviewed the plans she had already drafted. She had anticipated the Tassefi wanting a considerable safety margin, so she had worked out the energy budgets for detailed scenarios involving engineering spores and forty-seven different cometary clouds that fell within Tassef's jurisdiction. It took just seconds to identify the best one that met the required conditions, and she lodged it without hesitation.

Out on the streets, the Listening Party continued. For the billion pilgrims, this was enough: they would go home, return to their grandchildren, and die happy in the knowledge that they had finally seen something new in the world. Leila envied them; there'd been a time when that would have been enough for her, too.

She left her room and rejoined the celebration, talking, laughing, dancing with strangers, letting herself grow giddy with the moment. When the sun came up, she made her way home, stepping lightly over the sleeping bodies that filled the street.

‑‑‑

The engineering spores were the latest generation: strong bullets launched at close to lightspeed that shed their momentum by diving through the heart of a star, and then rebuilding themselves at atomic density as they decayed in the stellar atmosphere. In effect, the dying femtomachines constructed nanomachines bearing the same blueprints as they'd carried within themselves at nuclear densities, and which then continued out to the cometary cloud to replicate and commence the real work of mining raw materials and building the gamma ray transmitter.

Leila contemplated following in their wake, sending herself as a signal to be picked up by the as-yet-unbuilt transmitter. It would not have been as big a gamble as Jasim's with Trident; the strong bullets had already been used successfully this way in hundreds of similar stars.

In the end, she chose to wait on Tassef for a signal that the transmitter had been successfully constructed, and had tested, aligned and calibrated itself. If she was going to march blindly into the bulge, it would be absurd to stumble and fall prematurely, before she even reached the precipice.

When the day came, some ten thousand people gathered in the center of Shalouf to bid the traveler a safe journey. Leila would have preferred to slip away quietly, but after all her lobbying she had surrendered her privacy, and the Tassefi seemed to feel that she owed them this last splash of color and ceremony.

Forty-six years after the Listening Party, most of the pilgrims had returned to their homes, but of the few hundred who had lingered in Shalouf nearly all had showed up for this curious footnote to the main event. Leila wasn't sure that anyone here believed the Aloof's network would do more than bounce her straight back into the disk, but the affection these well-wishers expressed seemed genuine. Someone had even gone to the trouble of digging up a phrase in the oldest known surviving language of her ancestral species: *safar bekheyr*, may your journey be blessed. They had written it across the sky in an ancient script that she'd last seen eighty thousand years before, and it had been spread among the crowd phonetically so that everyone she met could offer her this hopeful farewell as she passed.

Tassef, the insentient delegate of all the planet's citizens, addressed the crowd with some somber ceremonial blather. Leila's mind wandered, settling on the observation that she was probably partaking in a public execution. No matter. She had said goodbye to her friends and family long ago. When she stepped through the ceremonial gate, which had been smeared with a tarry mess that the Tassefi considered the height of beauty, she would close her eyes and recall her last night on Najib, letting the intervening millennia collapse into a dream. Everyone chose death in the end, and no one's exit was perfect. Better to rely on your own flawed judgments, better to make your own ungainly mess of it, than live in the days when nature would simply take you at random.

As Tassef fell silent, a familiar voice rose up from the crowd.

"Are you still resolved to do this foolish thing?"

Leila glared down at her husband. "Yes, I am."

"You won't reconsider?"

"No."

"Then I'm coming with you."

Jasim pushed his way through the startled audience, and climbed onto the stage.

Leila spoke to him privately. "You're embarrassing us both."

He replied the same way. "Don't be petty. I know I've hurt you, but the blame lies with both of us."

"Why are you doing this? You've made your own wishes very plain."

"Do you think I can watch you walk into danger, and not walk beside you?"

"You were ready to die if Trident failed. You were ready to leave me behind then."

"Once I spoke my mind on that you gave me no choice. You insisted." He took her hand. "You know I only stayed away from you all this time because I hoped it would dissuade you. I failed. So now I'm here."

Leila's heart softened. "You're serious? You'll come with me?"

Jasim said, "Whatever they do to you, let them do it to us both."

Leila had no argument to make against this, no residue of anger, no false solicitousness. She had always wanted him beside her at the end, and she would not refuse him now.

She spoke to Tassef. "One more passenger. Is that acceptable?" The energy budget allowed for a thousand years of test transmissions to follow in her wake; Jasim would just be a minor blip of extra data.

"It's acceptable." Tassef proceeded to explain the change to the assembled crowd, and to the onlookers scattered across the planet.

Jasim said, "We'll interweave the data from both of us into a single packet. I don't want to end up at Massa and find they've sent you to Jahnom by mistake."

"All right." Leila arranged the necessary changes. None of the Eavesdroppers yet knew that they were coming, and no message sent the long way could warn them in time, but the data they sent into the bulge would be prefaced by instructions that anyone in the Amalgam would find clear and unambiguous, asking that their descriptions only be embodied if they were picked up at Massa. If they were found in other spillage along the way, they didn't want to be embodied multiple times. And if they did not emerge at Massa at all, so be it.

Tassef's second speech came to an end. Leila looked down at the crowd one last time, and let her irritation with the whole bombastic ceremony dissipate into amusement. If she had been among the sane, she might easily have turned up herself to watch a couple of ancient fools try to step onto the imaginary road in the sky, and wish them *safar bekheyr*.

She squeezed Jasim's hand, and they walked toward the gate.

9

Leila's fingers came together, her hand empty. She felt as if she was falling, but nothing in sight appeared to be moving. Then again, all she could see was a distant backdrop, its scale and proximity impossible to judge: thousands of fierce blue stars against the blackness of space.

She looked around for Jasim, but she was utterly alone. She could see no vehicle or other machine that might have disgorged her into this emptiness. There was not even a planet below her, or a single brightest star to which she might be bound. Absurdly, she was breathing. Every other cue told her that she was drifting through vacuum, probably through interstellar space. Her lungs kept filling and emptying, though. The air, and her skin, felt neither hot nor cold.

Someone or something had embodied her, or was running her as software. She was not on Massa, she was sure of that; she had never visited that world, but nowhere in the Amalgam would a guest be treated like this. Not even one who arrived unannounced in data spilling out from the bulge.

Leila said, "Are you listening to me? Do you understand me?" She could hear her own voice, flat and without resonance. The acoustics made perfect sense in a vast, empty, windless place, if not an airless one.

Anywhere in the Amalgam, you *knew* whether you were embodied or not; it was the nature of all bodies, real or virtual, that declarative knowledge of every detail was there for the asking. Here, when Leila tried to summon the same information, her mind remained blank. It was like the strange absence she'd felt on Trident, when she'd been cut off from the repositories of civilization, but here the amputation had reached all the way inside her.

She inhaled deeply, but there was no noticeable scent at all, not even the whiff of her own body odor that she would have expected, whether she was wearing her ancestral phenotype or any of the forms of ersatz flesh that she adopted when the environment demanded it. She pinched the skin of her forearm; it felt more like her original skin than any of the substitutes she'd ever worn. They might have fashioned this body out of something both remarkably lifelike and chemically inert, and placed her in a vast, transparent container of air, but she was beginning to pick up a strong stench of ersatz physics. Air and skin alike, she suspected, were made of bits, not atoms.

So where was Jasim? Were they running him too, in a separate scape? She called out his name, trying not to make the exploratory cry sound plaintive. She understood all too well now why he'd tried so hard to keep her from this place, and why he'd been unable to face staying behind: the thought that the Aloof might be doing something unspeakable to his defenseless consciousness, in some place she couldn't hope to reach or see, was like a white hot blade pressed to her heart. All she could do was try to shut off the panic and talk down the possibility. *All right, he's alone here, but so am I, and it's not that bad.* She would put her faith in symmetry; if they had not abused her, why would they have harmed Jasim?

She forced herself to be calm. The Aloof had taken the trouble to grant her consciousness, but she couldn't expect the level of amenity she was accustomed to. For a start, it would be perfectly reasonable if her hosts were unable or unwilling to plug her into any data source equivalent to the Amalgam's libraries, and perhaps the absence of somatic knowledge was not much different. Rather than deliberately fooling her about her body, maybe they had looked at the relevant data channels and decided that *anything* they fed into them would be misleading. Understanding her transmitted description well enough to bring her to consciousness was one thing, but it didn't guarantee that they knew how to translate the technical details of their instantiation of her into her own language.

And if this ignorance-plus-honesty excuse was too sanguine to swallow, it wasn't hard to think of the Aloof as being pathologically secretive without actually being malicious. If they wanted to keep quiet about the way they'd brought her to life lest it reveal something about themselves, that too was understandable. They need not be doing it for the sake of tormenting her.

Leila surveyed the sky around her, and felt a jolt of recognition. She'd memorized the positions of the nearest stars to the target node where her transmission would first be sent, and now a matching pattern stood out against the background in a collection of distinctive constellations. She was being shown the sky from that node. This didn't prove anything about her actual location, but the simplest explanation was that the Aloof had instantiated her here, rather than sending her on through the network. The stars were in the positions she'd predicted for her time of arrival, so if this was the reality, there had been little delay in choosing how to deal with the intruder. No thousand-year-long deliberations, no passing of the news to a distant decision-maker. Either the Aloof themselves were present here, or the machinery of the node was so sophisticated that they might as well have been. She could not have been woken by accident; it had to have been a deliberate act. It made her wonder if the Aloof had been expecting something like this for millennia.

"What now?" she asked. Her hosts remained silent. "Toss me back to Tassef?" The probes with their reversed trajectories bore no record of their experience; perhaps the Aloof wouldn't incorporate these new memories into her description before returning her. She spread her arms imploringly. "If you're going to erase this memory, why not speak to me first? I'm in your hands completely, you can send me to the grave with your secrets. Why wake me at all, if you don't want to talk?"

In the silence that followed, Leila had no trouble imagining one answer: to study her. It was a mathematical certainty that some questions about her behavior could never be answered simply by examining her static description; the only reliable way to predict what she'd do in any given scenario was to wake her and confront her with it. They might, of course, have chosen to wake her any number of times before, without granting her memories of the previous instantiations. She experienced a moment of sheer existential vertigo: this could be the thousandth, the billionth, in a vast series of experiments, as her captors permuted dozens of variables to catalog her responses.

The vertigo passed. Anything was possible, but she preferred to entertain more pleasant hypotheses.

"I came here to talk," she said. "I understand that you don't want us sending in machinery, but there must be something we can discuss, something we can learn from each other. In the disk, every time two space-faring civilizations met, they found they had something in common. Some mutual interests, some mutual benefits."

At the sound of her own earnest speech dissipating into the virtual air around her, Leila started laughing. The arguments she'd been putting for centuries to Jasim, to her friends on Najib, to the Snakes on Nazdeek, seemed ridiculous now, embarrassing. How could she face the Aloof and claim that she had anything to offer them that they had not considered, and rejected, hundreds of thousands of years before? The Amalgam had never tried to keep its nature hidden. The Aloof would have watched them, studied them from afar, and consciously chosen isolation. To come here and list the advantages of contact as if they'd never crossed her hosts' minds was simply insulting.

Leila fell silent. If she had lost faith in her role as cultural envoy, at least she'd proved to her own satisfaction that there was something in here smarter than the slingshot fence the probes had encountered. The Aloof had not embraced her, but the whole endeavor had not been in vain. To wake in the bulge, even to silence, was far more than she'd ever had the right to hope for.

She said, "Please, just bring me my husband now, then we'll leave you in peace."

This entreaty was met in the same way as all the others. Leila resisted speculating again about experimental variables. She did not believe that a million-year-old civilization was interested in testing her tolerance to isolation, robbing her of her companion and seeing how long she took to attempt suicide. The Aloof did not take orders from her; fine. If she was neither an experimental subject to be robbed of her sanity, nor a valued guest whose every wish was granted, there had to be some other relationship between them that she had yet to fathom. She had to be conscious for a reason.

She searched the sky for a hint of the node itself, or any other feature she might have missed, but she might as well have been living inside a star map, albeit one shorn of the usual annotations. The Milky Way, the plane of stars that bisected the sky, was hidden by the thicker clouds of gas and dust here, but Leila had her bearings; she knew which way led deeper into the bulge, and which way led back out to the disk.

She contemplated Tassef's distant sun with mixed emotions, as a sailor might look back on the last sight of land. As the yearning for that familiar place welled up, a cylinder of violet light appeared around her, encircling the direction of her gaze. For the first time, Leila felt her weightlessness interrupted: a gentle acceleration was carrying her forward along the imaginary beam.

"No! Wait!" She closed her eyes and curled into a ball. The acceleration halted, and when she opened her eyes the tunnel of light was gone.

She let herself float limply, paying no attention to anything in the sky, waiting to see what happened if she kept her mind free of any desire for travel.

After an hour like this, the phenomenon had not recurred. Leila turned her gaze in the opposite direction, into the bulge. She cleared her mind of all timidity and nostalgia, and imagined the thrill of rushing deeper into this violent, spectacular, alien territory. At first there was no response from the scape, but then she focused her attention sharply in the direction of a second node, the one she'd hoped her transmission would be forwarded to from the first, on its way through the galactic core.

The same violet light, the same motion. This time, Leila waited a few heartbeats longer before she broke the spell.

Unless this was some pointlessly sadistic game, the Aloof were offering her a clear choice. She could return to Tassef, return to the Amalgam. She could announce that she'd put a toe in these mysterious waters, and lived to tell the tale. Or she could dive into the bulge, as deep as she'd ever imagined, and see where the network took her.

"No promises?" she asked. "No guarantee I'll come out the other side? No intimations of contact, to tempt me further?" She was thinking aloud, she did not expect answers. Her hosts, she was beginning to conclude, viewed strangers through the prism of a strong, but very sharply delineated, sense of obligation. They sent back the insentient probes to their owners, scrupulously intact. They had woken this intruder to give her the choice: did she really want to go where her transmission suggested, or had she wandered in here like a lost child who just needed to find the way home? They would do her no harm, and send her on no journey without her consent, but those were the limits of their duty of care. They did not owe her any account of themselves. She would get no greeting, no hospitality, no conversation.

"What about Jasim? Will you give me a chance to consult with him?" She waited, picturing his face, willing his presence, hoping they might read her mind if her words were beyond them. If they could decode a yearning toward a point in the sky, surely this wish for companionship was not too difficult to comprehend? She tried variations, dwelling on the abstract structure of their intertwined data in the transmission, hoping this might clarify the object of her desire if his physical appearance meant nothing to them.

She remained alone.

The stars that surrounded her spelt out the only choices on offer. If she wanted to be with Jasim once more before she died, she had to make the same decision as he did.

Symmetry demanded that he faced the same dilemma.

How would he be thinking? He might be tempted to retreat back to the safety of Tassef, but he'd reconciled with her in Shalouf for the sole purpose of following her into danger. He would understand that she'd want to go deeper, would want to push all the way through to Massa, opening up the shortcut through the core, proving it safe for future travelers.

Would he understand, too, that she'd feel a pang of guilt at this presumptuous line of thought, and that she'd contemplate making a sacrifice of her own? He had braved the unknown for her, and they had reaped the reward already: they had come closer to the Aloof than anyone in history. Why couldn't that be enough? For all Leila knew, her hosts might not even wake her again before Massa. What would she be giving up if she turned back now?

More to the point, what would Jasim expect of her? That she'd march on relentlessly, following her obsession to the end, or that she'd put her love for him first?

The possibilities multiplied in an infinite regress. They knew each other as well as two people could, but they didn't carry each other's minds inside them.

Leila drifted through the limbo of stars, wondering if Jasim had already made his decision. Having seen that the Aloof were not the torturers he'd feared, had he already set out for Tassef, satisfied that she faced no real peril at their hands? Or had he reasoned that their experience at this single node meant nothing? This was not the Amalgam, the culture could be a thousand times more fractured.

This cycle of guesses and doubts led nowhere. If she tried to pursue it to the end she'd be paralyzed. There were no guarantees; she could only choose the least worst case. If she returned to Tassef, only to find that Jasim had gone on alone through the bulge, it would be unbearable: she would have lost him for nothing. If that happened, she could try to follow him, returning to the bulge immediately, but she would already be centuries behind him.

If she went on to Massa, and it was Jasim who retreated, at least she'd know that he'd ended up in safety. She'd know, too, that he had not been desperately afraid for her, that the Aloof's benign indifference at this first node had been enough to persuade him that they'd do her no harm.

That was her answer: she had to continue, all the way to Massa. With the hope, but no promise, that Jasim would have thought the same way.

The decision made, she lingered in the scape. Not from any second thoughts, but from a reluctance to give up lightly the opportunity she'd fought so hard to attain. She didn't know if any member of the Aloof was watching and listening to her, reading her thoughts, examining her desires. Perhaps they were so indifferent and incurious that they'd delegated everything to insentient software, and merely instructed their machines to baby-sit her while she made up her mind where she wanted to go. She still had to make one last attempt to reach them, or she would never die in peace.

"Maybe you're right," she said. "Maybe you've watched us for the last million years, and seen that we have nothing to offer you. Maybe our technology is backward, our philosophy naive, our customs bizarre, our manners appalling. If that's true, though, if we're so far beneath you, you could at least point us in the right direction. Offer us some kind of argument as to why we should change."

Silence.

Leila said, "All right. Forgive my impertinence. I have to tell you honestly, though, that we won't be the last to bother you. The Amalgam is full of people who will keep trying to find ways to reach you. This is going to go on for another million years, until we believe that we understand you. If that offends you, don't judge us too harshly. We can't help it. It's who we are."

She closed her eyes, trying to assure herself that there was nothing she'd regret having left unsaid.

"Thank you for granting us safe passage," she added, "if that's what you're offering. I hope my people can return the favor one day, if there's anywhere you want to go."

She opened her eyes and sought out her destination: deeper into the network, on toward the core.

10

The mountains outside the town of Astraahat started with a gentle slope that promised an easy journey, but gradually grew steeper. Similarly, the vegetation was low and sparse in the foothills, but became steadily thicker and taller the higher up the slope you went.

Jasim said, "Enough." He stopped and leaned on his climbing stick.

"One more hour?" Leila pleaded.

He considered this. "Half an hour resting, then half an hour walking?"

"One hour resting, then one hour walking."

He laughed wearily. "All right. One of each."

The two of them hacked away at the undergrowth until there was a place to sit.

Jasim poured water from the canteen into her hands, and she splashed her face clean.

They sat in silence for a while, listening to the sounds of the unfamiliar wildlife. Under the forest canopy it was almost twilight, and when Leila looked up into the small patch of sky above them she could see the stars of the bulge, like tiny, pale, translucent beads.

At times it felt like a dream, but the experience never really left her. The Aloof had woken her at every node, shown her the view, given her a choice. She had seen a thousand spectacles, from one side of the core to the other: cannibalistic novas, dazzling clusters of new-born stars, twin white dwarfs on the verge of collision. She had seen the black hole at the galaxy's center, its accretion disk glowing with X-rays, slowly tearing stars apart.

It might have been an elaborate lie, a plausible simulation, but every detail accessible from disk-based observatories confirmed what she had witnessed. If anything had been changed, or hidden from her, it must have been small. Perhaps the artifacts of the Aloof themselves had been painted out of the view, though Leila thought it was just as likely that the marks they'd left on their territory were so subtle, anyway, that there'd been nothing to conceal.

Jasim said sharply, "Where are you?"

She lowered her gaze and replied mildly, "I'm here, with you. I'm just remembering."

When they'd woken on Massa, surrounded by delirious, cheering Eavesdroppers, they'd been asked: *What happened in there? What did you see?* Leila didn't know why she'd kept her mouth shut and turned to her husband before replying, instead of letting every detail come tumbling out immediately. Perhaps she just hadn't known where to begin.

For whatever reason, it was Jasim who had answered first. "Nothing. We stepped through the gate on Tassef, and now here we are. On the other side of the bulge."

For almost a month, she'd flatly refused to believe him. *Nothing? You saw nothing?* It had to be a lie, a joke. It had to be some kind of revenge.

That was not in his nature, and she knew it. Still, she'd clung to that explanation for as long as she could, until it became impossible to believe any longer, and she'd asked for his forgiveness.

Six months later, another traveler had spilled out of the bulge. One of the die-hard Listening Party pilgrims had followed in their wake and taken the short cut. Like Jasim, this heptapod had seen nothing, experienced nothing.

Leila had struggled to imagine why she might have been singled out. So much for her theory that the Aloof felt morally obliged to check that each passenger on their network knew what they were doing, unless they'd decided that her actions were enough to demonstrate that intruders from the disk, considered generically, were making an informed choice. Could just one sample of a working, conscious version of their neighbors really be enough for them to conclude that they understood everything they needed to know? Could this capriciousness, instead, have been part of a strategy to lure in more visitors, with the enticing possibility that each one might, with luck, witness something far beyond all those who'd preceded them? Or had it been part of a scheme to discourage intruders by clouding the experience with uncertainty? The simplest act of discouragement would have been to discard all unwelcome transmissions, and the most effective incentive would have been to offer a few plain words of welcome, but then, the Aloof would not have been the Aloof if they'd followed such reasonable dictates.

Jasim said, "You know what I think. You wanted to wake so badly, they couldn't refuse you. They could tell I didn't care as much. It was as simple as that."

"What about the heptapod? It went in alone. It wasn't just tagging along to watch over someone else."

He shrugged. "Maybe it acted on the spur of the moment. They all seem unhealthily keen to me, whatever they're doing. Maybe the Aloof could discern its mood more clearly."

Leila said, "I don't believe a word of that."

Jasim spread his hands in a gesture of acceptance. "I'm sure you could change my mind in five minutes, if I let you. But if we walked back down this hill and waited for the next traveler from the bulge, and the next, until the reason some of them received the grand tour and some didn't finally became plain, there would still be another question, and another. Even if I wanted to live for ten thousand years more, I'd rather move on to something else. And in this last hour . . ." He trailed off.

Leila said, "I know. You're right."

She sat, listening to the strange chirps and buzzes emitted by creatures she knew nothing about. She could have absorbed every recorded fact about them in an instant, but she didn't care, she didn't need to know.

Someone else would come after them, to understand the Aloof, or advance that great, unruly, frustrating endeavor by the next increment. She and Jasim had made a start; that was enough. What they'd done was more than she could ever have imagined, back on Najib. Now, though, was the time to stop, while they were still themselves: enlarged by the experience, but not disfigured beyond recognition.

They finished their water, drinking the last drops. They left the canteen behind. Jasim took her hand and they climbed together, struggling up the slope side by side.